THE MOMENT IT WOULD BEGIN . . .

"Maybe you should put together your own band."

"Are you serious, Melinda? This could"—Christa hesitated—"this could take us to some strange places."

Melinda knew instinctively that the harper was not talking about Poughkeepsie or Los Angeles, but she stood her ground. "Yeah, I'm serious."

"It could be dangerous."

Very deliberately, Christa turned to the table that held the shrouded harp. It was as if she were conversing with the instrument, questioning it, receiving answers.

Strange places. The idea made Melinda shiver.

Christa turned back. Her eyes were bright and determined. "I'm game, Melinda. Let's rock. . . ."

GOSSAMER AXE

Gael Baudino

A ROC BOOK

ROC

Published by the Penguin Group
Penguin Books USA Inc., 375 Hudson Street,
New York, New York 10014, U.S.A.
Penguin Books Ltd, 27 Wrights Lane,
London W8 5TZ, England
Penguin Books Australia Ltd, Ringwood,
Victoria, Australia
Penguin Books Canada Ltd, 2801 John Street,
Markham, Ontario, Canada L3R 1B4
Penguin Books (N.Z.) Ltd, 182-190 Wairau Road,
Auckland 10, New Zealand

Penguin Books Ltd, Registered Offices:
Harmondsworth, Middlesex, England

First published by ROC, an imprint of New American Library, a division of
Penguin Books USA Inc.

First Printing, August, 1990
10 9 8 7 6 5 4 3 2 1

Permissions

"Don't Tell Me You Love Me" by J. Blades. © 1982 On the Boardwalk Music
(BMI). All rights controlled by Kid Bird Music. Used by permission.

"Hollyann" by T. Schultz. © 1986 Hideaway Hits (ASCAP). Used by permission.
All rights reserved.

"Metal Health" by C. Cavazo, K. DuBrow, F. Banali & T. Cavazo. © 1983 The
Grand Pasha (BMI). Used by permission. All rights reserved.

 ROC is a trademark of Penguin Books USA Inc.

Printed in the United States of America

BOOKS ARE AVAILABLE AT QUANTITY DISCOUNTS WHEN USED TO
PROMOTE PRODUCTS OR SERVICES. FOR INFORMATION PLEASE WRITE
TO PREMIUM MARKETING DIVISION, PENGUIN BOOKS USA INC., 375
HUDSON STREET, NEW YORK, NEW YORK 10014.

This book is dedicated to the memory of:

Genevieve Bergeron
Helene Colgan
Nathalie Croteau
Barbara Daigneault
Anne-Marie Edward
Maud Haviernick
Barbara Maria Klueznick
Maryse Laganiere
Maryse Leclair
Anne-Marie Lemay
Sonia Pelletier
Michele Richard
Annie Saint-Arneault
Annie Turcotte

You are loved. You are missed.

Sometimes, rock and roll dreams come true.
                    —Popular Mythology

Acknowledgments

Many people, knowing or unknowing, had a hand in this book, for it was the living of it that made the writing possible.

Shawn McNary taught me rock and roll and what volume controls were all about. Therese Schroeder-Sheker turned me into a harper, revealing in her teaching and her life the holiness of music.

Bethanny Forest and Laura Henning were my bandmates. They listened to my occasional ravings about magic and kept me focused on the serious business of making noise.

Mike Marlier told me horror stories of musicians on the road. Wendy Luck read each chapter with approval and cheers. Nancy Keogel read the first draft and suggested a critical change. Kyira Brooke kept the faith. Paulie Rainbow checked the revised manuscript. My beloved Mirya provided encouragement, made sure that I ate, and reminded me that chapter 14 is *always* a bitch. Toward the end, the Maroon Bells Morris kept my feet light and my face smiling.

My thanks to all. And especial thanks to Eugene O'Curry, whose exhaustive lectures, given in Dublin from 1857 to 1862, provided much of the foundation for the book.

CHAPTER ONE

Chick with a harp.

Her hair was the color of an angry sunset, and it fell to her waist in ripples of copper and red. Her steps—deliberate, prideful, measured—took her eastward along Evans Avenue through clouds of dust raised by the summertime street repair. People stared at the small, wire-strung harp she carried tucked under her arm. She did not appear to notice.

Shielding his eyes from the June sun that glared through the tinted windows of the guitar school, Kevin Larkin watched her. Blue blouse, beige slacks, red hair: she looked as summery as the day, and he smiled in spite of his headache and rested his eyes and his mind on the pretty harper. From an office down the hall drifted a simple arrangement of "Wildwood Flower" on acoustic guitar, the sweet country strain an appropriate soundtrack to accompany her along the dusty street.

But with that harp—and that hair—the tune should have been Irish. Something ancient. Kevin recalled the Ossianic ballads that his grandfather used to sing, the old man's resonant voice belying the frequent gasps of unchecked emphysema that interrupted his song. How did that one go? It had been years now, and Kevin—millennia from Ossian and decades from his grandfather—struggled a moment to remember, his hands falling to the electric guitar slung from his shoulder, picking out attempts at the melody in an unamplified whisper:

Stiurad me dod mho . . . something . . .

Cia nach ollamh . . . eigir . . . how was that?

. . . di . . . dum . . . di . . . But it would not come. The cadences were strange, and his inner ear, conditioned by years of rock and roll and by the involuted simplicity of the blues, lost the melody and left him

11

stranded and groping. He felt stale, empty. The music that he knew and taught had long ago been worn smooth and featureless with overhandling, and his grandfather's song eluded his grasp.

In the background, "Wildwood Flower" finished in a light strum and the crystalline spark of a harmonic.

"Nice, Dave," Kevin said aloud. "Do you know anything Irish?"

"Don't you?" came the voice of the other teacher. "You're the Paddy."

"Gave it up for Lent."

"Oh, sure." Dave whacked out a raucous series of chords, and after a moment his voice rang out in a sardonic imitation of an Irish tenor:

"Oh, Danny Boy . . ."

"Stuff it," Kevin yelled. A denim-and-leather-clad student who was waiting for a lesson looked up at him, startled. Kevin realized that there had been genuine anger in his voice. "Uh . . . sorry, Jake," he said. "Be with you in a minute." Mortified, he ducked into his office and closed the door.

Ossian was far fled now, and Kevin regretted it. Something about that melody. Very Irish—Celtic, rather—very clear, very pristine. But his grandfather had died and taken the songs with him, and Kevin's father and mother cared little for anything Irish except the Church.

Kevin ran his hand along the slender neck of his guitar, grimacing. Ossian had been forgotten, and music too, and perhaps also a son who had possessed the audacity to tell old Father Lynch to go piss up a rope.

Gave it up for Lent. Oh, sure, a nice Catholic boy. Glib as a tinker with a pint, and thrown out of the house for it as an example to his three sisters and his little brother, Danny.

He tipped his chair back, kicked away some of the clutter on his desk, and propped his feet up. Danny had, he supposed, gone on to the seminary. Jeanine, Marie, and Teresa had probably married. He did not know for sure. It had been twenty years.

A poster of Jimi Hendrix stared down at him from the wall beside an old slide guitar that hung from a piece of red twine. Kevin felt for the Ossianic strain unsuccessfully. Coming as it did from another land and another age, the music was very different from rock and roll. Maybe there was something about it that he could use to break the petrification growing within him. He was feeling desperate, afraid that, one fine day, a student like Jake was going to point at him in mid-lesson and call him a fraud, an old man who had lost the music, who had no business teaching rock and roll.

Malmsteen was playing tomorrow night. Heavy metal and Paganini. Wild combination. It might break the spell.

But Malmsteen was tomorrow. Today he hunted for Ossian. For a moment, he rested his mind on the image of the girl with the harp. Summery. Lovely.

A ghnuir anglidhe . . . what was it . . . no . . .

Damn.

The brass bell above the door of Best's Guitar Laboratory clanged once, twice, then settled down to a mellow reverberation that faded in the warm air. Roger looked up from the Les Paul that lay on the carpeted counter and nodded to the young woman who had entered. "Afternoon, Christa. I'll be with you in a min." He noticed then what she carried. "No problem with the harp, I hope."

"None, Roger. It's only some stain I need and I want to be sure of the color." Christa sat down on the rickety chair by the front window and laid the small harp across her lap. She glanced curiously at the young man who, in wild hair, a ripped T-shirt, and pink jeans, stood across the counter from Roger.

Roger grinned at her, flicked his short ponytail back over his shoulder, and bent over the guitar again. "This has seen some hard times, Tony," he commented.

"Well, like I found it in this pawnshop up on Broadway," Tony explained. "The guy didn't know what he had. I saw the PAF pickups, and I knew it was for me."

"PAFs give a nice sound. . . ." Roger lifted the instrument by its headstock and squinted down the neck. "Ummm . . . frets are kind of funky."

"I'd be funky too if I was hanging up by a heater for a couple years. Can you make it right?"

Roger estimated with a luthier's instinct. Probably a

'58. Good year for a Paul. He could have looked up the serial number, but he was fairly sure of it.

He ran his hand across the scarred face of the guitar, his fingers tracing gouges, splits, cracks, dents. Why did people treat instruments like this? Even the cheapest piece-of-shit import deserved better than to be left hanging by a heater. The wood, already dry from the arid Denver climate, had dried even more, shrinking, breaking the bindings, splitting the fingerboard. . . .

The Buddha is everywhere, he thought. But if he's in front of a hot ventilator, he's not smiling.

His hands continued to probe. Electronics could be repaired easily enough. And the pickups seemed fine. But the soul of a guitar—of any instrument—was in the wood.

"I can't make it perfect," he said, laying it gently down on the carpet as though to make up for the abuse it had suffered. "I can make it playable. But I can't say for sure what might happen in the future. Could split wide open someday."

"You're not sure?"

"Can't say. Things can happen."

The young man hesitated. Roger had worked on his guitars for several years, and he knew that Tony had probably committed himself to living on beans and fruit cocktail for several weeks in order to buy the Les Paul. Even a partial restoration would increase the period of beans and cocktail to two or three months. And then if the guitar died anyway . . .

Roger looked over at Christa. She had been staring at the harp, her face troubled, her thoughts obviously far away, but she raised her head. "Is it help you need?"

"You want to take a look?" Roger stepped back with a nod to Tony. "Christa knows wood. She does all her own work on her harps."

"Is that what that thing is . . . ?"

Laying her instrument aside, Christa came to the counter, rested her hand on the guitar. She was silent for a better part of a minute, then: "Oh dear." Tony started to speak, but she shushed him and bent her head.

After another minute, she straightened, shaking her head. "The heat has done it, I'm afraid," she said. "The damage is great, and there is a weak patch of grain—

look: you can see it here." She indicated a spot near the bridge with the tip of a long fingernail. "This will be giving way in about a year." She turned to Tony. "You said something about the . . . pickups?"

"Yeah. They're PAFs. The sound is just . . . awesome."

"Perhaps you can salvage them, then. Don't worry. The spirit is gone. There will be no pain for the guitar."

Tony looked at her, bewildered. Roger could not blame him. Christa could be a little scary at times. "I can take them out for you, Tony," he said. "It's no problem to drop one or both into your main axe." He noticed that the harper's eyes were hollow, tragic. "Are you okay, Christa?"

"I'll be well in a moment," she said. She shook her head, and the tragedy dispersed.

"I'll bring in my old Kramer," said Tony. "The rhythm slot's empty."

Roger nodded and helped him case the brutalized guitar. When the young man had left, he nodded to Christa. "Thanks for the help."

"It's sad." Her eyes were large and blue, and he wondered how they could ever have looked so bleak. "Didn't you feel that it was dead?"

"I think so. But I figured you'd know for sure. I'm surprised you can tell so much about an electric guitar."

She picked up the little harp and set it on the counter. "Music is music. That guitar came from a factory, but it had a spirit nonetheless. And now it's gone. That's sad for any instrument, not just for harps."

"I know what you mean." Roger was looking over the harp. There was a scratch along the length of the soundbox, but the damage had been expertly smoothed and buffed. Christa's work. "What's this?"

Christa sighed. "I'm sorry, Roger. One of my little students bumped into it and knocked it down. I did what I could, but I don't have the same stains as you."

Roger nodded slowly as he ran his fingers along the scratch. "It's kind of an oddball color. When I built the wife's first harp, I wanted it to look as though it was still alive, so I mixed this up, and I got to like it. I can give you a little, if you want to finish the job."

"I do, surely. I'm ashamed to bring one of your children back like this."

"No problem. Things happen. C'mon, I'll show you the workshop."

He led her down a short hall and into a large room full of tools, electronic parts, and cans of lacquer, stain, and varnish. Hanging from pegs and hooks, and lying on benches and tables, were a number of guitars in various degrees of completion. Rosewood and ebony glowed in dark shades of sable and brown. Maple gleamed yellow, and brown heart and amaranth shown with ruddy color.

Roger selected a can of stain, pried it open, and poured a bit of the dark liquid into a clean bottle. "There you are," he said, capping it. "Anything else? How about an electric guitar?"

He was proud of his work. His guitars looked alive, and surrounded as he was by his instruments, his pain at the mutilated Les Paul dimmed a little. Order and disorder. His job was to mold a little art out of chaos, something that would hold together for a while and bring a little joy to someone. But, yin and yang, everything had to come around again, and he had long ago accepted that whatever he made would have to return eventually to its beginnings. His art lasted only for a few instants of eternity: a blink of the Buddha's eye. Change was inevitable. Sad it was, but wonderful too.

Christa peered at the guitars just as Tony had stared at her harp. Roger smiled at the contrast between the quiet harper and the electric instruments about her. He wondered sometimes if she had been raised in a convent.

"No harps, Roger?" she said, turning around.

"No orders. The last one I built was for that girl you sent to me a few months back. What was her name? She's a rocker . . . plays bass . . ."

"Melinda Moore?"

"Yeah. Melinda. Good bass player. Anyway, that was it. Now, for guitars I have lots of orders. Fortunately."

"They're lovely, Roger," she said. "It's like walking through a forest. I thought, though, that electric guitars were supposed to be . . ." She paused before a nearly complete instrument, cautiously picked a steel string with the tip of a fingernail. ". . . strange colors."

"MTV guitars?" He frowned, shook his head. "Wood's pretty enough, even for heavy metal. It'd be easy to slap on three coats of day-glo polyurethane and call it done, but I want my kids to look alive. Kinda . . . druidical, if you know what I mean."

Her eyebrows lifted for a moment, but she smiled. "Well, not exactly druidical. But . . . sylvan."

"Let me know when you want to start rocking, Christa. I've got some beautiful wood sitting in back. I can really see the kind of guitar I'd build for you."

For years he had played with the idea, letting his imagination range about while he sanded, or buffed, or soldered pots and capacitors. What kind of guitar would he make for this pretty harper with her sweet voice and strange manners, who appeared so young but who seemed at times so old? It would have to glow with all the luster of her hair, and he knew he would have to give to it the feeling of ancient forests, of standing stones and misty dawns. Nothing else would be appropriate. Nothing else would fit.

Christa was laughing. "I really cannot see myself in pink jeans and spiked hair, Roger. But if ever I need an electric guitar, you'll be the one to build it."

"Hey, I'll hold you to that. About when hell freezes over, right?"

"Oh, I don't think it will be that soon. Do you?"

Roger shrugged. "Things happen. Never can tell."

As she parked in front of Christa's house and switched off the ignition, Melinda noticed that her hands were still shaking. She was not surprised. It had been a bad day all around, started by a sleepless night, sustained by morning traffic and heat, climaxed by the office manager's complaints about the way she dressed. She decided for the fifth time that week to quit the damned job and get back into a band.

Her stomach was knotted, her head ached, and she knew that the insomnia was going to be back tonight. Tomorrow would doubtless be a wretched affair. She rubbed at her stinging eyes, debating whether or not to give away her two tickets for the Malmsteen concert. It did not look as though she would be in any shape for it.

After a final rub, she got out of the Mustang with her harp and crossed the grass to the house. Christa was waiting for her at the door. "You look tired," she said, waving her in. "Is it the insomnia come back?"

"Bad night, bad day," said Melinda. She followed Christa back to the studio. "Would you believe they're bitching about my clothes again?"

Christa was pulling up a chair and a music stand, but she stopped. She looked at Melinda, lips pursed.

"Okay," Melinda admitted, "so maybe spandex pants aren't the thing for an office-supply company. I'm being rebellious."

"Oh, it was the hair and the handcuff belt I noticed more."

"I miss the rock and roll. I hate my job."

"And you've the shakes again."

"Yeah."

Christa gestured at the chair. "Sit down and tune up, Melinda. I'll get you something to drink." '

Melinda uncased her harp as Christa went into the kitchen. She heard the refrigerator door open, the clink of ice cubes in a glass. Sighing, she set the harp on her lap, grabbed it as it nearly slid off the slick spandex, repositioned it, and gingerly plucked at the bronze strings to check the tuning.

It felt good to be in Christa's house. The studio faced the backyard, and its large windows were shaded by tall willow and cottonwood trees. The sashes were raised because of the heat, and birdsong and the whine of a cicada drifted in from the garden.

About the room, lying on shelves and tables, were Christa's harps, modest-looking instruments of various sizes and woods—willow and oak and mahogany and cherry—wire strung and gut strung. They were uniformly small, meant to be held on the lap or set on a stool, for Christa taught the older styles of harping that had evolved before the instrument grew from a slender maid into a grand lady of gilt wood and corinthian pillars.

One harp, though, Melinda had never seen, for it was covered with a blue velvet drape. It stood alone and upright on a low table in front of an open window; and now, looking past it, she noticed that it was exactly framed by two trees in the garden. The arrangement was too symmetrical to be anything but deliberate.

Christa reentered with two glasses. Melinda took one and sipped. "What is this?"

"Medeclin," said Christa, taking the other chair. "Honey and water and some mint from the garden. Will it do?"

"Uh . . . fine." Melinda's stomach was settling, and the calm atmosphere of the room was easing the trembling in her hands. She laughed a little. "I might actually be able to play."

"Hmmm." Christa thought for a minute, then reached to a shelf and picked up a harp. She felt the side of the soundbox carefully. "Good. It's dry. Let's see if we can't do something about the shakes today, Melinda. After all, that's why you've been coming for lessons."

"I knew it'd be a shot in the dark."

Christa adjusted the pitch of two strings. "I think your aim might be better than you think. There's an old tune I'm thinking of. It's called a *sian*. Mothers used to sing their babies to sleep with it. I'll teach it to you today, and you can see if it helps tonight."

"I don't think I'll be able to play it that soon."

"It's best on harpstrings, but I'll write it out for you, and you can play it on your bass guitar for now if that will work better. Do promise me, though, that you won't rock it up: the rhythm is important for the effect."

The harper sounded a chord, the bronze strings sweet and bell-like. The melody she played was simple and short: a theme, an answer that was almost questioning, and then the theme again. By the end of the third repetition, Melinda's hands had stopped shaking, her headache had fled, and she was drifting off into vague daydreams about Christa—so familiar now, as though she had known the woman for years—and a forest, and a cluster of houses that looked like overturned baskets by the side of a still lake . . .

"Melinda?"

The room came back, but the headache and the shaking did not. Her head was clear, without a trace of pain. "How did you do that?"

"I'm a harper," said Christa. "That's part of what harping is."

Christa wrote out the *sian*, pointing out fingerings and stresses within the rhythm, suggesting interpretations. Melinda had only studied harp for a few months, and some of what her teacher said was technically beyond her. But she was enough of a musician to know what Christa meant even if she could not herself play it.

"This isn't coming," she muttered as her left hand struggled with the second section.

"It's a little grace followed by a turn," said Christa. Her voice was quiet, reassuring. "Break it down. Put your right hand in you lap, and just play the upper-hand notes slowly."

With concentration, Melinda stumbled through the phrase.

"Now, pick it up little by little. Not until you have your left hand do you add the right: a woman is free unless she gives herself willingly. Treat the turn as an independent section. You'll find you can use the same figure elsewhere, in other pieces."

Melinda brightened. "Like a guitar lick?"

"What is that?"

"A set bunch of notes that you can fire off without thinking," Melinda explained. "That's how some of those guitar heroes play their leads so fast. There's actually not much original stuff in what they're doing. It's mostly just licks strung together. You've heard it done, haven't you?"

Christa shook her head slightly.

"You haven't? But—"

"I have my harps, and my music," Christa explained in her soft voice.

"But . . . don't you ever go out or anything? Rock it up a little?"

"Really, Melinda. Could you see me in the outfit you're wearing now?"

"Well . . ." Melinda examined Christa. "As a matter of fact, I could. Someday, I'll take you out to one of the metal clubs in town. And one of these days I'll get back in a band, and you can come see us play. Sound good?"

"Someday." Christa smiled. "But you're quite right: it's very like a guitar lick."

They spent the rest of the lesson working on the piece, and by the time Melinda cased her harp, she could falter through it slowly. "You know . . . I think I'm going to sleep tonight."

"Good," said Christa. "But as I said, try not to turn it into rock and roll."

"Don't worry." Melinda's eye fell on the shrouded harp again. "Is that special?"

Christa nodded, but made no move to uncover the harp.

"When I was sitting down, I noticed the trees out there. Did you plant those so that—"

"The apple and the yew?" Christa's voice was only a little above a whisper, and her face was troubled. "I did."

Melinda noticed the change immediately. "Hey, I'm sorry. I didn't mean to get personal."

The harper wiped at her eyes. "I'm well, Melinda."

Melinda felt a pang. Christa had been helping her for months, not only as a harp teacher, but as a friend. Though Melinda hardly knew this quiet woman, she cared for her. "Can I . . . can I do something?"

"I'm all right."

"No you're not. You're upset." The strap of the harp case was sliding off her shoulder, and she hitched it back up as she tried to think of something with which to make amends. "Tell you what. I've got two tickets for the Malmsteen concert tomorrow night, and I was thinking about giving them away, but I've got a better idea. Why don't you come with me? It'll get you out of the house."

"Who is this person?"

"Yngwie Malmsteen. Swedish boy. One of those crazy metal gods. You've got to see him play the guitar. You'll like it: he uses a lot of classical stuff in what he does. Paganini."

Christa had been looking out at the two trees. "You want me to go to a rock concert?"

"Sure. You helped me with that lullaby. I think I can help you with rock and roll." Melinda felt her own enthusiasm building. Christa seemed too quiet, too introspective. She needed something that was as close to pure, mindless fun as was possible. "Come on. It'll be a blast."

The harper was still looking out at the trees. "It's . . . Midsummer. To the day." Her voice was barely audible.

"Well?"

Christa smiled, tiredly. "Why not? Sruitmor always

said that if one could not learn from one's students, one had no business teaching them."

"So you'll do it?"

Christa nodded.

Melinda headed for the front door. "Pick you up at six tomorrow night. And don't worry: I'll bring the earplugs!"

The door closed behind her. A meadowlark scattered an arpeggio across the backyard.

Christa sat down slowly on the chair, staring out at the apple and the yew that framed the shrouded harp. "To the day, Judith," she said. "I'm still here. And I won't give up. By all the Gods of Eriu, I won't give up."

CHAPTER
TWO

Under the dark, starless sky, the palace of the Sidh stands as if carved out of glass, its milky pinnacles illuminated by torchlight and firelight. Gossamer banners float in the ebony wind. A pale oriflamme drifts leisurely from a spire far above the polished tile of the courtyard: a wraith proclaiming the dominion of wraiths.

Orfide, the bard, is playing for the king and the court this endless evening, and his thin fingers caress the golden strings of his second-best harp. He has played this melody countless times before in this same way, and the crystalline, petrified beauty of the performance repeated exactly—note for note, nuance for nuance—is a tribute to his immense skill. He is immortal. He is a consummate bard. He cannot improve upon the performance he gave at the beginning of time. Like himself, like his people, like this entire Realm of twilight and gossamer, it is changeless.

About him, the Sidh are silent, listening. Orfide plays. The dark sky weighs down from above. Fingernails that gleam like mother-of-pearl strike strings, ripple chords and arpeggios into the perfumed air as he weaves a spell of timelessness and eternity. The sounds glance from polished stone, reverberate from pillar and pinnacle, caress the opalescent skin of his listeners.

The last note shimmers, fades, falls into silence. The court stirs. Fragile garments sigh as the Sidh rise from their seats. Pale, elfin faces nod approvingly. White hands applaud the bard.

Lamcrann, the king, stands beside his queen. "We are honored, master bard, by your song."

Orfide bows, his silver hair glimmering in the half light. "As I am honored by you, O king." He bows also

23

to Cumad, the queen, and ignores the mortal woman
who stands behind them with a clenched jaw.

Lamcrann turns and takes the hand of the woman.
"Do you not agree, Siudb? Does not our bard exceed
himself with each performance?"

Siudb starts to turn away, but the king's grasp detains
her. "Very nice," she says. "Nice it was the last time,
too. And the time before that. And the time—"

Cumad steps between Siudb and Lamcrann. "Leave
her be. I beg you." Her voice catches. "She is a . . .
child."

Lamcrann does not seem to notice his queen. "Ah, my
lovely mortal maiden. You could be happy among us.
Why not give up your stubborn ways? At my word,
Orfide could—"

"At your word, Orfide could allow me to return to my
own people. I am a free woman of the Gaeidil. You have
no right to keep me here against my will."

A purring edge of steel gleams in Orfide's soft, dulcet
voice. "As I recall, free woman of the Gaeidil, you and
your friend Chairiste sought out our realm of your own
free will."

She turns on him. "We did not seek to enter."

"You came to listen to my harp, mortal. What com-
plaint do you have now? I play for you often. You may
listen to the music of the Sidh as much as you like."

"Your music is the music of death." Siudb's brown
eyes are bright. "It neither lives nor grows. You have not
changed one note of any of your songs since first I heard
you, because you cannot. The clumsiest novice of the
Corca Duibne school could best you there."

"Please." Cumad looks restlessly this way and that. Her
frost-white hair rustles across her silken gown. "Please . . ."

Casually, Orfide takes his tuning key from a pouch at
his side, sits, and softly sounds a few strings, listening.
"Ah, novice harper . . . and so how is it that you have
not departed from our hospitality on your own?"

His words are meant to wound, but Siudb stands straight.
She knows Orfide's pride as well as she knows her own.
"Chairiste did. And your best harp she took with her."

The tuning key falls to the tiled floor and rings shrilly
for an instant. Orfide's mouth is suddenly set.

Lamcrann lifts a hand. "Gentle Siudb, pray give up

these thoughts you have of returning to the Gaeidil. You cannot return. Your people are no more. Years and centuries have passed outside the Realm since you came here, and you would fall into dust and ashes the moment you set foot outside."

"Chairiste did it. She survived."

Orfide cannot restrain himself. "But she left you behind. Does Chairiste Ní Cummen not care for her woman lover? And where is Chairiste now? Can a mortal live forever, my little *timpanach*?"

"Shut up."

"Chairiste is dead, mortal. She has been dead for centuries now. She lies rotted in the ground and shares the customary fate of your race."

Siudb is white-faced, but she has learned to brave the taunts of this Sidh bard. "If Chairiste is dead, then it is in the Summerland that I will find her, and the Goddess Herself will bring our hands together that we may be reborn, and meet, and remember, and love again. But you, Orfide, will fade, and it is a misty hand you will lift to your harp one day, and your bloodless voice will be unheard—"

"Enough." Lamcrann takes Siudb's arm, leads her away toward the open doors of the palace. Cumad toys fitfully with the lacy hem of her sleeve. Orfide watches for a moment, then bends over and retrieves his tuning key as Siudb breaks away from the king and runs off into the twilight meadows that surround the palace.

When Orfide looks up again, Cumad is still there. She meets his eyes, and her lips work soundlessly for a moment before she turns and follows after the king.

Christa was dreaming of Ireland.

Curled up in her bed under a light sheet, the windows open to the cool night air and the distant sound of traffic on Colorado Boulevard, the harper dreamed of her girlhood in Corca Duibne. Once again she wanders barefoot and barelegged across the wide green fields, climbs the embankment about her father's steading, peers through the hedge of crabapple and elder. She leans her back up against an old rowan tree and stares off at the sea, wondering if what the old storyteller said the night before is true: that the Summerland lies a league out and a foot above a tall man's head.

And with the illogic of dreams, she knows at the same time that she is dreaming, that she is both Christa Cruitaire, the harp teacher of Denver, and Chairiste Ní Cummen, by this dream a little girl again, who sits on this earthen bank and wonders about the Summerland.

And she knows also that this is not Ireland. Ireland is the creation of another people, of another language. This is Eriu: land of the Goddess, land of the Gaeidil. There is still a king at Cashel, and Christianity is but a new arrival come to contest the rule of the Gods.

Christa's hands clutched at the sheet, and for a moment she thought she saw her bedroom, the glow from the LED display of her clock radio turning everything into pale-blue abstractions, light from the almost-full moon patterning the wall with horizontal shadows from the blinds. But she wanted to dream. It was Midsummer, and she wanted to remember.

And she did. The rowan tree comes back, and the hedge, and the steading. The piquant smell of a wood-and-peat fire drifts through the clear air.

She is older now, no longer a little girl. Harpstrings have been often under her fingers these last years, and men and women come from distant steadings to hear her play. The sky is blue, the sea gray; and now she sees Siudb crossing the pastureland, running, her dark hair streaming out behind her and her tunic flapping about her thighs.

"Chairiste!" she calls. "Come and see! Father and Donal are out to catch the brown bull in the north field, and he is not coming, and father is so angry he looks like Cu Chulainn getting ready to fight the men of Connaught!"

But Chairiste, hurt and angry after yet another argument with her mother, does not reply. She waves to her beloved Siudb and motions for her to come up on the bank.

Arms about one another, the two young women look out at the sea. The harper of Denver wept in her sleep at the touch of her friend's hand and the feel of Siudb's brown hair mixing with the copper and red of her own. Siudb had been gone for a long time. Dreams were all Christa Cruitaire had left of her.

"Mother is talking about marriage," says Chairiste.

"Is she leaving your father then? I cannot say but that

it would be a good idea, with himself holding to the old ways and your mother taking up the new."

"No, she is not leaving father. She wants me to marry."

Siudb looks shocked and hurt at the same time. Her hand tightens possessively on Chairiste's shoulder. "Is that not your choice? Her people have the ear of many kings, but they have not recast Brehon Law yet."

"That is what I think, and that is what father thinks. But it seems the Christians do things differently. Mother wants me to be a Christian."

"But you are not a Christian!"

Chairiste plucks a piece of tall grass and, in the timeless manner of children who stand gawkily at the door of adulthood, chews absently on the sweet stalk. "I want to be a harper. Mother disagrees: Christian women stay at home and tend their men."

"And so?"

"And so I have decided to run away to the harpers' school to the north. People say that I play well, and maybe I do. But I want to do more than just make music. Any *timpanach* can do that. I want to learn to heal, to work magic with the harp. I cannot learn that here.

"I am thirteen, I have been proclaimed a woman. I am old enough to be taken as a student. Sruitmor is the master of the Corca Duibne school, and I saw him once at the Great Fair. I heard him play, too. He seems . . ." Chairiste smiles, impulsively presses her lips against Siudb's cheek. "He seems a strange man. Like a Druid, and yet not. Stern and kind both."

Again, Siudb tightens her hand on Chairiste's shoulder. "If you are running away, then so am I."

"But, your singing—"

But Siudb's hand fades, and Chairiste has only enough time to throw her arms about Siudb before the bedroom in Denver came back, flickered in and out of existence as Christa blinked at it with tear-filled eyes, then vanished again as the harper buried her head in the pillow and willed herself to sleep—and dream—again.

Midsummer Night. Crickets. Bonfires showing starlike at the tops of surrounding hills. Song and laughter across the miles, across the fields and pastures.

O dear Goddess, not this! Gracious Mother—

Older by four years again, Chairiste and Siudb, having

leapt the flames of the fire together, scamper away from the light. Under their arms they carry the harps that they painstakingly built during their first year of study. They are rude instruments, made by inexpert hands, but their tone is sweet.

Dear Goddess, no!

But the dream continues, unfolding methodically. It is a reckless, foolhardy thing they do, but they are young; and Chairiste sincerely believes that she can do anything, even unto listening with impunity to the music of the Sidh.

Go back, Judith. Go back. O Brigit, she doesn't hear me! She can't hear me. It's already over.

They approach the fairy mound and hear the crystalline tones of harp and voice. Chairiste looks at Siudb, puts her finger to her lips, then kisses her. Siudb giggles. The full moon burns down on the land, laving the mound in silver.

Chairiste touches several strings of her harp lightly, trying to follow a strain of the Sidh music. There is magic there, more magic than Sruitmor can ever teach her. The sequence of notes turns outward, then in on itself. She feels her arms tingling. Yes . . . yes, this is it. There is something *here*. . . .

Siudb gasps. The tall, silver-haired figure of the Sidh bard is stepping across the grass toward them, a gaping archway of darkness open in the hill behind him. His eyes glitter as though a piece of the moon lies in each one, and the harp in his hands glows palely.

He sounds a few strings. The mortals wilt before him.

In her bedroom, Christa screamed. "Judith! Run!"

But her friend was centuries away. Christa sat up, mouth dry, and switched on the bedside light. "Siudb," she whispered. But the Gaeidelg name came uneasily to her tongue. She had been speaking English for too many years. It was much easier to call her lover *Judith*, to call herself *Christa*, to call her instrument not a *cruit* but a harp. The old names were gone, and the old ways along with them.

She hunched over in bed, hands to her face. "Judith. Judith." But Judith was still with the Sidh, still a captive of that realm of twilight and shadow, still a dweller in that cursed palace of ice and moonlight.

The Realm was everywhere, and yet nowhere. Judith could have been within the reach of her arm, but that made no difference. She was with the Sidh. She was in another world, another universe.

Weeping, Christa looked out through her window at the full moon that was just touching the summits of the Rockies. "Goddess. Beloved Brigit. I stood in Your presence when I entered the circle of women and took the chalice from the hand of Your priestess, Aoine. My mother would not bring me. My father was allowed to by the good will of the women of my clan. You provided for your daughter then. Help me now. It's been over two hundred years since I've touched her. I haven't even seen her. O Mother of the *Cruitreacha,* guide me!"

On the nightstand beside her, the alarm went off in shrill chirps. She started and cried out before she realized what it was, then ruefully shook her head and silenced it. Time to get up.

Outside, the sky was turning blue, the moon fast disappearing behind the mountains as the sun rose to begin the longest day.

Siudb wanders through the shadowy meadows, seeing by the half light that pervades the Realm. Her gown whispers across the grass and the pale flowers. The gleaming fabric makes her mortal skin look dull and muddy, but even Chairiste was not flattered by the garments of the Sidh.

Near the center of the formal gardens, there is an alabaster bench by the side of a silent fountain. Siudb sits, face in her hands, thinking of Chairiste. There is no day here, nor really any night: merely a twilight, a continuing. Siudb finds that she cannot estimate how long she has lived among the Sidh, how long it has been since Chairiste, armed with Orfide's best harp, pried open a gate into mortality and so escaped into a sunlit landscape that neither Gaeidil recognized.

Siudb shudders, remembering how Chairiste reached back for her. But the harper was not strong enough. She had learned enough of the magic of the Sidh to save herself, but she could not help another. Immortal hands seized Siudb and dragged her back into the twilight, and the gateway closed on Chairiste's agonized face.

And is she dead then? Siudb wonders. Is Orfide certain? Or is he merely hoping?

She does not know. She knows, however, that she cannot die in this unchanging realm, and that if Chairiste has gone ahead into the Summerland, then she must return to the mortal lands herself, die, and so find her friend.

She looks at her hands. She has not touched a harp in a long time. Harps are forbidden her. Orfide is taking no chances.

"I will have to steal one," she mutters. "And if Orfide likes it not at all, then he can go to the Christians' hell."

Showered and dressed, Christa descended the stairs to her studio. Outside, the garden glowed in the morning light, and she smiled at the trees and flowers as she removed the blue drape from the solitary harp.

With the drape removed, the harp shone suddenly in a blaze of burnished wood, jeweled inlays, and golden strings.

day

"Indeed, it is day," she said to the harp. "Midsummer. Brigit bless you, Ceis."

bright

The harp's remark did not seem to require an answer, and after running a hand affectionately along its shoulder, Christa went into the kitchen to make breakfast.

students

"Not yet," she called over her shoulder. "Susan's my first, and she won't be here for a while." She heated milk on the stove and added oatmeal and a little chopped leek. "I'll eat quickly and then I need to sit with you. I've an idea."

speak

She stirred the porridge and left it to simmer. She had baked bread the day before, and she cut a piece out of a woman-sized loaf and put it in the toaster, set butter and honey on the table. "I'm thinking that I might be able to work with the tree calendar."

**

"Hear me. Thirteen moons, thirteen modes—counting the plagal forms—from *beth* to *ruis*."

fourteen

"Indeed, fourteen modes, but it's that point I'm making. The moons begin with birth, end in death, and commence again with birth. Since the modes overlap the moons by one, I could work with an ascending melodic pattern that would mutate through the modes, starting with C ionian in the plagal form. I'd use the symbolism of the tree month as a basis for each mutation. When the moons would indicate rebirth, the superfluous mode would be B locrian, in the authentic form. Death again. If I could catch Orfide within the cycle, I could lead him into death . . . and leave him there." Her voice held an edge.

Ceis sat silently, held upright in its polished wood support. It was essentially neutral in its loyalties. Existing only to be played, it allied itself with the player. It was more than capable of killing Orfide . . . if she herself had the strength, and the skill, and the raw power to defeat the Sidh bard—but she could feel that it was hesitating.

The response came at last. *anticipated*

The harp said no more, and Christa took her food to the table and put porridge and bread into her mouth, hardly tasting either. If the Sidh bard knew of the deadly cycle of modes, then he could easily nullify any magic she attempted with the idea. In fact, Orfide was subtle enough that he could possibly use the spell against her, twining her in her own music, forcing her to play the fatal strain against herself.

She tossed the idea on the rubbish heap of rescue plans that had been accumulating in the back of her mind since she had escaped from the Realm. Some she had actually tried. In 1811, in Cornwall, she had opened the gates and battled Orfide. And she had lost. Again, in Scotland in 1853. No success.

She felt herself running out of ideas. In order to win, she had to become as good a harper as Orfide. But the Sidh bard had nothing to do but play, and he had been playing since the beginning of time. Christa, though she could keep herself young and alive over the years, had to live as a mortal—eating and sleeping, working, paying bills.

She washed up, dried her hands carefully, rubbed a bit of olive oil into her nails. She needed something else, something so radically different that Orfide would never anticipate it, something with which she could wrench open the gates of the Realm and force the Sidh to give her lover back to her.

She entered the studio, picked up Ceis.

age

"Is it showing? Last night was hard, my friend. I'd not be surprised at all if I looked older."

help

She smiled at the harp's offer and accepted it. She had allowed herself a few additional years so as to survive better in a world that respected youth little more than it honored age, but overall, with the exception of dress and cosmetics, she looked much as she had when she escaped from the Realm. Judith would recognize her. It was important that Judith recognize her.

tears

She sighed. "A long time it's been."

play

She settled Ceis on her lap, rested it against her left shoulder. The tune she played was an old one, one that reminded her of her childhood with Judith. They had been close friends from infancy, and it had surprised no one that, as young women, they had fallen in love. Such an occurrence was unusual, but unremarkable. It was only the Christians who disapproved. . . .

Chairiste

"I'm sorry, Ceis. I was thinking of mother."

play

Her concentration was better this time, and the melody grew under her fingers. The sweet notes washed through her like a cool stream, leaching away the years.

"Not too much, old friend."

play

In many ways, Ceis was wiser than she, and she had learned to trust it. But it was taking several additional years from her this time, and, linked with it in magical union as she was, she could not easily stop the process on her own. Under such circumstances, it was difficult to say who was playing whom.

The melody at last wound down, the final notes shimmering into the quiet air of the studio. Christa sat, a little stunned, the magic slowly clearing from her head.

When she felt she could walk, she set Ceis back on its stand and made her way shakily to the bathroom mirror.

She was almost shocked: she had not been this young in a long time, not since she had stumbled out of the Realm and into France of 1782.

"Old friend," she said, "what have you done? I hardly look eighteen."

good

"But why?"

Ceis was silent. The doorbell rang: her first student of the day. Hoping that Susan would not comment on her appearance, she threw the drape over the Sidh harp and ran for the door. Her steps were light, youthful, as though she were, once again, the young woman who knew nothing of Sidh palaces or American cities, but only the green meadows and pastures of Eriu.

CHAPTER
THREE

The morning sun topped the peaks on the east side of the valley and splashed its light across the meadows around Kevin's house. Indian paintbrush glowed red-orange on rocky slopes that led up to pine forest, columbine was a blue and white maiden in the shade of aspen trees, wild roses twined along the split-rail fence beside the road.

Kevin washed his face in the kitchen sink to clear away the sleep and looked out from his front door while he dried off. Saturday morning in the Rockies. Blue sky. Yellow sun. Green fields. Old Wester's mare had foaled that spring, and now the mother and child were having a fine run along the stretch of pastureland that ran beside the big pond where birch and cottonwood grew. The foal slowed near the fence and reared, his forelegs beating the air and his hooves flashing in the new light.

"Hey, dude," said Kevin. He smiled and waved at the animals. Bless them, he thought. They've got nothing more to do than be horses.

While his eggs were cooking, he wandered into the living room and picked up the old slide guitar that he had brought back from the school. Since the night he had been given it in a dressing room in Cincinnati, it had always been with him; and every scratch and dent in its battered body was a story about the long-dead bluesman who had once played it. A chip on the neck came from a rickety stage in Detroit where the old man had played nearly doubled over from the ulcer that had killed him a few years later. And there was a burn in the headstock from the time that Frankie had shoved the filter end of his cigarette under the taut strings behind the nut—*Just a minute, Kevvy: gotta show you something.*—while he demonstrated some old lick, forgetting, as he showed the skinny white boy how to play the blues, that the cigarette was there until it had burned down and scarred the finish with a brown smear the color of old coffee.

Kevin took up what had once been a bottle of Coricidin, fitted the empty glass cylinder onto the little finger of his left hand, and lightly touched the strings with it while he picked, scraping short, taut glissandos out of the old guitar. Blind Frankie. No one could play the blues like Frankie. No one. Not B.B. Not Clapton. Not Duane. No one. It was one of the incredible but unremarkable ironies of the music business that Frankie had died in a slum bar on the outskirts of Cincinnati, unknown, unrecognized.

Kevin scraped away at the strings, searching for the same response, the same feeling that had sprung so effortlessly from the hands of the old black man. This guitar had cried, wailed, wept when Frankie had played; and in the dim corners of smoky bars from Harlem to New Orleans, bars ripe with the odors of whiskey and cheap cologne, people had cried, wailed, and wept along with it, bright tears starting from dark eyes, running down ebony cheeks.

Frankie had always played the same songs, but they had nonetheless always been different, changing in a thousand different ways that Kevin still could scarcely name. Now and again, the old man had shoved the guitar and slide into Kevin's hands, and there had been indulgent smiles throughout the bar at the sight of the white boy on the stage. But Kevin had played anyway, and one night a tall man in a fur coat had come up to him afterward.

"You play . . . uptown," he had said, his teeth glittering white in the darkness. And with a smile and a bow, he had vanished into the smoke and the shadows.

But that was a long time ago, and Kevin could not even remember what he had played that night, or how he had played it. "Stormy Monday"? Had he in those early years possessed such gall that he had picked the classic? And—even supposing for a moment that he had—where had he gotten enough feeling that the tall man had pronounced his playing *uptown*?

Or rather; where had that feeling gone?

Sighing, he put the guitar down and tossed the slide onto the sofa. Wherever it had gone, it had undoubtedly taken out a long lease and was not intending to return any time soon.

Irony. Frankie had died, unknown, in his dressing room, and this pasty-faced honky had gone on into rock and roll, cut himself a little bit of a name, even gotten a contract offer. His feeling was gone, but that did not matter. The irony had taken over long ago, and so it was perhaps not overly surprising that, after showing enough honesty to turn down the contract, he had put together a guitar school where he taught others to play music for which he himself had lost any empathy.

He stared out through the front door at the horses running back and forth in their pasture. He envied them their freedom and their purpose.

What, he wondered, was that lick the old man had showed him ages ago? If it was important enough that Frankie had scorched his guitar, then perhaps, like the Ossianic ballad that had escaped him, there was something to it that would break the music free once again, entice it away from the Florida condo that it was probably sharing with such things as inspiration and love. . . .

The odor of something burning seized his attention. Running into the kitchen, he found his eggs charred and unrecognizable, a brown smear of color of old coffee.

"Hmmph?"

It took Melinda a moment to realize that she had the wrong end of the phone receiver to her mouth. Half in, half out of her waterbed, she hitched herself up on one elbow while she attempted to turn it around. Mistake. It slipped from her fingers, bounced once on the side rail, and hit the floor with a thud. Across the room, the strings of her harp thrummed in response.

Leaning over, she grabbed the phone by the cord and pulled it up as she fell back among the rumpled sheets. "Hang on," she called hoarsely, hoping the caller could hear her, though in her opinion anyone who called at the ungodly hour of—she squinted at the clock—eleven in the morning deserved no courtesy whatsoever.

She got the receiver to her ear finally. "Hello?"

"Hey, how'ya doing, Melinda?"

The caller was a man, and he knew her name. She

figured that she must know his. "Okay," she said. "Listen, I'm a little sleepy. Who is this?"

"You gotta be kidding."

"I'm not kidding. It's eleven A period M period, and you got me out of some nice dreams—"

"Was he good?"

"Fuck you." She started to hang up, but the man squawked loudly enough that she put the handset to her ear again.

"Hey, I'm sorry. It's me, Tom."

"Tom? Tom who?"

He sounded exasperated. "Tom Delany."

"Oh, *Jes*us. What the hell are you bothering me for?" Now she remembered why she did not recognize his voice: she had tried to forget it.

"I've got some contacts out in L.A.," he said, "and they're interested in bankrolling me. I'm going to put a band together."

"Real nice. Count me out."

"You're the best bass player I know."

"Yeah, because I'm the only one willing to cop to knowing your name. Forget it. I want to get back into a band, but not that bad."

"Melinda—"

"Look—"

"Just a—"

"Will you buzz off? The only thing I ever got from you was screwed. Your idea of a band is a mobile dope ring that plays music . . . sometimes."

"Whatever happened to the Melinda Moore I once knew?" His voice was that of a patient man faced with an unreasonable female. "My gosh . . . she'd do anything to make it . . ."

Melinda winced. He had not even been that good in bed.

". . . work hard, practice, rehearse six nights a week. She had stars in her eyes—"

"And a fucking vacuum in her brain!"

"Melinda, be reasonable."

"I *am* being reasonable. Yeah, I want to make it. Yeah, I want to get a record contract and get checks for tons of money. But the times when I'd go after something just because of somebody's so-called contacts are long gone. I'm over it. Got that?"

"Melinda, you're going to be stuck in an office job for the rest of your life—"

"It's better than getting shit-faced and stoned every night at one of your so-called rehearsals."

Tom was silent for a minute. "Okay, Melinda. I give up. You still got my Strat?"

"Yeah, I still got it."

"Can I have it back?"

"You owe me four hundred and fifty bucks in rent and bills from when we lived together, remember?"

"I'll pay you later. I really—"

"No. No later. I got a bellyful of that two years ago. I told you when I threw you out that I was keeping the guitar in payment, and you said that was okay."

"I was wrong."

"You sure as hell were." In the back of her mind she was trying desperately to hang on to that last fading memory of the dream that the phone call had shattered. "And you know something else? You're a bad fuck, too."

Satisfied, she slammed down the receiver and jerked the plug out of the wall.

Tom had all the right moves and all the right words. It was tempting to believe him, very tempting. But Tom was a road that led to big words, grandiose plans, and nothing else. Oh, yes: sex too. Lots of that. And drugs.

It was a part of her life that she was trying to forget, one that pricked her conscience in the dark hours of the night and kept her from sleep, one that made her hands tremble with suppressed rage and frustrated hope. Tom's guitar was, perhaps, representative of it all: custom painted a faintly ridiculous avocado green, it stood in her front closet, leaning against the wall behind her coats like a corpse hastily buried.

"I ought to sell the damned thing." She slouched forward, scratching at her scalp. She pulled a strand of hair from her mouth. Terminal hairspray, she thought. The stuff feels like balsa wood.

A few minutes later, she was brushing out hairspray and backcombing as she tried to remember her lost dream. It had been pleasant, peaceful; and with Tom's voice still buzzing in her ear and dredging up old unhappiness, she wanted even more to recapture some fragment of it. But, like most dreams, it slipped and slid away from her, flitting into obscurity, daring her waking mind to relive the events of the night.

She tried for a general image, letting her mind find its own way into its fantasies. Green fields and a lake. And a little cluster of houses . . . huts, rather. A girl in a loose white cape was playing a harp, and her hair was long and red and unbound.

Melinda had been bending over while she brushed, but she abruptly stood up straight, her blond hair falling over her face and half choking her with the powdery remnants of hairspray. The girl had been Christa. In fact, the dream was very similar to the momentary vision that had come to her at her harp lesson.

Why should I be dreaming about Christa?

Well . . . why not? The lullaby had certainly helped her to sleep that night. Maybe it was gratitude, a tip of the hat to the harp teacher from her frontal lobes.

She recalled the Malmsteen concert that night and nodded inwardly at the thought of getting to know Christa a little better. She found that she was immensely flattered that the woman had accepted her invitation, and hoped that she would not be offended by the experience of a heavy-metal concert.

"Can't forget those earplugs," she murmured to herself as she headed for the shower.

As she turned on the water, she idly wondered what Christa would look like in stage clothes, and the thought of the gentle harper clad in leather and spandex, draped with chains, her wrists wrapped in studded bracelets and her red hair backcombed and spiked, made Melinda laugh amid the clouds of steam.

If your students are not your children, then you've no business touching harpstrings. There is a reason that our order is called the Cruitreacha, *that the name takes the same plural suffix as* mother. *Think about it.*

So Sruitmor, master of the harp school at Corca Duibne, had taught. So Christa lived. Though angry at Orfide and frustrated with the limitations of mortal life, she nonetheless had smiles and kind words for her students as they passed in and out of her front door. Perhaps their fingers were less skilled even than those of the rank novices of the Corca Duibne school, and perhaps they did not have the same dedication, but she loved them. And if they heard in their comparatively clumsy music, even for an instant, the magic of harpstrings, and if that gave them joy, then she was satisfied.

But her days were long, and this day, Midsummer, was a constant reminder of Judith, of the Sidh, of the arrogant bard who had consistently thwarted her struggles to free her beloved. The sight of the apple and the yew, tokens of two Gaeidil lovers who were fated never to meet in life, but who had met nonetheless, dimmed her smile and clouded her eyes. When her last student left, she shut the front door and leaned heavily against it.

If your students are not your children . . .

"They are, master," she murmured. "They're all I have." In her mind, she saw the old man leaning toward her, lifting an admonishing finger as he lectured.

The same suffix as *mother*. Had he not, in spite of his stern words and his lifted finger, mothered her throughout her time at the school? Manly he had been, and yet womanly too, as though Brigit, the order's Patroness, had given him something of Herself through the music he played.

But he was gone. Gone to the Summerland. Everyone was gone, swept away by the endless cycles of change that flowed throughout all that was mortal.

She went into the kitchen and filled a cup with wine. On an impulse, she lifted it. "To you, Sruitmor, with thanks. And maybe I'll reach the Summerland myself one of these days." She drank, set the cup down. Her eyes clouded again. "Some days I'm so tired of being alive."

The doorbell rang. She looked up. "Who on earth?"

Melinda

She had forgotten about the concert. "Thank you, Ceis," she called as she went down the hall. "But maybe you could have reminded me earlier?"

**

She opened the door. "Goodness."

"Hey, this outfit is conservative," said Melinda. "You should see me on stage. Are you ready to rock?"

"Ah . . . does that include single combat?" Christa hardly recognized her student. Black spandex jeans gave way to boots that rattled with lengths of chain. Leather jacket. Studded belts. A T-shirt that had been deliberately slashed into a borderline state between legality and indecency. Bandannas fluttered from ankles, elbows, wrists. Melinda had added perhaps a good six inches to her height with a teasing comb and a liberal application of hairspray. Her blue eyes sparkled at Christa from within dark wells of eyeliner and shadow.

"Relax," she said, "half the fun of this is dressing up."

Christa looked down at her pale silk blouse. "I won't do as I am, will I?"

"Well . . . you're not exactly rock and roll, but . . . you got some jeans and a T-shirt?"

Christa beckoned her in, poured her a glass of wine, and went upstairs to change. As she ran a brush through her hair, she studied her reflection in the bedroom mirror. Eighteen. Hardly more. She might well have been, once again, the young woman who had prepared to go off to another kind of concert in sixth-century Ireland, one that had ended in disaster and loss.

She felt around inside the dresser drawer for something to confine her hair, and her hand came up against a flat box. Her old jewelry.

Well, why not? Half the fun is dressing up.

But she noticed that her eyes looked sad as she coiled the *buinne* around her ponytail and slipped the open bracelets over her wrists. She had worn these same ornaments the night that the Sidh—

"Christa!" called Melinda from below. "We're pushing time a little."

"I'm ready," she called back. Ready for Malmsteen, perhaps, but not for the Sidh.

Melinda lifted her glass as Christa came down the stairs. "That's better." She took off a zebra-stripe bandanna and knotted it about Christa's ankle. "Gotta do something about the general effect. I mean, people are gonna talk if they know I'm hanging around with a *harper*."

"To be sure."

Melinda drove, heading south on Colorado Boulevard, then east on Evans. When they paused at a stoplight, Christa noticed that the man in the car next to them was staring. Melinda saw also. She bared her teeth at him, and he looked away quickly.

"Give him something to tell his grandchildren," said Melinda. "Oh, yeah: in the glove box, Christa. There's some earplugs there. This stuff gets loud."

Christa found the plugs, examined them for a moment, slipped them into her purse. She felt uneasy, and her stomach burned with the wine she had drunk. In contrast with the reckless optimism with which she had approached the Sidh hill on that fatal evening centuries ago, she found now that her nerves were on edge.

She fidgeted with her bracelets, farewell presents from her father when she had set off for the Corca Duibne school. *You take after your great grandmother, my little cruitaire. She was a harper too, and the high king himself gave her these* failge *after she played to heal his son. Take them now: they are all I have to give. Brigit bless.*

"I need to thank you," Melinda said. "That tune you showed me was dynamite. I slept real well. In fact, I had a dream about you. It was pretty strange."

"Hmmm?" Christa was watching the traffic. Ahead, the Rainbow Music Hall came into view.

"There was this lake," said Melinda, "and these little houses made like baskets . . ."

Christa stiffened.

". . . and you were there playing a harp, like that old one you've got that's made of willow." Melinda glanced at her passenger. "Come to think of it, you were wearing jewelry like you've got on now. And a white cape. You looked real young."

"Indeed?" Christa kept her voice steady. "And did you dream anything else?"

"Nah. This bozo that I used to know called me and got me up."

She found herself envying Melinda. Summerland, and rest, and then the sweet oblivion that accompanied a new incarnation and a fresh start. New friends and perhaps an old lover returned with a different name and a different face. She smiled sadly. "It's quickly you've picked up the harp, Melinda," she said. "I can't help but feel that perhaps you've played it before. In another lifetime."

The Mustang bumped into the parking lot. Christa glanced at the line of young folk waiting outside the door of the music hall. Leather jackets, pale faces. Hair that ran the gamut from shaved to spiked.

Melinda found an empty space in the rapidly filling lot, parked, and shut off the engine. "You mean, like reincarnation? Huh. Maybe. Are you some kind of a Buddhist?"

Christa shrugged, opened the door. "No," she said. "I'm a Heathen."

"Hey, sounds great. Wild parties?"

The harper smiled.

The line started to move shortly after they joined it, and Christa blinked as a police officer frisked her at the entrance. "Melinda? Was I right about the single combat?"

"It's okay. This is normal."

Amplified rock was already pouring from the sound system, and accompanying videos flashed on fifteen-foot screens to either side of the stage. Christa fumbled for the earplugs, but the volume was only a small part of her distress: in this crowded hall, the packed adolescent energies crawled like hot spiders across her skin. She sensed youth, but also anger, and rage, and a frantic grasping at power and release; the ability to scream . . . and be heard.

She stumbled, blinked, gripped Melinda's arm as they fought their way through the tossing crowd toward a pair of vacant seats. Sitting down gratefully, she closed her eyes and took a deep breath. She mentally ran through the *sian* that she had taught Melinda, taking it through several variations she knew to be effective against fear. When she opened her eyes, even the sight of a demon face on the video screens was tolerable, and, muted by the earplugs, the steadily pulsing rock seemed oddly reassuring.

Melinda looked concerned. "You okay?"

"I'm fine now."

The vidoes faded, the lights dimmed. "This is going to be Fant'mbalz," said Melinda in the silence that had fallen abruptly over the audience. "It's a local all-girl band—real good, too—and they're opening for Malmsteen. Nice break for them."

About them, people were climbing onto the seats.

"Looks like it's a standing-up concert." Melinda helped Christa up. "Stay forward or the seat'll fold. You sure you're okay?"

Christa nodded. Despite the *sian*, she still felt a vague apprehension. Something was going to happen.

The sound system switched to full, and the stage lights flared in parti-colors. The drummer smacked her sticks together in a four-count and the crowd's cheers were drowned out by a wave of sound that crashed through the room like a white-hot sea. Christa felt it as a solid mass that went straight for her heart, ripping through her chest, grappling with her body and her mind.

"Brigit!" But she could not even hear her own voice. A guitar blasted out of the whirl of music, notes climbing one over another in a shrill, rising cascade; reaching up, screaming . . .

And something *was* happening. Midsummer. There was something *here*. . . .

CHAPTER FOUR

One of those days.

Starting with the burned eggs, Kevin's Saturday had progressed juggernaut-like from one niggling but aggravating disaster to another. In loading his car for the trip into town, he had dropped Frankie's guitar and added another dent to its patina of injuries. He had been late for his first student at the guitar school, thereby delaying each subsequent lesson by thirty minutes. Come evening, his car battery had died, and somehow his gas tank had, in addition, mysteriously emptied itself. When he had finally reached a service station, he had discovered that he was low on cash.

So this night was perhaps appropriate for a heavy-metal concert. For a few hours he could scream out his frustration and slide into a world where pounding music and an overwhelming sense of sheer power would wipe out the annoyances of the day in a cathartic rush of volume.

He arrived late.

The doors were shut, but he could hear the bass lines pulsing out of the building from across the parking lot. It was all right after all. Fant'mbalz was still playing. He had not missed Malmsteen.

The girl behind the ticket window looked up from bundling stubs. "Hey . . . Kevin!"

He squinted at her through the heavy glass. "Liz, how are you?"

She shrugged. "Doing okay. The old man's got a gig up at InsideOut tonight, the baby's with my mother, and I'm making a few bucks. You here to see Yngwie?"

"Yeah . . . some head-banging to top off the day. Good crowd?"

"All sorts—come to see the maestro. We even got

some kids from the guitar school at D.U. Kinda geeky. But Ken's here. And Bethanny and Laura. You remember Melinda?''

"I think I met her once. Little blonde?''

"That's her. She brought a friend. Young chick.'' Liz laughed. "Looked totally weirded out when Harv frisked her. But . . .'' She touched her brown curls. ". . . boy, what I wouldn't give to have hair like that.''

Applause from within, screams, shouts. She glanced over her shoulder. "Break time. You probably should go in, but don't expect to find a seat. Real full house.''

Kevin shrugged. "They're all standing up anyway, right?''

Liz laughed again and gestured to someone in the darkness behind her. The door opened, and Kevin slipped into the intermission crowd.

Acquaintances tapped him on the shoulder, shook his hand, waved good-bye—the men lean and shaggy, the women sensual and aloof. Glitter and glam, spandex and denim. A few hours ago these same superstars had doubtless been working construction and waiting tables.

Kevin shouldered through knots of teenagers clutching tour shirts and quart-sized Cokes, slid past clumps of young men with shaved scalps who compensated for their lack of hair with an abundance of leather and chain.

"Hey, Kevin.''

"How'ya doin', guy?'' Proffered hands, backslaps, a half-timid, half-fierce cordiality that made him wonder what they had been saying three seconds before.

Of course they shook his hand, called him by name, asked with all sincerity how he was. He had once been offered a contract. And in the intricate mythology of popular music, that meant that Kevin had connections, that he must *know somebody,* that anything was possible if one were his friend.

He continued on his way, his scalp dampening with the heat in the room. Looking up, he saw Melinda, suitably attired in the very best metal fashion, and beside her—

He laughed to himself. It was the chick with the harp. Her fiery hair flashed over her shoulder in a blaze of bright color when she turned to Melinda to ask a question. Her eyes were bright, focused, intent, as though she were staring through a window at something unimaginable.

The lights dimmed. From behind the backdrop came a characteristic series of arpeggios—phrygian mode interchanging with harmonic minor—dark, exotic harmonies reminiscent of the florid violin of Nicolò Paganini.

Malmsteen.

People were screaming suddenly, raising hands, fists, jumping up and down, fighting their way back to their seats. Kevin edged his way past a girl in a T-shirt on which was painted *Yngwie is God* in scarlet letters that had run slightly, as though carved in living flesh. He climbed up the two-inch pipe railings against the rear wall and wedged himself in.

Darkness. *One-two-three-four . . .*

The stage exploded into light.

The courtyard is empty. High above, pennants and oriflamme flutter whitely against the dark sky. Silvery laughter spills out of an upper window of the palace, cascades down the milky walls, swirls amid columns of jasper and chalcedony, falls into silence.

As usual. As always.

Siudb peers through the archway. Orfide's harp lies beside the bench, unattended. She tries to calm herself. Even if she is caught, there is little that Orfide can do. Lamcrann is infatuated with her, and the bard would never risk the displeasure of the king by harming a royal toy.

She slips into the courtyard, follows the deeper shadows beneath the walls, nears the harp.

who

"Siudb Ní Corb. I would play upon you."

play

Her Sidh garments rustle as she lifts the ornate instrument. The strings sigh, and she feels a wash of energy across her skin.

play

"I shall, fair one. Might I know your name?"

Clesac

"I am honored."

play

The ornate harp pressed to her side, she makes her way through the shadows to the archway, then out into the fragrant gardens. Her own harp is of plain willow, uncarved, without decoration. It is, she supposes, within

the palace somewhere, perhaps resting among Lamcrann's
curiosities in the upper rooms where she is not allowed to
go.

Tears come to her eyes. She sang while she made that
harp, hoping that her song might bring to it more melody
than her hands alone ever would. It was the last music
she made with her voice, for, under Struitmor, the study
of the harp was all consuming, and she was not as skilled
as Chairiste.

Her voice was her strength. And she put it aside to
follow her lover.

Lost in her thoughts, she does not see a tall, silver-
haired figure move out of the darkness of the palace door.

. . . dark, violent whirlwinds of sound, of energy, spilling out in a murderous torrent, pouring through the
packed fans who, shoulder to shoulder, hand to hand,
crowded before the stage . . .

. . . light . . .

. . . music, or thunder, or the roots and branches of
terrifying oaks and yews, spectral in the blue-white flashes
of incandescence, reaching into other worlds, shattering
earth and sky . . . screaming . . .

. . . *Yngwie* . . . *Yngwie* . . . *Yngwie* . . .

. . . pouring out of an ivory-colored Strat and black
Marshall amplifiers . . . the fat, electronic shriek of circuitry pushing overload, vacuum tubes glowing red hot,
speakers vibrating in unnumbered frequencies, innumerable harmonics . . .

Music had changed since Christa had studied in Corca
Duibne. The stately, unmodulated modes had, over the
centuries, given way, first to the strict and predictable
division of major and minor, and then to the polymor-
phous fire of chromatics, the black flame of harmonic
minor and diminished scales.

But Christa had paid little attention. She had had her
instrument and her life. The branching, interweaving evolution of classical and popular music could not, would
not, affect her.

Until now.

Even through the earplugs, her head was ringing with
the volume and with the steady, pounding drive of heavy
metal. This was nothing like the rock and roll she had

heard from car radios as they passed her in traffic, the music distorting into a nightmare parody as it squeezed through three-inch speakers. This was real, immediate, an apocalyptic reification of sheer sound.

Trained in music as both art and magic, Christa felt and heard the energy that fireballed from one side of the stage to the other. Uncontrolled, without direction, it hovered on the edge of sight in shades of red and gold, of electric blue and near-luminous black. But, were it channeled, it could manifest, it could heal, it could do almost anything.

Malmsteen handled his guitar effortlessly, tossing it into the air, lifting his hands away from it to let waves of feedback inundate the hall while his vocalist stood his ground and spat lyrics at the audience.

She could not understand the words. English had deserted her. She was a Gaeidil again, and what thoughts she could muster in the hurricane of sound beating against her face were in her old language. But she understood the music, the energy, the fire, and the power of what was happening on stage; and she knew what she herself could do with them. If gates had to be opened, she would rip them off their hinges. If Orfide had to be defeated, she would bury him.

Her lover was being held captive by creatures of ice and twilight, and Chairiste Ní Cummen was, this night of Midsummer, finding it within her power to free her. She lifted an arm adorned with golden bracelets, her hand balled into a fist, and in a voice loud enough that Melinda heard it even over the sound of the concert and turned, half puzzled, half afraid at the change in her teacher, Christa screamed out her challenge to the Sidh:
"Rock and roll!"

The melody grows under Siudb's fingers, and Clesac, with aloyal devotion, strives in its own way to make her wishes real. On a hillside, looking off into the dimness of the Realm in which shadowy rivers flow through fields of muted color, woman and harp fight to bridge the gap between worlds.

Siudb's hands are stiff. Painfully, she makes her way through the turns and variations of the song, and the air before her begins to glow with the outlines of a gate: a wide archway, etched in blue flame.

Working from memory, she recreates the variations that Chairiste once played. This one, in triple time, works its way into the fabric of the worlds, and then, with the division of the rhythm into multiples of two, dissolves the barriers between them.

The ruddy glow of a setting sun suddenly invades the Realm, shadows of blue and gray fleeing before it. Siudb looks through the gate. A vast, golden plain stretches off to the horizon, an unbroken sea of tossing wheat.

The mortal lands. She struggles on, firming the gateway. She smells ripe grain and rich earth. Cirrus clouds burn scarlet on the horizon, their edges gilt with sunlight. The air that pours into the Realm is warm and dry, dusty and alive.

But her hands are aching already, and she has still an even mightier spell to harp into existence. For unless she can undo the effects of the timeless Realm upon herself, a single step into this land of sunset and wheat will be fatal.

And Chairiste *might* be alive. It is still possible, in spite of Orfide's words.

Again she turns to the harpstrings, fighting her hands. Clesac tries to help, but the fault is with the harper: Siudb cannot negotiate the intricacies of the spell.

The mortal lands are within her sight, but not within her grasp. Tearfully, she sets Clesac down, goes to the edge of the Realm, stands, hopeless, at the border. The warm wind is fragrant. The sunset glows on her skin.

She is very tempted to cast herself upon the dusty ground and accept the consequences. At least she would gain the Summerland. There would be a chance then. Chairiste would find her . . . someday.

But before she can decide, before she can act, she is seized from behind and pulled back. A practiced hand is playing Clesac, closing the gate. The land of wheat and sunset fades, and the Sidh guards turn her around and bring her face to face with Orfide.

The bard's face is a studied mask of indifference, though Siudb knows that he is raging within. "Little *timpanach*," he says softly, "would you leave us so suddenly? And without even apologizing for your words to me?"

"I have nothing to say to you, Sidh."

His long-nailed hands caressing Clesac, Orfide eyes her

up and down. "The king allows you too much freedom, I think. If matters were left to me—"

"But they are not left to you."

Orfide's jaw hardens, but in a moment he is indifferent again. "Perhaps," he says, touching a string of his second-best harp, "I should take away your knowledge of music." He looks down at her hands. They are still shaking with the strain of the magic she attempted to work. "But perhaps I do not have to."

He gestures to the guards. They release her. Carrying his harp, the bard starts back toward the palace, and the guards follow. Siudb stands for a moment, then turns silently and touches the ground where, a few moments before, she had seen wheat, and sunlight, and scarlet clouds.

Christa decided that she had become soft and passive over the years, taking refuge behind her harp, hiding from the changing world. The fierce Gaeidil woman who had run off to the *Cruitreacha,* who had challenged the Sidh and battled with their master bard, had become timid and uncertain. In striving for the same stasis as that which enveloped the Realm, she had, like the beings she hated, diminished.

If nothing else, rock and roll had shown her that. But its fierce barrage had also shown her both a way back to herself and a means of freeing Judith. As she sat in the fluorescent light of a Denny's, eating a late dinner with Melinda, her harper-trained mind was analyzing what she had heard that night: tearing the music apart, combining the sounds and the magics with what she already knew, synthesizing the whole into what she sensed could be a devastating weapon.

And at the same time she asked questions, probing at the history of rock and roll as she had once queried Sruitmor about the evolution of the harp and its music. Melinda answered her as she could. "I just play the stuff, Christa," she said over the rim of her milkshake. "There's a history to all this, sure, but it doesn't mean shit. Rock survives because it's always *now*. I can tell you that there's jazz in it, and blues, and there's hillbilly stuff in it from way back, but everything changed when it all came together."

"When did it come together?"

"Back in the '50s, with Elvis and Buddy Holly and the rest. But the stuff you heard tonight . . . well . . . some people say that it was Eric Clapton that started it. He was with this band called Cream, and he took blues licks and riffs and combined them with a heavy rock beat. That was in about '68. They played a tune called 'Crossroads' that way. Incredible. Blew everyone away. Led Zeppelin came along the next year. That was the first band you could really call heavy metal. But it was still based on the blues. There were classical influences too, all along, but later on some guys started to specialize in them. Uli Roth started working with diminished scales a few years ago, and then Yngwie . . . well, you heard what Yngwie does."

Yes, she had heard. Out of the sixth century had come intricately weaving melodies and countermelodies that contrasted and reinforced one another, chiming out of bronze strings plucked and muted by long nails and agile fingers. In the twentieth, the brute power of elementary chords and primal rhythms had developed into a firm foundation for harmonically sophisticated solos that blasted out of the meeting of plastic pick and steel strings.

Fatigue was plucking at her sleeve, but her rejuvenated body paid no attention. She finished her hamburger. "Have you records of this that I can listen to?"

"Christa, this is weird."

"Indeed?"

"You're a harper."

"I am, surely."

Melinda spread her hands. "What's going on?"

Christa smiled, stretched. She had been hiding too long. "I'm becoming a real harper, Melinda. And I need to go back to school." Melinda stared at her. "Now, about those records . . ."

Highway 285 wound into the mountains. There was only a little traffic, and Kevin kept his high beams on most of the time. The road rose to meet him, signs glowed out of the darkness, double yellow lines led him home.

Good concert, that. Malmsteen was everything they said he was, and his tendinitis did not seem to be slowing him down a bit. Kevin thought he had detected a few fumbles during the acoustic introduction to "Black Star," but fumbles were a hazard of the trade. Out of all those notes, a few could be incorrect without hurting anything.

The feeling was the important thing. Kevin had heard critics of the young Swede insist that he was no more than a technician, an automaton who hid his lack of emotion behind a flurry of notes. But there was feeling there, and it manifested as a clean precision that lofted the guitar leads and solos into rarefied heights. If Malmsteen was without passion, then so was his idol, Paganini. Different kinds of music, different kinds of feeling. People had said the same thing of old Bach, too.

And what about me?

He thought of old Frankie, of B.B., of Clapton and the rest. What about Kevin Larkin? Where had it gone? Where was it hiding? Passion. Feeling. Making music was like making love—Frankie had said that once—but he wondered if he had ever really made love. Guilt-ridden fucking in the back of his father's car in the hills west of Cheyenne had led on to anonymous unions and furtive partings in dark rooms above seedy bars in towns that were so similar that they had not possessed names, only vague recollections of stale smoke and sour beer, of blues drifting up from below. . . .

Christa sat on the arm of Melinda's broken-down sofa, swinging her feet in time to the music as she listened intently to the songs that Melinda played from her record collection. Some of what she heard horrified her, some she found amateurish and amusing, some was merely noise. But she also heard songs that made her heart pound as though she were back in the concert and listening to this music for the first time, hearing potentials, hearing magic.

She asked for more, always pushing in the direction of the violence and passion of heavy metal. Puzzled, bewildered, Melinda complied, and the hours passed, filled with everything from early Beatles to late Metallica.

The sky was lightening when Melinda finally snapped off the stereo. "I'm bushed," she said. "I have to take you home so I can crash."

Christa herself felt strong and free, her native attitudes

and pride stretching like long-unused muscles. She recalled the prayer with which she had begun this long day, smiled. "Where does one go to learn to play rock and roll?" she said, reaching for her purse.

Melinda slid a record back into its cover. "You used to have to take your chances with your local music store, but there's a place just opened a few months ago down on Evans. Guitar Tech. I've met the guy that teaches rock there. His name's Kevin Larkin. He's good: got a record offer a few years back. Big bucks."

"I see." Record contracts. Stardom. But her own goals were immediate and without complications. She did not want money or fame: she simply wanted Judith.

"Can't figure it out, though," Melinda continued. "He turned it down. I sure as hell wouldn't. Anyway, Kevin's a pro. He can teach you anything you want to know about rock."

Christa nodded as she scribbled the names in a small notebook. "Where do I buy an electric guitar?"

"Are you sure you want to do this?"

"Surely."

"Do you know what you're getting into?"

Did she? Had she known what she was getting into when she had run away from home? Or that night at the Sidh hill? Or that moment in the never-ending, static present of the Realm when she had stolen Ceis and won her way back to mortality? "Not in the slightest, Melinda," she said. "But I know what I have to do. Where do I get a guitar?"

The morning was growing outside, and the cheap white curtains of the apartment had paled enough to show their wear and stains. Melinda chewed silently on her lip as she stared at the door to her front closet, her eyes hollow within their dark makeup. She appeared to be remembering something unpleasant. "Yeah. Right. You need a guitar." She stood up, opened the closet, and pulled out a flat, rectangular case. "Listen: it's hard enough to buy something even when you know what you're looking for, and there's a lot of rip-off joints out there. If you want, I'll give you this. It's a funny color, but it plays okay."

She unsnapped the case and lifted out an avocado-green guitar. "This is a Strat. Like what Yngwie uses. An old boyfriend gave it to me."

Melinda plunked a few strings, tuned the instrument, and squinted appraisingly down the length of the fingerboard. Christa was reminded of Sruitmor: the old harper had examined her first, crudely made harp in just this same way, peering at it from one angle, then another. He had checked the heft, the tuning, the workmanship, and then he had . . .

Melinda held out the guitar. "Here. It's in good shape, even if it's the same color as a Waring blender."

. . . held it out to her.

Christa looked into Melinda's tired eyes. Where was Sruitmor now? In the Summerland? For so long?

She took the guitar and rested it on her thigh. Her left hand fumbled for a moment as it struggled to comprehend the frets. She could learn. It would not be easy, but she could learn.

Running a hand along the supple strings, she took note of the guitar. Twenty-one frets: a little over three octaves. It was a few notes less than her willow harp, but the guitar contained the sharps and flats also, which her harp did not.

She met the bassist's blue eyes again. *Sruitmor had blue eyes too, did he not?*

She could not quite remember. Goddess, it had been a long time.

"Thank you, Melinda," she said. "I'll try to be worthy of this."

"It's just rock and roll, Christa." Melinda shrugged, then laughed. "I've corrupted my harp teacher! I can't believe it!"

Melinda drove her and the guitar home and dropped them off with a wave as the sun rose over the eastern plains. The sky was a deep blue, promising a fine day; and when Christa let herself into her house, the mirror in the hallway showed her a young woman with a guitar. She looked very like the girl who had faced the Sidh with only a harp of willow.

Shrouded in blue velvet, Ceis stood on the table in the studio. It said nothing, but she sensed its approval.

CHAPTER
FIVE

The highway east of Bismarck was a gray line that lay ruler straight amid the gold of unrelieved fields of wheat. It receded into the distance, diminishing with perspective, turning into a vague heat shimmer just before it reached the horizon.

In the equipment bus, Lisa Donnatelli fumbled beside the seat for her jacket, fumbled some more into a pocket, and came up with a pair of sunglasses. The noon sun glared off the North Dakota plains, and though the glasses fogged the view as much as they darkened it, she grunted with relief once she had them on.

She checked the dashboard, then her watch. On schedule. The band would be in Bismarck by four, which left a few hours for setup—providing, of course, that they could find the club—and even some time to eat.

Her eyes felt dry and full of grit, her skin stretched and taut. She needed a full day of sleep in a real bed, in a real room that had a door she could lock. She had had enough of the roach-infested camaraderie of band houses and cheap motels.

But a day off was a half a week away, and for now she had to drive this endless strip of concrete with nothing to look forward to come evening save four sets in a smoky bar, abuse from the local rednecks, and two or three hours of comatose sleep.

She glanced over her shoulder. Her bandmates lay dozing on cushions beside cases and speaker cabinets. One turned over, belched loudly, and pried one eye open as he scratched at a stubble of beard. "You want me to take over, Boo-boo?"

It was the most civil thing any of them had said to her since the auditions. But she shook her head. "Go ahead and sleep, Max. I'm doing all right."

56

Max rolled back over and began snoring. After that argument about band funds in Fargo, she was not sure she felt safe enough to sleep among them. Anyway, driving was like drumming: once you got in a groove, it was easier to continue than to stop.

But was it maybe like living, too? She had been on the road now for six weeks, playing one tiny bar after another, and she had nothing to show for it save a dozen broken drumsticks and some extra lines in her face: a repeat of the tour before that, and the one before that and . . .

Sometimes, in the middle of endless drives like this, with the sun burning down on the plains and the interior of the bus turning close and stifling in spite of open windows and a cooler full of soft drinks, she found herself drifting off into daydreams about nine-to-five jobs and lifestyles in which she did not have to worry about money, a place to sleep, or strapped bandmates plotting to steal her equipment; in which she possessed a stability and fulfillment that eluded her in this life of pickup bands and coffee shops.

"Yeah, Boo-boo," she muttered as she reached back into the cooler and fished out a pop, "you're going to settle down and marry a rock star someday. Sure you are. And then what are you going to do? Bang your head against the walls? All you know is drums, girl, and there ain't no magic in the world gonna save you, no matter what your grandma said."

Groove? Or rut? She was not certain anymore. Was there even a difference?

She was tired. She checked her watch again. Four hours to Bismarck.

Danny Larkin watched the evening fall over the Bighorn Mountains. The sky just above the peaks still glowed with the last touches of sunset and, higher up, the stars came out to shine down on the city of Sheridan.

The day had been hot, but the breeze from the north was cool, and it sighed through the balcony railings and whispered through the curtains and the screens. Danny tried to forget the sound of the traffic below, tried, in fact, to forget everything except this balcony, and this night, and these stars. . . .

A clink of glass inside the apartment brought him
back. "Benji?"

"Right here."

"Would you fix me another drink?"

Benji examined him through the screen, sipped at a
glass of soda water. "I'd like to hold you to two, love."

Danny sighed. Benji slid the screen open and stood
behind him.

"It's pretty tonight."

"Yeah." Danny lifted his glass and let the last of the
alcohol slide down his throat.

Benji put a hand on his shoulder. "You okay?"

"Just thinking about the seminary. I can't seem to get
it out of my head these days. I keep wondering what
they're doing there now. Probably eating. Father Paul is
reading in that weird Georgia accent of his."

Benji leaned casually against the railing. His build was
that of a wrestler, compact and taut; and Danny wished
he could have some of Benji's presence, for he himself
was fair and thin, someone who, even after a year and a
half away from the seminary, still looked like a model for
the illustrations in a child's missal.

Benji touched Danny's head, played for a moment
with a lock of his hair. "Is that all you're stewing about?"

"No, only half. The other half is my parents."

"That was pretty hard on you."

"Yeah." Danny lifted his glass again, realized it was
empty, put it down. "They were so proud of me. Now
I'm some kind of leper."

He rubbed at his eyes. It was only a formality: his tears
had dried up long ago.

Benji frowned. "You're sweating. Have you got a
fever?"

"Nah. Just terminal guilt." Danny laughed, but he
found that he was shaking with a sudden chill. Sweat was
running down his forehead. He slumped in his chair. "It's
probably nothing."

Benji leaned closer. "You had a good sweat last night,
too. Your side of the bed was soaked."

"I'm just tired."

Benji poured his soda water into Danny's glass. "Drink
that. You need some fluids. You've been losing weight,
and now it looks like you've got some kind of virus." His

voice was a soft, concerned basso. "Would you do me a favor, loverboy? Would you take that cute little ass of yours and get it over to the clinic tomorrow?"

"Why bother?"

Benji touched Danny's head again. "Because I love you, you fearful little Jesuit. Enough to coax you out of the bar scene, enough to ask you to live with me, enough to want to keep you going." He knelt down beside Danny and wrapped him in his thick arms. Together they watched the last light fade from the sky. "Do it for me."

When Kevin Larkin got to the guitar school on Monday morning, he found a note tacked to his office door. *Christa Cruitaire—3:30*, it said in Dave's backhanded printing.

He plucked it off, walked round the corner, and stuck his head into Dave's room. The sandy-haired teacher looked up, as did an equally sandy-haired girl with an acoustic guitar on her lap. She blinked at Kevin with big blue eyes as though this rocker with the long hair and the ragged denim jacket were exactly the sort of person that her parents had nightmares about.

"What's this?" Kevin waved the note.

Dave squinted at it through his thick glasses. "Oh, her. Some girl who wants to play guitar like that Malmsteen guy you're always raving about. She called first thing this morning."

"She coming in?"

"Three-thirty, like it says. You had an opening then." Dave leered at his student for a moment, then turned back to Kevin. "Stay out of her pants, Kev."

"Huh?"

"We all know about rockers." He looked at his student again. "Don't worry, Rae. I'll protect you."

She nodded. "Right," she said resignedly. "That's all I need."

Kevin started back toward his office. "Don't believe a word of it, Rae," he called over his shoulder. "Folk guitarists are all animals. Why do you think there are so many folk?"

He glanced at the slip once more and then stuck it on his wall. It was to be expected, really. A virtuoso like Malmsteen could not possibly give a concert without triggering someone's interest. When Chris Parkening had played at the Denver Center a few months back, the school had received numerous calls about classical lessons. With Malmsteen, it was metal.

Another head-banging teenager who wanted to conquer the world with an electric guitar and a Marshall stack. Interesting, though, that a girl would be so inspired.

Reverently, he hung Frankie's guitar on the wall. "You're still the best, old man," he said. He plucked a string with his fingernail. "We'll see what you can teach me today, huh?"

As a girl, she had traveled to Corca Duibne on foot with a small, fat-bellied harp under her arm and Siudb Ní Corb by her side. Anything had been possible then, for the world was new and her fingers were talented. It did not seem in the least bit unrealistic to believe that, in twelve years, she and her lover would leave the cluster of houses and outbuildings by the lake and make their way through the five provinces of Eriu as master harpers.

But the plans for the future that she had made in Corca Duibne had collapsed, fallen into a timeless ruin; and today, to all appearances little older, she drove to Guitar Tech in her car, parked in the steaming lot in front of the modest office building, and climbed the steps with an electric guitar in her hand . . . alone.

She padded along the beige carpet until she came to a door with a small sign on it: *Guitar Tech*. Faintly, she heard a record playing: the blues.

Years before, when she had lived in New York and the Ninth Avenue El was still news, she had heard something similar one evening as she walked past the closed door of a black tavern: the sound of steel strings plucked and stretched in a bleak, minor pentatonic scale that somehow managed to sound joyful, as though even the deepest sorrow might be surmounted with the aid of a guitar and the will to make music. But she was white, and that door in New York had been closed to her.

This door was not. She turned the knob and found herself in a small lobby with an old sofa, two chairs, and walls that were light blue where they were not covered with posters of rock stars. Straight ahead, an archway opened into a large classroom containing a blackboard and a row or two of folding chairs. A short hall led off to the right. The blues seeped out from a closed door to the left: a scratchy, off-key guitar wailing alongside a near-unintelligible singer.

"Gonna buy this whole goddam town—
Put it in my shoe . . ."

A young man with a guitar was leaning against the wall, his fingers firing off licks and scales. He looked up when Christa entered and stared at her from beneath a shaggy mop of hair.

"Good afternoon," she said.

"Uh . . . hi."

"I have an appointment with Kevin Larkin."

"Uh . . . he's in the sound room right now." He nodded at the closed door. "He'll be done in a few." He was still staring. "You're . . . "

"I'm here to study rock and roll."

"Yeah . . ." His fingers buzzed for a few seconds, then: "What are you into?"

Christa's long hair rustled across her crepe de Chine blouse as she eased the guitar case to the carpet. "Heavy metal."

He blinked. "You sure?"

"My spandex pants, which I don't have, are in the wash today. So is my leather jacket, which I also don't have."

"Uh . . . yeah . . ." He went back to his scales, concentrating on his hands considerably more than he needed to.

A head stuck itself out of a doorway in the hall. It peered at her from behind thick glasses. "You're Christa?"

"I am, surely."

"A*ha.* I'm Dave Thomas." The head looked at the sound-room door. "Hey, Kev," it shouted. The stereo shut off. "Christa's here. Mind what I told you: keep your hands to yourself." The head disappeared, but from the open door came the sound of a nasal tenor:

"Wheeen Irish eyes are smiliiing . . ."

Christa felt her face grow warm. This was a music school? Well, she would show them what a harper from Corca Duibne could do.

The door to the sound room opened and a tall, dark-haired man came toward her, offering his hand. "Hi,

Christa. I'm Kevin Larkin." He stopped short and stared. "Hey, you're the chick with the harp—" He caught himself. "Uh . . . sorry."

She smiled as she clasped his hand. "I'm Christa Cruitaire. And I am a harper, true."

He was still embarrassed. "I saw you on the street the other day. You had a little harp with you. I . . . uh . . . didn't think anyone played those anymore."

"Some do," she said. "I teach harp." Kevin reminded her of some of the warriors who had now and again stayed at her parents' steading: tall, sturdy men who were more comfortable with weapons than with people, who cast themselves into the middle of frenzied combat but stood ill at ease before women.

"My grandfather had a harp something like that," he said. "I suppose it's up in my dad's attic now."

"A sad fate for a harp . . . or for any instrument."

"Yeah." For a moment, he seemed to be elsewhere, but he came to himself and gestured at the case by her feet. "Why don't you pull out your axe and come on back to my room. We can start your torture."

"Axe?"

"Your guitar."

"Oh. Of course." Bending, she unsnapped the catches and opened the case.

"Never seen a Strat that color. Was it a custom job?"

Christa straightened. "I don't know. A friend gave this to me."

She leaned the empty case against the wall and followed him into his office. There was just enough room in it for a desk, a filing cabinet, and two chairs.

Christa had spent most of Sunday examining the Strat, feeling out the relationships between hands and fingerboard and frets, the subtle curve of the neck and the height of the strings above it, the density of the body and the sound that the guitar made unamplified. She was a harper, but she came to her first lesson with the groundwork for her guitar technique already laid. Her left hand wrapped itself easily about the neck of the instrument as she sat down in Kevin's office, and the feel of a pick in her right was no longer totally foreign.

"Have you studied before?" said Kevin.

"I have not."

"You want to learn . . ."

"Heavy metal. I was at the Malmsteen concert Saturday night, and I liked what I heard."

"Electric guitar isn't harp, you know."

She nearly laughed. "I'm well aware of that."

"Okay then. Let's get started. We'll go easy until you get used to it and your fingers callus up a little."

He showed her basic chord formations and scales, added some standard blues licks. That would have been enough—more than enough—to keep most beginners busy for several weeks. But Christa was a musician who had been trained in the exacting methods of the Corca Duibne school. If she played a melody or a chord twice, she knew it. If she listened to the sound of a scale, she was instantly aware of its harmonic interaction with any accompanying chord.

Not satisifed with basics, she asked for more, methodically pressing Kevin for whatever he could give her. She noticed that he was suddenly scrambling to keep up with her demands.

"Are you sure you don't want to stop with this?" he said at last.

"Are we out of time?"

"No . . . but, hey, this is a lot of rock for you to absorb."

"Kevin," she explained patiently, "I have an entire week to work on this. What I've got now will take only a night or two."

"At least let me write some of this down."

"Write it down?" The idea seemed outlandish. She wrote out music for her students, but that was because they were students.

"You can't tell me you'll remember all of it."

"I certainly will."

He stared at her, then shook his head. "You're out of my league, Christa." He seemed almost afraid.

"Nonsense," she said softly. "It was not a part of your training. It was of mine."

"Yeah? Where did you study?"

She hesitated. "In . . . Ireland."

Kevin leaned back in his chair, rubbing the back of his neck. "You must have had one hell of a teacher."

Gently, she deflected the conversation. "Is there something by Malmsteen that you think would be suitable for me? I'd like to explore those sounds."

Kevin looked at her guitar, at her hands. "I'll tell you, Christa, I wouldn't dream of giving something like that to a beginning student. But if you're a beginner, I'm damned scared to think of what you'll be like when you're advanced."

She smiled thinly, hoping that she would also frighten a certain Sidh bard. "How about 'Black Star'? That had some wonderful harmonies in it. Very powerful."

"Let's see." He searched through a folder and came up with several scrawled pages of tablature. "I pulled it off the record a few months ago. It's tough." He handed her the sheets. "The lines are the strings," he explained, "the numbers are frets."

She looked, understood. "Do you have something I can listen to?"

"We can go into the sound room. There's a stereo there. You want to try it?"

"Please. If I may."

Guitar in hand, she followed him to the sound room. The student was still leaning up against the wall, and he eyed Christa as she went by. "How's it goin'?"

Kevin nodded at Christa. "Eddie Van Halen better move over, Jeff. This lady's fantastic."

Jeff snorted softly and went back to his practicing.

"Hey, remember," said Kevin. "You heard it here first."

"Yeah, sure."

The sound room contained a stereo, albums, tapes, and two very large speakers. Christa drew up a folding chair while Kevin flipped through the records. "It's in here somewhere."

"Is this any trouble for you?"

"No trouble at all. I do this all the time. There isn't much that's actually written down in rock and roll, so almost everything I teach has to be pulled off a record."

"Oral tradition?"

"Kind of." He found the album and cued it up on the turntable. "You just have to remember it all. There's no score, and it's always changing."

Absently, Christa picked at her guitar. The Sidh did not change. "It lives, then," she said.

He blinked at her choice of words, but he nodded. "Yeah. I know some players who never repeat a solo."

The music started them, and she opened herself to it, listening with concentration, mentally cataloging the melodies, the harmonies, the rhythms. Theme, countertheme, variation, free improvisation—she might have been sitting at Sruitmor's feet as he worked magic, or in the shadows of the Sidh palace as Orfide wove his timeless spells.

"Once more, please," she said when the cut had finished.

Kevin set the tone arm back to the beginning. When the music was done, Christa nodded and stood up.

"I'll have it ready for you next week," she said, handing back the sheets of tablature.

He stood as though struck. "You've got to be kidding."

"I'll have it."

Blankly, he looked at the pages. "All right, if you say so."

There was fear in his voice, though she could not understand why. Silently, she cased her guitar and picked up her purse. Kevin watched, his face drawn.

"Do you happen to know any of the Ossianic ballads?" he asked suddenly. "My grandfather used to sing them. I was trying to remember one the other day, but it just wouldn't come."

"The songs of Oisin, son of Find Mac Cumaill? I do. Which are you thinking of?"

"It's a hymn to the Virgin. It starts off: *Sturad me dod mholadh* . . . something or other."

"It is a hymn, surely," she said. "But not to the Virgin." She thought for a moment, picking up the thread of a mnemonic, then began to sing, her untrained voice reedy and thin:

*"Stiurad me dod molad
Cia nac ollam me am eígis,
A gnúis ainglíde, gan loct!
Tug sugad t'ucta dom réigteac."*

When she finished, there was silence in the school. Jeff had stopped his practicing. Kevin had his eyes closed as though trying to hold onto some inner vision.

Dave's head was sticking out of the doorway again. "What was that? German?"

"Gaeid—" She caught herself. She had given the words

the sounds they had had when she was young, when they had still possessed the corners and edges that passing centuries had worn away. "Irish."

"Never heard Irish like that before."

"It's . . . my dialect, perhaps."

"You sing well."

She smiled uneasily. "Not really. It's not natural to me. But . . ." She thought of Judith, of her incredibly pure, incredibly strong voice. How often had she heard it after they had begun their studies? "But I had a friend once who could sing. . . ."

She suddenly wondered what Judith had given up in order to remain with her. Her voice? Something so important?

Troubled, she picked up her guitar and left.

"Well, Kevin-me-lad," said Dave. "How did it go?"

Kevin's eyes were still closed. He sighed, rubbed at them.

"Well?"

Again, he looked at the sheets of tablature in his hands. "She's fucking scary, Dave."

CHAPTER
SIX

Close to midnight, Christa's studio was dark save for the dim glow of the city that filtered through the backyard trees. Ceis, unveiled, stood proudly, silently. If it had any opinion about the strange instrument of plastic and steel that had intruded into this sanctuary, it said nothing.

Under Sruitmor, Christa had spent twelve hours a day in utter darkness, alone save for her harp. Deprived of sight, restricted to a world of touch and sound, she had learned to let her hands guide themselves through the intricacies of polyphonic technique, and the notes that had chimed from her instrument had grown in meaning and weight until she had come to understand not only the subtle energies generated by her playing, but also the massive powers that those energies could control.

Suantraige. Gentraige. Goltraige. Sleeping. Laughing. Crying. But these traditional abilities of the harp were only a beginning. There was more to music, much more: powers to heal, to change, to create. And in her fourth year of study, Christa had begun to unlock those also. Her fingers were quick, her mind receptive, and the skills of the *Cruitreacha* had come to her almost effortlessly. Too effortlessly, it seemed, for she had decided that she could learn from Sruitmor and the Sidh both, and that arrogance had cost her everything.

But in the darkness of her studio in Denver, she was relearning music, relearning magic, preparing to win back from the Sidh what she had once lost; and as she had once practiced the harp, so she now practiced the guitar: in the dark, incessantly. Eyes closed, ears straining to hear each nuance of sound that came from the fretted and plucked strings, she explored the personality of a new instrument, the yearning earthiness of the blues, and the coruscating fire of harmonic minor. She had no amplifier, but no matter: there was time for volume later on. For now, she learned notes and scales, and she felt with elation the strange but potent energy that washed down her arm when she stretched a string up and shook it with a gentle vibrato.

Among the frets of the Strat, she found old songs and melodies from her training with Sruitmor, the straightforward modal airs of the Corca Duibne school. Layered throughout the familiar, though, were chromatic potentials: the sharps and flats that lay between the strings of her harp, unthought of by ancient harpers either mortal or immortal. With the addition of those extra notes, a familiar melody could suddenly explode in unexpected directions, modulate in surprising ways.

By day she was a harp teacher. At night she struggled with the guitar, her shoulders aching, her fingertips blistered from fretting the taut steel strings. The Malmsteen solo was easy to play, but playing did not imply understanding, and she fought her way through the lightning scales and arpeggios, striving to comprehend the flashes of blue and violet and emerald that erupted from the music.

At her next lesson with Kevin, she played "Black Star" note for note. Kevin watched, listened. He showed her how to pinch a note by striking the string with her pick and immediately muting it with her thumb. The resultant harmonic shrilled even without an amplifier. He listened again.

"Hang on a second, Christa," he said. He stuck his head out the door. "Hey, Jeff," he called into the lobby. "Come here a minute, will you?"

The student who had been lounging against the wall lounged up to the door. "Yeah?"

Kevin folded his arms. "Play 'Black Star,' Christa."

She played it. The pinched notes rang perfectly, the feeling and nuance were exactly right. She saw flickers of energy around her guitar and was careful to keep them unfocused, for as yet she had not penetrated very deeply into their use and control. Kevin Larkin could teach her rock and roll, but she would have to discover the magics on her own.

Sliding her hand down the neck, she fluttered the tremolo bar for a moment, then allowed the guitar to fall into silence. "Too faint it was to hear after that," she said, absently rubbing her smarting fingertips. " 'Twas not overly interesting, either."

Jeff was pale. "How . . . uh . . . long you been playing?"

"A week."

He paled even more.

"I told you," said Kevin. "You heard it here first." Jeff walked away, shaking his head, and Kevin closed the door. "That's fantastic, Christa. You must be some kind of natural guitar player."

"I'm a harper, Kevin."

But Kevin looked a little pale himself. "Yeah, well . . ." He leaned forward suddenly. "What's wrong with your fingers?"

Christa's flesh was less durable than her desire: blood was trickling down her left hand. "I broke a blister." She could play a healing spell on Ceis in less than five minutes, but she had been running late that day. "I'm all right." She reached into her purse, pulled out a handkerchief, dabbed at her fingertips. " 'Twill stop in a moment."

"Uh . . ." Kevin's brow was furrowed. "How much have you been practicing?"

She shrugged. "Six, perhaps seven hours a day. I have harp students."

"What are you doing, Christa? You're—"

"I'm learning rock and roll, Kevin," she said firmly. "If I can't put up with a little blood, what kind of musician am I?"

"You don't have to cut up your hands."

Twelve hours a day of harp had injured her fingers almost as badly. She could not understand what was upsetting Kevin. "The old harpers used to mark the first and fifth strings of each octave with their own blood. It gave life to their harps. I'm well within the tradition."

Kevin did not reply. He was looking at the wall above his desk where from a piece of red twine hung a battered guitar.

The blood stopped in a minute, and Christa put the handkerchief away. "I'll not be able to play anymore this afternoon, Kevin," she said softly. "Maybe you could show me something and let me listen to your records again?"

Kevin was still looking at the old guitar, as though he

sought advice from the mute strings. Christa sensed that he was afraid.

Where a lesser musician might have found terror enough in Christa's talent and abilities, anticipating the day when he would be surpassed by this woman who, by the look of her, was barely out of girlhood, Kevin felt that he had already been surpassed, and his fear stemmed from a sense of uselessness and futility.

Christa had the feeling. She had the passion. "Black Star" had never sounded so fluid and yearning as when she had played it in his office at the guitar school. He had no doubt that, had he that very day plugged her guitar into an amplifier, he would have wept.

So what could he teach her beyond a few techniques that she would probably figure out on her own if given the time? why had she come to him? Was this some kind of cruel joke?

The next week, she again came prepared, this time with a set of fiendishly difficult solos by Randy Rhoads. And again her guitar sang, the notes rippling out, the strings stretched and vibratoed with a crystalline purity that he had never heard before. Even Frankie had not sounded like that. The black man's music had been dark, earthy, ripped from his heart and presented to his listeners gleaming with his life's blood and the sweat of his hands. Christa floated, spinning strands of gossamer through space, her hands light, her music clear and graceful.

When she finished, Kevin pretended to look over the tablature of the piece. "You changed a few notes," he said, trying to be useful. "Did you know that?"

"Do you mean when I shifted the second section from aeolian mode to plagal mixolydian? The energy was wrong. There's no telling what—" She caught herself and was silent.

"Huh?"

"It . . . would not have sounded right to me."

He watched her for a moment. Why should the energy be wrong? There was no telling . . . what?

What kind of training had this girl been given? Blood on the harpstrings? Energy?

"Yeah . . . well, that's okay." He tried to keep the

shaking out of his voice. "Just so long as you know. After all, you'll be developing your own style. If you . . . haven't already."

Frightening. He thought about her when, as darkness fell across the eastern face of the Rockies, he drove home. Malmsteen was plugged into his car stereo and everything was cranked, as though with sufficient volume he could drive feeling and intensity through whatever armor plating was covering his heart and soul.

Christa seemed almost fragile—a slender young woman with the faintest hint of the old-fashioned in her English. But the fragility was deceptive, for he sensed about her something violent, something that would drive her to practice until her fingers bled . . . and think nothing of it.

Music and blood. Frankie had died of an ulcer that had festered in his belly for over fifteen years. Kevin had lost count of the number of times the old man had played with sweat starting out from his forehead from the pain. He had fallen down in Detroit, leaving a dent in his guitar. He had wailed in his sleep in a seedy motel room near Hyannis Port, sixteen-year-old Kevin sitting up frightened in the other bed and peering through the darkness to discover the source of the childlike weeping. But Frankie had neither money nor time for doctors. *The music, Kevvy. That's where it is. I go to the doctor, he tell me to stay at home and drink milk. And what do I do then? Go crazy, that's what.*

"Are you sure you're getting something out of these lessons?" he asked when, for the fourth straight week, she had come with an intricate lead flawlessly prepared.

She blinked at him. "I don't understand. Is my work not satisfactory?"

"It's damned satisfactory." He stood up, folded his arms, studied the halftone dots of the Jimi Hendrix poster. "I simply don't believe what I'm hearing, Christa. What the hell do you need me for?"

"I need you to teach me." Her voice was patient.

"You already know it all, girl."

Her eyes flashed a little. "I? Know it all?"

"Look," said Kevin, exasperated and fearful both, "I wouldn't normally talk to a student like this, but you're not really a student. If you can do one tenth on the harp what you've been doing on guitar, I'm scared to hear you play. You've got technique and feeling down cold. All you have to do is learn the songs."

The patience remained in her tone. "And all you have to do, Kevin, is teach them to me."

"What can I teach you?"

"It's a strange thing, music, in this place." Something about her choice of words struck him as peculiar. "I studied harp in Cor . . . in Kerry, and we learned there to pay attention to each note, to each sound we made or did not make. Here . . ." She cut loose a blinding flurry of licks that screamed from one end of the fingerboard to the other in less than a second. ". . . notes seem to be merely a means of filling up time. There are some lovely melodies buried among them, to be sure, but it's little attention I've heard anyone give them. I try to treat them with reverence. That's all. And because of that, you say you have nothing to teach me "

"I can't teach you that."

"I know."

He flinched. He had said too much. She knew. He was a fraud. He no more knew how to make music than did a player piano.

Christa watched him with her bright blue eyes. If she had guessed his secret, she gave no sign. "No one can teach that," she said softly. "You have to listen, Kevin. You have to listen to everything. But I don't know what songs there are to learn. I don't know which ones I should listen to, and my tendencies will always be to interpret them as a harper. I need to make sure that I stay within the feel of heavy metal." She looked at her guitar, stroked the neck. "I have a lot to do. You can save me a greal deal of time."

You have to listen, Kevin. Her words made sense, but there was a meaning lurking about their edges that eluded him. *You have to listen to everything.* Listen?

She lifted her head. "What should I learn for next week?"

"It depends." Kevin struggled to find his words. Glib little Irish boy—where was his blarney now? "Where do you want to go with this? You want to get into a band?"

"I believe that I will need to."

"And then what?"

She was silent.

"You want to be a rock star?"

She did not answer at first. Finally: "I have something that I must do, Kevin. Rock and roll will help me do it."

He was absolutely certain that he did not want to hear what it was. "Okay, you need to start listening to a lot of rock and roll, and you need to get some equipment together. Amplifier, effects, all that stuff. I'll put together a song list for you to learn, and I'll fish around out there to see if anyone's looking for a lead guitarist. You're hot. You'll have no trouble."

She smiled thinly. "I hope not."

Blood. Listening. That night, driving home along 285, he mulled over Christa's words as the mountain air cooled and the sky turned into a field of stars. Frankie's life and his music had been intimately bound up with blood, whether it was of the ulcer that ate at him or that which frequently spattered the floor of the cheap, violent bars in which he played. Blood. Passion. It was not noble, nor was it sublime: it had no claim to immortality. It was the blues. It was human, common, slippery with the grease of skin oil and sweat, fragrant with the ripe odors of life.

And Frankie had died, unknown.

Was that tragedy, Kevin began to wonder, or was that life? Did music have to be something for all time, something that built for itself an imperishable cathedral of spirit and adamant? Or was it more important that the music simply be played, that in a thousand common homes, a million apartments ranging from tenement to penthouse, someone with a guitar or a flute or a harp was letting the melodies flow straight from the heart, with no pretensions, no delusions of grandeur, no hope of permanence. Just the music. Just the honest blood, transformed into sound and sent forth into the world to exist for a moment, and then to fade away . . . until some other hand took up an instrument.

He turned his Beetle onto the stretch of dirt road that led to his door and pulled up in front of his dark house. When he shut off the engine, the quiet mountain sounds rushed in at him.

You have to listen to everything.

Everything. He got out of the car and stood on the earth, straining his ears. Crickets. An owl. Wester's mare whinnied uneasily across the fields.

And behind those sounds were others. Pine branches rustled, and aspen leaves made little papery noises. A mallard in the pond stirred the water with a webbed foot, and the ripple plashed at the borders of hearing.

And beyond that was the sound of mountains: the half-heard, half-felt presence of tree and rock and water that blended imperceptibly into the heartbeat pulsing quietly within him.

The sounds were always there, always changing. It was not important that they endured; it was important that they were made, that they continued to be made.

He realized that he was holding his breath, and he let the air out of his lungs in a long sigh that entered the nocturne being played about him, twined with the music as though it were a growing thing, and cadenced softly as a mockingbird took a brief solo.

Christa continued to practice in the dark; and as her hands loosened, the flow of magic increased. She began to experiment with the irridescent energies, playing passages at different speeds, changing individual notes within licks. She had much to learn, in spite of what Kevin had said, but her progress was steady and rapid, driven forward relentlessly by thoughts of her beloved.

Where was Judith? What was she doing? Did she play the harp still? Did she . . . did she sing? Christa found herself wandering through her house before she went to bed, examining the furniture, the appliances, the carpeting and wallpaper. Judith knew only the wicker houses of the Gaeidil and the glass palace of the Sidh. How would she react to all of this?

Possibility tore at her imagination, at her dreams. Starting up from sleep, she would search frantically among the sheets and pillows for Judith, knowing with all the befuddled confusion of the half-awakened dreamer that her lover was near, that the Sidh had hidden her, that if she only knew how to look, she would find her. But her senses would return, and sleep would flee, and she would spend the rest of the night curled up with the avocado Strat, practicing.

And perhaps it was because her thoughts were so intent upon her goal that, one night in late July, as she practiced in the darkness of her studio, she sensed a thin place in the warp and weft of the mortal world. It was some distance away, perhaps several hundred miles, but it was real: a potential doorway into the Realm.

The lands of the Sidh were everywhere, and yet they were normally accessible only when a combination of chance, magic, and will created a passage to them. In 1869, Christa had come to America because of an unmistakable feeling that the gates into the Realm were leaving the Old World and reforming in the New; and eighty miles north of New York, where folklore and superstition had invested the Catskill Mountains with an aura of the unreal and the impossible, she had found one. But she had never tried it. Orfide had nearly killed her by the shore of Lake Levin, north of Edinburgh, and she had become reluctant to battle the bard again without a greater hope of victory. She could do little for Judith if she were dead.

But at Midsummer each year, she had made her way out to the Catskills. There, within sight of a waterfall that had sent a long tendril of froth down the face of a bare cliff, shrouding the scene with an opalescent mist that seemed more of old Eriu than of America, Christa had put off the dull, stiff garments of the nineteenth century and had, once more, become a woman of the Gaeidil. Clad in the white mantle of a novice harper, her hair long and unbound, she had lifted a chalice of wine to the woman who lived just out of reach, in a castle of glass on the other side of the mist.

Heartbreaking gestures, futile commemorations. Later on, with the turning of the century, the gate had vanished, and she had followed her feelings to Colorado. But the grief had been building in her, and she no longer had the strength to confront the impossibility of what she wanted. The gate was . . . somewhere. She had not sought it out.

But what she wanted no longer seemed so impossible. The Strat was flickering with energy as she backtracked through the scale she was playing—a plagal variant of the dorian mode—and found the notes that emphasized her perception of the gate. Carefully, she pieced together a lick that contained them and, letting her hands move of themselves, repeated the sequence with machinelike rapidity.

She had a sudden vision of a mountain lake surrounded by pine forest. Behind it was a cliff with a distinctive mineral vein. Above the water was a faint, dark turbulence, as though the fabric of reality was slightly frayed.

She pushed herself, added chromatic fire to the lick, dropped in bleak, uncompromising pieces of the locrian mode to add weight to the spell. Her vision expanded. She saw miles of forest backed up by tall mountains that could only be the Rockies. The dusty thread of a fire road snaked through the trees, but there was no sign that people lived in the area.

A gate. A palpable gate. Somewhere to the . . . southwest. With the power she anticipated from amplification, she was sure that she could smash a portal into the Realm wherever she liked, but with a gate already in existence, her task would be easier. She would be able to concentrate on battling Orfide.

She had not yet mastered the guitar: after a minute, the vision shifted, faded, and dissolved in a sheet of pale fire. She blinked, saw the dark outlines of Ceis against the faintly glowing windows of the studio.

visit

"Not now, Ceis. Later. Perhaps at Lugnasad." She fingered the Strat. "It's enough that I know the gate is there." She pinched a harmonic and jerked up on the tremolo bar until it shrieked, then pushed the bar down and let the string drop into flaccid silence. "I need to talk to Melinda," she said. "I need equipment."

CHAPTER SEVEN

Devi stayed away from the guitar department at the Proshop. Her specialty was keyboards, and she had little reason to go to the other end of the store, especially since the boys in charge of Guitar had told her a week after she was hired that, in their opinion, keyboards were suitable only for firewood.

Their opinion meant nothing to her, though. If they wanted to bang away on their gaily colored bits of metal and plastic and annoy the neighbors, so be it. If they were gratified by the admiration of vacant-faced girls, fine. They knew volume and distortion—that was all. She had no use for them.

The essence of music—of everything—was control, the precise, exacting specification of each parameter to the third decimal, the willful shaping of frequency, waveform, attack, decay, and amplitude into a realization of what had been inwardly heard. Devi knew the touch of electronic keyboards, the intricacies of computer programs, the heady blending of passionate music and dispassionate microprocessors. She knew the fierce joy that came from evoking a storm of sound from a PA system driven to peak, a cresting wave of volume that obeyed the slightest touch of her fingertips.

". . . so I'll tell you, I got her upstairs to my room, and when I started coming on to her, I got this weird feeling. . . ."

She looked up from the operating manual she was reading. Two young men were passing by on their way back to Guitar. One of them carried a cased instrument. They did not notice her.

". . . and I asked her how old she was," said the taller of the two, "and she told me *thirteen*."

"What did you do?"

77

He laughed. "I told her that she was going to get one hell of a musical education."

"You mean you . . ." The conversation faded to inaudibility, and in the next room, someone began battering on a set of drums.

She slammed the manual closed. "Bastard."

It was a slow day: she had nothing but the manual to distract her thoughts, and that was insufficient for now. She looked out through the smoke-gray windows of the store, watched a light blue 4x4 wagon pull into the lot.

Too many memories. A girlhood full of them. Even before she had stood on tiptoe to reach the high keyboard of the old upright piano in the living room and pick out the organ solo from "Light My Fire"—her chubby, nine-year-old fingers faltering through the chords and the riffs that had come so easily to Ray Manzarek's adult hands—even before she had heard those seductive melodies seeping from the radio and had decided that she wanted to do that too, the memories were there: dark brown shading into the scummy black of an unwashed sink; her father, tall and strong, bending over her with a beckoning finger: *Come be daddy's little princess . . .*

. . . or daddy's little slut, which was what he told her later. No one would ever touch her, he said. She was polluted, corrupt. Bad girl.

And life went on. Sure it did. A six-year-old turned into a whore among her stuffed animals and the pink sheets with the print balloons. A thirteen-year-old taken for whatever she had to give in an upstairs motel room off Santa Fe Drive. Boys will be boys. It takes two to tango.

Control. Pull those faders down, Devi. Change those parameters. Make it go away.

Out in the parking lot, a woman got out of the wagon, her waist-length red hair as eye catching as a blue mohawk. Devi watched her, absently fingering her own dense black curls. The woman's movements were graceful, deliberate, proud. She climbed out of an AMC Eagle as though she had just bought the whole city of Denver.

The woman opened a back door of the wagon and pulled out a rectangular guitar case. Devi stared. A rocker? She was distracted from her thoughts and did not even notice the woman's companion until they had entered the store.

"Hi, Devi," said Melinda.

Devi recognized her. Years before, they had played in rival, all-girl bands. They had run into one another occasionally since then, but she had not seen Melinda in months. "How are you, Mel?"

"Doing all right." The standard lie, unless frustrated poverty was all right.

"Working?"

"Not in a band. The guys were giving me shit, so I quit. I'm in office supplies for now. What about you?"

Devi spread her hands to indicate the store. "This is it. I was playing out until a few weeks back. Got tired of the hassles." This was also a lie, though not so innocent as Melinda's. It had been an ugly night in the club, and during a break she had been cornered in a dark alcove by two drunks. They had not touched her, but something had snapped, and by the time the bouncer had arrived, Devi was nine again, and screaming.

She had spent the last set hiding behind her keyboards. White-faced, staring but seeing nothing, she had taken refuge in her music, in control, just as she had when "Light My Fire" was the only song she knew.

The red-haired woman was standing off by herself, looking over the electric pianos and the synthesizers. She carried the guitar case a little awkwardly, as though new to the instrument, but even her awkwardness was sure, and proud.

Devi envied her, refused to show it. She shrugged. "You know how it is."

"Yeah." Melinda looked over her shoulder. "Hey, Christa," she called. "This is Devi. We've known each other for years."

Christa came forward and offered her hand. "Hello. I'm Christa Cruitaire."

Devi flinched and pretended not to notice the hand. "Nice to meet you, Christa. I'm Devi Anderson. Welcome to the Proshop. What can we do for you?"

Christa dropped her hand with a soft smile. "I'm after taking up heavy metal," she said, "and I need an amplifier for my guitar and some equipment to go with it."

"You should hear her, Devi," said Melinda. "She makes the guys look sick."

"Most guys look pretty sick anyway," Devi said bitterly. She caught herself. "Excuse me."

Christa examined her for a moment. Her blue eyes were frank, without judgment. "There is no problem," she said.

"As far as amps and the rest go," said Devi, changing the subject, "you'll have to go to Scott in Guitar. Straight back. Don't let them give you any bullshit."

Christa nodded. "I understand."

And as Christa and Melinda made their way to the back of the store, Devi found herself with the feeling that Christa did indeed understand. A great deal. About almost everything.

But before she could dwell on the thought, she had to help a customer. The tall black man seemed at first a little perplexed by a woman who knew about FM synthesis and digital sampling, but once she had put several keyboards through their paces, he settled down to the serious business of talking music.

While Devi worked with him, though, she was hearing the sound of an amplified guitar from the other end of the store. Shimmering bends, runs that were anything but uncontrolled: the antithesis of the heavy-handed metal she usually heard from the boys. Melinda's friend?

When her customer tried out one of the synths, she took a moment to peek around the tall speaker enclosures that formed a wall around her department. Christa was standing in front of a cheap amplifier, a light-green guitar in her hands. She played a little, talked with Melinda, adjusted a knob or two, and played a little more. The sounds she made were graceful, lyrical; but Devi detected an edge, as of a hidden threat, behind them. Christa's sweetness was an illusion.

"Miss?"

"Oops, sorry," she said, turning back to her customer. She gestured toward Christa. "That's some guitar player."

"Yeah, I was listening too."

Devi made the sale, but she was only half conscious of it. She wanted to hear more of that guitar. She wrote up the ticket, pulled a boxed synth from stock, and, in violation of her custom, absently shook the man's hand before she sent him up front to pay. She hardly noticed the contact. Nor did she notice the incredulous look that Scott gave her when he saw her in the guitar department.

"What do you think of this, Melinda?" Christa was saying.

Melinda shrugged. "Not sure. It sounds okay, I guess."

"I can't help but think that it could be richer. Right here." She played a flash of notes in the middle register of the guitar. "It's a little weak."

"Maybe . . ."

Devi eased her way over to the counter. Scott was listening. "Pretty good, huh?" he said.

"How come you've got her on that piece of shit?"

"The DL-5? It's budget, sure, but it's good."

"Not that good."

"Stay with your keys, woman."

"You want to make a sale today? She's not going to take that. She's hearing the dropout in the midrange. That thing shelves down five dB per octave from one to five kilohertz."

"What do you want to show her?"

"The Laney A.O.R. Fix her up with a hundred-watt head and a 4–12 cabinet. She'll love it."

"What?" He finally stopped looking at Christa and turned to Devi. "She doesn't want stuff like that."

"Did she say so?"

"Well . . . no. But you know that kind. She's no rocker. Look at the way she's dressed. She's probably trying to impress her boyfriend."

Devi felt herself bristle.

"Or something," he added quickly.

Devi folded her arms and watched for a few more minutes as Christa tried to force the DL-5 to do something it could not. The midrange simply was not strong enough. Christa finally looked at Melinda and shook her head.

Devi turned to Scott. "Do you want to sell her the Laney half-stack, or shall I?"

"What the hell do you know about guitar amps?"

"Zip. Zilch. But I know sound, I've heard what those Laneys can do, and I've read the fucking service manuals."

He shrugged. "Maybe you're right. Go ahead, Devi."

In two minutes, Devi had Christa plugged into a one

hundred-watt Laney head and a cabinet containing four twelve-inch speakers. "It's a good solid rock setup," she explained while they waited for the tubes to heat. "And with the stacked preamps, you can vary the amount of sustain and distortion you get by punching them in and out with the footswitch."

Christa looked dubiously at the half-stack; then, with a shrug, she turned up the volume knob of her guitar. The amplifier tubes finished heating, and the speakers hissed faintly. "I suppose I have a great deal to learn," she said. "Whoever thought that a harper from Corca Duibne would come to this?"

And then she played. The middle register was solid, rich, the notes flowing like honey left out in the warm summer sun. Christa broke out into a bright smile, closed her eyes, and let the music come.

Devi was hearing control. It did not matter that Christa could not alter the substance of her sound, that she was limited to electromagnetic pickups, steel strings, and glowing tubes. Her expression and her hands made up for that.

Christa stopped, looked at Scott and Devi. "May I turn this up?"

"Crank it," said Devi.

"I don't know how."

Devi adjusted the Laney until Christa's guitar was overloading the preamplifier circuitry enough to produce a smooth, violin-like sustain. "If you turn this knob," she said, "you'll just get louder. Turn this other one, and you'll increase the distortion. Step on this switch, and you'll kick in another preamp."

Christa turned up and hit a chord that was like a spatter of bright metal. The air in the guitar department was suddenly alive, trembling. She flipped the pickup selector switch on the front of the Strat, adjusted a tone knob, and then went off into a series of cascading arpeggios that ranged from despairing to joyous in the space of a few seconds.

Nodding, she worked across the entire fingerboard, feeling out the response of the amplifier. She struck and held a chord. The rich harmonies shouldered their way through the room. Devi leaned her elbows on the vibrating counter and cupped her chin in her hands, watching, listening.

Christa stepped on the footswitch and increased her sustain. Her blue eyes narrowed as she went back into rapid-fire arpeggios and licks, and she seemed to be thinking of something that angered her. Sounds tumbled over one another, and Devi suddenly felt afraid. Who was this woman? Where had she learned to play guitar like this?

Devi had grown up with guilt and with shame, and those emotions had come to seem natural to her, an integral part of womanhood. Here though, holding a guitar and reeling off power chords and runs with a tight precision that was drawing a small crowd, was a woman who seemed to know nothing of either. Christa was proud—not arrogantly so, not with the posturing of the hundreds of would-be guitar heroes that Devi saw each month, but with a firm, inner conviction. No one, it seemed, had ever told Christa that femininity was a curse, that a woman's form was a weak vessel, a temptation, a burden. The idea had apparently never occurred to her.

Christa was lost in her music, in the waves of sound that she called up out of the Laney. Another sustained chord while she adjusted the sound, and she was off again. The air in the room felt charged, ready to erupt.

And in a way it did. For as Christa powered out a series of odd-sounding scales, lingering over occasional notes in a strange, deliberate pattern, Devi opened her eyes and saw a roiling, turbulent sheet of gray mist where there should have been a wall hung with guitars. It seemed to stretch off into the distance, as though a hole had been partly torn in the universe.

She gasped, looked back at Christa. The guitarist slammed home one more chord and then allowed silence to return. The gray mist vanished. The wall came back.

People were applauding. No one else had noticed. Christa turned off the amplifier and bowed to Devi. "I'll take it. Thank you. You have helped me greatly."

"You've changed a lot," said Melinda.

Christa eased the wagon through midday traffic. Behind, on the cargo deck, was the speaker cabinet and head, two digital delays, and her guitar. "Have I?"

"Oh, come on. I take you to one rock concert, and

suddenly you're Denver's next guitar hero. What happened?"

"I liked what I heard." Christa smiled at Melinda. She tried to remember when she had last had a friend besides Judith, drew a blank. Maybe her father. Maybe Dennis Hempson, the old blind harper who had helped her with her English. No one else. Had she been alone that long?

"You're not telling me everything."

"You wouldn't believe me if I told you. So I won't."

Melinda cast her eyes upward for a moment, shook her head. "Where did you say you were from?"

"Ireland."

"No: I mean, what planet?" Melinda laughed. "Where to now?"

"Soundtrack. I need a good stereo. Kevin told me to start listening to as much rock as I could—so as to develop my feeling for the idiom."

"You've got bucks, lady."

Christa shrugged. Two hundred years of thrift—and a little prescience—had given her a fair-sized bank account. She was making a sizable dent in it today, but she would have given up everything for Judith. "I want to thank you for all your help."

"No problem. Glad I can do something."

Christa pulled into the parking lot. "Excellent. You can do even more: you can help me carry the Laney down to my basement, and set up my stereo."

"I can? Gee, thanks."

"You're most welcome."

Melinda spread her hands. "You going to feed me?"

"Oatcakes and the champion's portion of the beef." And though Melinda stared at her, Christa laughed at her own joke.

In all her days at the school in Corca Duibne she had never dreamed of this: that she would spend a day driving the streets of Denver in the company of a woman as audacious as the most wild-eyed hoyden of the Gaeidil, enjoying a world far stranger even than that of curdled milk oceans and meat-clad doorkeepers in the dream of Anier Mac Conglinde.

She was opening up, and the darkness of her endless twilight memories of the Sidh had been riven by the blue sky of Colorado and the bright lights of a rock concert.

Renouncing at last the anesthetic life that had kept her loss from overwhelming her with grief, she was crawling out from behind her harp.

It was early evening by the time Christa pulled into her own driveway, and, with Melinda helping, she muscled the equipment inside and down the stairs. She had spent the last several days cleaning out her basement, trashing the accumulated rubbish of eighty years of Denver living, pitching old furniture, out-of-fashion clothes, cardboard boxes gritty with the talcumlike dust of the past. Now the sheetrock walls were covered with carpet scraps to keep down the echoes, and the otherwise empty room was soon occupied by the Laney, the delays, a new stereo, and several stacks of records that Melinda had insisted on lending to her.

"You're going to have to get used to listening to this stuff, Chris," said Melinda as she staggered down the stairs with a foot-high pile of cardboard and vinyl in her arms. "Might as well start now."

Melinda made Christa do the actual hook-up of the amplifier and the stereo, insisting that if she did not start learning about electronics immediately, she would be lost in rock and roll. Sitting amid a tangle of wire and patch cables, Christa puzzled through the directions while Melinda translated the unfamiliar terminology.

"Positive to positive and negative to negative," said the bassist. "Otherwise your speakers will be out of phase."

Christa held the speaker cord up to the light and examined the bare copper ends. "Energy is energy, Melinda. What is this positive and negative?"

"Take it on faith."

"You sound like a Christian."

"I *am* a Christian."

"My apologies." Christa squatted behind the stereo, squinting in the dim light as she attached the cables.

"You've never done this before?"

"Never. This is my first stereo."

"Brother."

"You have to understand . . ." Christa stood up. "I grew up in the sixth century."

Melinda made a face. "Yeah, sure."

Christa plugged in the power cord and snapped on the switch. KAZY blasted through the speakers. The Doors.

"Light My Fire." Manzarek's organ solo. It was dispassionate, aloof music, a lead that cared little for anything made of such paltry stuff as flesh and blood.

Christa listened, evaluated it. Everything that she heard, she could use, and though this lead lacked the brute force that characterized heavy metal, she heard the terrible potentials that it contained; for if Manzarek had changed his inflections just a little, held a note a trifle longer here, altered the emphasis there, the music, with surgical objectivity, could have killed.

"Good stuff," said Melinda.

Christa gestured at the speakers. "Do you hear it, Melinda?"

"Hear what? The organ?"

"Do you hear the magic?"

Melinda looked surprised, but she closed her eyes and listened intently. Finally: "I hear the music. They've got good chops. I'm not sure what you mean by magic."

The song ended. A commercial came on. Christa turned off the stereo. It was risky, but she had to ask. In order to win Judith, she needed to work with others: she needed a band. Her Celtic pride sneered at anything short of single combat with the Sidh bard, but that pride had been tempered by two hundred years of loss and by over a century of American practicality. Let Find Mac Cumaill and the Fianna concern themselves with personal glory. Christa Cruitaire now sought only results.

"Do you believe in magic, Melinda?" she said softly.

"Like what? Princes into frogs and that stuff?"

"Like what I talk about during your harp lessons. That *sian* I taught you: you can sleep now. Doesn't that seem like magic?"

Melinda was plainly uncomfortable. "Magic? Isn't it more like psychology, or something like that?"

Christa wanted to pick up her guitar, plug in, and do something. She was not sure what. Something that would show Melinda what she was talking about. But that would have been too much. "I suppose," she said, "that it has a lot to do with the way you look at the world. You can see it as solid and immovable; or as fluid, changeable. Music operates on a number of levels. The base is, of course, the vibrations in the air, but it also touches other worlds, other parts of ourselves. And it can change them."

"This . . . uh . . . sounds more like religion than music, Chris."

"They are the same thing, Melinda."

"But . . ." She was shaking again. "Religion is . . . like going to church, and being holy."

"Exactly. That's what I'm saying."

Melinda's blond hair had suddenly grown damp at the roots. "I'm a nice Lutheran girl, Chris. I don't understand this. When do we eat?"

Christa bent her head and discovered that, in setting up the equipment, she had chipped one of her nails. "We can eat now," she said, trying to sound cheerful.

They settled for fast food: there was a Burger King a few blocks away. A Double Whopper with cheese was a pale shadow of the champion's portion, but Melinda seemed satisfied with it. While they ate, they watched the traffic passing on Colorado Boulevard and chatted about harps and guitars and rock and roll, staying far away from such subjects as religion and magic.

"You got plans tonight?" Melinda asked.

Melinda's inability to understand magic hung like a lead weight at the back of Christa's mind, but she put it aside. There was time. For now, she had a friend, and she had advice and help. "I thought I'd go home and practice."

"You want to go out to a club with me? We can head up to InsideOut. Some cute guys there. Tom Del—" The name stuck in her throat. "Uh . . ."

Christa noticed her unease. "I'm not really in the market, Melinda."

Melinda shook herself out of her thoughts. "Whatever. Little Sister is playing tonight. They're hot. Good moves, good songs, the whole schtick. Kevin told you to listen to a lot of rock, but that's really only half of it. You gotta go see the bands. If you're going to perform, you have to work on your moves."

"Moves?"

"Like you saw at the Malmsteen concert. You have to jump around, play with your guitar, show the audience what you can do. You know: strut your stuff."

Christa laughed.

"I'm serious."

"I know you're serious, Melinda. I was just thinking what my harp teacher would say."

Melinda leaned across the orange formica tabletop and poked a finger at her. "He'd think you were hot stuff, girl. That's what he'd think." She finished her soft drink. "Tell you what: let's get crazy tonight. You want to borrow some of my spandex? I've got something in electric blue that would look great on you."

Her blue eyes were bright. They reminded Christa of someone she had known once—someone who had taught her the precision of the harp, just as Melinda was instructing her in the cocky insanity of rock and roll.

Stage moves. Spandex. It all seemed absurd, but Melinda would doubtless think that twelve hours a day of blind practice and the white mantle of a novice harper were absurd. Different worlds. And Anier had dreamed of a doorkeeper dressed like a side of beef.

Christa smiled softly. "Why not? It's been at least a century since I've been crazy."

CHAPTER
EIGHT

Orfide is playing.

Head bent, fingers agile, he recreates once again the timeless, limpid melodies that Siudb has heard so often that she knows every string, every pause, every rubato, every duration of every note. Had she a chance to practice, she too could play these pieces, evoke these magics. But time and opportunity are denied her, and so she must sit at Lamcrann's side, stifling the scream of frustration that wells up within her. She can only listen. She is a toy.

Orfide finishes, and—as usual, as always—pale hands applaud and the bard rises and bows. Lamcrann thanks him and takes Siudb by the arm. Siudb pulls away. Cumad intervenes as the mortal woman flees to the isolation of the gardens and meadows that surround the palace.

It disturbs Siudb that she has fallen into the endless repetition and the eternal theater of the Sidh. As well as she can predict each nuance of Orfide's performance, so she knows her own part in the ritual: she must listen, and then she must run. Perhaps she is being ensnared by some subtle spell woven by the bard. Perhaps she has already been caught, and, like her captors, can now only reenact prior motions.

She passes through the gardens, climbs a slope, enters a grove of myrtle. The trees are shadowed, fragrant, but she longs for the virile oaks and rowans of her mortal past. The forests of Eriu betokened change, honest sexuality, fertility; the Realm offers only perfumed invitations to endless, unfulfilled dalliance. Her garments rustling across the tall grass and the twilight-blooming flowers, she leaves the grove and finds herself beside a reflecting pool. The water is still, but there are no stars for it to mirror.

She has been here before, too. How many times? She

does not know. Merely a player she is, fallen hopelessly under the spell of the Sidh.

A footstep, a sigh of a sandal across the grass. A Sidh has followed her, one who is pleased to appear as a youth, a lad no older than herself. His hair is light, his eyes gray; but unlike the men of Siudb's folk, he is as barefaced as a woman.

He approaches her, bows. He wears the livery of the palace guard. "I am Glasluit."

"Siudb Ní Corb. What is it you want?"

He fumbles for a moment with his words. "I would speak with you, my lady."

Arms folded, she looks out across the blank surface of the pool. "Speak, then."

He is ill at ease, almost shy. "I . . . I have . . . that is to say . . ."

Surprised, she looks at him. His face is flushed.

"I am not accustomed to speaking in this fashion," he says. It is almost a confession.

Change. Of a sudden, out of nowhere, something is different. Terribly different.

Glasluit fidgets. "I want to help you."

Lugnasad. Away to the east, where the mountains gave way to the rolling plains that led into Kansas, the August harvest was beginning as fields of golden wheat and barley were gathered in: foodstuff for the future, nourishment from sun and earth.

But where the fields of Eriu had been cleared by brown-backed men and women wielding scythes and singing songs of the God Lugh, their coppery hair bleached as blond as cornsilk by the long summer, the fields of Colorado and the Plains were harvested by machine. Christa had seen them: dark, clattering reapers and roaring combines that spewed out a shower of yellow grain. There was no singing, no worship. A day's work, a good supper, and then a night's rest—no more. Worship was for Sundays, in church.

Christa snorted softly, but the sound was masked by the rush of air past the windows of her station wagon. She had been on the road since before dawn, following highway 285 to the south and southwest, taking the steep grade of Kenosha Pass down to the wide valley below just as the ever-rising sun called back the shadows of the mountains in a fast-receding tide of darkness that left herds of grazing cattle stranded upon wide green pastures.

distance

Ceis rested on the seat beside her, the lap belt slung loosely over its forepillar. Its gilt and gems flashed in the clear light.

" 'Twill be a ways, Ceis," she said. "From my feelings, it's at least as far as Gunnison we'll have to travel, maybe farther. We'll pick up U.S. 50 near Salida, but we'll do a check there and see if we can't triangulate on the gate."

mountains

"I daresay. We'll cross Monarch Pass, and there's a lovely view from there. Would you like to play a little at the Continental Divide?"

always

She paused for a quick breakfast at a truck stop in Fairplay. The burly, unshaven patrons in the diner looked at her curiously and stared at Ceis without reservation. A yawning waitress with a name tag that said *Bobbie* took her order for oatmeal, milk, and bacon, and paused for a moment before she left the table.

"What *is* that thing you've got there, honey?"

"It is a harp."

Bobbie shook her head. "Never seen one that small. You play?"

**

Christa smiled at Ceis affectionately. "I do."

While she waited for her food, she watched the morning grow outside. It was a fine day, the air warm, the sky clear and blue. Even Eriu had not possessed such a sky: a deep azure the color of a master harper's robe.

And from the kitchen came the crisp rattle of cups and plates, the slow, murmured drawl of the cook, the lilting, girlish tones of the waitress. About her, truckers read newspapers, lingered over coffee, grunted comments to one another. Christa ate, knowing full well that most of them were talking about the odd stranger who traveled with an even odder instrument, and she smiled inwardly with the thought that, carrying a harp, she was as outlandish to these people as she would have been had she walked in wearing the spandex she had donned the other night.

It had been a strange evening, as foreign to her usual lifestyle as the modern harvest was to the holy days of grain gathering. The club to which Melinda had taken her pulsed steadily with the harsh accents of hard rock, and the air was filled with tobacco smoke and a faint undertone of marijuana. Christa was clad in garments that made her feel almost naked, but the look in her black-rimmed eyes kept the curious and the prurient away as much as did the studded belts and chains that adorned her.

Stage moves. She watched the band. She learned. At first, she wondered what it would be like to play for such a party-minded audience, and then she considered what she might do against Orfide, who, immersed in the intricacies of a spell woven of twilight and harpstrings, could not but be unsettled by the gleeful, casual arrogance of a rock performer.

Near dawn, she had dropped Melinda off at her apartment. "Good night."

"Night." Melinda had reached for the doorhandle. "You know something, Chris? You're deceptive."

"Me? I don't understand."

"You come on all sweetness and light. But I can see now that you're definitely not someone to fuck around with." she had swung out of the wagon with a wave. "Later. See you at my lesson."

Christa had smiled. "Later."

She finished her coffee, hoping that Melinda was correct. Sweetness had helped her to survive throughout the years, but the violence and anger had been building. She hoped that Orfide would indeed find that she meant business, that she was not someone to fuck around with.

The waitress took her money at the front counter. She looked at Ceis again, her lips pursed, thinking.

Christa knew the look. She smiled in spite of Orfide and picked up the harp. "Would you like a tune before I leave?"

Bobbie shrugged apologetically. "It's been a slow morning. And the radio's busted. It'd be nice. Would you?"

"Surely." Making sure that she had a view to the south, she settled herself in a chair by the front window and put Ceis on her lap. "What say you, old friend?" she murmured to the harp. "Shall we?"

play

South and west. Putting her hands to the strings, she began one of the old melodies. It had been, perhaps, the first she had learned, a bittersweet mixolydian tune redolent of love and longing, but hopeful nonetheless, the flatted seventh tone leading graciously to a tonic that shone like a moonstone.

But while Christa played for Bobbie and the cook and the truckers, she was also playing for herself. She wove the melody into her awareness, into her view of the mountains to the south, and then—expanding the song, increasing the intervals between melody and accompaniment, contrasting ascending scales with descending arpeggios—she also increased her vision.

The diner went away. She saw mountains, valleys, forests of pine and aspen, fire roads, highways. With a discipline acquired through years of practice, she held the memory of the gate in her mind and let her instincts guide her hands until, with a shimmer and a sensation of opening in her mind, she saw once again the lake and cliff with the mineral vein.

And still the music expanded. From her vantage at the mountain lake, Christa looked back toward the truck stop, her split consciousness regarding itself over the intervening miles, taking notes of landmarks that would give her a true bearing toward the gate.

Satisfied, she returned to herself and let her fingers blur into an old jig that danced up and down, now high, now low. She smiled as she played a staccato run from the bass to the treble—harper's flash, nothing more—and finished in a rolling arpeggio and a splash of the highest strings.

Bobbie's eyes were closed. The truckers stared into their cups of coffee, one of them surreptitiously wiping his eyes. Even the cook had paused in his work, and aside from the crackling of frying eggs and the brown gurgle of the coffee-maker, the diner was silent.

"God." The waitress's word was barely a whisper, but it broke the spell and freed the applause. Christa stood, bowed, and turned for the door. "Wait a minute, honey." Bobbie opened the register and reached into the till. "You ain't paying for your breakfast after playing like that."

Christa shook her head. "It was freely given, and I have been well paid already." And she was out the door then, heading for the light-blue Eagle in the parking lot.

After strapping Ceis in, she reached behind her seat for a state map and a compass. She sighted toward the landmarks she had noted and traced a pencil line that slanted steeply to the southwest.

tell

"Somewhere between here and Durango. If we check in Salida and in Gunnison, we'll know fairly closely." A semitrailer rumbled by, and Ceis's strings thrummed in response. Christa, lips pursed, watched it fade into the distance. "And then it's just a matter of convincing a bunch of rockers to come help me kill something that's immortal."

She dropped the Eagle into gear and pulled out onto the asphalt, following 285 southward across the valley.

Glasluit's hand is strong, but his grip is not proprietary, like Lamcrann's, nor is it the cool, efficient touch of the guards who dragged her back from the land of rolling fields of wheat. He seems, instead, to hold to her mortality as a child might seize the skirts of his mother.

Siudb is puzzled. Since Chairiste left her, she has heard no offer of aid, has seen no hand extended in friendship. The Sidh do not know pity, and the eternal stasis that envelops the Realm bars their ever learning.

Or so she thought. Here is Glasluit, and here is his immortal hand, and here is his silvery Sidh voice. Help?

"Why?"

Glasluit answers with difficulty. "You do not belong here, Siudb Ní Corb. My people are not yours. You should be among your own kind."

"I have not heard the Sidh speak this way before."

"Maybe the Sidh do not. Maybe I am Sidh no longer." He gestures at the landscape, a gently rolling vista of hills and lakes and forests, all shrouded in twilight, all tranquil, still. "This is my home. I know it, and I wander through it. But it is dead."

"Dead?"

"It does not change. Do you understand, Siudb Ní Corb? Do you not know why the Sidh capture mortals and hold them in this place? Maybe the Sidh themselves do not know, but I can guess. It is because we crave their mortality."

Siudb does not understand. "But you have everything."

"Pah! We have nothing." He stops at the brow of a hill and looks off toward the distant glow of the Sidh palace. His eyes are damp. "We have this existence, this . . . prolongation. We ape the motions of the mortal world, for we have no substance of our own. We have no past and no future. I am not even certain that we really think, for how else could we endure this endless sameness, this consummate emptiness?"

Siudb hears the pain in his voice, the loneliness. Glasluit is forever estranged from his people, from his world. "Have you always thought this?"

"I have not. I said that we bring mortals here for their mortality. But we do not wish to partake of it ourselves. Therefore Lamcrann merely seeks to bed you, Orfide to torment you, Cumad to cling to you. They assume only the semblance of that which they crave. But you, woman of the Gaeidil, you are strong and vibrant with the colors and the sounds of your world. And though you may yourself be a captive of our spells, yet you have ensnared me. My world is pale, my people are mere shadows. I have watched you, and I have . . . changed." He looks up at the black, starless sky. "I want sunlight. I want seasons. I want lovers who pledge their hearts, not just the occasional use of their bodies." There are tears on his face, glittering like pearls in the half light. "I . . . believe . . . that I belong here . . . no longer."

She takes his arm. The Sidh do not weep, and yet he weeps; and as he has offered his help, so she is reaching out to him.

"But I myself have no home to which to return," he says. "There is no escape for me. I could die, perhaps. But I do not know how."

Even in sorrow, he is courageous. He weeps, but he weeps from admission, not from denial. Siudb finds that she has changed also, for until now she has hated the Sidh with all the hot temper of the Gaeidil; and yet her heart has softened almost to breaking with the sadness of Glasluit.

"I too have thought of death," she says.

He is almost frightened. "Do not, my lady. Live. You will return to your own."

"I have no great hope, Glasluit, even though you offer to help me. Orfide has lost patience: he would gladly make me forget everything. I am no master harper. In fact, I think now that I was never a harper at all, that I gave up my own strength to follow Chairiste. I cannot fight Orfide, nor can you."

"There is no need to fight Orfide."

"Stealth? I have no harp."

"I am of the palace guard. I know where your harp is." He has stopped crying. Once more like his people, he is almost passionless, but there is a purpose behind his words and his actions that delves deep below the shallow theatrics of the Sidh. "If I were to bring you your harp, at regular times, and if you were to practice without Orfide's knowledge, could you not eventually master the magics you need to win your freedom?"

She did not dream of this. "I could, but—"

"No one would know. I will have the harp back in its place when you are not using it. I ask but one favor in return."

"Name it."

"When your time comes to leave this place, I pray you take me with you."

"So be it." Siudb is weeping now herself. Glasluit's face blurs into a pale shadow.

But faintly, very faintly, Siudb hears the sound of a harp. It is not Orfide who plays, though. The hands that touch the strings are light, agile, but strong and mortal also, and Siudb recognizes the style, the tune, the quick turns and graces that come to her ears as though from an infinite distance. The distance between universes, maybe.

She turns, her eyes searching the twilight. She sees nothing. The harp sounds from beyond the Realm.

Her voice is hoarse. *"Chairiste."*

The Eagle jounced and bumped over the potholes and ruts in the trail, and Ceis was saved repeatedly by the seatbelt looped through its forepillar. The roads within Gunnison National Forest were not intended for casual driving.

Christa stopped near a picnic area, locked in the front hubs, and set the transfer case for four-wheeling. The terrain ahead—mountain slopes and muddy ditches—

looked even more forbidding than that through which she
had just passed.
    close
    "Are you sure, Ceis?" Christa unfolded a topographic
map, spread it out on the steering wheel. A bluejay
flitted across the clearing and perched in the window. It
peered over her shoulder at the lines and dots. Christa
glanced at it. "Good afternoon."
    certain
    The jay squawked once and took off, heading in the
driection of Sawtooth Mountain.
    follow
    She regarded the road—steep, rocky, overgrown—and
wrinkled her nose.
    follow
    With a shrug, she tossed the map into the back seat
and eased into gear. About her, forest closed in and
opened out, mountain vistas appeared and vanished. The
August sun was hot, but the air was cool and filled with
the sweet smell of pine and a trace of moisture from a
nearby lake.
    **
    "I smell the water, indeed, Ceis." An ugly pothole
threw the wagon to the side, and Christa fought with the
wheel for a moment. Looking up, she saw a cliff with a
mineral vein streaking it, and she swerved onto a narrow,
little-used road that was no more than two parallel ruts
amid the bushes. Branches scraped against the sides of
the wagon. Leaves and needles dropped in through the
open window and tangled in her long hair.
    The lake was a smooth oval of still water backed by an
almost sheer wall of rock. A broad meadow lay before it:
deep grass and kinnikinnick spotted with alpine butter-
cup and pink fairyslipper.
    When Christa switched off the engine, she heard the
jay calling over and over. "We're here, Ceis," she said.
She unstrapped the harp, lifted it out after her, and went
down to the edge of the water.
    Though she listened carefully, she heard nothing ex-
cept the wind, the birds, the pattering of distant falling
water. No dirt bikes, no chain saws, no sounds of speech
or horses. The last turn she had taken was almost over-
grown, and she sensed that campers did not often come

to this area. In order to be certain, she would have to use Ceis, but she had other matters to attend to first.

She settled herself on a rock outcropping above the water, put Ceis on her lap. "Gently now. This is but a test."

And with all her skill, she struck a chord that ran from one end of the harp's compass to the other, a rolling shimmer of sound that hung in the air like a curtain of mist. Before it faded, though, she was off into a gentle melody, one that always reminded her of Judith, of Siudb, the brown-eyed, dark-haired woman that she loved. It rippled out from the strings, and in her mind she felt out the extent and solidity of the potential gate.

There was something disquieting about this gate, and it was not long before she understood it: real though the gate was, it was less so than the one she had found in the Catskills. And that, she realized, had, in turn, been less solid than those in Britain.

The Realm had been drawing away from mortality, distancing itself further with each passing decade. The gates were closing, fading. Materialism, loss of belief, the cataclysms of two world wars and the horror of mass death were bricking them up, pushing the Realm back, relegating the Sidh to the status of dream and fancy.

And Judith was with the Sidh.

Christa's hands were shaking when she finished her work. Ten, fifteen years, and the doors would be shut forever. Judith would be beyond reach. She covered her face.

tears

"Indeed, Ceis," she said, wiping the eyes. "I nearly lost her." She thought of the prayer she had offered to Brigit, thanked the Goddess again for answering it. "It's next Midsummer I'll have to fight him. And I'll have to win. I have no more time for defeats."

She lifted her eyes to the faint turbulence that hovered above the water just at the edge of sight.

"Siudb. Beloved. I'm coming."

CHAPTER
NINE

In some ways, Christa changed. In others, she did not.

Kevin noticed that she had become more at ease in the company of the long-haired rockers at the school. She bantered with them while she waited for her lessons. She showed them licks and muting techniques that could only have been derived from the skilled manipulation of harpstrings. She watched appreciatively as they demonstrated their prowess with flash techniques and the tremolo bar.

Frequently now, with the heat of late August turning muggy, she exchanged her twill slacks and silk blouses for simple jeans and T-shirts, knotting a bandanna about her ankle to contrast brightly with her powder-blue sneakers. Her hair, long and flowing, still lent her an air of antiquity—just an old-fashioned gal at heart, someone his parents would have approved of—but she seemed to Kevin less distant, more real, as though she had finally stepped out of an Irish storybook and onto the gritty, concrete sidewalks of Denver. Legs crossed, eyes closed, unconsciously biting her lip as she worked to coax the last bit of emotion out of her Strat, she seemed human, vulnerable, a pretty young woman with immense talents and a kind heart.

But during her lessons she still spoke enigmatically of energies and powers, and she left Kevin with a feeling that if he were to actually hear all of what she had to say on the subject, he would finally give up, throw his guitar onto the rubbish heap, and turn to something mundane and useless at which he might actually do well.

"This section here . . ." She was back to Malmsteen again, commenting as she played. "He was right to shift to electric guitar . . ." Her hands blurred across the fingerboard. ". . . because if he had not, he would have

99

released the darker aspects of nightmare, and that kind of confrontation can be too destructive. I doubt he knew, though." Broken staccato chords now, interspersed with a high, wailing lead line. "I changed this to lydian. It is more of a woman's voice that way: life to balance death."

And on and on. He had given up any pretense of teaching Christa technique, for her command of her hands was flawless. And she took interpretation and emotion into aetheric realms that made him feel the beginner again. She was paying him for his ears and his experience, not for his lessons, and he was coming to the conclusion that she was paying him too much, that perhaps he should have been paying her, for he was more her student than she had ever been his.

"What do you mean by energy, Christa?" He sat facing her in his small office, his hands resting idly on his guitar. He never played during Christa's lessons.

She looked up. "Energy . . . is energy. It's the energy that makes things grow, that makes the seasons change."

"Like the sun?"

She shook her head slowly. "The sun is a manifestation of that energy, just like you are, like I am. It's something more subtle I'm talking about. I suppose that since it's always around us, and we see it every day we wind up not seeing it at all. The Druids . . ." She fell silent, biting her lip, frustrated with herself. "I'll put it this way: music grows. If I play a lead break, and I'm improvising, the music is growing like a tree, or a flower . . . or even like a mountain. Like sex. I'm giving to the music, and the music is giving to me. Together, with the back-and-forth flow of our energies, something comes into being. And with that can come changes in the world."

He looked up at the slide guitar on the wall. Music was like sex: Frankie had said the same thing. But changes in the world? "Are you talking about magic?"

She hesitated, then: "I am, surely. That's what music is."

Magic. He looked down at the guitar on his lap. Such a far cry from Father Lynch's sermons about the evils of Transcendental Meditation this was! "After my folks threw me out," he said, "I lived in Frisco for a while. Out in the Haight. There were some guys there into ceremonial magic. Aleister Crowley and all that. But music as magic . . . I never thought of it that way."

She was suddenly earnest, hopeful. "Could . . . could you? Think of it that way? Is it possible?"

"Rock and roll?" The idea seemed preposterous. The Beatles? Elvis?

"Anything. Harp, guitar . . . there were pipers who could raise a wall of flame from one side of Tara to the other. Once—" She stopped, shook her head. Her blue eyes were intent on him. "What say you, Kevin? Is it possible?"

"Well . . . anything's possible, I guess."

She dropped her eyes, faintly disappointed at his words, as though she had failed in some way. "Am I good enough to join a band?"

"Shit, Christa, you're good enough to own the world. There's damned few like you."

She did not look up. "I know." Her voice was faint, almost a whisper.

"Look," he said, trying to find something that would help, "we've all got our ways of looking at things, and if yours is magic, then more power to you. Look what the Eastern stuff did for John MacLaughlin."

"True."

"It's probably time for you to play some music with some other people. Sometimes you're a little rarefied, and rock and roll sounds best with some grease in it. I found some guys that need a good lead guitarist. You want me to give them your number?"

Her eyes were clouded. "You think I'm too . . . rarefied?"

He shrugged, feeling that it was almost a sacrilege to criticize such perfect playing. "Well, rock and roll's pretty down and dirty. A band would be good for you."

That night, in his cabin, he felt like a fool for having said it. Grease. Dirt and grit. Human beings: loving, giving birth, dying. The entire world was bathed in semen and sweat. And Christa, with her bloody harpstrings and her instinctive likening of music and magic and sex, was infinitely closer to the truth than was he.

Maybe her playing was aetheric, lofty. But maybe it would be good for rock and roll to have something spiritual in it besides the aesthetic posturings of early Yes and the bastardized classicism of Emerson, Lake, and Palmer.

And, dropping off to sleep with only the soft glow of a

waning moon slanting in through the windows to keep him company, he wondered: just how much did he himself really know about sex and blood? Guilt-ridden fucking . . . and Father Lynch's vitriolic lectures in the confessional . . . His parents had slept in twin beds for as long as he could remember.

Christa knew now what it was that so pained Kevin: he had lost all feeling for his music. He listened to the magic and he heard only the precision and clarity that was to be expected from any fourth-year novice from Corca Duibne. The real music—the melodies that grew and sang to the musician, to the listener, to the Worlds—had escaped him.

She was disappointed, but frightened also. Eventually—sometime before Midsummer—she would have to reveal herself to other musicians, and she would have to ask for their aid. But if no one could understand, if no one could feel, if no one would believe her, then she had already lost the battle with Orfide.

A few days later, she got a phone call from Ron, the vocalist in a band called Dark Power.

"Kevin Larkin put me on to you," he said. "He says you can really play."

"I—"

"Now, you know, I don't usually go for girls in the band. I'll tell you that right up front. All looks and nothing else, if you know what I mean. And they cause problems. But Kevin says you're good, so I'm willing to give it a try. What kind of equipment you got?"

His casual sexism rankled her. "I play a '78 Strat, and I run it through two Roland SDE-2500 delays for chorus and a little slapback echo to fatten it up. I use a Laney half-stack."

He was carefully unimpressed. "Well, that's pretty good. Listen, why don't you come over tomorrow night and we'll jam a little."

"Who, may I ask, is *we*?"

"Me and you."

"The band won't be there?"

"Well, I thought I'd give you the once-over by myself. No sense using up a full audition when I don't know you. Y'see, we're into some serious rockin' here, we're out to impress people, make a statement—"

It was her turn to interrupt. "I have harp students tomorrow evening," she said with a distinct edge, "and I am unwilling to cancel their lessons just so that you can give me the 'once-over.' If it's an audition you want, it's an audition you'll have to give me. Do you need a guitarist, or do you not?"

"Well . . . yeah . . ."

"When is your next rehearsal?" She was half of a mind to tell him to go tweak Bricriu's beard, but out of loyalty—or perhaps pity—for Kevin, she would audition.

"Thursday night. Seven."

"What songs do you want me to know?"

He named several. Some Quiet Riot, some Ozzy, some Metallica. They were obviously pieces intended to daunt her, but she knew most of them already, and the rest she could pull off Melinda's records in an hour.

"I'll be there," she said as she wrote out his address in neat Gaelic letters. But her heart was heavy as she hung up. She was going to explain magic to someone like Ron? Dear Goddess!

It had been a bad tour all around, and Lisa Donnatelli had given up on it several weeks before it actually broke down. Beer-swilling bar patrons, abusive club owners, miles of North Dakota wheat fields, and less than adequate sleep had piled one on top of another in a deadening heap; but she had nonetheless continued pounding on her kit night after night. Four smacks of her black graphite drumsticks started each set, and the songs followed in sequence thereafter, ground out with mechanical precision. It was not her idea of music, but it got her through the night.

But band economics continued to be a cause of disagreements that erupted into loud, vicious arguments in impersonal motel rooms. Her bandmates spent their money on beer and women. Lisa stuffed hers into savings. Expenses inevitably came up, and Max and the others expected her to make up for their lacks.

The final rift came in Billings, over lunch in a Mr. Steak just off Interstate 90. "You're paying, aren't you, Boo-boo?"

"Huh?"

"We're out of money." Max looked sheepish; so did Art and Monty.

She was more than annoyed. "You mean you brought us here for lunch, ordered top sirloin and all the beer, and you knew that you couldn't pay your own tab?"

"I didn't think you'd mind."

"I sure as hell do mind."

"Hey, take it easy . . ."

"What do you mean, take it easy? I've been buying meals for you guys since Bismarck. You think I'm made of money? I've got to re-head my snare pretty soon, and I'm already short because I've been springing for all the food. You guys want to play without a back-beat?"

Max sighed, looked at Art. Art looked at Monty. Monty looked uncomfortable and stared at his french fries. "Uh, you don't have to worry about your snare," he said. "We got you a brand-new one."

Her stomach started to hurt. It was not the food. Her grandmother would have called it prescience, or intuition, or something weird that a *strega* would say. Lisa called it gut feeling. "What do you mean?"

"It's really nice," Max put in quickly. "Matches the rest of your kit and everything."

Now she felt cold, too. "What did you do with my snare?"

"Well . . . uh . . . see, Monty needed some grass last night, and we worked out . . . this . . . uh . . . trade . . ."

Had the table not been in the way, she would have been on her feet and at his throat. "You traded my snare for some goddamn weed?"

"I told you, take it easy," said Max. "It's all right. You on the rag or something?"

"No, I'm not on the fucking rag. I'm something." She got up and threw down her napkin. "You can call it what you want. I call it fed up to here. I quit. Got it?"

"But we've got tonight . . . a-and the rest of the tour—"

"Right. How 'bout that?" And she walked out of the Mr. Steak and hitched a ride back to the hotel. The boys being held up by the unpaid tab, she had just enough time to grab her drums and suitcase and pile them into a taxi for a trip to the Greyhound station.

Goddam fucking rock and roll bands.

Unwashed, her hair stiff with spray, and traces of makeup from last night's show still smudged around her eyes, she stood before the ticket counter with a stack of cased drums. Her family was in New York, but they did not want to see her unless she had a diamond on her finger—minimum weight: one-half carat.

So New York was out. The fare was too much, anyway. She ran her eyes down the route map on the wall. Sheridan. No: middle of nowhere. Caspar and Cheyenne, likewise. Denver?

Didn't she know someone in Denver? There had been a girl at the NAMM show a year back. The one who had been drooling over the Pedulla basses. Melinda . . . Moore. They had eaten lunch together: female rockers trading horror stories. They had traded phone numbers, too.

"Give me a ticket to Denver," she told the man at the counter. "And how much is the freight for my babies here?"

Ron's address led Christa to a small house in a blue-collar neighborhood off South Broadway. The front lawn was dry and neglected. Paint was peeling off the shutters, and the yellow stucco walls were stained.

She pulled into the driveway in the early evening. Rock and roll was playing on a stereo inside, and she had to ring the doorbell and knock several times before a man with masses of curly brown hair and a stubble of beard came and peered at her through the screen door. "Yeah? You must be Christa."

"I am, surely."

"I'm Ron. Come on in. Our drummer's not here yet, but we can get your equipment downstairs."

He swung the door open, and she stepped into a cluttered room that smelled of smoke and too many people. Two blond-men watched a television that was competing unsuccessfully with the stereo, and a dark woman with bleach-damaged hair lounged in a corner.

"Christa," said Ron, pointing. "Fred and Jerry. Monica. Fred's our bass player, Jerry's on keys."

Christa bowed slightly. "Blessings."

Fred and Jerry nodded absently in return. Monica seemed hostile. "Come on," said Ron, "I'll show you where we'll put your stuff."

"Can't she carry her own equipment?" said Monica.

"Hey, babe, she's a girl."

Monica's tone was ugly. "She can carry her own fucking stuff. What's the matter, you already sweet on her?"

Christa turned to Monica. "I do not wish to cause difficulties." She kept her voice even, polite. "But I cannot lift my cabinet by myself. A woman friend has helped me before, but she is not here. Would you care to help?"

Monica snorted and turned back to the television.

Ron steered Christa toward the back stairs. "Don't pay any attention to Monica," he said loudly. "She's just being a spic bitch today."

Monica whirled. "Shut the fuck up, Ron."

Ron grinned at Christa and took her down the stairs to the basement. A large set of drums was set up in the corner. Synthesizers and amplifiers were arranged to either side. A mixing board stood against the wall, and cables snaked from it out to large PA speakers.

In ten minutes, the men had carried in her amp, speaker cabinet, and delays. Paul, the drummer, arrived a little later. He grinned and offered a large hand when introduced to Christa. "Sorry I'm late," he said. "I was helping with my kid sister's birthday party and had to run some of the little monsters home."

Monica kept to herslef, filing at her nails. She avoided looking at Christa, but she had followed the musicians down to the basement and had found herself another corner.

Christa powered up her amp and her effects and plucked a few notes to check the sound. Fred offered her a tuner, but she declined. "Give me an A, please," she said.

He played the note. Christa struck a single chord, listened, adjusted a string. She toed a footswitch, and the hum from her amp turned into an electric hiss as the preamps kicked in.

"I'm ready."

"What'cha want to do first?" Ron had said nothing further about his opinion of women in bands, but he had made it clear already.

Christa felt herself in the company of patronizing men and a hostile woman. Not even Colum Cille had treated a harper from Corca Duibne in such a way. She sighed. "Let's do some Ozzy. 'I Don't Know.' 'Twill loosen me up."

Monica snorted.

Christa turned to her. "If you do not treat your sisters with honor, Monica," she said quietly, "then your lot will be no better than that of a slave."

"What are you, some kind of a dyke?"

For a moment, Christa smiled to herself, thinking of Judith. "I am a woman, Monica. And I play the guitar." She looked at Paul. "Master drummer?"

He blinked at the title, found his wits, and smacked out a four-count. Christa slid into the opening rhythm hook, rapid-firing the notes at the members of Dark Power. She looked up briefly to see Fred watching her incredulously. He was so unnerved that he almost forgot to come in with the bass figure, but he caught himself in time. Christa grinned at him, nodded to Paul, and popped off a string of harmonics without looking at her hands. Harper's flash, guitarist's flash.

In spite of their opinions, the men were competent musicians and knew their parts well. Even the tricky slow section came off, with Jerry's keys shimmering out in background swells while Christa plucked clean runs and arpeggios.

Then the drive came back to the music, and Christa was off into her lead, opening with a high, shrieking wail that dropped immediately into a string of blues-influenced licks, then into rapid runs, rising trills, and long, sustained notes.

Randy Rhoads had written this lead two years before his death in 1982, and the young guitarist had been pushing the limits of his instrument and his technique, expanding both into new worlds. Christa treated his music with reverence, playing it note-for-note, changing only the last four measures so as to echo a *duchand*, a lamentation that the bards used to sing for champions fallen in battle.

Another verse, another chorus, and it was over. Christa turned her volume down, tossed back her red hair. She looked at the other. "Well?"

They were staring at her. Paul set his sticks down on the head of his floor tom and folded his long arms. "How long have you been playing, Christa?"

She wiped the sweat from her forehead. "Two months."

He laughed out loud. "Goddammit, Ron, hire her!"

CHAPTER
TEN

Grease.

Sleep was eluding Kevin tonight, and the sound of crickets and mockingbirds was loud outside his window as he sat on his sofa with his guitar, staring out at the obscurity that had enveloped the valley, a darkness as profound as the pupils of Frankie's eyes, blind in life, long closed in death.

Grease.

He fingered notes, thinking of Frankie, thinking of Christa. Somehow—and the connections kept slipping away from him, but he knew they were there—the lusty, pain-ridden bluesman and the pale, intense harper had paired themselves in his thoughts, more like than unlike in spite of their surface differences.

Grease.

He was crying. Crying for Frankie, dead and unknown in a Cincinnati bar when his music should have been a part of the lives of millions. Crying for Christa, who seemed to have more ability than her small body ought to contain, who strove to express ideas that he could not understand. Crying for himself, for music that he could not make, for thoughts and feelings that had long been lost in the eddies and cul-de-sacs of the years between his present and his past.

Grease.

What had she done, that Celtic girl whose blue eyes shone like the edge of a razor? How had she played that Malmsteen piece? That slow, harmonic minor arpeggio, with the third and the seventh lingered over as a lover might linger over a beloved, staring down into her eyes as the moonlight washed over the bed in waves of silver and white . . .

His fingers were on the guitar strings, and in his mind

he saw Christa looking up at him from the tousled sheets of his bed, her eyes blue and full of moonlight, her hands reaching up to touch his face. And he loved her. And through the arpeggio that he played—harmonic minor, third and seventh lingered over and shaken with just the faintest touch of vibrato, the notes shimmering through the air and touching it with life—he told of that love more eloquently that he would have found possible with such dull things as words.

He saw her again, reaching up to him, her eyes as deep as a summer Colorado sky. Music was like sex, like magic. Like blood. Like the twining of flesh against flesh. But now in her eyes he saw something more than an offer of love, physical or otherwise. He saw a command—imperious, urgent—a call from a Goddess to a mortal. *Come. Come now. Come to the altar, or else be lost. For if you have hands, and will, and do not make music—whether your song be as sweet as the milk of my breasts or as bitter as your deepest sorrow—then are you bereft of all. Come. Quickly.*

He awakened to the sun streaming in through the window. His fingertips were blistered and cut, the strings of his guitar slick with blood.

It was a band, but it was not the right band. But with the gateways into the Realm closing, with Judith slipping farther from her reach with each passing day, Christa wanted to believe otherwise.

She learned Dark Power's songlist in a few days, dazzling the other members of the band with her abilities; and she came faithfully to rehearsal, week after week, braving Ron's persistent condescension and Monica's continuing hostility.

But she played with a growing certainty that she would never be able to tell these musicians about the magic, about the Sidh, about Judith. She had absorbed new ideas and new melodies, but that was small comfort when, in the bleak hours after a practice, she found herself depressed and unfulfilled, facing a future loss as bitter as it would be permanent.

A month into rehearsal, after a particularly unsuccessful attempt at Night Ranger's "Don't Tell Me You Love

Me," she turned to Jerry. He was fiddling with his key-boards, shaking his head.

"It's not the patch, Jerry," she said.

"If I can just get this sound right," he muttered, "it'll fall together."

"It won't."

He looked up in annoyance. "What the hell do you mean?"

"You're not listening, Jerry," she said, already feeling the futility. "The music grows during that quiet part. Think of a tree. Think of a river. Don't think about your hands. You could play that part on a piano and it would sound right if you brought the right image to the music."

He shook his head. "Think of a tree? This is bullshit."

"Y'see, Christa," Ron said as he flicked cigarette ash onto the floor, "these days, when you're going out, you got to sound like the record. Now, we want to make it, and I think we can. I told this friend at an agency about this hot girl we've got on guitar. He's real interested. Quite a gimmick and all that."

"Gimmick?" She had thought that a harper from Corca Duibne could be many things . . . but a gimmick?

"Yeah. Don' you see? You usually use the girls for window dressing—tits and ass for the guys to look at and all that—but we've got someone who's a terrific looker, and she can shave the heads of the first ten rows, too. Think of it."

She turned her volume knob down. Her amp hissed quietly, the sound blending into the faint, electronic whine that filled the basement. "I am."

He did not notice her tone. "It's going to be great. You need to get yourself something really sexy to wear on stage. That's something I've been meaning to talk to you about. You dress like a school teacher. You need to dress metal."

"I thought," she said, "that this was rehearsal."

"It's all a part of it. Metal is a lifestyle. You can't really play it unless you're into it."

"I see. And I have not been playing it, I assume."

"Well . . ." He took a drug, threw the butt down, and stepped on it. "You've been doing all right. And you've got the moves. But . . . can't you dress sexy? I mean, you've got a nice little body."

"And what about you gentlemen?"

"Aw, that's the way it is. Guys dress power, girls dress sexy."

She glanced over at the corner that Monica usually occupied. Tonight it was vacant: Monica had apparently decided that Christa was not competition. "Would you be telling me this if your lady were here?"

He colored, and his jaw clenched. "I'm telling you this for your own good. We can go out cool, or we can go out stupid. I intend that we go out cool."

Ron was, in many ways, correct. He was describing the heavy-metal culture exactly, and was only expecting conformity from her. But her Celtic pride balked at being so treated, and she felt loyalty to her school and to what it stood for. A harper from Corca Duibne treated like a piece of pretty meat? Better her harp be shattered!

"I will dress appropriately for the style of music we play," she said. "But I will be the judge of what is appropriate."

"Look, Christa—" There was threat in Ron's voice.

Paul spoke up from behind his drums. "Ron, this isn't really the time to get into this. We've got weeks of rehearsal ahead of us before we have to worry about it."

Ron whirled on him. "This is my band, guy. Remember that. You can be replaced."

"It's a hard time you'd have of it," said Christa. "Paul knows what he's doing."

Ron stood for a moment. Then: "Shit." He switched off his microphone, stuck it in its stand, stomped upstairs.

"Okay, guys," said Paul. "Let's call it for the night."

Christa shut down her amp and effects and cased her guitar. Fred and Jerry were already ascending the stairs, talking quietly to one another. Jerry cast a look back at Christa. He was angry.

But Christa was also angry. If she had wanted predictability and stagnation, she could have stayed with the Sidh. She grabbed her guitar and headed for the stairs. "See you on Thursday," she said to Paul.

"Hey, Chris."

She stopped, one foot on the bottom tread.

Paul stuck his sticks into a leather case. "Take it easy," he said. "I've been in a lot of bands, and things like this always happen. You're hot, and you can call the shots a lot more than Ron thinks. But you'll have to go through a bunch of shit before you find what you want."

"I don't have time for that, Paul."

He shrugged. "You're young. Just starting out. Music is a crazy business, you know that already. And if you're going to go anywhere—and I know you are, Chris—it takes awhile. Just play your guitar. Relax. Enjoy the ride."

She looked up toward the top of the stairs where the light from the kitchen shone smoky and yellow. The decision was staring her in the face. She could not conceive of any combination of events that would bring Dark Power to confront Orfide and the Sidh. But she could not think of anything else to do. Paul had as much as told her that in another band she would face the same problems. "Thanks, Paul," she said. "But I really don't have the time."

"Sorry, Chris."

"Blessings." Unwilling to deal with Ron any more that night, she went up the stairs and let herself out the back door. She made her way along the driveway, scuffing through the unraked autumn leaves.

As she neared the street, a car pulled in. It approached, stopped, and Monica stuck her head out. "You guys breaking up already?"

"Some . . . ah . . . disagreements."

Monica's eyes narrowed. "Ron after you?"

"I think that he would like to be. I'm not interested. I'm sure you know that."

Monica tapped her long nails on the wheel for a moment. Finally: "Yeah. I know it. You're gay, aren't you?"

"I love a woman, Monica. If that means I am gay, then so be it."

Monica nodded. "I gotta respect you for being honest. Listen: can we talk? I . . . I mean, I'm not into women, I just need some adivce. I . . . uh . . ." She shrugged. "You seem to know what you're doing."

"I wish I believed that. Surely."

Christa put her guitar in her station wagon and followed Monica to a coffee shop a few blocks away. The lights were pale and cast few shadows, and the coffee was weak and without depth, but Monica had not come there to drink anything.

She was a dark woman, and her bleached hair was a stark whiteness against her Latino skin and eyes. But her face was drawn as she slumped in the booth. "Ron's always pulling that shit," she said after a time. "That's why I was so mad at you when you auditioned."

"I guessed that," said Christa.

"What can I do . . . to keep him with me?" Monica fidgeted with her coffee, dripping in cream and watching the patterns puff across the surface like clouds in a brown sky. "I mean, he's after everything in a skirt, and when he's with me I feel like his whore. What do I do to make him care?"

"Is it so important," Christa said, "that he care? Is it himself you must have in order to be happy?"

Monica looked puzzled. "I love him."

"Are you sure?"

"What do you mean?"

"Love is like music. It has to flow. It has to give . . . and be given in return. If you love him, and he does not love you, is there really love there at all?"

"But . . ." She looked confused. "But I need him."

"That is a different thing. Need is not love. Need might come from love, but then again it might not. Why do you need him?"

"Because . . ." She started hastily, groped for a minute, then shrugged her thin shoulders. "I . . . just do."

"Would you be less of a woman if you had no man?"

Monica stared into her coffee, struggling with unaccustomed thoughts. "No . . ." she said slowly. "But . . . it's . . . I . . ." She lifted her eyes. "I don't know what I mean."

"Think about it, Monica. Give yourself when you wish to, but know that when you give yourself willingly, you are still your own." The Gaeidil was coming out too strongly, and Christa softened her words with a wink and a smile. "Don't let Ron push you around."

"Okay." Monica nodded slowly. "I think I understood that last part."

And, driving home, Christa understood also. Love was like music. Music was like love. If it did not flow, it was nothing.

She was not—could never be—a part of Dark Power. For the men in the band, she was an attractive guitarist, no more. There was no flow, and therefore no growth. Jerry could not understand her advice, and Ron could not understand her needs. Even Paul fell far short of the goal, for music had become a job for him, and he had come to expect nothing else.

Since there was no real music, she was wasting her time. Perhaps no hope was better than a false one. Orfide could only be defeated by music, by musicians, by a band that was knit together by something more than economics and the desire to play out six nights a week.

The lights along Colorado Boulevard were harsh, garish, distant. She needed a band. The right band. But could such a thing exist?

Kevin had watched Christa's growing depression, but there was little that he could say. Not content with the erratic convolutions of fate and chance that governed the formation and dissolution of rock bands, the red-haired girl wanted results immediately; and she was blaming herself when they did not come. Kevin was beginning to fear that she would leave rock and roll entirely.

His fingers were still scabbed and sore from his unconscious, all-night solo when she came in for her last lesson of the month. She was late. That in itself told him a great deal, and the look in her eyes—bleak, shadowed—told him everything else. He did not need her spoken confirmation: "I quit the band."

"Problems?" He did not have to ask. He knew there had been problems.

"Indeed." She hardly looked at him. "I am a harper, not a centerfold."

He blushed in spite of himself, remembering his vision: Christa, naked and holy, in his bed. "Uh . . . yeah. You run into a lot of that."

"And . . ." She bit her lip as though unwilling to express the thought. "They do not understand what music can be."

"There's damned few that do, Christa."

"Do you?" Her blue eyes were intent upon him. He could have felt their gaze through a cinder-block wall.

That all-night solo: impossible licks and melodies had been ringing in his ears when he had come to himself. His fingers had been mutilated, wounded, but that was of no consequence: for the first time in years, he had played music. He did not know if he could do it again, but the knowledge that he had done it at all was a warm comfort in his heart.

He looked at his left hand. Brown scabs patched his fingertips. "Yeah . . . I think I do."

She followed his eyes, reached out and took his hand, examined it. "How came this?"

"I was playing. Really playing. It was . . . great. Like magic. I must have been in some kind of trance." And the thought of what had carried him into that trance made him blush again.

She was nodding. "It's often like that. Music can be a demanding Goddess who calls Her priest to Her altar and possesses him utterly."

He started at her metaphor. "It . . . must have been pretty intense. I don't remember much, though. Haven't been able to play for most of a week, either." He held up his hand, flexed the fingers, dropped it into his lap. "So I think I can say that, yeah, I'm starting to understand."

"Would anyone else, do you think? Could they?"

She had asked much the same question a few weeks ago, and he had put her off with a cop-out. Now . . .

"I dunno," he said. His hand strayed to the fingerboard of his guitar, touched the strings. He winced, gave up. "People are into music for different things. The bottom line is that you've got to eat, of course. But, higher motives . . ." He laughed quietly. "The most that rockers want is to have a good time and make some noise."

Christa did not give up. "I'm not asking for much more than that. Is it so impossible?"

A week ago he had thought that he could never really play the guitar. "Anything's possible, I guess." This time, his words were an invocation to hope, not a casual dismissal. "But you've got to understand, Christa: you take music into places that most people can't even think about, and you're going to have to look long and hard for people who can keep up with you." He paused, glanced at his hand. "For myself . . . I can't teach you anything more. If anything, you've got to start teaching me. I'm not going to let you waste your money on useless lessons."

He was telling her the truth for the first time since she had walked into Guitar Tech. And he felt relieved. No more hiding. No more fears. Just the truth: up front, right on the line.

For Christa, it was one loss on top of another—first her band, then her teacher—but she was thoughtful. "You know more rockers than I," she said. "Will you keep your eye out? This is important. I don't have much time."

"Sure." Once, he would have shrugged off the whole affair. *That's the breaks. That's the way this crazy business works.* But now he was convinced that this crazy business had to start working differently or it would lose something precious. "You'll stay in touch with me?" *Please* . . . "I like to think that we're friends."

Christa's eyes were still clouded, but she smiled. "I will indeed, Kevin. I still need advice and knowledge. And I need friendship most of all. But you have given me something today, and so I want to return the gift before I go. If you want to play music, you will need a sound hand."

She told him to put aside his guitar and close his eyes. Wondering, he did so, and he heard her start to play her Strat, the unamplified instrument chiming like a quiet harp. The melody sounded ancient, Irish, something like the ballad she had sung for him weeks ago. . . .

He opened his eyes, blinked, shook his head. Christa was gone. The clock told him that only a few minutes had passed. "Must have dozed off," he muttered, rubbing his eyes.

But something seemed strange, and when he realized what it was, he snatched his hands from his face. The pain had fled. His left hand was sound and whole, the fingertips pink and healthy, without a trace of a wound.

At her harp lesson, Melinda noticed that Christa was subdued. She was as attentive and supportive as ever, but she seemed to have something on her mind.

"You're doing quite well, Melinda," she said after listening to her play. "Your hands are relaxing. That's the most difficult part of learning a new instrument: relaxing. Once you show your fingers that they don't have to fight one another, you all can sit back and enjoy the music."

Melinda nodded, pleased. "It's been great. I even played

for my roommate. She thinks I'm a little weird, but . . . well, she hasn't met you."

"Roommate?"

"I thought I told you. This girl I met once showed up on my doorstep. Her name's Lisa, but everyone calls her Boo-boo. She was touring up in Montana, and her band fucked her over, so she quit." Melinda shook her head. Lisa's drums were still stacked in the middle of her small living room. The drummer had not touched them since she had brought them into the apartment. "She's pretty depressed about it, but she doesn't want to show it. You know the kind: tough as nails, heart like butter."

"Mmm." Christa nodded slowly, almost to herself.

"The harp seemed to cheer her up."

"Not hard: the harp is a healing instrument."

Christa fell silent then, staring out the window at the apple and the yew. Her eyes were troubled. Melinda was reminded of another lesson with Christa, near the middle of June. "You're dying inside, lady. What's wrong?"

"The band didn't work out."

"It happens."

"Indeed. But it was a bitter parting." Christa's mouth tightened. "The vocalist had the audacity to tell me that I was leaving because I was not dedicated enough to music."

"Asshole." A thought was forming in Melinda's mind. "What . . . what are you going to do now?"

"I don't know, Melinda. I need a band, but I need a band that can understand me when I talk about music. I need people who are willing to concern themselves more with how they play than how they look. It might not be a particularly commercial venture, but that's the way it has to be." She sighed. "I'm not sure such a thing exists."

"Maybe you should put together your own band."

"Me?" Christa smiled sadly. "I don't know anything about putting a band together."

"But I do." Melinda's hands were shaking. Ever since she had handed Christa the green Strat, this was something she had fantasized about. "I've been in a bunch of bands."

Christa lifted her head.

"A-and you're gonna need a bass player, Christa." The words tumbled out. "And maybe I don't know what you're talking about, but I'm willing to listen. I don't care if it's commercial. I just want to rock."

"Are you serious, Melinda? This could . . ." Christa hesitated. "This could take us to some strange places."

Melinda knew instinctively that the harper was not talking about Poughkeepsie or Los Angeles, but she stood her ground. "Yeah, I'm serious."

"It could be dangerous."

"Hey, what are friends for?"

"Do you understand?"

Melinda grimaced. "No, I don't. I just want to play. And I know a drummer who's just about given up—but I know she wants to play, too. There you are, Chris. Most of a band. Are you game?"

Very deliverately, Christa turned to the table that held the shrouded harp. It was as if she were conversing with the instrument, questioning it, receiving answers.

Strange places. The idea made Melinda shiver.

Christa turned back. Her eyes were bright and determined. "I'm game, Melinda. Let's rock."

CHAPTER
ELEVEN

The breeze that floats across the Realm is no more than a strengthless movement of the tepid air, incapable of stirring Siudb's long dark hair as she sits beside the reflecting pool, practicing.

It is her own harp she holds on her lap, the one she made long ago in Corca Duibne. The joinery is crude, and the finish shows the mark of an inexpert hand, but it is dear to her: an old friend returned in time of need, a symbol both of her achievement and her sacrifice.

She does not think about singing now. Once again she is a harper, and she works methodically, eyes closed. Slowly, she finds her way through the exercises given to beginners at the school; and she fights back tears as she realizes how stiff and uncooperative her hands are. Siudb Ní Corb, a harper? Absurd. Sruitmor could sooner teach a cow to play.

But harper she must be. Somewhere, Chairiste is waiting for her, perhaps herself working to release her from the bondage of the Sidh. Siudb does not know. She can only practice.

In the distance, hidden among the branches of the myrtle grove, Glasluit stands guard. Siudb is not of his people, and her dark skin is gritty with the dust of mortality, but he thinks her beautiful. Willful, free, passionate —she is everything to him that the Realm is not; and though he loves her, he knows that his love will never be returned except out of gratitude.

Still, that is something, and he falls to musing about the mortal lands. Will he someday sit upon a grassy hill in the company of Siudb and Chairiste, talking lightly of these unchanging and endless moments in the Realm, living some unimaginable existence among humans? Could it be?

He looks at his hands. Mortal, with red blood coursing through his veins? Brown dirt under his opalescent nails?

Siudb practices. Glasluit muses. And Orfide . . .

The bard stands in an upper hall of the palace, examining a niche once occupied by a crudely made harp of willow and alder. In the light of the ruby lamp that hangs high above him, his dark garments are the color of old blood.

Beside him, Lamcrann is bathed in the same light, and the diamonds ornamenting his fingers flash with crimson fire as he reaches out and touches the empty niche. " 'Tis true."

" 'Tis gone." Orfide lays his hand on the king's shoulder. "And I know who took it."

"Not Siudb, surely!"

"Not Siudb. The mortal has no access to this place. There is a certain lad, though . . ."

Lamcrann studies the bard's face. "She has been wasting here, Orfide. Perhaps it is no more than a gesture of kindness."

"Kindness? You have been listening to your mortal pet overlong, my king. Siudb wishes to leave us. With her harp—" He struggles with the thought, dismisses it. No, the Gaeidil cannot master the intricate music that would free her. The gate she called up was an illusion. Chairiste managed only by chance. "I am not concerned," he says, but his fists are clenched.

Lamcrann's eyes are on the bard's hands. "You are certain?"

"Glasluit and Siudb can amuse themselves as they wish. The possibility of something unacceptable being done exists, of course. If so, I recommend discipline."

Lamcrann is still looking at the bard's hands. "If there is discipline, dear Orfide, I will be the one to impose it."

"Of course, my liege."

But the bard's face is expressionless, a mask of lurid flame, his silver hair and beard sparkling as though strewn with the dust of rubies.

Lisa hated the snare. Christa noticed that almost immediately, even while the dark, sturdy woman was still hauling her equipment into the basement. She carried the

drum with repugnance, as though it embodied some failure, personal or otherwise, that she could not escape.

And when she had set up her kit, the snare, although it
had the same glossy black finish as her other drums,
seemed separate: a pariah among the brahmans. Lisa
adjusted its stand brusquely, and she smacked the head
to check the pitch as though she would rather have broken it. "Ready on the firing line."

Christa turned her amp on. In a minute, the Laney's
hiss had joined the quiet hum of Melinda's Marshall, but
Christa watched Lisa for a moment more. The drummer's
broad shoulders were hunched. She slumped on her throne,
staring moodily at a crash cymbal. "Do you want to do
this, Lisa?" asked Christa gently.

Lisa regarded the snare as though she held an alligator
between her knees. "Yeah. Let's do it. What do you
want to play?"

Christa shook her long hair back over her shoulders to
keep it off her strings. "Melinda?"

"You're the boss, Chris."

"Well . . . There is a new Quiet Riot album out, but I
don't know anything on it yet. I do know 'Metal Health'
though."

Lisa looked up. "The one that goes *Bang your head*?"

"That one. Indeed."

The drummer cracked a smile, the first Christa had
seen. "Boy, you sure don't look the type."

Christa's pale pink blouse matched the polish of her
nails and reflected warmly in the gold *failge* adorning her
left wrist. She had intentionally dressed conservatively
for this first meeting to see whether Lisa would judge her
clothes or listen to the music.

"That's what I kept telling you, Boo-boo," said Melinda.
"She's okay."

"Yeah . . . whatever you say . . ." Lisa straightened.
"You want a count, or should I just start?"

"Go for it," said Christa. "I'll follow."

Lisa nodded and opened the song with a quick fill that
slowed until her drumsticks hung, poised, above her cymbals, waiting . . .

She looked at Christa. Hoping . . .

Christa saw the sticks begin to descend, and as the
cymbals crashed, she blasted out the opening hook, trying

to put something as fragile as hope into thick, stupid bar chords.

Hope? Lisa was hoping, and Christa was hoping too. Midsummer was only a little over nine months away, and rock bands were unstable, vaporous things that ordinarily came together and fragmented with terrible regularity. But Christa could not afford the ordinary. This band would have to stay together. It would have to work.

She played, supported by the drums and the driving bass. Melinda's black Fender Precision made the small blond woman seem even smaller, but the sound she produced belied her stature. She knew what was wanted, and she supplied it: a firm, punchy rhythm that reinforced the drums and contrasted with a fiery syncopation of the guitar. Christa grinned at her. Three women making noise, making music, making magic.

And it was working. Christa felt it, and Lisa, she was sure, felt it too. The drummer had been playing with strength, but when Christa took the lead break, Lisa laid the groundwork for her with a high-speed fill that pounded from one side of her kit to the other in a moment, crashed through her cymbals, and left the air shivering as Christa's first note screamed out of her amplifier like a fat blue spark.

Pink blouse and nails, golden bracelets, long red hair, Christa piled flash and technique into the break, adding wild bends and pick scrapes to an already pungent solo; and she finished it off by jamming the Strat's headstock against the side of her amp until the feedback eclipsed even the wall of percussion that Lisa had raised.

And without losing a shred of momentum, she fell back into the rhythm hook. She cycled through the chord progression twice, held the final chord, and let her volume fall until only the bass and drums were left.

She looked at Melinda with pursed lips. In the next section of the song, the vocalist and the guitar entered into a call-and-response pattern. But there was no vocalist present today. This was a first meeting, a tentative joining of musical energies to see what might happen.

Melinda gave her a wink, went to the microphone, and screamed out the lyrics. She was not a singer—her voice was hoarse and it shattered on the high notes—but the spirit was there.

Bang your head!
Wake the dead!

"Do you hear, Orfide?" Christa said to herself. "Do you hear? It's a hard time of it you'll have sleeping through this." And, answering Melinda, she snapped out short, angry blues licks, her strings shrieking with hostility.

The chorus came back then, and Christa let the final chord ring until Lisa, her mouth turned down at the corners as though she wept, smashed through a last fill and a flourish, whipping at her cymbals until the sound was a taste of metal at the back of Christa's throat.

Silence backwashed into the room, smothering the hiss and whine of electronics. Melinda grinned. "Far out."

Christa wiped her forehead on her sleeve. Lisa's eyes were closed, her half-open mouth seemingly caught in mid-sob.

"Lisa?"

Lisa's voice was a whisper. "My friends call me Boo-boo."

"All right. Boo-boo?"

Lisa shook her head. "God, that felt good." And when she at last looked at Christa, her brown eyes were indeed filled with tears. "You are . . . utterly fantastic. You want me?"

"Indeed," said Christa. "You have a great heart."

Lisa turned to Melinda. "Does that mean yes?"

That's the breaks. That's the way this crazy business works.

But Christa was putting together her own band, and that also was the way the crazy business worked. And if the quiet harper-turned-guitarist could do something—and whatever it was, Kevin was not going to ask, because it still scared the hell out of him—to heal his hand, if she had that much (he had to say it) *magic* in her, then this crazy business might not turn out to be quite so crazy for her . . . or, rather, it might just be crazy enough. Whatever.

He pulled into the parking lot of the Proshop and ran for the door with his collar up. The thin denim jacket did little to keep out the October cold, but he wore the garment more for its looks than for its warmth.

The store was quiet. The woman at the front desk waved at him. "Hi, Kev."

"Howdy, Barb. Did my tubes come in?"

"You'll have to ask Scott down in Guitar. He was taking care of it. The truck dropped off a bunch of stuff from the warehouse yesterday afternoon, but I didn't see the paperwork."

He started for the guitar department, but Barb spoke again.

"Wait a minute." She checked a blackboard on the wall. "Scott got that Taiwan flu that's going around. Sick as a dog. Devi's covering for him. She's usually in Keyboards, but she knows her stuff."

"Would she know about my order?"

Barb shrugged. "I don't know, Kev. Sometimes I think she knows everything."

The woman behind the guitar counter was thin and pale, as though a young sorceress—coaxed away from a midnight desk strewn with old palimpsests and grimoires—had been persuaded to mind a music store for a time. Black hair, black eyes. "Are you Devi?" Kevin asked. "I'm Kevin Larkin."

He offered his hand, but she did not take it. Her smile, he noticed, was insubstantial, thin—like butter that had been scraped across too much bread.

"Yeah, I'm Devi." She eyed him for a moment. "Wait a minute. Weren't you in the Violators a few years back?"

He blinked. "A few years back? More like ten. Where'd you see me?"

"Herman's Hideaway up on Broadway." For all her intensity, Devi seemed fragile. A strong wind might snap her. "I was underage, but I sneaked in with a girlfriend. You were great. Are you still playing Hendrix that way?"

"I . . ." As far as Kevin could tell, he was not playing anything that way anymore. The years of sterility had intervened, and now, with Christa's influence, his playing had changed again. "I don't know. You'll have to listen sometime."

"Are you gigging?"

"Not for now. Maybe . . ." Outside, snow began to fall, hard and pebbly. It hissed against the plate-glass windows. The cars on Colorado Boulevard had their headlights on. "Maybe sometime soon."

"I'll look forward to it." Again the insubstantial smile. "This time I'll be legal." She pushed aside a stack of service manuals. "What can I do for you?"

"I'm retubing my amp. Paul ordered some 12AX7s for me."

"Hang on. I think they came in, but I'll have to climb around in back for a few minutes."

While she searched for the tubes, Kevin poked through the department, examining the guitars and the amps. When he had bought his Strat, a tobacco sunburst was thought to be high style indeed, but compared to the peacock hues of the instruments hanging on the wall— the intense pinks and blues, the tiger stripes and the iridescence—its brown and amber finish was subdued and drab. Still, it was the sound of an instrument that mattered, not the appearance. Christa had once told him that she had made her first harp herself, and that, though the workmanship was painfully crude, it had the sweetest tone of any mortal harp she knew.

Mortal harp. Strange that she had put it that way. What could she have meant by that?

He was still pondering her choice of words when Devi came back and handed him the tubes and the ticket. "Anything else, Kevin?"

"That's it, thanks. How come they've got you covering guitars?"

She laughed a shallow laugh. "I made the mistake of showing that I knew something. A girl came in a few weeks ago and they wanted to sell her a POS special. I could tell she wanted something better, so I took over. She went out with a Laney and a couple of Roland delays." She shook her head wonderingly, and her eyes flickered as though she remembered something almost frightening. "Damn, she could play."

"Yeah?" He was studying the tubes and the receipt, but something jogged his memory. "Wait a minute. Long red hair?"

"Down to her waist."

"That was Christa."

"You know her?"

"She went to my guitar school for a while."

Devi's eyes flickered again. "How well . . . how well do you know her?"

"Christa?" He stood with the tubes in his large hands, thinking. "She's hard to know. I mean . . . it's like she goes back a long way."

"Does she ever . . . do anything . . . with music?"

Do anything? "I'm not sure. She's pretty incredible. She's scared me a few times." His left hand, cupping the tubes, was sound and whole. Not a mark on it. "What do you mean?"

Devi was staring at the wall hung with guitars. "Uh . . . nothing, really. Just wondered."

Devi had seen something, and Kevin's hand tingled as it had on that afternoon when Christa had told him to sit back and close his eyes. "Yeah. Okay."

For an instant, Devi's gaze flicked down to his hand. "What's she doing now?" she asked casually.

"Putting together a metal band."

"What does she need?"

"Keys. Vocals. They'll have to be some pretty incredible people to keep up with her."

"Yeah." Devi looked at the wall. Her black eyes were intense, hot, and they reminded him of Christa. "You know her phone number?"

My fault.

Danny Larkin pulled his down jacket close to his body as a child might pull the sheets over his head to keep away the darkness. Snow was falling in Sheridan, large white flakes that stuck to street signs and curbs, that made the sidewalks slippery and caked up on automobile glass at the end of the wipers' travel. It flecked his lashes as he squinted up at the dark sky, and he shivered.

Always my fault. My fault that ma almost died. My fault that ma and da can't sleep together. My fault that they're going to hell. My fault that Benji's going to have a corpse on his hands in a few . . .

Though he was sweating, he shivered again; and he forced himself away from the entrance to the medical center and bullied himself down the walk to the parking lot. The windshield of his car was opaque with snow and ice, but he made no move to clear it off. He merely climbed in, closed the door, and stared at the whiteness, shivering.

It was something he should have expected after the

months he had spent cruising the bars, picking up fast-talking, skinny litte faggots who thought of liaisons in terms of hours and fist-fucking. He himself had been one of them, flitting from bed to bed, from bathhouse to bathhouse, rebelling against the lifetime that had been planned for him while he was still in his mother's belly, showing the seminary, his parents, and Father Lynch just what he thought of them. An angry little boy with a toy gun.

A fit of coughing took him, and he put his forehead against the cold steering wheel as he hacked uselessly. His lungs would not clear. They would never clear. And whether pneumonia or cancer or any one of a thousand ills killed him first, he had nothing to complain about, for he himself had marked out his future death from a failed immune system more unalterably than his parents had ever committed him to the life of a priest.

My fault.

He would have to get out of the car and scrape the windshield eventually, but for now he wept. The snow isolated him from the stares of the curious, and he pulled his collar up and huddled in the driver's seat, wishing that he could indeed pull the covers over his head and hide from the darkness.

My fault. What am I going to tell Benji?

CHAPTER
TWELVE

Christa's days were still filled with harps and harp students, but her evenings were devoted to a different music. As darkness fell across Denver—the shadows of the Rockies racing eastward, the lights of the city blinking on in star-scattered fields of tungsten yellow and mercury-vapor blue—her basement reverberated with the sound of drums, bass, and white-hot guitar. It was not a band . . . yet. But it was a beginning.

Devi showed up a week after Lisa had hauled her drums down Christa's back stairs. She pulled up in a white van, opened the side doors, and pulled out, piece by piece, an assortment of keyboards, stands, and cables that took her an hour and a half to assemble. By the time she was finished, she was virtually buried in electronics.

"I mean no offense," said Christa delicately, "but does it really take this much equipment to make music?"

Devi's mouth tightened. "Am I hearing the old *keyboards are firewood* routine?"

"Not at all." Christa squeezed through a narrow gap between two synthesizers and stood beside Devi. "It's not a great deal I know about such things. This is . . . impressive."

"You can do a lot with one good keyboard," said Devi. "But you can do a lot more with several." She gestured to the synthesizers around her. "I've got these three MIDIed together so I can control them with the MKB-1000 over here, and I brought the micro-computer because I've got a bunch of sounds stored on floppies. I can sample your guitar onto disk, for instance, and then I can keep a good crunchy rhythm going for you when you go off into a lead."

All the while she talked, Devi's black eyes constantly flicked back to Christa, examining, evaluating. Christa

could understand it to a degree, for there were two sides
to any audition: the band checked out the prospect and
the prospect checked out the band. She herself was main-
taining her silk-blouse-and-pink-nails persona, just as she
had for several other keyboardist auditions, but Devi did
not appear to notice such superficialities. She seemed,
rather, to be trying to pierce the mild persona that Christa
had built up over the course of two centuries: the civilized, socialized woman that hid, for the most part, the
wild Gaeidil.

Did she see? Devi herself, Christa sensed, was a carefully constructed mask, one that lacked depth but allowed its wearer to function from day to day. It was as
though, just beneath the soft features and rounded body
of a woman, there was a shell, an iron carapace that
blocked any deep knowledge or empathy. Who better to
recognize a mask than another mask?

Christa faced her. "You're good, aren't you?"

Devi's eyes narrowed as though she were examining
the question for a trap—an ounce of explosive, perhaps,
designed to sever a finger, or amputate a hand. Satisfied,
she nodded. "Yes. I am."

"Excellent. Let's make some noise."

"What do you want to play?"

"Do you know 'Don't Tell Me You Love Me'?"

"Night Ranger? Sure. Simple synth parts, though."

Christa smiled, her face responding to the orders of the
woman hidden within. " 'Twill be enough."

In Dark Power, Christa had been confronted with a
keyboardist who knew a little technique, a little feeling,
and a little synthesizer theory. Jerry had been an adequate player, but what Christa had wanted was beyond
his ability, and he had not been able to understand her
when she had tried to explain.

Devi was different. Christa was almost startled by the
surging chords that welled up out of the speakers. To
Jerry she had given the images ot tree and river, but Devi
seemed to have her own sources of inspiration. Head
down, eyes on the keys as though she were commanding
the sounds to come forth not through simple electronics
but rather by force of will, she made music that sobbed
and wept, as though jerked bloodily out of her heart.

And though there was no microphone stand before Devi, Christa saw her mouthing the words of the chorus.

Don't tell me you love me.

Don't tell me you love me.

She did not know to whom the keyboardist sang, but she knew from the expression on Devi's face that she uttered the words with a seething mixture of anger and hate that would not have been adequately conveyed by any amount of amplification.

Don't tell me—I don't want to know.

If the words had been razors, Devi would have hurled them.

The song ended. Christa nodded slowly, wondering at the emotion she had heard, then bowed to Devi. "You are indeed good."

The black eyes bored back at her from across the room. "Thanks. You're good too."

Christa looked at Melinda and at Lisa. They had already auditioned several keyboardists, and though one or two had demonstrated considerable skill, none had possessed Devi's abilities. Did they hear the difference?

Lisa nodded to herself. "That was good," she murmured. "That was it."

Melinda was grinning, lounging back against her speaker cabinet. The overhead fluorescents gleamed on the black Fender Precision. "Devi, you were always hot shit on keys, even back when. What was that band you were in when we first met?"

"Teenage Sluts From Hell." Devi smiled, but the expression went no further than the iron plates that rose up a quarter of an inch past her pupils.

"Yeah. That was it. You emptied a beer on my head in between two of our sets."

"What did you expect? You guys threw us out of the dressing room."

"Well . . . yeah . . . we were kinda rowdy. . . ."

"I trust," said Christa politely, "that we won't have any problems involving old band rivalries."

"Hey," said Melinda, "I owe her a can of beer."

"You sure as hell don't," said Devin. "You deserved that."

Christa turned to the keyboardist. "We rehearse three times a week, six to ten in the evening. We will be playing cover tunes, but I will be writing some originals, and I plan that they will eventually comprise about half of our material. I don't know how commercial this will be, so I would advise you to keep your day job."

"Are you intending to play out, or is this a basement band?" Devi was cool, professional, but Christa sensed her eagerness.

"We'll be playing out. But we won't be going on the road. I have . . . commitments."

"Fine with me."

Devi wanted something. Christa was certain of that. "The position is yours if you want it."

Devi nodded. "Thanks. I do. When is the next rehearsal?"

"Tomorrow. How quickly can you learn twenty-five songs?"

"Week. Ten days." Devi looked at her keyboards, then at Christa. An iron wall stood behind her eyes, and it seemed now to be glowing red with the intensity of whatever was shut up behind it.

Outside Christa's house, a cold rain was falling, pattering softly on the roof, rustling in the branches of the maple trees that were leaved in the blood of late October. The pages of the tablet before her glared whitely under the desk lamp, and she rubbed her eyes often.

Notes and melodies came easily to her, but words were halting things that struggled and fought with her pen. In neat Gaelic letters she tried to capture the songs she needed to write, songs that she would hurl against the opalescent walls of the Sidh palace; but it was hard, frustrating work, and she labored on into the night.

There was a sense of futility about the edges of her thoughts, though, for as yet she labored in a vacuum. Even after several weeks of constant auditions, the band was still without a vocalist, and the quality of the prospects had been uniformly low.

Lisa called them wanna-bes: attractive, stylish young women and men who knew nothing of music other than that they could sing along with the car stereo. It was easy, they thought. Anyone could sing. It took no equipment save a voice and a microphone, and it was a glamorous lifestyle.

"They're hard to find," the drummer had said. "A good vocalist is as hard to find as a good fuck. Better, too. Lasts longer."

Pessimistic sentiments. Christa had considered giving up the search, but her own voice was reedy and thin, unsuitable for anything more than back-up vocals. Melinda and Devi were little better. Lisa hardly sang at all.

Judith sang . . .

Christa straightened and turned toward the window to rest her eyes. The rain rustled on, threatening sleet and snow. A drop traced its way down the glass, and the streetlamp was a full moon patterned by tossing leaves.

Judith sang. On winter evenings at the steadings, when the families of Cummen and Corb had joined together to pass a few of the long, dark hours, Christa's untrained harping had accompanied her as she sang old airs and ballads in a voice as rich as the fresh-plowed earth of the fields. Even before she had reached womanhood, Judith's voice had possessed a warmth that belied her years, a depth that glowed like the amber of a priestess's necklace.

And Judith had given it all up.

Christa put a hand to her face. Did she still sing? Did she have anything to sing about?

Pattering, running down the windowpanes, rustling in the leaves, the rain continued. It sounded cold. As cold as the touch of a Sidh.

She went back to the tablet. The song she was writing was a challenge, something to let Orfide know that she was back. She whacked out a series of power chords on her guitar, mentally turning the faint, unamplified twang into the full-throated roar of the Laney. The words did not have to be Gaeidelg. They could be English. They could be anything: it was the music that would tell the Sidh bard exactly what she did not want to know.

Are you surprised to see me
Standing here at your door?
Thought it was over between us?
Thought you could forget about it all?

She struggled, weighing the sounds of the words. She wanted the feeling of heavy metal: the power, the anger, the straightforward, rough-hewn verses that were not so much sung as screamed. This was no place for the niceties of bardic convention. Let the old kings of Eriu sleep peacefully, their long-dead ears full of elegant phrases and skilled poetry. Orfide would hear something different.

Did you really think I'd just
Give up and walk away?
Did you really think I could?

The words yielded a little more, the colloquial idiom slowly adapting to the form she imposed upon it. She battered her way through the chorus:

I'm here
And I'm calling you out
So get your ass out here, boy,
'Cause it's time to get down
To the firing line!

Tipping back in her chair, she played the song through, singing the words under her breath. There was plenty of room in the melody for lead lines that would lash out at Orfide like keen blades. A challenge and a weapon both.

"Good," she murmured. "Another verse it could probably use, but this is a beginning." She looked at the time. Near midnight. She had students early the next morning.

She put her guitar aside, went into the kitchen, and poured herself a cup of milk. She had just set it in the microwave when she heard a car pull up suddenly in the street, brakes screeching faintly, tires sliding a foot or two on the pavement with the sound of wet gravel. A metallic slam, and a moment later someone was frantically ringing her doorbell.

Christa ran down the hall. The woman on the porch was shivering in the cold, her nightgown soaked with rain. Blood flowed from a cut in her face and one eye was swelling shut.

"Monica?" Christa hardly recognized her.

"Can I come in, Chris? Ron's after me, and he's really pissed." Monica glanced over her shoulder as a pair of headlights rounded the corner. "Omygod, he followed me!"

The harper pulled her in, slammed and locked the door. Monica was crying, tears mixing with rain and blood, mascara spreading panda-like over her dark face. Christa took her thick cloak out of the hall closet and cast it around the woman's shoulders. "Into the living room with you," she said.

"But . . . Ron . . ."

"If Ron has nerve enough to come to my door, I'll handle him. Come on, you're freezing."

In the living room, Monica huddled into a corner of the big sofa, looking small and frail in the wide blue Kinsale. Water dripped onto the shag rug from the hem of her nightgown. "I took your advice." Her voice was a whisper, and tears were close to the surface. "But he got mad when I told him it was over. He's been mad before, but he never hit me. This time . . ."

Her eyes widened and she gasped hoarsely at the sudden pounding on the front door. "Chris," she said, "he's drunk. Maybe you should call the cops."

Christa stood up, her face flushed. Ron had insulted her on several occasions, had questioned her dedication to music, and now he was at her door, threatening violence.

Violence? He did not know what violence was.

"Maybe," she said. "And maybe it's a poor excuse for a woman of my clan I'd be if I could not stand for myself, or for those that come to me for help." She went down the hall and paused with her hand on the deadbolt as another bout of pounding shook the door.

"Where the fuck are you, slut?" Ron shouted.

Christa turned the bolt, jerked the door open. Ron was a head taller than she, but the look in her eyes made him step back a pace. "What do you want?" she said.

There was threat in her voice, but Ron's bravado came back. "You know what I want, bitch. I want my woman."

"You have no woman, sir. She left you. And I'd suggest you keep a civil tongue when you talk to me."

"I'll fucking talk to you however I want. And you keep your dyke hands off her."

"So you can beat her up? I think not. Please leave."

He lunged for her. Her reactions were sluggish after decades of disuse, but she managed to grab his hair. Pivoting, she slammed his head into the doorjamb as he grappled for her throat.

"You fucking bitch . . ." For a moment, he staggered, and she drove in, slashed his face with her long nails, and sent him reeling back off the porch. He fell flat on his back. She was on top of him in a moment.

"The Romans found out about us, *fuidir*," she screamed as she pummeled him, "and by the Gods you'll find out too!"

He was struggling, but now he was clawing to get away from the raging Celt who had planted herself on his chest. He managed to turn over, and as she battered at his head, he inched his way down the brick walk.

He did not protest when she leaped off his back, seized his coat, and dragged him to his car. The odor of beer and cigarettes choked her as she shoved him in. His eyes were bloodshot and frightened, and they peered through the steamy window at her as he hastily closed and locked the door.

Head high, she strode back to the house through the freezing rain. Her hair was wet and matted with leaves, her blouse ripped and covered with mud, but a warm pride was burning within her. She was Chairiste Ní Cummen, a woman of her clan. She had not forgotten what that meant.

Monica looked up as she entered. "I watched through the front window. You're . . . fantastic. . . ."

Christa shrugged in reply and picked up the phone. She was still shaking with anger, and she fought to reestablish the quiet harper of Denver. The handset was of smooth beige plastic, and the numbers and letters glowed softly at her, reminding her of where she was, of who she needed to be.

"What are you doing?"

Christa took a deep breath, let it out slowly. The flush left her cheeks. The harper of Denver came back. "He's been drinking," she said. "I don't want him driving, but I don't want him staying, either." She riffled through the directory with a muddy hand, found the number she wanted, punched it in. "My name is Christa Cruitaire," she said into the handset. "I'm at 72 Eudora Street. There'a man in an old Impala out front, and I'm sure he's drunk. Could you have some officers come out and take a look? Thank you."

When she hung up, Monica was still wide-eyed. "Where'd you learn to do all that?"

"My father taught me. He thought that his daughter should be able to take care of herself. My mother, though . . ." Christa laughed quietly, sadly. Bretan Ní Coemgen had been well schooled by the bishops. Stay at home, take care of your man—whether he be father, brother, or husband—and you will, in turn, be taken care of. As a Christian man to his God, so the Christian woman to her man.

She shook her head. It never really worked that way. Absently, she began picking sodden leaves out of her hair. "What happened?"

Monica shrugged within the cloak. She had stopped shivering, and the cut on her face was slowly scabbing over. "Pretty much what I told you. I finally got fed up with Ron. He was drunk, and I was in bed, so I guess I was kinda stupid. We got in a big argument, and it took a while for me to get out. I found your address in the phone book. There aren't too many Cruitaires in Denver."

"Nor anywhere else, Monica."

Monica tried to grin, but it hurt too much. "I liked you. You talked to me straight. Ron and the others never did. Just a bunch of fucking games."

A soft creak from Christa's studio made Monica jump. "What's that? Is that Ron?"

The room was very quiet: the rain pattering outside and the ticking of the wall clock only intensified the silence. "Be easy. My harps are in the other room, and they become a little vocal when the humidity changes."

"I didn't know you played harp."

"Indeed. I am a harper."

"That's pretty neat."

Outside, a motor grew louder. Doors slammed. A police flasher lit the curtains with staccato bursts of light, and there was a squawk of a radio.

Christa went to the window. "Ron's being taken care of."

"That son of a bitch." Monica gasped, wiped at her face. "I put up with so damn much from him, and then he turns around and pulls this shit on me. Do this, and do that, and give up this, and feel grateful 'cause you're going out with a white man. . . . Fuck."

"It's over. You're your own again."

Monica sniffled. "Haven't got much."

"Do you have a job?"

"Yeah. Receptionist. Dumb, pretty meat that fills a hiring quota and gets paid zip. I gave up the singing for Ron."

Christa suddenly felt cold, but not because of her sopping clothes. "Gave it up?"

"He said he didn't like the way other guys looked at me up there."

Christa had picked a handful of limp leaves out of her hair, and as she wandered into the kitchen and tossed them into the trash can under the sink, she noticed that the cup of milk was still in the microwave, still warm. She brought it back with her and put it into Monica's hands. "What did you sing?"

Monica sipped at the liquid. "Warm milk? Jeez, I haven't had this since I was a kid and ate *menudo* for lunch." She laughed. "I was in a band. We did hard rock and metal. I've got one of those nasty Lita Ford voices. It was fun. We had a bunch of bookings—almost got to open for Van Halen when they played Red Rocks." She touched her swollen eye, winced again. "Be a damn long time before anyone'll hire me for singing with this mess. Besides, Ron's got connections."

"Not with everyone, I daresay."

"I'd be stuck in some basement band. We'd never get out."

I gave up the singing for Ron. And what had Judith said to herself as she struggled with harpstrings in the pitch darkness of the practice cells? *I gave up the singing for Chairiste?*

"I'm . . ." Christa bit her lip, turned half away. Rain streaked down the windows. "I'm putting together a metal band. We need a vocalist. Would you like to try out?"

"But Ron said—"

"Ron said a great many things."

Monica deliberated. "You're . . . real good, I know."

"Do you want to try out?" *Is that what you said, Judith? O Brigit!*

Monica shook her head a little. "I'm out of practice."

"The remedy for lack of practice is practice," said Christa. "And I can promise that you won't be stuck in the basement."

Wrapped in a cloak that seemed overlarge, her feet tucked under her, Monica sipped at the cup of milk. "I dunno. I guess . . ." She blinked her dark brown eyes at Christa. "I guess I can give it a try. What's the name of your band?"

"We don't have one yet."

"Ummm. You ought to get one. Maybe put something about harps in it. That'd be classy."

Something about harps. Later in the night, with Monica warm and safe beneath the covers in the spare bedroom, Christa, bathed and in a robe, stood in the doorway of her studio, drinking cocoa, thinking about it.

The band needed a name. Up until now, she had been reluctant to discuss or consider such a thing. It was enough that she was finding the musicians she needed. To name the band before the personnel had been found seemed to be the action of a wanna-be, or a *crossain*. Names were holy, not to be used wantonly.

In the night, shadowy and indistinct, the yew and the apple framed Ceis. The Sidh harp was silent. Its wires glinted in the spill of light from the kitchen, a web of gold, a gossamer net that could enmesh the mightiest spells.

Across the room, her Strat answered the gleam of Ceis's wires with its own strings of steel. Her axe, Kevin had called it. She laughed softly at the term.

Something about harps. Indeed, that was a good idea. And though the thought of naming the band had seemed premature when she had sat down to write a song earlier that evening, now it was almost urgent. She had her vocalist. She was sure of that.

Ceis and the Strat glittered at one another across the darkness, and the name came together, holy and appropriate both.

Gossamer Axe.

CHAPTER
THIRTEEN

"Good. Very good. Let's do that again. And this time, Melinda, can you bring up your treble during the lead break?"

"You sure you want that, Chris? That's going to load the midrange a lot."

"It will, but your overtones will mesh with mine and I'll have more energy to work with."

Christa approached heavy metal with the same care and effort that she expended on the harp. Every note counted. Every rhythm had to be right. The quality of sound had to be weighed against the eventual effect upon both a human audience and the immortal Sidh. But for all her planning and arranging, she left ample opportunity for her bandmates to express themselves freely, for without spontaneity, magic would be impossible. She guided, and she suggested, but she entrusted the final interpretation of her ideas to her fellow musicians.

"Lovely, Devi. That hissing quality you're getting out of the MKB-1000—it's rather hot in the top end. Can you bring it down just a trifle? I really liked what you did with your solo."

"It wasn't like the record."

"That's quite all right. If I wanted the record, I could go out and buy it. Is there any chance you can work a major-sixth feeling into that A chord in the third measure of the break?"

"I think so. Say . . . that'd sound hot, wouldn't it?"

Monica's voice was out of condition, and it failed midway through her first two rehearsals. But Christa was right: the remedy was practice. Every evening after work, Monica was downstairs in the basement with microphone, stereo, and PA, working on the difficult sections of songs, smoothing and polishing the easy parts.

Christa did not begrudge her the time. Monica had moved back into her own apartment, but she was still afraid of Ron, who, shouting and threatening, had attempted to bother her at work several times. Christa's home was a refuge for the singer, a place where she had found a friend and a defender.

Day by day, Monica was relaxing, regaining her voice and her stage moves; and at her third rehearsal, she startled them all with a performance of "Metal Health" that might have melted steel. In contrast to the thin, vulnerable receptionist, Monica the singer turned out to be all fire and brass.

I got the boys
To make the noise,
Won't ever let up,
Hope it annoys you!

She strutted, sneered, bared her teeth; and Christa thought of Orfide as he fingered the golden strings of his harp—his second-best harp—musically savaging her in Cornwall and in Scotland.

"Nastier on that last chorus, Monica?"

"Sure."

And Judith . . . giving up her song . . .

"Jump out of that fill just a tad quicker, Boo-boo. We'll cut their measure short. The unexpectedness will be worth it."

Though the music they played was raw and angry, the evening's end would invariably leave Christa with a good feeling, a satisfied fullness in her heart. Gossamer Axe had become a band, and, moreover, it had become a family in which the members cared for one another and knew each other's ways.

Devi was razor sharp, pained and impenetrable, a wizard with sounds and electronics. Lisa was slow and steady, at times almost taciturn, but she worked out at the local Y three nights a week so that she could hit like the boys. Melinda was brash and sensitive at the same time, with a head full of dreams that repeated disapointments had not banished. Monica was cheerfully unsophisticated, almost childishly grateful for any kindness. Christa . . .

Christa waved good-bye as Devi's van pulled away from the curb. How did they see her? Though she wore the mask of modern America, she came from a different place and time. She might don T-shirts and jeans, play rock and roll, tie a bandanna about her ankle, but she did so formally, carefully, hiding behind yet another mask.

Masks had been her life since she had left the Realm. The quaint little harper kept as a novelty by a nobleman of France had become the governess and music teacher of nineteenth-century London. America had made little difference in her life: she was still quiet, still polished, still hiding. Despite the occasional outbursts of the Gaeidil, she had, over the course of the years, grown almost innately conservative. It had been a matter of survival.

But the matter of Judith's rescue demanded that she drop her reticence. Gossamer Axe: it was going to be quite a band. It *had* to be quite a band. The masks would have to come off. All of them.

change

"Indeed, Ceis," she said, closing the front door. "The ladies may well flee in terror. And I might also."

"You know," said Melinda, "I'm going to be glad when I can give up this nine-to-five shit." She squeezed toothpaste onto her brush and plunged it into her mouth.

Lisa was plumping the pillows on the sofa. It was not much, but it was a place to sleep. "Sounds like you're planning ahead."

Melinda rinsed her mouth before she answered. "Hey, this band is going places."

"I'm keeping my day job," said Lisa. "I like being a flagman, and I like the idea of eating three times a day."

"You're a pessimist."

Lisa pulled on the oversized Mötly Crüe T-shirt that she slept in. The room was cold, and she shivered a little as she crawled under the comforter. She edged her back around to miss the lumps in the sofa and settled in with a sigh. "I'm being real. There's lots of bands. They come and go. Yeah, this one could make it big, but chances are that in ten years we'll still be playing bars . . . if we're together that long."

"I don't think we have to worry. Christa's absolute dynamite with that guitar—and you should hear her on harp."

"Heavy-metal harp. I can imagine." Lisa buried her face in her pillow. "Good night."

"You're not listening to me."

"I'm tired, Mel. We just practiced for four hours without a break, and my arms are ready to fall off. I want to be awake enough to go to that party tomorrow night."

"Pansy wop."

"Dippy blonde." Melinda wanted to talk, and Lisa finally conceded defeat, turned over on her back, put her hands behind her head. "Christa's a slave-driver," she said. "I've never worked that hard at a practice before."

"She's different."

"I'll say. From what Monica said, she tore into old Ron like a SWAT team." Lisa looked up at Melinda. "What does she mean when she keeps talking about energy and stuff like that? I can't follow her. She sounds like my grandmother sometimes."

Melinda was pulling on a tattered bathrobe. "What does your grandmother have to do with it?"

"Old-country Italian. She was a *strega*. A witch. Everyone went to her for herbs and stuff. She healed people, read cards . . . things like that. She never learned much English, but she used to baby-sit me when I was little. She talked about spirits in the garden, and she went on about energy just like Christa does. She said once that magic was going to save my ass someday." She hitched herself up on one elbow. "Is Christa some kind of witch, do you think?"

"Nah. She just plays harp. But . . ." Melinda stopped suddenly, looked down at the floor.

"But what?"

"She once asked me about magic—if I felt magic in music."

"What did you say?"

"I said I didn't know." Melinda's voice dropped to a confidential whisper. "But I'll tell you this, Boo-boo—and I haven't told anyone else—she gave me this little harp piece to help me with my insomnia, and the damn thing works. Like . . . like . . ."

"Like magic?"

"Yeah, kinda."

"This is giving me the creeps." Lisa shuddered, turned back over. "Maybe we should take her with us tomorrow night and scare everyone to death."

"I already asked her. She said she's busy. It's a holy day or something like that."

"Halloween?"

Melinda shrugged. "Complaints?"

Lisa shook her head. "She's cool. I'm glad we hooked up with her."

"If we push a little, we can make it big."

"Yeah, with a witch on lead guitar. Will you stow it? I'm tired."

Melinda paused at the bedroom door. "G'night, Boo-boo. My little *strega*."

Lisa threw a pillow at her.

But when Lisa thought about it—the lights off, the streetlamps glowing on the thin curtains, the old sofa insisting on putting its lumps exactly where she did not want them—she knew that Christa was a good deal more than cool.

Christa was different. Like her grandmother, there was a sense of age about her, a feeling of solidity, of years that went back behind the actual person, as though she were a direct link with something far distant, an embodiment of old ways that others had forgotten.

Lisa tossed and turned for a minute, trying to get comfortable. She heard Melinda take down her harp in the other room, heard the gentle strains of the tune she used for her insomnia. Good bassist. Not bad on harp, either. She wondered what Christa the harper sounded like.

Suddenly, she found that she was happy. A good job, a place to sleep—her own apartment would have been nice, but that could come later—and a good band. What more could she ever want?

"Hey, God," she said softly, "this isn't bad. I'll even buy the magic, if that's what it takes."

"Fucking bitch."

The music that poured off the stage was too loud for Ron to hear his own words: they reached no further than his thoughts. Tucked into this little corner of the club, alone in the darkness of this tiny balcony overlooking the dance floor, he nursed his beer, nursed his anger.

Monica had left him. He knew all the lines, all the ways to make girls do what he wanted, but she had torn herself out of his hands in the middle of the night, grabbed her purse and car keys, and fled. Her nightgown had clung to her dark little breasts as he wrestled with her in the parking lot, and the greasy water had allowed her to writhe away from him like the snake she was. If he had not tripped and fallen over the concrete wheel-stop, she would not have gotten away so easily.

He drained the last of his beer, leaned over the railing, and signaled to the waitress for another. He should have known she was going to look for Christa. Little red-headed bitch. It was Christa who had given Monica ideas about leaving—he was sure of it.

The dyke. And now Monica was probably getting felt up after practice every night, soft little hands prodding at her crotch, lipstick-coated lips seeking hers. *Come on, Monica, how can you say you don't like it if you haven't tried it?*

He shut his eyes, but the image would not go away. Damn them both. It was Christa's fault, too, that Dark Power had fallen apart. Paul had quit a few days after Christa, and Fred and Jerry had stopped showing up for rehearsals. Too busy, they said. Besides, what good was a rehearsal without a drummer and a guitarist?

The waitress brought him another beer. He counted out her money and stiffed her the tip. When she was gone, he lifted the bottle and sucked at it.

Well, Christa had hit him where it counted. She had gotten her revenge. Or so she thought. She thought, too, that she was putting together a band. Stupid. Girl games. They probably spend most of their time talking about tampons or douche or something like that.

Short little fingers feeling into the waistband of designer jeans, pink nails sparkling in the half light of a frilly bedroom. Stuffed animals watching. The sweet scent of perfume and baby powder.

He stared at the bottle in his hand for a moment, then raised it and hurled it at the wall. But the crash was lost in the steady, pounding music, the foam invisible against the white paint. An amber splotch, that was all, trickling to the parquetry floor, puddling as though a dog had urinated in the corner.

Snow was falling on this last day of October, and it flecked Kevin's long hair and spotted his denim jacket.

He squinted into the flakes. The weather would keep

the trick-or-treaters in, but it was otherwise appropriate for Halloween. Father Lynch would have called it witch-weather, and would have approved greatly. *Let the children stay in. Much better that old godless customs should die. All Saints' Day is tomorrow. Think about that.*

"You old bastard, Lynch," he muttered as he went up Christa's brick walk. "Are you still alive? Still scaring the hell out of little kids with your stories about eternal damnation?"

Kevin felt a little foolish showing up on the harper's doorstep without warning on a Friday evening, but he ran the bell and waited anyway, half expecting that there would be no answer. Christa was young, pretty, undoubtedly popular. Some fellow probably had her on his arm tonight, maybe at some Irish-club party. Lucky stiff.

But no, the door opened, and Christa stood there in a white robe, blue eyes inquiring. Her red hair still fell to her waist, but it had been layered around her face, and it feathered back to either side. She looked, if anything, younger.

"Uh . . . hi," said Kevin.

"Hello, Kevin. Blessings."

"Sorry for just showing up like this. I lost your phone number, but I had your address at the school."

She smiled. "I'm in the phone book."

"Yeah . . . well . . . you were on my way, too." He shuffled his feet for a moment. Snow was still falling. "I like your hair."

She laughed. "Come in and have something hot to drink. There's no sense in you being frozen."

She took him into the living room, sat him down on the sofa, and went off to the kitchen. Her house rather surprised him. From her age, he had expected something small, something rented, something temporary. But this was obviously a home in which someone had invested time and money. The decor was mature but eclectic, with a predominance of earth tones and burnished wood. "Nice place, Christa. How'd you wind up with this?"

"I've been saving for a long time," she said as she reentered with two cups of hot cider. She handed him one, and he noticed that her robe was bordered with white-on-white Celtic knotwork: intricate meanders that caught and held the eye.

He sniffed. Something in the air.

"Dittany of Crete and apple bark," she explained. "I use it for incense."

"I've interrupted something, haven't I?"

"Not really. I keep some of the old ways, and Hallows is a special day. The children usually keep me busy in the early evening, but with the snow and all, I thought that this year I might start before midnight."

Father Lynch would have reddened with outrage, but Kevin nodded slowly. "It's one of the old Irish holidays, isn't it?"

"Samain—" She caught herself. "I mean, Samhain." She altered the pronunciation, slurring through the aspi-rated *m*. "It marks the changing of the seasons. The seam between summer and winter, if you will."

His parents had kept what they called the Irish ways: mass every morning, parties on Saint Pat's day, strict observance of their religion. His grandfather sang some of the old songs, and he had a harp, too, though Kevin was sure that the old man did not know how to play it. Wakes, weddings, and *never forget you're a Larkin, Kevin.*

But the tree had long ago been severed at the root. Ireland had been broken, and broken again. Even as a child he had sensed something hollow about the pride, about the tenacious clinging to a heritage of defeat and exile.

Never forget you're a Larkin, Kevin. Never forget you're Irish. But what did that mean—Irish? What difference did it make? Any semblance of an Irish culture had been submerged long ago. Even the language was gone: Irish Gaelic was dead or dying, clinging to a vestigial and eroding existence on the rocky shores of bays and inlets the names of which he did not know and could not pronounce even if he did. What was a culture without even a language of its own?

And yet here was Christa, a harper, preparing to cele-brate a holiday that predated all the troubles, predated even the advent of Christianity. The tree had withered, but she had not clung to the branches. She had instead held to the deep roots that tapped down into something vital, something nourishing.

"I feel like an idiot," he said softly. Christa was a queen, and he had shuffled to her door in a snowstorm as though she were a commoner like himself.

"I don't understand."

He shrugged sheepishly. "I came here because I was going to a party. A dumb Halloween party. Loud music and a bunch of drunk rockers. I thought you might like to go." He laughed with self-deprecation. "Stupid, huh?"

"For going to a party?" Christa sat down in an armchair, settling the robe about her as though she had been born to it. "Better the day have some commemoration than none at all."

He shifted uneasily and found that he did not know what to do with his hands.

Christa smiled kindly. "Relax, Kevin. Stay a little. I have time."

"Haven't heard from you in a while," he mumbled. "I didn't want to lose touch. That's another reason I stopped in."

"I'm . . . rather glad you did."

"How's the band going? Any bookings?"

"Nothing concrete. The other ladies want to play out by December. I'm willing."

It was not the time to talk about rock and roll. Harps, maybe. But rock was too new, too recent to fit in with this night of snow and incense. He drained the cider hurriedly and stood up. "I guess I'll take off, then. If there's anything I can do to help with the band, let me know. I know a few of the club owners in town. They might listen to me. You'll stay in touch?"

A fool. A total fool. All he had to offer was mealy-mouthed promises that could have come from anyone. *I know a few of the club owners*. . . . Sure. And he knew a bunch of record executives, and . . . and . . . the mayor of New York . . . yeah . . . and . . .

"Sit down, Kevin," said Christa. "You're upset now, and I won't have you leaving my house in such a state."

"What am I supposed to do? I interrupted something special for you. You're busy."

She considered, looked at the clock, thought some more. "It's been a long time since I've gone to a party," she said.

He felt, if anything, worse. "Aw . . . it's just stupid."

"That it is not." She stood. "Is it too late to accept your invitation, Kevin? I ask only that you get me home by midnight."

"Yeah, I can do that. Uh—"

"Let me go and change. Make yourself at home."

She went upstairs, and he heard closet doors and drawers opening and closing, the faint clink of jewelry being doffed and donned. It was tempting to think that she cared for him enough to put aside her own plans for the evening, but he knew that, even in acquiescing, Christa was keeping her own counsel. Delaying her celebration of the holiday fit in somehow with larger plans that only she knew.

His cup was empty, and he found his way into the kitchen. A kettle of spiced cider sat on the stove, kept warm by a low flame. "You're damned amazing, Christa," he murmured, dipping the ladle. "Where the hell did you come from? Not from any Ireland that I know of."

Behind him, a doorway opened off into a dark room; and when he had filled his cup, he peered through it. Christa's studio. Harps . . . and a guitar. On the desk, a coal glowed on a ceramic plate, incense sputtering in the red heat. On a table across the room . . .

He leaned closer. It was a harp, but it was unlike any he had ever seen, certainly nothing like his grandfather's. Ornate, gilt, glittering with gems, it stood upright on a table, its polished wood gleaming in the faint light, its strings of . . . gold? Who strung harps with gold?

"Its name is Ceis," said Christa from behind him. "The name is Old Irish. It means a number of things. Harmony. The interaction of notes. The full voice of the harp in all the Worlds. The understanding of the harp's music. Ceis, this is Kevin Larkin."

He turned around. Christa stood in the bright kitchen, dressed in spandex and leather. She zipped up her jacket. "I believe I'm ready."

"Brother. You've changed."

"Indeed. But I play in a heavy-metal band, and I don't want to embarrass my ladies. I believe it's called . . . ah . . . image?" She smiled, and though at first glance he thought the combination of her sweet face and her black leather jacket to be unexpected, even absurd, he saw a little deeper tonight and noticed the glint in her eyes. Unexpected, perhaps. But not absurd.

"It's rather fun, too," she added.

*   *   *

Devi's door was double, triple-locked. Her lights were out, and she was hiding in her bedroom, heart pounding, tensed, waiting for her doorbell to ring, for knocks, for shouting.

Halloween night was never easy for Devi. There was too much casual interaction that bordered too frighteningly upon violence. Too many people wandered about, came to her door, demanded something from her. Reaching hands, masks, faces . . .

Snow was falling heavily outside, and that was some comfort, for people would be less likely to venture outdoors in such weather. Nevertheless, she stayed wrapped in her covers, head buried under her pillow, listening to the muffled ticking of the alarm clock on her nightstand.

Come be my little princess, her father had said on a Halloween night years ago. Breathless and pink-cheeked from her dash home amid the falling shadows of evening, her paper sack bulging with candy and apples, she had entered the house in gown and gossamer wings, a tinfoil wand in her hand. *Come be daddy's fairy princess . . .*

She shuddered, rolled herself tighter in the blanket. Here there were no faders, so LED read-outs that she could change with a turn of a knob, no patch cords to be jerked loose and rerouted. Just herself, and a dark room, and the memories.

The phone rang, the sound shrill and sudden. She flinched and cried out, then tried to ignore it, but it continued to ring—ten, fifteen times. Slowly, reluctantly, as if putting off armor, she unwound the sheets and blankets and picked up the handset.

"Devi," came Melinda's voice, "how the hell are you?" She was a little drunk. The music and laughter of a party swirled in the background.

"Hey, Melinda." Devi tried to sound calm. Just another night. No one knew about the terror-filled evenings that she spent alone in her apartment. "What's going on?"

"What's going on? Why, just the best fucking party you've ever seen. What'cha doing tonight? Why don't you head on over?"

"I . . ." Searching for an appropriate lie, finding nothing. "I'm busy . . ."

"That's what Christa said. And you know what? She

showed up anyway. And—Jesus fucking Christ—you should see her." Laughter. "Lisa and I look like potatoes beside her. She went out and got a haircut and a bunch of new clothes. She's all metaled up, and she looks so damned hot—"

Faintly, in the background, Devi heard Christa's voice. "Melinda, please."

"Aw, come on, Chris. Flaunt it."

There was a scuffling with the receiver at the other end of the connection, and Christa came on. "Hello, Devi."

Devi tried to keep her voice steady. "Hi."

"Busy?"

"Uh . . . yeah . . ." *Come be my little princess . . .*

A pause. Metallica was playing in the background, loud. Devi had to strain to make out Christa's soft voice. "Is something wrong?"

"I'm okay. Really. I'm . . . just busy . . ."

Christa did not push. "All right, then. Be well. I'll see you on Monday."

"Sure."

With a good-night, Christa hung up. Devi stood by the nightstand, phone to her ear, listening to the dial tone. Outside, the snow swished, and the cars that passed in the street made hissing noises on the wet asphalt.

Christa. So sure, so calm. But beneath the gentler qualities that she wore like a light summer dress was a sense of power. Devi had felt it radiating from her like heat from a stove, had heard it seething in her music every rehearsal, had seen it dissolve reality into gray mist.

Power—and violence too—melded together, balanced as exactingly as the parameters of a complex synthesizer voice.

"If you need to make a call, please hang up and try again. . . ." The recorded voice was metallic, tinny. Devi put the receiver into its cradle and turned back to her bed.

Come be daddy's fairy princess . . .

Christa had strength. Christa had control. Christa had everything. Devi hid again, wondering when the doorbell would ring, when the shouting would begin, when the hands would reach out, grasping.

CHAPTER
FOURTEEN

Chick with a guitar.

Snow was still falling the day after Samain, and it patterned Christa's leather jacket with white flakes as she made her way along Evans Avenue. Guitar case in one hand, cloth-wrapped bundle in the other, she pushed through the weather as though it were a bramble thicket.

Across the street was Guitar Tech, the office building a hazy blue outline in the falling snow. It was early afternoon: Kevin would be teaching. She stood for a moment on the wet sidewalk, wondering which window might be his.

She had parted from him at the turning of one day into another, giving him a kiss for luck and blessing. He had been long without a woman, long without love, and she knew now that he hoped that she might be that woman and that love. Looking up at him as she had, reaching out and touching his stubbled cheek, she herself had wondered if that might be the case—for a little while. He had blinked, his eyes a little cloudy with beer, and he had hugged her. And she had let him.

With a small shake of her head, she hitched up the bundle for a better purchase and continued on her way, her boots squishing through puddles of melt.

Like parties and feasts, lovemaking had always been a part of Samain. But she would not have been able to explain to Kevin what they did and what they celebrated; and, for him, a love consummated in an evening and then left unpursued would have been more an occasion for pain and regret than for joy.

A touch of the cheek then, one final kiss, and they had gone their ways—he to his home in the mountains, she to the rites she kept for the holyday: incense and harp, and ancient words that offered welcome to ghosts long since reincarnated.

The guitar case scraped against the doorframe as she pushed into Best's Guitar Laboratory with both hands full, and the bell above her head rang shrilly as though it embodied the cold day. She shivered: leather and denim was not an over-warm combination. The thick wool Kinsale would have been better.

But the room was warm and dry. Familiar too: she had known Roger for over—what? She thought quickly as she unwound the scarf from her neck. Six . . . no, seven years. It was important to remember, for since she did not age, she had to set limits to friendships. Another year, and Roger might start asking questions that she could not answer.

"Hang on," he called from the back room. "Be right there."

Another year? Another year and it would not matter. The gates were vanishing. Another year, and Judith would either be with her . . . or that would be the end of it. Another year, regardless, and she would let time have its way with her.

Roger came out to the counter, wiping his hands on a rag. He looked at her without recognition. "What can I do for you, ma'am?"

She lifted the bundle to the counter, shook the snow out of her hair, unzipped her jacket. "Is it a stranger I am, Roger?"

"Christa?" He stared, then laughed. "Goddam . . . and with a guitar. What are you doing now?"

"Playing in a rock band."

A slow smile spread over his face. "I guess I was right, eh? Anything can happen."

"I needed reminding, Roger. About change. It's a good thing."

"What can I do for you then, Christa? You need a harp built?"

"Indeed not. You were right about something else, too. It's a guitar I want, Roger."

Her own harp had made her realize the need last night. It was a crude but sweet instrument that she had carved of willow when she had first reached the harpers' school, but two hundred mortal years were hard on perishable wood, and she rarely played it now. Nonetheless, it had been made carefully—as carefully as skilled hands could manage—and every line of the instrument was flavored with hope and the expectation of its future use.

The Strat, though, was a production-line instrument, put together not without care, but with an objectivity that could not but affect the music she produced with it. In the fury of a final contest with Orfide, she could not afford to be playing a disinterested guitar. She needed passion. She needed energy. She needed hope.

Roger was laughing again. "This is fantastic! I've still got that wood in back, Christa. And I meant what I said when I told you I had something in mind." He stopped with his mouth open, shut it, grinned apologetically. "If it's to your taste. It'll be your guitar, after all. If you don't like my ideas, you can tell me to take a flying one."

"Oh, there are a few parts of the design that I need to specify," she said. She bent, unsnapped the guitar case, took out the Strat. "For example: this is a wonderful guitar, but Mr. Fender designed it to fit a man's hand. The back of the neck curves too sharply for my taste, and I think the radius of the fingerboard should be different."

"Just tell me what you want, Christa."

"There are a few things. But most of all I need your interest and your enthusiasm. The guitar must have the right kind of energy, the right . . . feeling." Here it was again: she was trying to speak of spiritual needs in a world of materialists. Roger, though, was nodding with understanding, and she went on. "I can't build this for myself. I need you to build it for me. But I need you to build it with the same love with which I made . . . this."

She set down the Strat, opened the bundle, and took out her first harp. Roger cleared away the wet wrappings and set the instrument reverently on the carpeted counter. In spite of the years, the willow was still smooth and white, and the tuning pins were firm. "It looks like a sweet little harp, Christa."

"The first one I made, Roger. It's been a good friend to me, though I confess I blush now at the woodworking."

He felt the forepillar, touched a string to listen to the sound. "You should have seen my first guitar. My dad was a luthier too, and he let me make all my mistakes on scraps." He chuckled. "I made this thing that looked like a Strat. Sounded terrible—kind of like the Wild Dog setting on a Jim Burns guitar. Totally unusable. But I loved it. I painted it with white house-paint and stuck a little American flag on the upper horn."

Christa rested her hand on the harp. "I was tempted to try some carving," she said. "But then I took a good look at the instrument and decided that I did not want to torment it any further."

Roger was lost in the harp. "Fascinating. The soundbox is just a solid block that's been hollowed out."

"At the time, it was the best way."

"Damn . . ."

"Do you feel it though, Roger? What this harp meant to me? I was just beginning my studies, and I had . . . wonderful thoughts about the future."

The day was bleak and snowy, but the willow shone like pale sunlight. She remembered a day when she was working on the harp, fitting the neck to the forepillar. Judith was near, smoothing a bronze pin, humming a slow song under her breath in time to the strokes of the file. Across the fields to the north of the school, the ground fell away suddenly into rocky cliffs, and the gray sea crashed against the stone. Beyond were the islands where the Christians had built their hermitage, and then open ocean to the horizon . . . or to the Summerland.

Twelve years of study lay between them and the rank of master harper, but they were confident, and they were lovers. . . .

. . . and they might be lovers again.

Roger's fingers were stained with varnish and dyes, rough with the wood and the tools that he used, but they caressed the little harp as though it were his only daughter. "I know what you mean, Christa. This meant a lot to you."

"Can you build a guitar for me with that in mind? That it has to mean a lot? With thoughts of a wonderful future?"

Roger knew wood, and he knew instruments. He smiled softly. "I think I can, Christa. It won't be the same. It just can't. But I'll do the best I can."

Christa nodded. "There's one other thing." Her first harp. It had been with her at the school, in the Realm. It had wandered with her through France and across England. It had been her companion the one time she had returned to Ireland, only to find her homeland ravaged and wasted. "Can you . . ." She felt the tears welling up, touched the harp gently. "Can you take the wood from this harp and build in into the guitar?"

He looked up, surprised. "Why, Christa? You're proud of this harp."

"For that very reason, Roger. So the guitar will embody what I want, so it will be a part of everything that I am."

"But—"

"It has to be that way. What I must do with this guitar—" She stopped, bit at her lip. "It just has to be."

Roger pursed his lips, examined the wood thoughtfully. "There's a lot of possibilities," he said after a time. "If you want a through-the-body neck, I can build it up out of sections of the forepillar. The soundbox can go for stringers to either side. I can color the wood for variation —it would look sweet with brownheart and amaranth. And then there's inlay work. I like to use a sustaining block under the bridge. . . . I can melt down the tuning pins for that. You want a tremolo?"

"I do. A Kahler."

"Okay. Then it'll be more of a plate, but you get the idea. Purfling, ornament. I can use quite a bit of it, maybe all of it. You're sure you want to do this?"

Mortal harps did not speak. But this crude harp of willow was no longer altogether mortal, for it had existed for too many years. With her hand on the soundbox, Christa sensed a faint, almost subliminal emotion in it. *I trust you.*

She wiped at her eyes. Her harp . . . she was going to break up her harp. Change was inevitable, but did it have to hurt so much?

I trust you.

"I trust you too, Saille," she murmured. To Roger she said, "I'm sure. It's for the best."

He was engrossed in the wood. "You say you made this harp, Christa?"

"I did, indeed."

When Roger straightened, he looked puzzled. "Then I really don't understand this at all. This wood: from what I can tell, it's over two hundred years old. The harp too.

There was a fellow in here once who played a fiddle with the Denver Symphony. He had a Stradivarius, and he let me look at it. It was only a little older than this."

Christa felt her face color. "It's the harp I made when I started school, Roger. I can't lie to you—you're going to build my guitar."

He looked at the harp, then at her. "Who . . ." His fingers traced a faint crack in the soundboard. "Who are you, Christa?"

Kevin had asked her the same question the night before. *Who are you?* She had not been able to answer. It had been too dark. The Solstice was still weeks away. *Not tonight*, she had said. *It's not the time. Not now.*

She lifted her eyes, met his. "I can't tell you, Roger. You wouldn't believe me if I did. Can you accept that?"

He had paled a little. "Okay. If you're sure then." He wiped at the sweat that had gathered on his forehead, composed himself, took a deep breath. "I don't ask any more questions."

She touched his hand. "Thank you."

"I'm not kidding you, Carl. These girls know what they're doing. If you miss this chance, you're going to be kicking yourself for the next ten years."

Carl Taylor sighed and drew the last of a cigarette into his lungs. "Ten years you say, huh?" The smoke floated up toward the white ceiling to gather in a hazy inversion layer.

"Damn straight. It's not everyone who gets a chance to start the next Van Halen."

"Titty bands aren't Van Halen, Kevin." Carl was playing hard to get, and he knew it, but owning a club could turn anyone into a cynic. Agents called him every day with the next Van Halen.

But he reminded himself that it was not an agent on the other end of the line, it was Kevin Larkin. Kevin had taste. He would not recommend anything unless it were really something. Maybe even the next Van Halen.

"It's not a titty band," Kevin insisted.

Carl's cynicism remained. "You said it was all girls."

"Yeah."

"So what's the deal? You sleeping with the lead guitarist or something?" Carl covered the mouthpiece and waved to catch the attention of the man across the room. "The oak bookcase, Dennis. Third shelf. Behind the Karnow book on Vietnam. Help yourself. But watch out: it's good stuff."

"The lead guitarist," Kevin was saying, "makes anything you've ever heard sound like shit."

"What's her name?"

"Christa Cruitaire."

"Weird name. Never heard of her."

"Look, man, will you just give them a listen? I sat in on one of their rehearsals last night, and they blew me away. Their covers are perfect, and their originals are . . . are—"

"They playing anywhere?" Across the room, Dennis had located the Karnow book. He reached behind it, extracted a slab of glass and a small tin box with a tight lid.

"Good stuff, you say?" Dennis gestured with the box.

Carl nodded. "The best. There was this girl last week—"

"You listening, Carl?" said Kevin.

"Yeah. Yeah, I'm listening. Have them get me a demo, will you? It's not like I don't trust you, Kev, but . . . shit, man, if I hired every band that plays InsideOut on the basis of someone's word, I'd lose my customers. And my shirt."

"Yeah, sure," said Kevin. "Like you don't have any other sources of income, Carl."

"Come on, you know what I mean."

"I'll get you a demo. Thanks for the listen."

"Anytime. Bye." Carl hung up and propped his feet on the desk. There was a disadvantage to working out of your home: everyone knew where to find you.

Dennis was transferring white powder from the box to the slab with a small gold spoon. "You're generous, Carl."

"Hey, friends are friends."

"Who was that?"

Carl leaned forward. "Hey, go easy on that stuff, will you? I said it was good. We're talking ninety-five percent pure."

"You're kidding." Dennis looked down at the white caterpillar that he had scratched into shape on the glass.

"No shit. Like I was saying, I picked up this girl last

week, and we spent the evening having a fine time. She didn't think she wanted to fuck at first, but that stuff changed her mind real quick."

"Okay, okay." Dennis closed the box, scratched the caterpillar into two halves. "But who was that?"

"Kevin Larkin. Remember him?"

"The guitar player? Sure do." Dennis pulled out his wallet and fished through the bills. "Good stuff? Let's make this an occasion, then. You got anything big?"

"In the Karnow book. Page one hundred."

Dennis went back to the book. "Whoa. Big time." He took out the bill and rolled it into a tube. "Anyway, the guy who worked A & R before me called him the next Hendrix. No one at the label could figure out why he turned the contract down."

"Some people are crazy."

Dennis paused with the tube. "He managing a band now?"

"No. He's just a friend of one of the girls. He says they're the next Van Halen."

Dennis blinked and set the tube aside. "Kevin Larkin said that? What's this band called?"

"Gossamer Axe."

Dennis stared at the rolled-up bill, lips pursed.

Carl rubbed at the back of his neck. Screwy business. He got up and strolled to the window, his hands shoved into his pockets. Snow was coming down hard, and the cold seeped off the glass in an invisible sheet. "Come on, man, you're out here for the skiing, not to find a band."

"But don't you see? Kevin Larkin isn't the kind to go on like that unless there's something there. Remember what Hendrix said about Billy Gibbons."

"He's probably balling the guitarist."

Dennis settled down with the rolled-up bill again, held it poised above the white line of powder. "Tell you what, Carl," he said. "If you get a demo from them, you get me a copy. Okay?"

"Whatever." Snow. Heavy snow. Carl liked the snow and the cold—the girls coming into the club wrapped in coats and jackets and then shedding them to reveal clinging spandex and jeans, fishnet tops, female flesh fragrant with musk and rosy with blush and makeup. . . .

*   *   *

The mid-November skies were vicious with snow, and the streets were icy as Kevin edged his Beetle through the evening traffic. It was tense, white-knuckled driving, and when he finally pulled up in front of Christa's house, he had to sit for a few minutes before his heart stopped pounding. Beyond the bare maple trees in the front yard, her living-room windows glowed yellow, and he could make out the wall clock ticking away, telling him that he was a little late.

Carrying his Strat and Frankie's old guitar, he made a slippery path up to her door and rang the bell. He was expected. Christa smiled as she held the door open. "How is it that it's always snowing when you come to my house?"

"Just another kind of blarney." He set the guitars down as she shut out the cold. "If it's snowing, I look more pathetic, and you're more inclined to take me in." His smile was crooked.

She stared at him curiously, and he felt as though she were looking through him. As usual. He thought of his healed hand and wondered at his courage.

"And is it pity I'd need to ask you into my house, Kevin?"

He shrugged and tried to see her merely as a woman, a friend. He found that he could not. "Sorry. My Catholic guilt is showing."

"Guilt?"

"Well, you know."

She shook her head, and her hair moved softly. "I don't. You asked me out tonight, and I accepted freely. There is no guilt."

Would she say the same thing, he wondered, if she knew that he still dreamed of her in his bed, flushed with the glow of recent lovemaking? Well . . .

He managed to look at her face and was shaken. Probably even so. And he—oh, Divine Fool!—had actually been permitted to hold her in his arms for a moment.

He felt a blush rising, looked for something with which to rechannel his thoughts. "You . . . uh . . . have any thoughts about that demo for Carl?"

As though she understood the change of subject, Christa nodded. "I called Melinda. She's booking some time at a studio. She says it has good rates." She indicated the guitar cases. "Did you want to jam tonight? I thought we were going to a movie."

"I didn't want to leave them out in the cold."

"It's that bad out, is it?"

"Driving's terrible. Black ice all over the place."

"Hmmm." She went to the front windows and peered out at the storm. "Did you have your heart set on a movie?"

"You have something else in mind?" It was his date, his offer, but thoughts of bald tires and glassy asphalt were not at all inviting.

She turned around with a wry smile. "Why don't we just send out for a pizza and relax? My last student was going on about what she called *real music*. As opposed to rock and roll, you understand. I was about ready to scream, so I'm not up to driving either."

"Fine with me."

While she made the call, he took off his coat and hung it on a peg by the front door. The snow dripped from the soaked denim and smacked into the carpet below. From the kitchen, Christa's clear voice carried to him as she ordered dinner.

He did not think that he was very far off when he called Gossamer Axe the next Van Halen. His own nerve and his music had failed him, but if he had needed a success in his life to balance that defeat, he had it: he had guided Christa Cruitaire into rock and roll.

I knew her when.

When she was a harper. When he could dream that she might someday be his lover. When he could stand in her front hall and listen to her order a pizza on the phone. Even though he had found that his own music—though still halting, like a language long unused—had broken free, she would always outdistance him. He could not predict what would become of her, but as surely as he had, dreaming, seen her in his bed, he knew that it would be glorious.

Christa came back into the hall. She was wearing a sweater and jeans, and her figure was young and shapely with the soft mortality of human flesh. Whatever else she was, Christa, like the blues, was for a short time only. Years would pass, and she would be gone. But, again like the blues, like music, the importance of her existence

was not the duration, it was the bare, simple fact that she
was, that she, once upon a time in Denver, had touched
his life, had touched the lives of others, had made music,
songs, melodies that lilted from her harp and screamed
from her guitar.

And on this particular night of that once-upon-a-time,
she apparently thought it good to spend some time with
him—talking, laughing, lounging on the living-room sofa
with a fire burning on the hearth, her hair spilling over
the upholstery like a copper wave.

She said nothing about her girlhood or her family. He
did not recall that she had ever mentioned anything to
him about such things. Her references to her birth or to
her past were always reluctantly made, inevitably pref-
aced and followed by an almost embarrassed silence; and
for all that she had revealed about herself, she might
have sprung forth fully grown like a Goddess, a harp in
her hand and a guitar slung from her shoulder.

Tonight, she asked him of his past, and he told her
about growing up in Cheyenne, about getting thrown out
of the house at fifteen, about Frankie, about the road.
He tried to keep the tale light and flavored with humor,
but toward the end his voice began to catch in the middle
of sentences, and he had to lubricate the words with
frequent pauses.

"You've never been back home?" she said when the
ticking of the wall clock had grown loud in yet another
silence.

"No." He finished the last piece of pizza, washed it
down his tight throat with a swallow of beer. He was
unnerved to discover that his other arm was about Christa's
shoulders. "I . . . uh . . ."

Her eyes were kind and blue. He decided to leave his
arm where it was.

"I never went back," he said. "I guess I feel about as
far away from Cheyenne as you are from Ireland."

She shook her head slightly, but said nothing.

"All that bullshit they'd handed out to me just ate at
my guts for years," he said. "Still does, I guess. My
sisters all toed the line—nice little Irish girls, all lined up
to get married and have more babies than they could
ever manage—and my brother Danny wanted to be a
priest from the beginning."

Christa was slender, but strong too. He felt her strength as his hand tightened on her shoulder: a lean, focused power, with nothing extra, nothing superfluous—like everything else about her.

"But me . . ." The beer touched his laugh with bitterness. "I couldn't leave anything alone. I had to push. I had to show off."

He finished the bottle and set it aside. "I was an arrogant little snot, wasn't I?"

Christa's eyes were elsewhere. Nowhere in the room, he was sure. Nor anywhere in Denver. "And you lost everything," she said.

"Well . . . yeah. But I found other things. I found Frankie."

The look in her eyes was still distant, and it suddenly told him something about her, about the past of which she did not speak.

His voice caught again, and when he freed it, it was only a whisper. "What did you find, Chris?"

A tear pulled itself together at the corner of her eye. "I found friends. I think. Maybe another family."

"Does that make up for it?"

He waited for her answer, hoping. He had no family. He had walked away from its ties, its burdens, its heritage. But, he wondered, how much of his disdain was only more blarney, the idle creation of a beer-soaked tongue? How much of a past did he want . . . or need?

Christa let her head fall against his shoulder, and he gathered her into his arms. She was crying. And if he was still in any way afraid of her or of what she could do, that fear melted now in the wash of her tears. She was human. She was mortal. Regardless of her music or her magic or her past, she was as fragile—and as needy—as he himself.

"Never," she said. "Never."

CHAPTER
FIFTEEN

The atmosphere of the recording studio was as rarefied as one of Sruitmor's exacting quizzes on the precise symbolic meanings of the fourteen modes. Although the decor was relaxed, even sensuous—thick shag carpets, dim lighting, textured walls of wood and rock—it could not disguise the fact that the studio was a laboratory in which sounds were created specifically to be recorded, scrutinized, and, if necessary, rejected and rerecorded.

Through the thick glass window, Christa saw the engineer in the control room nod to her. Her headphones hissed. "All right, Chris," he said. "If you're ready, I'm rolling four measures before the break."

Precision. Everything was precision. The demo that the band recorded would be its representative in the back rooms and offices of club owners and booking agents throughout Denver. It had to be right.

Christa reached up and freed a strand of her hair from the headphones. "I'm ready," she said.

Behind the engineer, Melinda waved, and Devi watched intently. Christa smiled at them, turned up her Strat's volume, and readied herself. Her new guitar would not be ready until March, on the Equinox, but the Strat was a friend, and she did not doubt its abilities.

Suddenly, her headphones were filled with music: Lisa implacably beating out the rhythm, Devi interrupting with staccato bursts of suspended chords in unison with Christa's guitar track, Melinda thumping away on bass. Monica was snarling:

"So get your ass out here, boy,
'Cause it's time to get down
To the firing line . . ."

Alone in the room save for her amplifier and her guitar, Christa launched into the lead. Eyes closed, biting at her lip in concentration, she made the Strat's scream mesh with Monica's, echoed the main melodic line of the chorus, then went off into free improvisation, climbing up the fingerboard until she ran out of frets, bending the top string so as to eke a few additional steps out of the guitar's range.

But though, her body swaying with the waves of emotion, she threw all the passion she had into the lead, she worked to keep the energy mundane. This was a song about a woman who had been jilted. That was all. The woman was angry, and she wanted to fight. There were no cosmic dimensions to the disagreement.

Nonetheless, Christa found herself automatically dropping into some of the licks that she had planned to use when, in the final battle with the Sidh bard, this song would tear open a hole between one reality and another. Before she could reroute her fingers, she felt the floor in front of her waver almost imperceptibly. She stabilized it in an instant, and she finished the solo perfectly, but when she looked up at the control-room window again, she saw Devi watching her intently.

Did she see it? Roger had sensed something, and so had Kevin. Did she have to add Devi Anderson to the list of those who suspected that there was more to Christa Cruitaire than harp and guitar?

The music stopped, her headphones hissed, and the engineer came back on. "Real good, Chris. You satisfied?"

She might have discarded the entire track because of her slip, but she decided not to. Playing it back would probably change the sound enough to dissipate the magic. "I am," she said. "Let's keep it."

"Okay. You're the boss." Her headphones continued to hiss: he was keeping his finger on the talk-switch. "Uh . . . and I think I owe you an apology. These have been some of the most painless sessions I've done. You guys are pros. Sorry about that crack about girls not knowing how to rock."

"I'm sure it's all right, Hank," said Christa as she switched off her amplifier. "You probably were unaware that I didn't play my guitar with a penis."

He laughed. "Come up and have a listen, then."

During the initial playback, Christa was relieved to find that the magic had not been captured on the tape, but she was pointedly aware that Devi was still watching her.

She saw. I know it.

The songs they had recorded over the last three days were complete now. A final mixdown would take hours of critical listening while Hank manipulated the volume and quality of each track and instrument until they blended perfectly. But that would be tomorrow night. For now, he could give them a rough idea of the final product.

Monica was curled up in an overstuffed chair like a bleached-blond kitten. She listened, but she was content to let the others deal with the mix. She did not pretend to know about equipment or about sound quality, but she knew her voice. Alternately raging and choking off syllables with a chirp of rising sexuality, she had cut all the vocal tracks in one night.

Christa brought her a cup of coffee while the tape wound out to the end of the reel. "Thanks, Christa." Monica looked into the cup. "No warm milk this time?"

"Ron bothering you again?"

"Well . . . not really." Her nose wrinkled at her own lie.

"What's happening?"

"He . . . he's not coming to my door anymore, and he's not bothering me at work. But he's . . ." Her brown eyes flicked up to Christa, childlike, questioning. "He's around. I know it. It's like I see him out of the corner of my eye; but when I look, he's gone." She laughed nervously. "Maybe I'm just jumpy."

Lisa had overheard. "What do you say we just go out and pound the son of a bitch?"

"Hey," said Hank, "I said I was sorry."

Lisa patted him on the shoulder. "It's OK, we're not talking about you." She grinned. "Different son of a bitch."

The clock said four in the morning when they left the studio. "Who's for breakfast?" said Melinda.

"Don't you have to sleep?" said Lisa.

"I sleep at work. Doesn't everyone?"

Lisa was frowning. "Aren't you worried about little things like job security?"

"Are you kidding? This demo is going to open doors for us. That job of mine is strictly temporary."

"Get real."

"Hey, I know what I'm talking about."

Lisa sighed. "So do I, Mel." She waved over her shoulder as she went to her car. "I'm out of here."

Lisa's exhaust steamed in the blue glow of the streetlamps as she pulled away. Monica decided to go home also, for her nagging worries about Ron were sapping her strength. "And I want to keep my job," she added.

Devi turned to Christa. "What about you?"

Christa had students, but not until noon. "I think I'd like some food."

"Can I ride with you? My van's full of keys and amps, and I don't want to haul it all over town." Devi's reason was plausible, but her eyes were searching.

Melinda led the way in her Mustang. Christa followed with Devi in the passenger seat. Though she had asked for a ride, Devi seemed tense, watchful, as though Christa might turn into an unexpected threat.

"Did you like the mix?" said Devi.

Christa huddled into the warmth of her Kinsale. Off to the right, the Platte River gleamed in the light of a waning moon. "I think we have something good there."

"That last lead track was hot."

"Thank you."

Devi shifted in her seat. "How . . ." Her voice was hoarse, as though the words came forth unwillingly. "How do you do it, Christa?"

"Do . . . what?"

But Devi did not answer immediately. She had turned away. Her shoulders might have been shaking. Fear?

But her response was unexpected. "You're so . . ." Her voice caught. "You're so proud. You're not ashamed of anything."

Christa blinked. She had misunderstood Devi, misunderstood everything. "Why should I be ashamed?"

"Because . . ." Devi's voice trailed off into the silence of engine noise.

"Devi?"

Devi turned back, and for an instant, as a stoplight hovered on red and finally, reluctantly, flicked to green, Christa saw behind her shell. The black eyes were pain-filled, imponderably sad, hopeless.

Devi did not speak until Christa had pulled into the

parking lot. Beyond the plate-glass windows, lights were bright, coffee steamed, the waitress's uniform was crisp.

"Whatever it is you've got," she said. "I wish to hell I had some of it."

Devi did not want the magic. She wanted instead what the magic was grounded upon: a sense of purpose, a knowledge of intrinsic power, a claim to one's own life. Christa faced her in the dark car. "Can I help?" An honest offer. One woman to another.

"You do pretty good with walls and floors. How are you at dissolving childhoods?"

Melinda pounded on the window, and they both jumped. "Hey! You guys want to freeze?"

Devi's wall rose again like dull iron. "We were waiting for you."

"I'm here. I'm here." Melinda's teeth were chattering. "Let's get inside. I don't want to die before I've made my first three platinum albums."

But as Devi opened the door, Christa touched her hand. "I'm here, too," she said softly.

"Thanks. Just let me watch, huh? Maybe something will rub off." Devi's words smoked in the cold air, hung for a moment, and dispersed without a trace.

The telephone on Kevin's desk was disturbingly reminiscent of the one in his parents' kitchen. It was the same design, the same color, and years ago he had poked at its counterpart with stubby, little-boy fingers, adding grime, fingerprints, and the remnants of peanut-butter sandwiches to the patina of scratches of dust that had been forming on the device since before he was born. Today his fingers were different, but he was still poking: picking up the handset, putting it down, flicking idly at the dial.

What would he say? What could he say after almost twenty years? Hello?

Even though her tears had been wordless, Christa had continued to teach him. Angry though he might be, resentful though he surely was, he could not walk away from fifteen years of his life.

His memories now, blunted by time, tempered by Christa, seemed almost sadly funny, emblematic of a continuous, near-comic sequence of misunderstandings:

the classic bewilderment of the old when confronted with the young. Once he had been sitting on his bed with the tobacco-sunburst Strat, determined to learn "Purple Haze" note for note. The record had been playing, and his fingers had been sore. His father had stumped up the stairs on legs that were bent and crooked from years of carrying sides of beef. Arms akimbo, blue eyes hard and glinting, he had surveyed his eldest son and the electric guitar.

"So, we're playing nigger music now, eh?"

Prodding at the black phone, finally picking up the handset and dialing, Kevin actually laughed about it. Maybe it was worth a try, even after twenty years. Christa could not go back: she had as much as said so. But he could.

Dead air. Hissing. A click and the sound of a ring. They might have moved. It was possible.

But the second ring was cut short. "Hello?"

His mother's voice. It was older now, sere with age, but he knew it. He found that his mouth was dry. "Uh . . . hi, ma. It's Kevin."

"Kevin?" He wondered if his name had been expunged from the family records. A heretic. Gone forever now. "Kevin? Oh, dear God, Kevvy?"

"Yes," he said. "It's me."

There was no depth to the evening sky: it might have been a dark gray plate set on top of the city, or the lid of a chest freezer that had been fastened down securely, the light switching off automatically as the rubber gasket thumped into place.

Melinda's hands were numb on the steering wheel. The car heater had been broken for months, but her job did not pay well enough for her to have it fixed. She shrugged inside her jacket: winter was not all that long. And besides, there was a chance—a good chance—that comparatively soon she would have money sufficient to replace the entire automobile.

"This is it," she muttered as she made the turn onto Virginia Avenue. "We're going to make it. We just are. Carl, if you can't hear what's on this cassette, then you're deaf and ought to be tethered out to die."

She believed in the band. She believed in Christa.

One break was all they needed, someone at some record company who would listen fairly to the demo. And then . . .

"Blammo!" She was grinning. Gossamer Axe had to start with local clubs and bars, but that would not last long. One break.

The parking lot at InsideOut was almost empty. Monday nights were usually lean, and the evening had just started. She parked close to the door.

"Hey, Melinda!" The voice was familiar, and she felt a dry prickle run down her spine. She hurried toward the entrance, hoping that the caller would figure he had made a mistake.

"Melinda Moore!"

She gave up and stood her ground. Tom Delany was waving at her from the stage door.

"How the hell are you?" He jogged toward her. "I been wondering what you were doing." He spoke quickly, in bursts of words that ran together. "Hey, you're done up, aren't you? You here to see my band?"

He had not changed. "What are you on, Tom?" said Melinda.

"Little coke. Little speed. We had a party last night to celebrate our first gig." He grinned sheepishly, his blond hair falling into his eyes despite a layer of hairspray. "Didn't get much sleep."

He seemed faintly ridiculous to her. "Well," she said, "good luck."

"You know, if you'd taken my offer last June, it'd be you playing with me."

She nearly laughed in his face. What Tom had offered was nothing compared to what she had now. "Actually," she said, "I'm in a band. I'm here with a demo for Carl."

"Oh, yeah? Who's playing guitar?"

"Christa Cruitaire."

"Never heard of her."

"You will, Tom. You can fucking bet on it." She grinned at him, felt the hot contempt rise. "See you later."

She pushed in through the glass doors and asked for Carl. The girl at the front desk examined her from beneath dark blue eyelids, asked her name, and pointed to a door at the end of a short hallway. "He's expecting you. Just give a knock and go right in."

Melinda stepped into a sitting room with two over-stuffed chairs and a sofa arranged around a teakwood coffee table. Cigarette smoke hung in a soft haze and glowed like a halo about the ceiling lights.

She had met Carl Taylor years ago, and, like Tom, he was a reminder of a period in her life that she was trying to forget. Then, as now, he had owned a club, and he had booked the better bands. Carl was a part of the milieu, a background figure that remained constant no matter how the props and costumes changed. If you were in Denver, and your business was music, then sooner or later you dealt with Carl.

She wondered if he would remember her, hoped he would not. She had made quite a reputation. . . .

Carl rose from a chair. "How are you, Melinda?"

"I'm okay, Carl."

He regarded her for a moment. She was suddenly conscious of her body. Did the spandex look good on her? Was she putting on weight? Too many lines around her eyes?

But Carl seemed appreciative. "Back into music, are you?"

He remembered. She tried to shrug it off with a forced laugh. "Can't kick the habit." The cassette was a lump of fire in her pocket. The past was gone, over. All he had to do was listen. It was only the beginning.

He dropped an arm about her shoulders and guided her to the sofa. Maybe the spandex was a mistake, too much a reminder of the stupid girl she had once been. "What do you have for me tonight, Melinda?"

Her hands were shaking. She extracted the cassette, fumbled with it for an instant, then handed it over. "I won't give you any hard sell. You know me too well for that. Just listen, huh?"

"That's my job." Carl went to a rack of stereo equipment that stood against the wall. "If I didn't listen to demos, I wouldn't have music, would I?" He laughed and slipped the cassette into a player. LEDs glowed, and the speakers hissed faintly.

He sat down with her while the leader ran out. She felt his eyes on her, felt his body heat through her spandex.

The tape opened with a brief improvisation by Christa, who double-stopped two-part polyphony up and down the neck of her guitar, weaving together two discrete tunes. The sound, overdriven and chorused, was massive, but the melodic lines were clean, separate, and perfectly balanced.

"You've got two guitarists?"

"No," said Melinda, "that's just Christa. And that's live—no overdubs. She can do that on stage."

Carl's eyebrows lifted.

Christa's solo ended with a series of power chords that segued into the first of a sampling of cover tunes from the songlist. Carl listened, his elbows on his knees and his chin in his hands. His eyebrows lifted again. Melinda tried to hide her smile.

In the silence between songs, he turned to her. "The band sounds good, but that's some guitarist you've got."

"That's Christa. She's terrific, isn't she? This next one is an original. It's called 'Firing Line.' "

And the speakers exploded again with sound, a burning, turbulent rhythm that leaned into each beat as though with a battering ram. Monica's voice was a call to battle:

*"Are you surprised to see me
Standing at your door?"*

When the music faded, Carl sat for a minute. The tape ran out silently. "Well . . ."

"What do you think?" Melinda tried to sound disinterested, but her pride kept breaking through.

He strolled over to the stereo, rewound the cassette, took it out, and hefted it in his hand. "I think I'm going to hire a band, Melinda. This bunch that's playing tonight: they're due back mid-December, but I'm going to toss them for Gossamer Axe. I'll give you girls a week, starting Friday the twelfth. If the patrons like you, we'll talk about the future. How does that sound?"

It was happening, but it was only a beginning. "Sounds good."

"You guys come on down to my house tomorrow night," said Carl. "I'll have the contract ready."

Melinda nodded, stood up. She held out her hand for the cassette.

"How about I keep this for a little?" he said. "That's quite a band you've got. I'd . . ."

He looked at her, smiling. Suddenly, she was glad she had worn the spandex. She was still young; she could still rock and roll. And she knew that any lines around her eyes were invisible.

"I've got some friends in L.A. who'd like to hear this." She smiled back at him.

"Tell you what," he said. "I'm having a little party on Saturday. Why don't you—don't worry about the rest of the band, just you—why don't you come on by? We'll have some fun. I'll introduce you to some friends."

Her hands were not shaking at all. "That sounds real nice, Carl. Thanks. I'd like that."

CHAPTER
SIXTEEN

The marriage was going downhill. No, not going. If he had to argue with Kelly over a favor to a friend, it had already bottomed out.

Bill Sarah leaned on his steering wheel while he watched the young folks dribble up to the door of the club in twos and threes and fours. The weather was mild—not unusual for Colorado's unpredictable Decembers—and the sky was clear, but the piles of snow at the edges of the parking lot were reminders of the storm that had hit the city earlier that week.

He thought about how people changed. Once, yes, he and Kelly had been inseparable, and the sight of her face had been enough to hold his attention to the exclusion of all else. But over the years the marriage had firmed, solidified, and settled into routine. There were other things to do now, other people in the world besides her, and Kevin Larkin was one of them.

Kevin had helped him manage his first band. That had led to other bands, and eventually to a career, and money, and security—if anything in music could ever be called secure. Kevin had never made it big himself, but Bill Sarah was not the kind to forget debts.

Maybe Kelly was different. Bill flicked cigar ash out the open window and onto the pavement, thinking. He had no idea how she ran her business. He had never asked. To be sure, interior decorating was of no interest to him—a domain of excitable flits and frilly artistes—but surely after ten years he might have picked up something about her work.

Strangers they had become, he realized, strangers who knew little of one another save the shoes at the foot of the bed, the overcoats hanging in the closet, the names of the magazines left on the coffee table. The compromises had been cast off and left behind, the promises and the love rent by acquired indifference.

When Bill saw Kevin walking toward the club, he got out and hailed him. Kevin seemed a little more frayed around the edges than when they had first met, but his height and his long hair were much more a part of the rock-and-roll style than Bill's own stocky roundness. Too bad he had turned down that record contract. Lost his nerve, maybe. It had happened before.

And Bill found himself testing Kevin's grip as they shook hands, as though by doing so he might confirm his nagging suspicion that Gossamer Axe was nothing more than Kevin's dream; that, unable to believe in himself, Kevin had focused his hope on someone else. That also had happened before.

"How are you, Kevin?" Tragic. And he had shouted at Kelly because of another man's fading hope.

"Glad you could come, Bill." Kevin's grip was strong, his smile too.

"I'll tell you, Kev, this better be good." Bill laughed a little as he loosened his tie. What on earth was he doing with a tie? Where were those days of 501s, paisley shirts, and a few beads? But here he was, a round little man in a suit and a tie and a foundering marriage, come to listen to heavy metal.

He paid the cover for both Kevin and himself and noted with embarrassment the cashier's amused look. She probably thought he was Kevin's father.

Routine marriage, routine life. Now he was indistinguishable from the maggot-folk who crawled along the downtown sidewalks with their wool-blend suits and Yves San Laurent briefcases, mouthing the right words and the right prejudices, their little behinds as well scrubbed as their faces. Shuffle, shuffle. *Ain't no room for no rev'lution here, brothah!*

He took a table in a dark corner and tried to forget the suit, the dismissive look in the girl's eyes. "So, where did you find these girls, Kevin?" he said. He had to shout over the taped music, and he noticed with distaste that whoever was running sound was abusing the graphic equalizers. Like the weather, this was nothing unusual, but it always annoyed Bill that millions of dollars of studio time and engineering went to waste because the disc jockeys insisted upon boosting the bass and treble into unintelligibility. The same fate befell the live bands, for the stage microphones and direct outputs ran into the house PA, and the result was an undistinguished mass of mud and hiss no matter how good the musicians.

"The guitar player was a student of mine," Kevin replied. "But I can't say I taught her anything: she blew me away after her first lesson. You'd better get ready: this is no T and A band. These ladies can cook."

Bill tried to keep an open mind, but his doubts were crawling out of their hole again. One of Kevin's students. Yeah, sure. Kevin was not the first teacher to lose perspective.

Across the big room, on a platform twenty feet in the air, were the sound board and the gentleman who was abusing the graphic EQs. LEDs and illuminated dials formed bright constellations in the dim light, and a young woman in leather and spandex was climbing the flight stairs to the platform. Bill could not help but notice her: her red hair had been backcombed into a fiery mane.

"Hey," said Kevin. "That's Crista."

She gained the platform, tapped the man on the shoulder, and spoke to him. At first he shook his head, but the red-haired girl was adamant. Bill felt her presence even though he could hear nothing of her words.

With a dismissive gesture, the man turned away. Christa seized him by the jacket and lifted him out of his chair. Now he was listening.

When she released him, he turned and made adjustments to the rack of equipment at the side of the board. The sound of the PA altered, bass and treble diminishing and settling into proportion with the midrange. The music sparkled. Harmonies were clean. Songs were recognizable.

The girl descended the stairs and vanished through the door that led to the dressing rooms.

"Got balls, doesn't she?" said Kevin.

"How well does she play?"

The lights on the stage went out, and the canned music shut off. Kevin sat back. "You're going to hear, Bill. I hope you're ready."

In the darkness, Bill saw shapes moving on stage, heard the buzzing of amplifiers. The drummer smacked out a four-count, and the stage turned incandescent with light and music.

And Kevin was right. The ladies could cook.

From the impersonal sterility of the dressing room, Christa had stepped into the glitter and flash of the stage. The quiet lakes and sea-battered shores of Corca Duibne were far away now. Here was volume that the sea itself would have been hard pressed to match, and here was music that had never sounded from bronze strings and willow soundboxes, music that screamed and rumbled, music that filled the club as strong mead might fill a wooden cup.

Christa hardly looked at her guitar, for, like her harp, it had become familiar territory. With the cocky smile she had taken for her stage persona, she looked her audience in the eye as she chopped out rhythms, bounded from one side of the stage to the other, bounced up on Lisa's drum risers, down to rejoin Monica at the microphone for a chorus, down again to the dance floor to play a lead break among the club's patrons. Her spandex was soaked by the middle of the first set, her hair wilting in spite of its coating of spray, but still she moved with energy, grinning with a surety and an openness that would have startled her fellow students at the harpers' school.

But her smile was not all affectation, for its roots were sunk deep in a genuine satisfaction with her band. The sound was good, the feelings were good, the music was good: the work of five women, five musicians, blending together into a heady, sensuous mix of noise and passion and—though the patrons were unaware and the rest of the band might only have guessed—magic.

In contrast to the biting energy of the music, it was a gentle spell she wove about the club. True, Corca Duibne was far away in distance and in time, but though she could not return to the green and fertile fields of Eriu, she could bring some of her home and her memories into this club, into the lives of the people for whom she played.

During the break between sets, she called a short band conference in the dressing room. "It's sounding wonderful," she told the others. "I want to thank you."

Lisa shook her head. "Shit, we ought to be thanking

you, Chris. You know, I always thought that this was the
way a band should be, but I never could find it before.
It's like . . ." She blushed. "It's like having sex with
someone you really love."

Devi dropped her eyes, looked in another direction;
but when Christa touched her hand, she did not draw
away.

"That's what music should be, Boo-boo," said Christa.
"That's what it always should be."

"Does that mean we're all lesbians?" Monica giggled
as she adjusted a studded belt, her fingernails the color
of blood against the gun-metal gray leather. "God, Ron'll
be pissed if he hears about this."

Melinda was not paying much attention. Her thoughts
seemed to be somewhere else as she faced a mirror and
added backcombing to her hair with short, rapid strokes.

"What do you think, Mel?" said Lisa. "Are we hot?"

"Real hot," she replied. "Real fucking hot. What did I
tell you?"

"Hey, this is InsideOut, not Capitol Records."

"Give it time. I know what I'm doing."

Something about her manner struck Christa as odd. In
her mind, she went over the set, considering; and when
the others left—Lisa and Monica to mingle with the
patrons, Devi to adjust equipment and double-check
programs—she held Melinda back. "Are you well?"

"Sure. Perfect. Whatsamatter?"

"You're a trifle before the beat tonight. I imagine it's
just excitement, but can you please be careful? I have
that big solo this next set, and I'll need you to be in the
pocket."

Melinda grinned. "No problem, Crissy. I got it all
worked out." The bassist gave her a light punch to the
shoulder and walked out of the room.

Christa winced. Her name was Chairiste. She was willing to compromise on Christa, tolerated Chris out of
affection. But *Crissy*?

Her satisfaction with the band was still a warm glow in
her belly, but Melinda's response had tempered it. She
could not say that something was wrong, but all the same
she could no longer abandon herself to the utter certainty
that everything was right.

She pushed out through the door and edge through the

crowd, accepting compliments, declining drinks. She found Kevin in a dark corner with a stout man in a business suit.

"Christa, Bill Sarah," said Kevin. "Bill's been a friend for a long time. I asked him to come by and hear some good metal."

Bill seemed an unlikely person either to know Kevin or to have the faintest interest in heavy metal, but Christa shrugged off the incongruity. Six months ago she herself had been unacquainted with leather and studs, and guitars had been far from her mind.

"I hope you're enjoying the show, Bill," she said, taking a chair beside Kevin.

"It's . . ." Bill seemed to be choosing his words, and Christa noticed that Kevin was watching him carefully. "It's pretty impressive," he said at last. "I haven't heard many bands as together as you girls are. And there's power there, too."

"What did I tell you?" Kevin slipped his arm about Christa's waist. She had no objection. Since she had cried in his arms, the unspoken loneliness of two centuries finally catching up with her, she had rediscovered the comfort of another's touch. She was as loyal to Judith as ever; but, like Devi, she needed a human, mortal hand.

And Kevin had apparently felt something similar: where she needed others, he needed a heritage and a past. He had talked to his mother and father for the first time in a score of years, and he was planning, albeit with some anxiety, to spend Christmas with them in Cheyenne.

Under the table, she took his hand and gave it a squeeze. Fourteen centuries separated their births, but they were nonetheless alike. "Thank you," she said to Bill.

"You played a couple originals in there."

"My compositions. I'm no master poet, I'm afraid."

"Doesn't matter. They sounded good. Most of the time, a band plays originals, I can't tell what's coming down. You know: I only hear the song once in a live performance. There's not enough time to say if I like it or not." He tapped a small cigar out of a case and lit up. "Now, your stuff, I'm remembering. I might not know the words, but I'll bet you I can hum that entire tune . . . the one with *Get your ass out here, boy* in the chorus."

Christa smiled. "It's pleased I am to hear that." She still wondered who this man was, but from his words she knew that he heard a little more in music than did most. Still, the suit . . . and his hands were not those of a musician.

"Good stuff. Keep it up." Bill signaled to the waitress for another beer, glanced at Christa and made it two. "I think I'm going to stay the evening."

Kevin grinned broadly. She felt the warmth of his arm as it tightened on her waist.

And later, many minutes later, in the middle of the second set, she still felt the warmth. Kevin was an honorable, honest man, tall as one of the Fianna, gentle as a harper. He had been there for her tears, had asked nothing of her, and in his own way he seemed to be trying to learn what he could about music and magic.

Melinda was still anticipating the beat, but Christa found that her heart was full as she began her solo lead. If she could bring nothing else to this club full of the jaded and the flirting, she would bring a sense of love, of honest, giving affection. Love for Judith. Love for Kevin. The love of one Gaeidil for another.

Most of the time, Jessica felt isolated and embattled, as though the office she occupied at Adria Records were hedged in by rings of land mines, barbed wire, and reinforced concrete walls. As the sole woman in the Artist and Repertoire department, she occupied a precarious and delicate position that was open to judgment and prone to harassment—sure, she had slept her way to the top; that was why the top was so saturated with female executives, right?—a hefty paycheck and an incipient ulcer her only rewards.

But sometimes she wondered if she were simply filling a position at a desk, screening tapes and musicians, keeping the yokels away from the big boys. Or maybe it was the real talent that she turned away. It was hard to tell sometimes. That hick from Des Moines who was in the other day could have been the next Springsteen. The metaled-up trio last Wednesday might have turned out to be the next Triumph. In either case, they were gone now.

Tonight, she sat with Dennis at a table in the corner of a Denver rock club, nursing a bloody mary and an ankle that still throbbed from yesterday's skiing disaster. Her injury warranted aspirin and rest, but she had heard the demo that Dennis had brought back to L.A.—full of static and flutter from his portable tape player but bursting with hot metal—and she was willing to ignore the ankle, or at least to dull it with the bloody mary, while she listened to a band called Gossamer Axe.

The covers were solid and well executed, the stage show one of the best she had seen. The girl who played lead guitar covered the stage with her indefatigable presence, and though the singer's voice cut through the wall of sound like a chain saw ripping through balsa wood, still the guitar was always there, doubling vocal lines, powering out block chords for emphasis, shrieking out leads that melded anger and vicious joy.

Jessica tried to be objective. Returning to L.A. with an enthusiastic recommendation for an all-girl band was bound to affect her status at the label. Was she perhaps seeing in these five women an image of herself? Maybe it was Jessica Conway who should have been on stage—hair spiked, body clad in spandex—jiggling her tits at an audience she could not see for the spotlights. Nice fantasy. Would it sell?

Near the end of the evening, the singer stepped to the front of the stage, shook back her peroxide-blond hair, lifted the microphone. "We'd like to thank you all for coming to hear us," she said. "You've been a fantastic bunch of people, and we really enjoyed playing for you. We've got one more song before we call it for the night . . ." She smiled, her eyes flashing in her dark face. "It's an original by our guitarist, Christa Cruitaire—"

Someone whistled, and there was applause. The woman with the flame-colored mane waved. The singer grinned, threw an arm about Christa's shoulders. "What do you think, guys? Isn't she great? And she plays harp, too!"

Cheers and more applause. "Atta girl, Chris!"

"Anyway," she continued, "Chris wrote this, and we'd like to dedicate it to all of you who've found someone they really love tonight. Our best wishes to you, and a big thank-you from *Gossamer Axe!*"

The song was a rock ballad. Supported by synthesizer and piano, the guitar lilted fills and licks. The drums were even, steady, the bass rich and full; but in contrast to the instruments of the 1980s, the words sounded almost ancient.

I do not know how to praise you, O my love,
For I am no master poet who can claim the twelve
branches.
Your hair in my hands was sweet as new milk,
Your lips against mine like the rich mead of kings.

Sensual and yearning both, the singer's voice drifted out, borne up and echoed by masterful guitar playing; and something about the song spoke of a love more tender than Jessica had ever hoped to find in a world of plush carpet and false smiles. She felt her eyes start to tear and she glanced surreptitiously at Dennis. His cheeks were damp. She looked away quickly.

Unlooked for, maybe forgotten, I have come
To win you, who, once won, graced my arms
With your presence.
Unthought of, perhaps dispaired, I return
From lands which, though mortal, are alive
And waiting for you.

And as Christa's guitar lofted out a melody that seemed an embodiment of whole-hearted affection, Jessica felt the barbed wire and the battlements dissolving, taking with them the hard, tense knot that lived habitually in the pit of her stomach. Something melted, flowed, glowed warmly within her.

The song ended, the stage lights darkened, and the women of the band left for bed or for celebrations. But Jessica remained at the table. She ordered another drink to ease the lump in her throat, and she was almost afraid to look at Dennis for fear that he might see how vulnerable and sad she really was.

"What do you think, Jessica?" Dennis's voice was faint. "Was I right?"

She smiled. He sounded like a small boy asking his mother if he could keep a turtle. "You were right, Dennis. Let's take that demo and see what we can do back at the label." She shook her head. "I'm just afraid that no one's going to believe us."

I do not know how to praise you, O my love. . . .
The melody and the words and the emotion they expressed came back to Bill Sarah as he climbed the stairs

to the bedroom. In the dark silence, he could hear Kelly's soft breathing, and he leaned against the doorframe,
listening.

He could not see her, but he knew that she lay among
the sheets, her breasts, as firm as a girl's, poking up from
the white satin, her face composed and tranquil in sleep.
Once, long ago, he had awakened just as the early morning light was paling the sky, and he had watched her for
an hour, maybe two, wondering at this woman who had
given him her life, who had vouchsafed to take his hand
at the altar.

Your hair in my hands was sweet as new milk. . . .

It could not all be gone, that sweetness of their youth,
that honeyed, hot love that had turned sex into a sacrament, that had allowed him to hold her body as though
his hands cupped a chalice. Somewhere, it was there to
be found again . . . indeed, he had begun to find it
already, through the music of, impossibly, a heavy-metal
band.

Your lips against mine like the rich mead of kings . . .

Kelly stirred, groped for the light switch.

"It's all right, darling," Bill said quickly. "It's just
me."

Sleep had obscured her memory of their argument.
"You coming to bed?"

"In a minute. How was your meeting?" He had not the
control over his voice that Christa Cruitaire had over her
guitar, but he tried to put into his words something of
what he had heard in her music. "I hope it went all
right."

"Yeah . . . it was fine. I got the contract."

"Great." He smiled in the darkness. "I'm . . . I'm
proud of you, Kelly."

She laughed sleepily. "You, Bill Sarah, are full of hot
air."

"Yeah . . . maybe so." He laughed too. "But I'm still
proud of you."

"Come to bed, man."

And when he was spooned against her body beneath
the covers, he buried his face in her hair and put his arms
about her.

*Unlooked for, maybe forgotten, I have come to win
you. . . .*

"How was the show?" she murmured.

"I can't describe it."

"Oh, come on."

"No. No, really. It was . . . well . . ." He looked toward the window. In another hour, maybe there would be enough light so that he could see Kelly, so that he could watch her—just watch—for a while. "Do you remember that movie we saw way back? Polanski's *Tess of the D'Urbervilles*? With that shot of Stonehenge coming up out of the mist?" She did not reply, but he went on. "It was like that. It was . . ."

Folded in his arms, Kelly was snoring gently. He smiled. "And I'm crazy as hell," he whispered. "But I think I might just call them to see if they want a manager."

He touched his lips to her hair and laid his head down on the pillow. Another hour or so, and he could watch her.

CHAPTER
SEVENTEEN

Cumad, the queen, is distracted, upset. She tosses back and forth in her chambers like a ship moored in an unquiet sea, her pallid hands wringing one another, her hair rustling across her shimmering garments with spider-like whispers.

"I saw a willow tree," she says, rushing to the window as though to look again. "Its leaves are dark and green. It is the same tree each time I look at it. It is no different. It does not change."

"That is the way of our Realm." Lamcrann's voice is soft, low. "There is no death here." His jewels flicker in the light from the wall sconces as he turns his head to track his wandering queen.

She grips the sill of the window as though to anchor herself. The view is of twilight—it always is—and the sky is starless. In the distance, the horizon is limned by the corposant glow of a sunset that never was, of a sunrise that cannot be. "There is a rose in the courtyard, white as my skin."

"That is true."

Cumad turns, buffeted, heeling over in a wind of thought. *"It is always the same rose, my king."*

She has shouted at him. This has not happened before. Lamcrann finds himself staring at her, speechless.

"It has never dropped a petal, never opened. It has never grown." She turns back to the window, to the endless dusk. "I am tired," she says softly. "I want to sleep."

"We do not sleep, Cumad."

She does not seem to hear him. "I want to sleep."

Cumad will say no more, and Lamcrann leaves in a swirl of cloth-of-gold and filigreed robes. The door slams soundlessly behind him.

Staring into the half light, the queen struggles with wants and needs to which she can give no names. It is not the willow she desires, nor the rose. It is something else . . . something that eludes her.

How many times has she stood at this window and regarded an unchanging landscape of shrouded lake and hill, of distant myrtle grove and even more distant reflecting pool that images nothing? There are no yesterdays to count from. There is no progression of light and dark to determine before and after, to set events in order . . . there are, in fact, no events to set in order.

And perhaps this non-knowledge that has grown from a vague emptiness to a demanding void has driven her slightly mad; but she—poor queen!—has nothing with which to combat it. Even Siudb, the mortal woman, has no sense of time in the Realm: how then should a Sidh comprehend days, moons, the movements of stars and suns that exist only in another world?

"Something must change." Cumad is unaware that she speaks aloud. "Something, anything, must die. I . . . I wish I could sleep."

North of Denver, Interstate 25 straightened out on the plains. The Rockies bent away to the west and receded to a shallow backdrop: a tumble of hills and summits speckled with December snow. Kevin's Beetle protested at the constant freeway speed, and he was not sure himself why he was pushing: 35 was fast enough for a homeward journey.

In two hours he was taking the offramp at Missile Road, skirting the line of high-tension towers that marched in skeletal ranks alongside the highway. The stores at the corner of Missile and Frontage had been remodeled, their plaster facades replaced with modern brickwork and streamlined signs, but he recognized them and, with a right turn, entered the little web of residential streets.

But as the streets and the houses became more familiar, he began to wonder how much of this homecoming he actually wanted. He had laughed to himself about his childhood and youth, but here, immersed as he was in the source of his memories, with the white church peering at him through the bare crabapple trees, the laughter was fading quickly.

He parked in front of his parents' house, grabbed his suitcase, and almost ran to the door for fear that his nerve might suddenly fail and send him back to his car, back to Denver.

Back to Christa.

His hand hovered over the doorbell. She had cried in his arms, but even her tears were strong. "Wish you were here, Chris," he murmured.

But the door opened, and his mother was there: older, drier, her brown hair pale with incursions of gray, her blue eyes crinkling behind her steel-rimmed glasses as she smiled. She put her arms up to her tall son and brought his head down to hers. "Jesus and Mary, look at you, Kevin," she said. "You're a man."

"Well, ma, I grew."

She brought him into the house, and his father laid aside his newspaper and stood up from his chair. He offered his hand, and Kevin took it. Iron-haired and square-jawed, Martin Larkin looked him up and down, grinned thinly. "Still playing nigger music, Kevvy?"

"Yeah. Still." The handshake was strong—the grip of a laborer—but although his father's words were hearty, the turning of an old wound into a new joke, Kevin was conscious of the thinness of the humor.

Had he only imagined a bridge between himself and his family, then? Had he gilded a dream and taken it for the truth? The living room seemed smaller now, and the religious pictures on the walls had faded to vague out-lines. Kevin made out the image of a thorn-crowned heart, of a man dying as his mother sorrowed in silence.

"God's mercy on you," Martin was saying, "but I guess we'll have to . . ." His jaw trembled for a moment. "I guess we'll have to get used to it. You seem strong enough. I'm glad we raised . . . no sissies."

"Come into the kitchen, then," said his mother quickly. "I've lunch ready."

His parents asked him about his school, and his father spoke admiringly when he found out that Kevin actually made money. Kevin told them about the years he had spent wandering around the country, from San Francisco to New York, and he could not help but dwell on his time with Frankie.

"You . . ." His mother looked at his father, then at

the picture of the Sacred Heart that hung above the table. "You liked Frankie, did you?"

"Oh, ma, if I could play blues like he did, I'd think that maybe I was a real musician."

"I'm sure you're a fine musician, Kevin. But . . . was there . . ." Donna Larkin fell silent. The electric clock whined through the seconds. "Was there anything more . . . between you?"

"What do you mean?"

"Well . . ." She shook her head to dismiss the subject. "Never mind. I'm glad you had such a fine teacher."

Kevin's father had retired. He now spent most days in his garden or his woodshop. "I'm making cabinets and tables," he said. "I sell them at the flea market, and now and again I get a call for something special. It's turning out well."

"Tell Kevin about what you made for Father Lynch."

"Ah, it wasn't anything, Donna."

"It was too," insisted his mother with pride. "Before he died, Father Lynch asked your father to make a new credence table for the sanctuary. It's lovely. We see it every time we go to church. You'll see it too, at Christmas Mass."

Kevin looked up. "He's dead, then?" Almost feeling cheated out of a possible confrontation. "Father Lynch?"

Donna blinked at his tone. "He passed away a few years ago. The whole parish turned out for the funeral. He'd done so much for all of us."

"Yeah . . . I guess so . . ." Kevin had his own memories of Father Lynch. His parents exchanged glances, and his father bent his head and sighed.

Kevin expected some kind of reproof, some admonition to honor the priest, but none came. The clock continued to whine, and unspoken sentiments lay thick upon the table beside the cold roast beef. He was almost puzzled, for Martin Larkin had never been one to bite back words.

Off the kitchen, near the back door, a flight of narrow steps led up to the attic. Kevin groped for a change of subject. "You haven't . . . given any thought to rebuilding grandpa's old harp, have you?"

The silence thawed, but Martin had to think for a minute. "Why, I even forget we had it. It's up in the attic still, I guess."

"Could I . . . could I get it down? I'd like to look at it."

"You taking up the harp?"

"Well, I doubt I'd have much luck. But I know a girl in Denver who's a harper, and . . ." Kevin did not know what to say. Christa suddenly seemed far away. Why had he come here?

"A girl? Are you courting her?" Donna seemed hopeful, almost eager.

"Uh . . ." The idea seemed preposterous. One might as soon court the sea or the Rockies as make overtures to Christa Cruitaire. "We're . . . friends."

"A-*ha!*" said his father.

There was a palpable sense of relief in the air, but Kevin felt as though he had inadvertently diminished Christa. "How is everyone else?" he said quickly. "Teresa, and Marie, and Jeanine?"

"They'll be here for Christmas dinner," said Donna. "Jeanine is Sister Jeanine now, and she'll fly in from Chicago come Wednesday morning, and Teresa and Marie are up in Casper. They're married." She smiled at Kevin. "Some fine children they have, Kevin. But there's no one to carry on the Larkin name."

Kevin nodded abstractedly and chewed at a roast-beef sandwich. He should not have mentioned Christa. He could sense a wedding being planned: Christa blue-eyed and Irish and in a white gown, himself in a tuxedo, the family gathered around with approving glances.

He shuddered, floundered, groped again for a different subject. "What about Danny?"

Silence. His father's mouth was suddenly set. His mother looked away. "Danny . . ." She spoke with difficulty. "Danny won't be here."

"What's the matter? The Church won't let him come?"

Martin set down his fork a little too hard. "Your brother won't be here, that's all."

"But—"

"That's all, Kevin," he repeated. "The matter's done."

Kevin knew that tone. *The matter's done.* There was simply no more to be said—about music, about church, about anything. He looked from his mother's lined face to his father's. A glacier had descended upon the kitchen table.

He cleared his throat. "Good lunch, ma. Where should I take my suitcase?"

"We've got your old room ready, Kevin." His mother's voice sounded distant, as though the lid of a sarcophagus intervened. "I hope it will do."

Danny's high-school yearbooks were missing from the bookcase in the living room, and his pictures had been removed from the family album. His old room had likewise vanished: Donna had taken it for her own bedroom. Kevin found that in itself vaguely disturbing, for despite their twin beds, Martin and Donna had, in his youth, been an affectionate couple. Now they not only slept in separate rooms, but they also hardly ever touched.

As Christmas approached, Kevin explored the house, and although he found it outwardly unchanged, inwardly it had become as chill and grieving as if his parents were waking a corpse in the living room. The weather was mild and the sun made the sky blue and the foothills brown, but Donna Larkin went through the motions of her day with a thin, brittle smile. Martin labored in his woodshop, but seemed bent under more weight than that of a 2x4 or a sheet of plywood.

Wednesday morning, mumbling something about old things that he wanted to find, Kevin climbed the stairs to the attic and lifted the hatch that was thick with dust and cobwebs. As much as he sought his grandfather's harp, he was also looking for something that he could name as Danny's.

He had hoped to make peace with his entire family this Christmas, Danny included, but that desire was being denied him. It was useless to ask questions. If he were going to find any sense of belonging or of home, he would have to find it himself. And he would find it not among the present and the living, but scattered amid the possessions of the absent and the dead.

In a graying box, he found some of Danny's old school papers. Childishly printed, the pages were superscribed with *J.M.J.* and filled with copied questions and answers from the Baltimore Catechism.

Why did God make me?

God made me to know Him, to love Him, and to serve Him.

Up at the top: *Daniel Larkin. Grade 2. Room 3.*

"Where are you now, Danny?" he whispered. "What the hell happened?"

A faint gleam caught his eye, and he found, tucked between two stacks of clothes, an old harp. It was larger and heavier than one he had seen in Christa's house, and it was certainly less ornate, but he lifted it reverently.

He tested the strings. They would barely sound. Many were broken. The soundbox was cracked, and some of the dusty wood was rotten and patched with mildew. Oxidation caked the brass plate that ran the length of the harmonic curve, and he did not have to try the tuning pins to know that tarnish and corrosion had frozen them in place.

He looked over the instrument with a sigh. *A sad fate for a harp,* Christa had said, and she was right.

Sitting on the floor of his parents' attic, examining the remnants of his brother's life and the ruin of his grandfather's harp, Kevin let his mind rest for a minute on Christa. He felt hollow and unfulfilled by this attempt to regain his family, and the thought of the harper's blue eyes and sweet face nearly sent him down the stairs for his suitcase and his car keys.

A knocking from below. "Kevvy! Are you up there?"

His voice was tight. "Right here, ma."

"Your father and I are going to the airport to pick up Jeanine. Will you be all right?"

He held the harp in his arms as he had once held Christa. "Yeah, I'll be all right."

"I've left some money out on the counter," she continued. "Can you run to the store while we're out and pick up a ham for tomorrow? The whole family will be her for dinner, and I want to be sure there's enough for all of us."

He clutched the harp. "Sure . . ."

Jeanine had grown from a shy girl into a strapping woman. Since the Church reforms of the sixties, her order had abandoned its habit, but Kevin was still surprised to see her in slacks and a blouse. A crucifix on a gold chain glinted oddly against the soft bare flesh of her throat.

She sighed when she met her brother, but she was

smiling. "Well, Kevin, your hair is still longer than mine."
And then she hugged him. He noticed, though, as she
chattered to Martin and Donna about the family and
about him, that she did not ask about Danny.

He left the matter dead until their parents had gone to
bed, when he and Jeanine were sitting up for a few
minutes after the eleven o'clock news, alone in the living
room.

"I'm being wicked," said Jeanine as she stretched her
legs. "We're usually in bed by ten."

"Orders from On High?"

She looked at him as though unsure whether he was
making fun of her. "No," she said. "Our day starts
early."

For the last quarter hour, Kevin had been turning the
pages of a magazine without seeing anything of it. Now
he tossed it onto the coffee table. "Sounds like we're
having the whole family in tomorrow."

She nodded. "Dear God, yes. It'll be wonderful. You've
made ma and da so happy, Kevin, coming home like
this."

"I thought it was about time. But . . ." He stole a
glance at her. "But it doesn't sound like the whole family
will be here after all."

"What do you mean?"

"Where's Danny?"

"He . . . won't be here."

"What happened to him?"

Silence. Then: "What did ma and da say?"

"Da said the matter's done. You know that tone of
voice he gets."

"Well then, I can hardly disobey him."

Kevin stood up. "Dammit, Jeannie, you're going on
forty years old. Don't give me this crap about disobedi-
ence. You're an adult."

She regarded him for some time, not eye to eye and
freely like Christa, but with her head lowered, as though
brooding over something. "Danny decided that certain
things were more important to him than his family and
the Church."

He snorted. "Goddam. He had some balls after all."

Jeanine rose. "I don't have to stay here for this, Kevin.
Good night."

Kevin listened to the sound of her steps in the carpeted hall, heard her brush her teeth and crawl into bed in the spare room. He too had decided that certain things were more important than family and religion, and as a result he had absented himself from both for twenty years.

But his own pictures had never been removed from the photo album, and his single yearbook was still on the shelf. His family had obviously hoped that he might, someday, return. But not Danny. Danny was gone. Forever. And they wanted it that way.

Jeanine said nothing about Kevin's questions the next morning. She appeared to have forgotten the entire discussion. The matter was done. She and Martin and Donna readied themselves for Christmas Mass as though Danny were far from their minds. Kevin knew better.

He had not brought a suit, but he dressed in a sweater and clean slacks for church, and as the sun rose over the eastern plains, he climbed into the family car with the others.

Jeanine looked at him with mock distaste. "Well," she said, "at least your hair's combed."

"Aw, sis, you're just jealous." But his eyes threw the question at her again. *Where the fuck is Danny?*

Jeanine looked away quickly.

The priest who celebrated Mass that morning was a young man, blond and slight like Danny had always been. He wore the satin and gilt vestments as though new to them, and Kevin was not surprised at his voice: a thin tenor.

But Kevin noticed more than the priest, for having been so long away from the trappings of Catholicism, the Mass was for him not so much a sacrament as an environment. He was acutely conscious of the men and women and children who surrounded him, and in spite of his past denials he felt unwillingly subsumed into the congregation. It was as if, by his mere presence, he were repudiating his life, returning, humble and repentant, to the fold.

But in his mind he was scrambling away from the church, away from the people, away from Cheyenne. The sermon spoke of love and redemption, but what was all that beside a page of childish handwriting from a vanished brother? Danny's birth had been as real as that of any Savior. Why then did the Larkins commemorate Christmas while they methodically erased his memory?

Kevin wanted Christa. He wanted her in his arms, wanted her eyes and her face before him, wanted her voice in his ears. Even though her comments were frequently obscure, sometimes frightening, he would rather hear honest words that he could not understand because of his own stupidity than equivocations deliberately constructed to hide the truth.

You have to listen, Kevin.

Yes, he could listen, but what was he hearing? *The matter's done.* But that was foolish: nothing was ever done. The lead break finished so that the guitar could return to rhythm playing and leave room for the vocals. A twelve-bar blues progression ended with a dominant-seventh chord that pulled the music back to its beginnings.

And the evening before he had left for Cheyenne, over dinner, Christa had told him about the Solstice, told him that the seasons worked the same way. Of course they did: it was obvious to him now. Like music, like the blues, winter led to spring, which turned to summer, then to autumn, and then back to winter and the beginning again.

The atmosphere of the church was stifling, but Kevin smiled. Christa was close, for her words and her thoughts lived within him. He could not lose them, nor could another's tacit assumption take them from him. He remained aloof, apart, separate. His heritage was a snare, but it could not claim him.

But why, then, he wondered, had he come home?

He looked to Christmas dinner for some answer to his questions. As the plates of ham and roast beef made their way down the length of the dining-room table—Jeanine's pale white hands yielding the platters to her sisters' ruddy ones, the children's grubby fingers clutching at each morsel—he examined the food earnestly, as though he could find in sliced meat and mashed potatoes some intangible validation of his homecoming.

In truth, he was not hungry. And the fact that Martin and Donna referred constantly to the assembled family as though it were whole and complete soured his stomach with anger. The Larkin clan lived a lie. He had come home, certainly, but it occurred to him that salmon also returned to their birthplace . . . to die.

"So glad you came back, Kevin," Marie was saying. "I'm sure you're finding everything quite strange after so long."

"Yeah . . . you might say that . . ." Jeanine caught his tone, and so did his parents. Marie, though, took no notice. She seemed dull and frayed from the stress of marriage and children, and was content to allow her husband—whose name, like that of Teresa's mate, Kevin had forgotten in five minutes—to tell her what to do. Tall, with a braying laugh and a red face, Marie's man had shaken Kevin's hand, but had remained distant and supicious. A musician? Well, everyone knew about that kind.

"Da says you're courting a girl down in Denver."

The comment sat in his belly like a lead brick. "I'm not courting her," he said flatly. "Christa's a friend. A good friend. She's a harper."

A chuckle went round the table. Kevin kept back his words with clenched teeth.

"Mmm," Marie went on. "I'm glad she keeps herself busy. You might have brought her with you."

He had wished many times during this week that he had done just that, for her presence would have been of infinite comfort to him. But for now, he was glad that she was safely in Denver. Better he be alone and confused than Christa find herself trivialized and sullied by the complacent ignorance of his family.

And whether he liked it or not, this was indeed his family. All the frustrations, all the denials, all the rebellion came swarming back to him, and he was fifteen again, and angry, and looking for the person who had hurt his brother.

Never forget you're a Larkin. . . .

And what about Danny? He was a Larkin, too.

"Maybe next year," said Teresa.

"Probably not," said Kevin. "Probably never." He noticed that his mother looked up at him, eyes wide and frightened. She shook her head slightly, pleading.

"Come on, Kevin," said Martin. "We're trying to patch things up. It's been a long time, and you've been hanging around some strange people. Don't look down your nose at us." The words ended with a bitter twist.

Kevin set down his knife and fork. Martin picked at his food. Donna had given up. The others rattled on through the meal.

Mouth dry, Kevin framed the question he had already asked. But this time, he was resolved that he would have an answer.

"Where's Danny?"

His father looked up, flushed. "I think I told you that—"

"I know what you told me. Where's Danny? He was the family saint when I left, and now you don't even want to hear his name."

Martin's eyes narrowed. "That's right. So do what I say."

A silence like a chill fog had fallen on the table. Even the children had quieted at the tone of the exchange. "No, I won't," said Kevin. "That's why I left twenty years ago, remember? I didn't come back to tell you that I'd toe the line. I came back because . . ." He stopped short. Heritage? He had no heritage here. Religion? His faith lay as dead as Father Lynch.

Marie's husband spoke up. "Why the hell did you bother?" His tone was ugly, an attempt to put the city boy in his place.

The challenge only increased Kevin's bravado. "I came back for a lot of reasons. Maybe one of them was to find Danny." He turned to Martin. "Where is he, da? What happened?"

Donna Larkin shoved back her chair and fled to her bedroom, hands pressed to her face. "Jeanine, go help your mother," said Martin without looking.

"Aw, look at yourself, you spoiled brat," said Marie's husband. "Who the hell do you think you are?"

"Ken," said Marie, "take the children out of here."

He stared at her. "What are you telling me?"

Her eyes flashed, and for a moment Kevin saw behind the dutiful mask his sister had assumed. "Take them out. This is Larkin business." She herded the rest of the others through the door, then followed.

Kevin and his father remained at the table, alone, glaring at one another across half-finished plates. "Okay, da," said Kevin. "I asked a question."

"I ought to take you outside and give you a thrashing."

"I'm too big for that, now. It looks like Danny was, too."

Martin's jaw trembled for an instant, then squared itself. "We had to send him away, Kevin. He couldn't stay here."

"He left the seminary?"

"He . . . he left everything. The seminary, the Church, his family, God . . ."

"What did he do?"

Martin struggled. "He's queer, Kevin. It makes me sick to say it, but that's the truth." The words dribbled out of him in a muddy stream. "He was sleeping with men in the seminary, and he came to doubt his vocation."

"He's got his own life to lead, da," said Kevin. "And I left the Church myself. So he's gay. So what's the big deal?"

"You wouldn't understand."

Kevin rose, smashed the dishes and glassware from the table, leaned toward his father. *"Tell me!"*

Martin ignored the wreckage. His eyes were unflinching. "It goes back a long way."

"So do I."

"What would *you* do with a son who was so selfish that he'd sooner condemn his parents than forgo his vice?"

The words left Kevin confused. "Da, Danny's gay. That's Danny's business. It has nothing to do with you and ma."

"It has everything to do with us." His father had opened up finally, and he seemed to be wielding the words like clubs. "When Danny was born, your ma almost died. The doctors said another child would kill her for sure. We didn't know what to do." He silenced Kevin's words with a lifted hand. "So Father Lynch gave us permission to live as brother and sister on the condition that Danny be given to God."

Kevin was baffled. "Permission? What did he have to do with it?"

"He was our priest."

"Goddammit, da, there's such a thing as birth control!"

"It's not allowed. You've lapsed so far in your faith that you don't remember what's a sin and what's not."

"And dumping your own son isn't a sin? What kind of shit did Lynch give you, da?"

"He gave us the word of God."

"Fuck that bullshit. I'd just as soon go piss on his grave."

Something that looked like fear flashed across Martin's face. "Don't talk like that, Kevin. You'll only suffer for it. Danny did. He's caught that disease that queers get. He's beyond saving."

Worse and worse. "AIDS? He's dying? For crissakes, da, he needs us!"

"It's . . ." Behind Martin's words, Kevin sensed the words of a dead priest, words that now could never be unsaid. "It's the justice of God."

Faced with the utter starkness of his father's statement, struck with the full weight of his futile homecoming, Kevin swayed on his feet. "If that's your God, da, then you can keep him." He felt empty. His hopes had disintegrated.

"Kevin . . ."

"You threw me out twenty years ago. I gave the whole schmeer one last chance, but you haven't done anything except make me remember why I hadn't come back. Now it's final. Satisfied?"

"Get out."

"Me and Danny both: the rocker and the queer."

"Get out!" Martin's fear was a white face pressed against his eyes. "For God's sake, get out!"

Kevin went to his old bedroom and stuffed his clothes into his suitcase. The house was silent. It might have been deserted.

He loaded his bag and the harp into the Beetle, climbed in, slammed the door. The house stood against the afternoon light. Windows were dark, curtains pale and ghostly and rustling in wayward drafts.

His family was dead. All of them. Lynch had buried them, tamping the dirt down firmly on their hearts, their love, and whatever shreds of Ireland had remained after the centuries of defeat.

The highway was deserted and lonely, arrow-straight and southbound. He could not weep. Tears demanded something more than numb shock. Tears demanded a past.

CHAPTER EIGHTEEN

The Solstice had come and gone, the Sun returning in rebirth, rising up upon the broad eastern plains like a young King in the arms of his Mother. The days were growing longer now, winter giving way, minute by daylight minute, to spring. The land could look towards summer.

Christa looked towards summer too, not only in expectation of yet another turning of the year—the King dying on the longest day, yielding his life to the increasing darkness—but also in the certain knowledge of a battle that would determine the remainder of her life. Judith was in sight.

But the nights were still long and cold. The band had dispersed to spend the holidays with family and friends, and Kevin was off to Wyoming.

Often now, Christa found herself wondering at him, at her feelings for him. On her thirteenth birthday, she had taken the cup of womanhood from the hand of her priestess, and since then, the giftings that she had made of her body—to Judith most often, but also to some of the gentler harper lads of the school whom she had loved as she now loved Kevin—had been colored with a sacredness that, despite differences of culture and history, she had hoped to share with Kevin.

Kevin, though, had gone to reclaim his own heritage; and in rejoining his people and their ways, he could not but be distanced from her. Christa could not say that his action was an evil one. She could only regret the loss and consider sadly what the Solstice might have been for both of them.

Christmas Day would have found her alone had Devi not called in the afternoon. She, too, was alone. For all the keyboardist had ever said, her family might have been as vanished as Christa's.

"What'cha doing today, Chris?"

"Ah . . ." Aside from the social observance, the day meant little to the Gaeidil. But it was hard to live by oneself in America and not be touched by loneliness on Christmas. She shrugged. "Hanging around. What about you?"

"The same. Tell you what: I'll pick you up. We'll find some place that's open and have a burger."

Christa still heard the wall behind Devi's words, but the wall had developed a few cracks recently. Devi needed friends, family, and she had turned to Christa.

A burger? Indeed not. "Why don't you come over here?" said Christa. "I've got some steaks in the freezer."

"Steaks? Whoa. I'm in. You're sure no vegetarian, are you?"

Christa smiled. "It runs in my family."

It was a simple dinner she prepared: meat, mealcakes flavored with honey, vegetables, and cider. Devi thanked her, but kept her mask in place. "You think our gig up at InsideOut went well?" she said as she started on her beef.

Christa set an uncut loaf before her—a *bairgin banfuine*, the portion of an adult woman—and put the butter beside it. "Very well. In fact, I got a phone call day before yesterday from a gentleman named Bill Sarah. He wants to manage us. He already has a return booking for us at InsideOut if we want it."

Devi stared. "Bill Sarah? Jesus Christ! He's a big name in Denver. How come you didn't tell us?"

"Almost everyone's away, Devi. I decided it could wait until next rehearsal. Bill seems an honorable man, and he's willing to deal with our preference for in-town work."

"Damn. Maybe Melinda's right. Maybe we're going places." Devi broke the *bairgin*, spread butter on it. "Speaking of Melinda though . . ."

"That Friday? I noticed."

"I hope she doesn't make a habit of that. I mean, a lot of people do coke, but if she's going to mess up on stage, we've got problems."

"I spoke to her. She didn't want to talk."

"Shit. Sounds like the same thing she pulled years ago."

Christa poured cider. "There was a problem?"

"She really screwed herself over—like she thought the way to the top was to sleep with everyone and shoot up. I have to give her credit, though: she turned herself around. Been clean for years . . . until Friday at the club."

Some of the reasons for Melinda's sleepless nights were becoming clear to Christa. "There was no difficulty the rest of the week," she said, "so I assume it was a one-time thing."

"Damn well better be." Devi sampled the mealcake. "This is really good, Christa. Is this what people in Ireland eat?"

"It was, once. Before the conquests and the famines. I was a little lonely today . . ." Strange: she was even admitting it now. ". . . and all this reminds me of my family."

Devi was silent for a minute. "Do you see much of them?"

"Nothing. It's been a long time."

Bairgin in one hand, knife in the other, Devi sat, unmoving. "Same here," she said finally. "I . . ." Her mouth worked. "My father—" She broke off suddenly, bent her head. The wall crumbled.

Devi did not have to explain. "Where I come from," Christa said softly, "the High King would have had the man put to death."

Devi did not look up. "You don't come from around here, do you, Chris?"

"I do not."

"It's supposed to be my fault."

"Who told you that?"

"He did."

"You believe him?"

"I'd . . ." The wall remained down, and Devi's childhood seethed acridly in the open. "I'd like to not believe it. But that seems to be the general opinion."

"It didn't used to be."

Devi wiped at her eyes. "What do you think?"

Christa searched through a foreign language for words that might help to undo the damage of a foreign culture, but English was not Gaeidelg, America was not Eriu, and words were only empty things in any case. "You were abused," she said gently. "You're not anymore, though. A woman is free until she gives herself, and when she takes herself back, then she is free once more. Take yourself back, Devi."

"Easier said than done."

"It is, surely." In the face of Devi's past, words were nothing. But once, at her passage from childhood into womanhood, Christa had been given more than words. "Here," she said, refilling Devi's cup. "Here is an image for you. The cup is a symbol of the Goddess, of women. It contains everything, but it isn't controlled by what it contains. Rather, it gives its contents form and shape. Reality . . . if you want to call it that."

Aoine, the priestess, would have smiled at the rephrasing of the mystery, but Devi stared at the cup, her lips pressed together in a crooked frown. "I . . ."

"You can think about it later," said Christa. "For now, just believe. Pretend. It's the same thing. That's your cup, Devi. That's you. What do you want to contain?"

Devi looked up at her, eyes streaming. "What kind of a question is that?"

"What do you want to contain? What do you want to make real?"

"You're talking about magic, Christa."

"I am, surely. What do you want to make real?"

Devi stopped her tears seemingly by force of will. "How about some fucking self-respect?"

The harper offered the cup to Devi as, long ago, Aoine had offered it to her. "Take. Drink. This is self-respect. This is the beginning of the end of fear. This is yourself, whom you now take back."

For a moment, Devi hesitated; then she grabbed the cup, brought it to her lips, gulped the contents. The cider was strong, and she coughed violently for the better part of a minute, face flushed, eyes clenched.

When she was done, she wiped her eyes with a tissue, blew her nose, shuddered. "Did it work, Chris?"

"You took the cup by yourself."

Devi blew her nose again. "I guess I did."

"It's a beginning."

"Yeah." The keyboardist suddenly looked stricken, as though she realized how thoroughly she had revealed herself. "You know, I really didn't come here tonight to cry all over you."

"I said I was here. I meant it. I still do." Christa gestured at the table. "Eat now."

"But—"

"Don't worry about it. Just remember it." Smiling, Christa poured more cider.

Every woman is a priestess, Aoine had told her after her passage. *Every woman can heal with her hands, with a word, sometimes with just a smile.* In her pursuit of the mysteries of the *Cruitreacha,* she had forgotten the mysteries of her own body. But, on Midsummer Eve, a prayer to Brigit and the memory of Aoine's chalice had brought her to rock and roll and to hope. Perhaps now, at Midwinter, it was time to remember again.

Devi was shaken, but they finished their meal together, and Christa noticed that her smile was a little warmer now, a little stronger. And though the wall was rising again, it did not seem quite so high, nor so thick. Nor was it needed so much. A beginning.

"A priestess now," Christa murmured as she watched Devi's van pull away into the midnight darkness. "And what else must I be, my Goddess?"

The phone rang, and her heart caught. She had a little prescience. She knew that it was Kevin.

Siudb's hands have loosened, and the sound of her old harp rings clearly in the twilight air of the Realm, echoes off the still blankness of the reflecting pool, hangs shimmering among the leaves of the myrtle grove. The old magic is returning, the powers of the notes and intervals falling easily beneath her fingers. She has surpassed anything that she ever achieved at the harpers' school, has broken through the spell of continuity that holds the Realm. Soon she will be ready to open a gate into the mortal lands, to shield herself from the deadly years, to step, with Glasluit, into freedom.

On the bench beside her, Glasluit watches and admires. Were it flawless, immortal harping that he wished to hear, he could listen to Orfide, for the bard's playing is nothing save bloodless precision. But Glasluit is finished with perfection, and Siudb's music is redolent of the mortality to which he is drawn: the transience of seasons, the unending but ever-changing cycles.

She plays, lost in the inner world she creates as her nails strike the bronze strings. Glasluit feels—sees—the dead limbs of the winter forest grow green with the leaves of spring and flower with the heat of summer. Orfide's music speaks only of an everlasting present, but as Suidb continues, the forest darkens, drops its leaves and fruit, retires again into deathlike sleep.

The last chord quivers. Siudb comes to herself. "It is a song my teacher gave me," she says. "The first song that novices are given upon entering the school at Corca Duibne." She runs her hand along the strings as once she touched Chairiste's body: gently, almost fearful of the holiness of flesh and music both. "It is said that a harper can spend a lifetime perfecting it."

"I do not wish to hear it played perfectly."

Her smile was fond, gracious. "Then your wish is granted, because it cannot be."

He seems to her at times to be something other than Sidh, as though the shallowness of his immortal heart has been—by desire or by her music—deepened, enlarged. He might be now no more than a Gaeidil lad, a straw-haired, richly clad *flath* come to listen to a harper maid and lose his heart to her.

If he loves her for her mortality and her strength, she in turn has come to love him for his devotion. She did not think that she could ever desire a Sidh, but Glasluit, perhaps, is now as mortal as she. In defiance of his nature, in defiance of the Realm, he has grown, changed, become something else.

She sets her harp aside for a time. To become something else. For a time.

Christa pulled to the side of the highway, flicked on the dome light, puzzled over the directions to Kevin's house that, hastily scrawled in accordance with his hoarse dictation, were now almost unreadable. Her neat handwriting had disintegrated with concern, and she could hardly focus on the paper long enough to put the words together.

Parmalee Gulch Road . . . In— . . .

It was cold outside, and the air smelled of frost. Her

white wool robe was warm, her big blue Kinsale even warmer, but she shivered anyway. Perhaps it was not the cold. Perhaps it was horror.

"*In—*, Ceis? Do you remember what I said?"

Muffled under a thick comforter to keep the cold away, the harp deliberated. *Inca*

"Inca Road. Good. Right or left?"

left

With Ceis's help, she followed the road into the Indian Hills community, found Inca, and then took the turnoff that led to Kevin's home. The house itself was dark, almost invisible in the shadows of the mountain night, but her headlights picked up the familiar shape of his Volkswagen. She pulled in beside it, switched off her engine.

Silence. And cold. And the beating of her heart.

Holding Ceis under her arm, she picked her way to the door. "Is he here, Ceis?"

here

Christa knocked, then pounded. The oiled wood shuddered. Snow spattered down on her from the eaves. "Kevin!"

No answer.

When she tried the knob, she found the door unlocked. She swung it open and fumbled for the light switch. The yellow glare showed her a small living room: butcher-block furniture and cushions neatly arranged, Frankie's old guitar propped in a corner. An empty glass on the coffee table. A few issues of *Guitar Player* magazine.

And on the floor beside the sofa was an old harp, dusty, its brass corroded, its wood rotten. It was of the kind she had seen played at the Belfast competitions in 1792, where, during her single, heartbreaking visit to an Ireland she no longer recognized, she had paused in search of something familiar. But the harps were different, the music was different, and only venerable old Dennis Hempson still played wire strings with his nails.

She touched the instrument; and as though it recognized that a friend had come to it, it responded with a kind of a fluttering life, like a wounded bird come out of the winter snow into a warm house, frightened at first, then unbelieving of its fortune.

"Poor dear thing," she murmured. "A long time it's been for both of us." She straightened. "Kevin?"

"I'm here."

She made out his form in the dining alcove where the light did not quite reach. He was slumped in a chair, his head in his hands, but at her call, he rose and tottered into the living room.

His face was gray, wasted. "I'm an idiot," he said softly. "A stupid kid, calling you up in the middle of the night. Selfish— "

"You said you needed me." She set Ceis on the chair, doffed the Kinsale, and laid the cloak beside the harp. "You sounded like you did."

"Yeah, well . . ."

She went to him. "You sound like you still do, Kevin."

He dropped his eyes.

"What happened, man?"

He broke, sobbed dryly. She put her arms about him, guided him to the sofa, held him while he shook. As the harp, so Kevin.

"What happened?"

"Everything's dead up there," he whispered. "Dead. Ma and da don't even touch, my sisters are all fucked in the head, Danny's dying somewhere. Lynch is dead, but he still runs that family. If you can call it a family anymore."

He told her what had happened, choking out the words, his voice catching in mid-sentence as it always did when he spoke of his family. But this time there was a finality to his tone that made each pause a small death, and Christa was torn between a civilized pity and a savage rage at the tale.

"I told them to keep their God," he said as he finished. "And I told them I was gone for good, that they wouldn't see me any more. I'd thought that I could go back and find my family, but I just found everything that I hate. I haven't got a family, I haven't got a God, I haven't got anything. I'm just empty.

"Coming home down I-25, all I could see was my father. All I could hear was him going on about the justice of God, about how Danny got what he deserved. I imagine I'll get it too, sooner or later. And I'll probably do it to myself . . . just like Danny did. . . ."

Christa took his head in her hands, forced him to look at her. "That's not true, Kevin."

His eyes were blank. "Maybe it isn't," he said. "I'd have to believe in something for that. And I don't. I don't believe in anything." He looked at Frankie's guitar propped forlorn and abandoned in the corner; at the harp, old and pleading and hopeful. "I don't think I even believe in music any more."

White-robed, clad in flesh that, for all its years, was still hardly older than that of the girl who had accepted the cup and had thereby become a woman, Christa tried to find in herself the divinity that she had faced during that passage. A woman could heal by a word, but she felt that words would be, for Kevin as for Devi, only a beginning.

A word, a touch . . .

Sweat dampened her forehead, gathered at her temples. Kevin was dying as she watched. Could she apply the mystery of the cup to her own body?

She spoke the words. "What do you want, Kevin?"

"I wanna die."

She touched his face, shaking at what lay before her. "What do you want?" And her tone said that she would not accept an easy, despairing answer.

He could not look at her. "I want . . . I want to belong somewhere. I want a family that doesn't condemn my brother because he's gay, that isn't an asslicker to a bunch of priests. I want to believe in a God that doesn't hate everything I do . . . or think. I want my life back."

What he asked, she knew she could give. Indeed, she wanted to give it; for whether Kevin knew it or not, she owed him a great debt: he had guided her into the music that could bring her lover back. He had helped her, he had helped Judith, and, in the process, he had begun to grow.

There was too much music left in Kevin—she would not turn her back on him. And though she was no more an ordained priestess than she was a master poet, she was a woman, of flesh and blood, and she loved him. And that was enough.

Christa rose, shook back her hair. "If that's what you want, Kevin, take it. There are other Gods, and Ireland has a heritage that reaches back well before the coming of Patrick. For a family . . ." She thought of her land, gone now, and the tears came for a moment. "Harpers once wandered the length and breadth of Ireland, free to go where they would. There was a reason for that. Everyone was their family."

He did not look up. "I'm no harper, Chris."

"You are not. But you're a guitarist, and these days that's the same thing." She tried to remember how Aoine had looked. Soft, gracious, strong, replete with the Goddess, the priestess had smiled at her, offered the chalice, offered everything.

"Ah, shit, Chris. I'm too fucked up."

"Look at me, Kevin." Her voice had picked up strength. "Look at me. If you want something else, take it." She reached up to her throat, pulled loose the tie of her robe. The garment slipped off her shoulders, fell. "Take it," she said proudly. "Take me." Her words, like harpsong, seemed to echo through the room and beyond, resonating throughout the Worlds. "Take my people. Take my heritage. Take my Gods."

He looked at her at last, his face worn as if by years. He struggled with words. "I . . ."

She heard his reluctance and knew that it came not from him, but from the inheritance of shame that he was leaving. Her eyes flashed, her head tossed imperiously, and she understood then that it was not simply Christa Cruitaire who stood, naked and holy, before a man who had asked for rebirth. Nor was it Chairiste Ní Cummen. "Sin or sacrament, Kevin," she said. "Which is it? Which do you want it to be?"

She held out her hands to him—offering, commanding— and after a time, as though he suddenly recognized her, he took them.

CHAPTER NINETEEN

For the first time since Devi had come to a sense of memory that was something more than the hazy and unsequenced recollections of childhood, she awoke in the middle of the night without an instinctive sense of panic. Her bed was no longer a reminder of times past, of plastic clothesline knotted about her wrists, of her pajamas pulled up over her face. It was merely a bed, a place to sleep; and if she had curled herself into a soft ball beneath the covers, she had, apparently, done so because it felt good.

Drowsy, she shook some of her curly hair out of her face and drifted back among the luminous images of her dreams. Christa was there, garbed in a mantle of sky blue, and behind her was an arch of unhewn stone that rose up from a green lawn to frame, precisely, a still lake. She held a cup, and beside her was an ornate harp, carved and gilded and begemmed.

"Im here, Devi," she said. "I've always been here."

"Chris . . ."

"Take the cup, Devi. You're grown up now, and it's time for you to know that. Take the cup. Take yourself."

Devi opened her eyes, turned over, and was again awake. Rubbing her face, she got up and used the bathroom; and she drank a glass of water as she stood before the mirror, eyeing herself, squinting in the glare from the white tile.

It seemed quite strange to her that she could feel so markedly different without there being, at the same time, a visible manifestation to reflect the inward change. But then again, that she had achieved such a profound alteration by drinking a cup of cider seemed more than strange: it seemed utterly ridiculous.

A part of her wanted to rebel at the thought, for the

208

openness and irrationality into which she had thrust herself at dinner was both uncharacteristic and terrifying. But Christa had not hurt her. In fact, she had done her nothing but good; and when Devi turned around and faced the dark doorway that led into her bedroom, the shadows looked restful. She was not afraid. Her father was . . . someplace else. She could go back to bed.

As she settled herself under the covers, the memory of the harper was a warm presence that blanketed her like a down comforter. She saw the arch of stone again, saw Christa.

"I'm here, Devi. You're grown up now."

Devi curled up, drifting into quiet memories of a land she did not know. "Yes," she said. "I am."

Somewhere, downstairs in the kitchen, a floorboard creaked. Or maybe the stove, cooling now after a day of cooking for the Sanchez and Lucero clans, gave up some of its accumulated heat of a sudden, metal sliding against metal: an abrupt, hollow clank.

Monica's eyes flew open, and she was already sitting up in bed before she was aware of herself. "Ron?"

But no, the house was again inhabited only by the customary night sounds: her father snoring, the *tik-tik-tik* of a cooling water pipe, the rumbling of trucks on Speer Boulevard. Ron was . . .

She shuddered and clutched the blanket about her shoulders. Ron was somewhere. Earlier that evening, he had been at the front door, but Angel had promised him a broken arm if he did not leave. Strong and military, Monica's brother was quite capable of carrying out the threat, and Ron had left.

But Ron had found her parents' house, and so that was yet another haven denied her. He did not appear often these days, but when he did, it was obvious that he was now blaming her for everything from the disintegration of his band to his growing drug habit. He was still angry, and Angel could not be around all the time.

She put her head back down on the pillow and tried to sleep, but her ears were straining and she dozed fitfully, mouth dry, eyes burning. That window by the front door: was it really locked tight? The back door: was the chain on?

She might have left town, fleeing to Los Angeles or to Chicago to stay with relatives. There were other bands in the world. But what she had in Denver was more than an assemblage of musicians out to make a few dollars. It was even more than a family. Christa had given her respect and honor; and, singing with Gossamer Axe, Monica was not just pretty meat, she was a woman—something important, something powerful.

Titty band? Someone had called them that during their very first set. Christa had smiled ironically at the term and had blistered out a lead break that had rooted the dancers to the parquetry and turned them around to watch the woman who was making such music.

Monica's response to the guitarist had gone beyond gratitude. It had become a matter of loyalty and of love. No, she would not leave. Ron had driven her away from music before. She would not let him do that again.

Towards dawn she fell asleep, and she dreamed of clubs, of concerts and stardom. And if there was a dark, shadowed figure lurking up in the balcony, she felt that, somehow, Christa was guarding her just as much as had Angel.

Melinda had finally cleared out the spare bedroom, and Lisa had moved in as a resident. After months on the road, the drummer found it utter luxury to have her own bed, her own dresser, and a room to herself. Without crabs.

But the apartment seemed a little too quiet tonight, for Melinda had gone out early in the afternoon—she had not said where—and she had not come home. True, she was a grown-up girl, and if she kept late hours, it was none of Lisa's business. But Lisa considered her a friend, and she worried about her. Particularly after her rather addled performance on the first Friday of the InsideOut gig.

Coke? But Melinda had given that up a long time ago. Drugs were out. A little beer, maybe, but hard stuff? Forget it. Until recently.

Lisa got out of bed, stumped across the room, and opened her bedroom door. The light in the living room was still on. Melinda was still out. If she was doing coke—and she seemed to be doing a lot of it—then she had to have some fairly well-off friends, because no one made enough money in office supplies to suck up that much nose candy and still pay the rent.

Steps, a key in the lock. Lisa glanced at the clock: three in the morning. Quietly, she closed her door and crawled back into bed. She heard Melinda moving clumsily in the living room, crashing glasses in the kitchen, talking to herself.

The crashes gave Lisa an excuse. She cracked the door. "Hey, Mel."

"Hey yourself."

"You okay?"

"Jes' fine."

Lisa pulled on a robe and tottered into the kitchen. Melinda was stuffing a cold hot dog into her mouth. "Is that Christmas dinner?"

"Nuh . . ." Melinda chewed, swallowed, her movements choppy and quick. "Had that earlier." Her makeup, thicker than usual, had smeared. Her lips were a red slash. "Got hungry again. Was I making noise?"

"Uh . . ." Lisa stuck her hands in her pockets, shrugged. "I think I just had to go pee. I'll remember in a minute."

Melinda nodded, lifted the hot dog again. "What'd you do today?"

"Saw my cousin and her kids. They filled me up with pasta and turkey. Shit, she's younger than I am and she's got a family already." She broke off, stared. "What's wrong with your wrists?"

"Huh?"

"You're all bruised."

Melinda examined the purple abrasions. "Jeez . . . I guess I must have jerked a little." She laughed, and the sound was harsh. "He likes to tie me up. I go along with it."

"Uh . . . sure." Lisa started toward the bathroom, stopped, turned around. "Who's the lucky guy?"

"Oh . . . someone . . ."

"Anyone I know?"

Melinda whirled on her suddenly, eyes hot. "Why the fuck do you want to know?"

Lisa blinked. "Sorry."

"Just don't push me, okay? I'm doing this for you."

"For me?"

"Don't fucking push me."

Lisa retreated to the bathroom. She heard Melinda slam the refrigerator door, then the door to her room.

She rubbed at her face, sighed. "Hey, God," she whispered. "You there?"

Conjoined with Christa, Kevin felt himself to be embracing the world, and the look in her eyes that took him back to his inner vision—now reified in tender caress, in passionate climax—was but a confirmation of what he had known since he had felt himself grasped by a divinity that was one with the touch of her hand: that this union, this bond of flesh and spirit, was not simply with a girl of Ireland, nor even with the woman that Christa had come to be to him. No, he had seen her as Goddess, and Goddess she was.

Come, she had said. *Come to the altar.* And he had taken her hands, and she had led him to a place of safety and of hope, had taken him into herself and birthed him anew.

But, Goddess though she was, she was, nonetheless, still Christa, fragrant and soft, her hair spilling across the sheets and pillows in waves of sunset. Human and mortal as ever, she moved beneath him, sought his lips, wrapped her arms about him, gasped in the sudden rush of joy. Outside, in the night, frost crept along the windows, and the crystalline air seemed poised upon fracturing with the cold. But inside, in his bed, enfolding him, the warmth triumphed like a sunrise after a long night.

Spent then, floating upon the tenderness that had found him, he drifted into dreams that, even as he lived them, he knew to flow from her memories. A green land, wide and fertile under a blue sky, unrolled to meet him. The sun was yellow, the lakes shone like mirrors, and the forests lay dark with the mystery of their holy leaves.

Had she told him in words what she was and from where, his belief might have flickered in and out, his reason battling with his trust. But these dreams, he knew, were truth, and no doubt crossed his mind as, with Christa—Chairiste—he walked the meadows and forests of Eriu, called music forth from harps, touched Siudb with gentle hands in the moonlit brilliance of the

Midsummer night, journeyed to the foot of the Sidh mound . . .

With her he saw France boil into a cauldron of revolution and blood, the burning châteaux of the land streaking the summer sky with black plumes. With her he fled to England, wandered Ireland, journeyed to America, discovered rock and roll . . .

. . . met Kevin Larkin . . . and healed him.

He opened his eyes and found that the windows were gray with dawn, the windows opalescent with new light. Christa slept, her head pillowed on his shoulder.

Gently, he touched her hair. An Irish girl. But more. Much, much more.

Silently, joyfully, he wept. Pledged, devoted to another, she had given him this night because she loved him, because he was worthy. There was no question of possession or of jealousy: she had already given him everything. He could not but give in return.

Christa stirred, murmured in her sleep, and her hand on his chest clenched, relaxed, lay quietly. He stared at her hand, at the long harper-nails that glowed pink with polish in the rising light. How old was her hand? How many years had it seen? How many harpstrings had it touched?

Meaningless maunderings. Covering her hand with his own, he kissed her head, slid back into her dreams, and awoke to morning and the sound of a harp in the next room.

His memory of the evening and of the night slowly returned, and he was at peace. If he had awakened with Christa by his side, the morning would have been perfect. But nothing was ever perfect, and in any case he was glad of the chance to hear her play, so the imperfection was good, too. The harp chimed on, and in its song he heard more songs, and those in turn led on to others. It was very simple. It was very good.

Rising, he stretched the stiffness out of his body and wrapped himself in a robe. He smelled coffee and the scent of burning pine, and when he went to the door, he saw a woman in a white robe playing a harp strung with gold. Her hair was red and flowing, freshly washed and lustrous, drying in the shimmering heat from the wood stove.

She did not notice him. She was occupied with her music; occupied also with the battered old harp that lay on the floor at her feet. The song wove in and out, and Kevin sensed that she was trying to comfort the instrument.

Magic. He smiled. She had told him about that. He understood now.

She finished the song, bent, and touched the old harp. The brass was still corroded, the wood was still cracked and rotten, but it seemed more alive now, as though its spirit had returned.

"Chairiste," said Kevin softly.

At the name, she looked up; and then she gasped when she realized what he had called her. Slowly, she nodded to him. "Good morning, Kevin. Brigit bless."

She was lovely. She might have stepped out of his dreams that night. "Good morning. Brigit . . ." *Take my Gods.* He smiled self-consciously, ran a hand back through his hair, scratched at the stubble on his face. Why not? "Brigit bless."

"I made coffee."

"Thanks."

He filled two mugs and sat down with her by the stove. The heat was friendly and warm, and the pine logs crackled and snapped. From outside came the wet sound of melting snow. "That's my grandfather's harp," he said.

"A sad harp it is," she said, touching it again. She had apparently cleaned it up a little before she had played, and with the dust and dirt and broken strings removed, he could see carving along the side of the soundbox:

In the time of Noah I was green,
After his flood I was not seen,
Until 17 hundred 07—then I was found
By Cormac Kelly, under ground:
He raised me up to that degree,
Queen of music you may call me.

"1707," he said. "It's been a while."

"It's an old harp."

"Old, Chairiste?"

She dropped her eyes, bit at her lip.

"Why didn't you tell me?"

She set her harp across her lap and picked up her coffee. Her hand was shaking as she sipped. "Would you have believed me?"

"I might have."

"Oh, sure."

"Hey, anything's possible. I'm one of those crazy Irish boys, remember?"

Christa smiled. Her eyes were, he thought, even bluer than in his dreams. "I remember. And it's glad I am that you know. It's been a long time since . . . since . . ." She gave up. But her hand was steady again.

The silence lengthened. The harp was old. Christa was older still. He was a child in comparison. "My history isn't too good," he said. "Those houses, the school—when was that?"

"The sixth century." Her hand strayed to the jeweled harp. "As far as I can tell, I was born about 551."

"And Si—" He stumbled over the Gaeidelg name. "And Judith is . . ."

"She's still in the Realm. It's been about two centuries—our time—since I left. I don't know what it's been for her. Time doesn't really exist there."

"And you're going to use metal to get her out."

Christa nodded. She ran her hand along her harp's forepillar. "I can only do so much with Ceis. I have to make up for my lacks with sheer power. By his nature, Orfide can learn nothing new. He will neither understand the music nor be able to fight the volume."

Kevin laughed softly. "You're going to blow his socks off, Chris."

"He's subtle. He's won before. He might be able to match even the volume with his skill." For an instant, the razor flashed in her eyes. "But he'd best be on his guard, for it's no simple harper he'll face this time."

"Can I help?"

"You've helped already, Kevin," she said. "You gave me my tools. And more." The expression on her face was that of the Goddess he had seen. "It's up to me to use them."

In the morning light, Christa and her harp shone like a stained-glass window, at once distant and close, antique and immanent. But Kevin thought now that it was silly to draw such distinctions. The sacred, the holy, was immediate, perceptible. If he perceived distance, it was something of his own creation, something he could, with effort, see beyond. As he had last night.

He felt strong, complete. "I owe you, Chris," he said. "I owe you, and Judith, and your teachers. And your Gods, too. You turned me around last night. I want to help." He started to reach out, hesitated, then hugged her and felt her lips against his cheek. "You're not alone anymore, Chairiste. There's two of us."

three

He heard the voice within him, blinked, shook his head. He realized that it belonged to Ceis. "It can talk?"

She leaned the harp against her left shoulder and struck a soft chord. "It's a different world you've come into, Kevin. Ceis is a Sidh harp. Of course it can talk."

Clesac is Orfide's second-best harp, and though it is richly adorned with gems and gold and carving, still it is a constant reminder of Ceis, lost to him now. It reminds him, too, of Chairiste, and of her escape.

The Realm does not change. Angry at the cheek of the Gaeidil, humiliated by his loss, Orfide must exist with those emotions forever. He cannot grow beyond them, and therefore his resentment gnaws at him like a canker within the lily.

But if, as he plays for Cumad, he dwells upon his injuries, his face and demeanor show nothing of it. He is a bard, and his king has asked him to play for the queen, to soothe her concerns, to quiet the questioning voices within her.

And so, outwardly impassive, he weaves his spell, the strains of melody and counterpoint twining about the queen, seeking to stem the sudden onslaught of the new and the strange. Since eternity began, since the Realm unfolded into being with all of its past, present, and future contained in an immediate, changeless *now,* Orfide has been its guardian in just this way. The Realm will not change. It cannot change.

As he plays, though, he feels the changes growing about him nonetheless. Rents, tears, the gradual tattering of the fabric of stasis: in his mind's eye, Orfide sees it all as though a veil were being slowly shredded. Cumad's ailment (dare he, even to himself, call it madness?) is but a symptom of a more widespread disease.

It is Siudb that is the problem. Lamcrann considers her a toy, an amusement; but Cumad is beginning to look to her for inspiration, and Glasluit has already been hopelessly corrupted. Tears, rents. If Orfide played constantly, filling the Realm with unending, imperishable music, yet would he be unable to contain the contagion that Siudb spreads.

The Gaeidil must be stopped, must be made more of a substance with the Realm before she destroys it. Her nature must be changed.

Orfide has given this thought, and he knows that he can accomplish the desired end. Holding him back, though, is the potential displeasure of his king. Lamcrann actually likes Siudb's novelty . . . in small doses.

And so the bard must be patient. Lamcrann will enjoy a nearly successful escape attempt on Siudb's part no more than a proposed change in her nature; but, faced with the former, he will, most likely, prefer the latter. Better to have a docile Celt than no Celt at all.

On her throne, Cumad sits, hands folded in her lap, eyes closed. Siudb is not with her. Orfide knows where she is. His face a careful mask of calm, he sparkles through the music, through the spell, and the final cadence glows like a double handful of fire strewn upon the palace floor.

Cumad opens her eyes. "My thanks to you, master bard."

Orfide rises, bows. "It is my honor, O queen."

But she looks troubled. Her hands fidget with the hem of her sleeve. "But you have played that song before."

"I have, my queen."

"It has not changed."

He stands, speechless, his hand tight on his harp. His second-best harp.

Cumad rises from her throne, eyes wide. "It is the same song."

"My queen—"

But she has already turned and rushed out of the room. Her footsteps clatter down the stairs, across the courtyard. Orfide goes to the window in time to see her pale figure fade into the shadows that surround the palace.

He passes a hand across his face. Changes. And even if Siudb were altered, that itself would be another change, another tear in the gossamer fabric of the Realm.

And as he stands at the window, staring out at the dim world, a flicker of something bright catches his eye. A twinkling star burns near the zenith of the overarching vault of darkness that encompasses the Realm. It vanishes in a moment, but its afterimage burns in his brain. A star.

The night wind turns cold.

CHAPTER TWENTY

Bill Sarah's word was good, and Gossamer Axe was back at InsideOut immediately after the holidays. Attendance at the club was growing steadily, and Bill used that fact to good advantage, securing both an article about the band in the entertainment section of the *Rocky Mountain News* and an interview with Christa in one of the local music tabloids.

"Cindy Holmes from *Rockbeat* is coming out to talk to you, Chris," he said when he phoned with the news. "She's an okay gal. Polite and all that. You know, some of these people get sort of pushy when they've been in the business for a while."

"Pushy, Bill?" Christa laughed.

He laughed also. "Come on, Chris, you know me. Anyway, she's going to talk to you about your style. She's been out at the club a few times, and she thinks you're hot. Of course, that's to be expected. But try not to scare her."

"I'm not sure I understand you."

"Well . . . you've said a few things about music that curled my hair. What I've got left of it. But . . . wait a minute, I've got an idea." He deliberated, humming tunelessly. "On second thought, tell her whatever you want. Everyone's always turning metal into satanism, but you've definitely got something else going. And it's healthy: it makes people feel good. Go on, weird her out. Good promo. Keep 'em guessing."

"All right, Bill." Good promo. Was that what her religion had become? "Is everyone happy at InsideOut?"

"You really need to ask? You're blowing them away. Carl should be pretty excited. It isn't every club owner who gets to start the next Van Halen."

"I'm not Eddie Van Halen!"

"I know. You're much prettier, especially since he cut his hair. Oh yeah: Bangles wants you in two weeks. I told them yes so they could make their ad deadlines."

"Oh, Brigit . . ."

"Relax, Chris. Enjoy the ride. And . . . loosen up, will you? This is rock and roll. This is fun, remember?"

"Ah . . . thanks, Bill."

She hung up and stood by the phone for a minute, feeling torn. She was a harper. Rock and roll was something that was going to rescue Judith, no more. To keep her band together, though, she had to allow her guitar to influence ever-larger portions of her life, and she found herself confronted by a growing list of club dates and small concerts. It was unnerving, unsettling.

But as the days lengthened toward spring, it became more than that, for many of Christa's harp students began to cancel their lessons. Their excuses were varied and somewhat predictable—time, money, commitments—but she could sense the real reason: harp and heavy metal did not mix. A harper who suddenly espoused a more violent and modern music, who showed a growing preference for leather pants and boots, for streaks of crimson and purple in her hair, for metallic blouses and barbaric jewelry, could expect nothing else than to lose students.

A bitter taste came to be in her mouth when she donned her stage clothes and prepared for a show. By their actions, her students were as much as telling her that her work with them had been wasted. She had loved them as her children, had tried to share with them the joy and fire that she found not only among harpstrings, but in all music, and they had rejected her.

Kevin met her backstage as she warmed up one evening. Lisa was changing the head on her much-hated snare while Devi was helping Monica with her microphone stand. Melinda was missing, but that was not unusual: she was making a habit of showing up at the last minute with a vagueness about the edges of her eyes that worried her bandmates.

Kevin's grin was reassuring. "How's my Celt?"

She wrinkled her nose. Two more students had canceled that afternoon, and one had been quite frank about his reasons. "I'm after finding out that the more metalheads I get for fans, the fewer harp students I'll have." She told him what was happening. "Dear Goddess, Kevin, it's just music!"

He shook his head. "I guess I should have warned you that first day at the school. A lot of people out there want rock and roll to go away. It's been that way from the beginning. You've thrown in with a pretty scruffy bunch."

She snorted and banged out an unamplified chord. "They'd think our whole people was a pretty scruffy bunch. At least these days we only spike out our hair with lacquer."

"What'd we use back when?"

"Lime." She smiled at the thought. "Like cement. And some of us went into battle naked."

"Be a hell of a show, wouldn't it?"

He made her laugh; but on stage, with the music and the energy flaring around her, she brooded on the matter. Her solos took a darker, more reflective turn, and during the first break, when she paused in the dressing room to fix her makeup and hair, her reflection disturbed her. Where was the quiet Christa Cruitaire of the crepe de Chine blouses and the khaki slacks? Gone. Her place had been usurped by this figure in tight leather and boots, a woman hardly out of girlhood with deep-shadowed eyes, a mane of red hair, and breasts that strained against barely concealing spandex and lace.

Beside her, Monica was applying a lipstick that turned her mouth the color of an open wound. "You're looking good, Chris," she said with a wink. "What happened? You get yourself laid?"

Pale, Celtic skin showed blushes better than any other complexion. "Why . . . why do you ask?"

"Because ever since the holidays, you've been practically glowing. And the way you're playing just about gives me wet pants." Monica finished with the lipstick, picked a bit of fuzz out of her mascara. "That's pretty neat. Good for you."

Monica went toward the door to the club, paused with her hand on the knob, came back. "Would you . . . uh . . . mind if I sort of stuck with you during break?"

Christa heard the tone. "Ron?"

Monica lowered her voice. "Yeah. He was hanging around my car this afternoon when I got off work. He took off when he saw me, but I've kind of wondered . . ."

Beneath her makeup, Monica's face was haggard. Christa knew that, unable to change her work schedule to accommodate late nights, she shorted herself on sleep and slept in on weekends, eking out her stamina with an occasional amphetamine. Ron was something extra that she did not need on her mind. "Surely." Christa slipped an arm about her waist. "Stay with me. And if he shows up, I'll give everyone a good show."

"You crazy dyke. You'd do it too, wouldn't you?"

Out in the main room, the patrons seemed fascinated by Christa. Strangers shook her hand and wanted to talk to her. Napkins and pens were pressed on her for autographs. A girl—underage by the look of her—with hair dyed black and eyes that were all liner and shadow, just stared. On her T-shirt was painted *Christa is God*.

Christa noticed that she kept her nails short, and that her hands looked stronger than was usual for girls her age. "You play guitar?"

The girl looked almost frightened, but she forced herself to nod. "Yeah. I . . . uh . . . I got a Charvel."

"I've seen them. They're nice."

"Oh . . . wow . . ."

"Do you have a band?"

"Just . . . uh . . . oh, jeez . . . We're just starting out. We don't sound too good right now."

Christa smiled. She had failed as a harp teacher, but perhaps she could make a difference here. "Keep at it. Just play. That's the important thing. And remember that you can do almost anything with music." She looked at her earnestly. "Almost anything. Do you understand?"

The girl nodded, wide-eyed. "Yeah. I've heard you do it."

Christa clasped her hand for a moment. "Brigit bless," she said, the girl broke out in a smile and scuttled away to her friends.

"You've arrived, Chris." Monica was shouting in her ear to be heard above the recorded music. "*Christa is God*. How about that?"

Christa saw Kevin at a table on an upper level and steered Monica in his direction. "Shouldn't that be *Goddess*?"

Monica laughed. "You're wild."

"Honestly, don't you think so?"

"I think it would be hot to be a Goddess," said Monica as they climbed the stairs. "Instead of a slut."

Christa stopped her halfway up. "So be one."

The canned music surged around them, the flashing lights speckled Monica's hair with gold. "What?"

"Be a Goddess."

Monica shook her head wonderingly. "Chris, you're wild."

Kevin had left his family, left his religion, left all but the roots of his heritage in the pursuit of a vision of Divinity that he had at last attained through the intercession of a young woman from another time and place. He had been a boy before, but now he was a man. He did not question that, did not feel the slightest need to prove it, and with wide arms he embraced his new life.

Come Imbolc, the beginning of Spring, the weather was mild, as though the waxing light were indeed making inroads on the cold season. Kevin joined Christa at dawn for the simple rite, and though he did not understand the ancient language, he knew he belonged there. Christa blessed a cup of wine, offered if to him, and once again he looked into the eyes of the Goddess to whom poets and healers and smiths and harpers owed homage.

But afterward, over breakfast, he was quiet. "Old memories?" said Christa.

"Kinda." He spooned his oatmeal around in his bowl. "I've been trying to find Danny. He needs a family, and I'm all he's got left. No luck. My relatives don't know or won't tell, and I'm out of ideas. It's a big world. He could be anywhere. He could have changed his name. He could . . ." His voice broke for an instant. "He could be dead already. He needs to know that someone cares."

"Did you try calling his seminary?"

"Are you kidding? They'd probably prefer him dead."

Christa poured milk into her coffee. "Today is traditionally a time of purification," she said, "a time to get rid of all the dross and impurity in our souls. I've brooded on the fact that the Christians more or less destroyed my culture. You've spent your life angry at Father Lynch and his Church. But maybe all of that is blinding us and making us forget that there are some sincere people out there who just happen to worship a foreign God."

Kevin shrugged. "I'll grant that."

"All right, then what about Danny's school? Maybe someone there knows and cares. Let's forgive what's gone before and get ready for Spring."

The task was nonetheless difficult. Kevin did not know where Danny had studied. A visit to the offices of the Denver archdiocese produced a long list of seminaries in the United States, and there was nothing for Kevin and Christa to do but work their way through it.

More waiting, more frustration. But finally, as Christa—guitar in hand, garbed in the black leather and sensuality of rock and roll—was heading out the door to yet another performance, a return call came in from a Father Paul Lennox. Yes, he said in a soft Southern accent, he had known Danny Larkin. And he knew where he was.

The highway to Sheridan was trimmed with ribbons of blowing snow and hazy with flakes that swarmed down from an overcast sky. It took Kevin past Cheyenne, but he avoided looking at the Missile Road turnoff. A single Solstice, a single Imbolc, could not undo a lifetime.

The dark clouds were growing darker, and the wind from the north had taken on a bitter edge when Kevin knocked on the door of Danny's apartment. Waiting for an answer, his stomach clenching and unclenching, he tried to think of something he could say to his brother. Twenty years, and Danny dying. What could he say? What could anyone say?

He wished again that Christa were with him. She had, unwillingly, remained in Denver, almost overwhelmed by a full schedule of performances. But had she come to Sheridan with him, she would doubtless have given him the same advice she had already.

"Tell him that you love him," she had said.

"Then what?"

"Say it again. And again. And again. Until he understands."

Sleepless, her makeup smudged with the exertions of five hours of rock and roll, she had seen him off in the early morning; and just before he had climbed into his car, she had pulled one of the *failge* off her wrist and put it on his. "For luck. For you."

He touched the bracelet as he waited. The twisted gold was smooth and warm. He covered it with his hand as though embracing her.

Benji opened the door. He was a short, well-muscled man with brown eyes and a smile that was almost winsome; but his eyes were tired, and his smile did not conceal a sadness that was at once profound and incurable. "Kevin?"

Kevin stuck his hand out. "That's me, Benji."

Benji led him into a sparsely furnished living room. Even after so many years, Kevin knew that Danny had chosen the décor. Always the monk. But on the white walls there were no religious pictures, sun bleached and faded with years of contrition; just a few prints by Picasso, one by Van Gogh, and an incongruously comic serigraph by Michael Bedard.

"How is he, Benji?"

"Sleeping right now, I think." Benji shook the snow from Kevin's jacket and hung it in the front closet. "This last couple of weeks, he's been at a plateau. We've got something of a routine going. A friend who isn't so badly off yet comes by while I'm at work and cleans him up if he needs it. A couple times . . ." He looked away, passed a hand over his face. "A couple times we've found him on the floor. He doesn't want to be a problem and keeps trying to make it to the toilet by himself."

"How long . . . how long does he have?"

"It's hard to say. A month, maybe. Maybe two."

Softly, as though filtered through distances or years, a voice drifted in from another room. "Benji?"

"It's your brother, Danny," Benji replied. He gestured at a short hallway, and Kevin nodded.

Benji showed him to the bedroom and quietly retreated while Kevin hesitated with his hand on the knob. Christa knew what to do, and she could do it. But she was a harper. He played guitar. Not the same thing at all. Not even close.

When Kevin entered, Danny was sitting up in bed, his back propped on a pile of pillows. Kevin was almost shocked: Danny's age was strange enough to him, but added to the accumulated years was the wasting effect of the disease. Danny seemed old: hollow cheeks, sharp nose, sunken eyes. His hair was thinning, and some of it had gone prematurely gray. He had the look of a damaged angel.

"Kevin."

Kevin forced his lips to move. "Hey, Danny."

"You've gotten big." Danny groped for a glass of water on the table by the bed. Kevin picked it up and put it in his hands.

Danny's skin was dry, cool, like that of an old woman. There was a tremor in his fingers as they closed about the glass. Kevin was afraid to look at his eyes.

"It's okay, Kevin," Danny whispered between sips. "Thanks for coming." His voice was listless. "Have you seen ma and da?"

"I was up there for Christmas. Well . . . for part of it." Kevin shrugged. "I pulled one of my famous scenes. I'm . . . not welcome there anymore."

"I'm not either." Danny seemed resigned. Like a painting in a museum, he seemed caught under glass, frozen in time, hollow cheeks forever sunken in El Greco asceticism, eyes mirroring . . .

Kevin finally looked. Eyes mirroring nothing. If they were bright, it was no more than a hectic side effect of the AIDS, a daub of silver added by a cynical artist to suggest life where there was none.

The insight frightened Kevin. He pulled up a chair and sat down. "Danny, talk to me. What's going on?"

Danny shrugged. "Why should anything be going on, Kevin? I'm dying." He laughed softly. "Set myself up real good, too. Lynch would love it."

"That doesn't sound like you, Danny."

"You don't know me."

Danny's words were all too pat, as though he had rehearsed them for the benefit of a straight brother who came with prepackaged bourgeois solace for the queer. "Dammit," siad Kevin, "we're brothers."

Danny shook his head. Resignation. "Kev, you went your way, I went mine. Don't think that you know me, because you haven't had a chance to. That was what the problem was all along: everyone thought Danny was a pious little nitwit, ripe for the priesthood. They were wrong. I'm not letting that happen again. I don't have time: I'm dying." He grimaced. "It's fucked: I have to apologize for it."

"Okay. Maybe you're right. Maybe I don't know you. So tell me. What happened?"

Danny shrugged offhandedly. "Got AIDS."

"No, really." *Brigit, Chris: What the hell do I do?* "Tell me. I care."

Danny's eyes flickered as if to say *yeah, sure.* "Not much to tell, really." He stared at his thin hands, flexed the fingers as though amazed that they still obeyed his commands. "I don't think I ever really thought about what ma and da had planned for me. I just did what I was told, paddled after them to church, and always figured I'd be a priest. But when I got to the seminary, it just didn't seem right; and on top of everything else, I started to realize I was gay. I wound up in bed with a few of the novices who were willing, and I started asking questions about what I was doing at the school; but I never got decent answers from anyone. Even Father Paul had too much invested in his religion." He smiled wryly. "It probably hurt him when I left. I sent him a card to let him know about what happened. Maybe he'll pray for me."

"He did better. He turned me on to where you were."

"Is that how you found me? Christ . . . maybe he really cared."

The news seemed to make Danny think, and so made Kevin hope. But Danny resumed his tale ploddingly: "Ma and da flipped out when I told them, and I finally wormed the whole story of my birth out of them. They figure they're going to hell now. Or maybe since I'm dying, they figure that I'm the one going to hell and it'll be all right for them. I don't know." He stared at the blank wall for a moment. "I tried once more: when I found out about the AIDS. They won't even talk to me. No one will." The derision was thick in his voice. "Real nice family. You don't act like a sweet little Catholic boy, and they want you dead."

Kevin finally understood: Danny had not left his family in Cheyenne. Instead, they were all clustered here in this small bedroom that smelled of antiseptic and stale urine: mothers and fathers and grandparents and ancestors crowding shoulder to shoulder, bending over Danny's bed, cursing the apostate, condemning the fallen priest.

What did Kevin have that might stand against so many? what could he say to Danny that might counter the anger of generations?

Take me. Take my people. Take my heritage . . . my Gods . . .

Christa had offered him the chalice that was herself, and he had taken it; and with it had come something that now bolstered him, that planted its feet between Danny and the multitude, folded its arms, and defied the condemnation. The old ways and the old Gods had been felled, but in Christa they lived still, and in Kevin they had taken root once again, lifted leaves to the sun, blossomed and endured even in the middle of a winter night.

Kevin lifted his head. "What do you mean, no one?" he said. "What about Father Paul?"

Danny did not respond.

"What about Benji?"

"He's probably got this too."

"What does he say?"

"He says he still loves me." Danny moistened his sore lips with more water. "He says that I gave him a lot of love, and he wants to give me as much of it back as he can."

"Isn't that something?"

"Hey, queers have to stick together."

"Would you say that to him?"

"You know what I mean."

"I don't think I do, Danny." Kevin kissed Danny's hand. "And what about me? I'm here. And I'm not here because I feel guilty, or because I'm trying to put some trip on you. It's been twenty years, and there's been a lot of bullshit gone down, but . . . I . . ." He struggled with words, struggled with the knowledge that, as the divine had spoken through Christa, now it had to speak through him.

But it was simple, really. Christa had already told him what to say, had, in fact, said the same thing to him, over and over again in a hundred different ways, finally speaking with her body when he refused to understand words.

"I love you, Danny."

Danny bent his head. Kevin felt the ice melting. Or maybe he was only hoping. Which was it? Which did he want it to be?

"I've heard that before." Danny was almost suspicious, as though unbelieving that anything at once so profound and so unconditional could be offered him. "You mean it? You know what it means to say that?"

"Yeah, I mean it. And what it means is that there's two of us now."

Danny shuddered for a moment and held himself stiffly until the seizure passed. AIDS was painful. "I'd like to believe that."

The *fail* on Kevin's wrist gleamed softly. "Remember when we were growing up?" he said. "Ma and da had those stupid parties where everyone would get drunk and talk about Ireland? They told us never to forget that we were Irish. But when they started putting strings on love, they missed the whole point." He lifted Danny's hand, still clasped in his own. "This is what it means to be Irish. This is what it's always meant."

Guilt was killing Danny as surely as was the disease, and Kevin could do little about that, for there were too many pointing fingers, too many words that could never be unsaid. But he could stand between Danny and those who pointed; and if he could not cure, he could at least comfort. There was still time for that.

He folded his dying brother in his arms.

CHAPTER
TWENTY-ONE

Though the loss of her students left Christa free to throw herself further into the world of rock and roll, she did so silently, without comment, her reticence masking both the pain of her loss and her hope for the future. But if she still concealed from her bandmates her reason for playing heavy metal, the overall mask she wore was thinner these days, the Gaeidil closer to the surface.

Truly, she realized, it could not be otherwise, for as she had led Devi into adulthood and Kevin into rebirth, so had she transformed herself. She had channeled divinity through her very being, and by doing so she had achieved the most profound goal of the *Cruitreacha*. A step had been taken, a door had been passed, and she who had once been a child, and then a woman, was now something that was a little of both, and yet neither.

Kevin's harp understood and recognized the change in her status, and while she worked to restore the old instrument—cleaning brass and repairing cracks and scraping away rot—she felt the trust that radiated from it: the instinctive response of a creature of art to a consummate artist.

Master.

Mortal instruments did not speak, but they had spirits, and the title the harp gave Christa was a sense of fullness near her heart and a glow in the wood beneath her hands that could not have been uncovered by sandpaper and steel wool, but only given freely by a harp to a master harper.

"Do you have a name, old one?" she whispered softly as she worked. But the harp made no response. It had been asleep for a long time. If it had ever had a name, it had forgotten what it was.

Toward afternoon, she heard her front door open.
"Kevin?"

"Yeah . . . it's me."

"I'm in the workroom." Shoving a strand of hair out of
her face with the back of a hand, she blinked at the
window. Cold gray weather, snow hissing against the
glass. How long had she been working? Without a constant stream of students to break up her day, the time
slid by unnoticed.

She heard Kevin rattle through the kitchen as he poured
himself a cup of coffee. He entered the workroom a
minute later. "How's it going?"

"Progress . . . that's about all I can say right now."

He shuffled to the workbench, peered at the harp.
"Do you think you can . . ." He pressed his lips together
as if thinking of something else. "Can you save it?"

"I can." She watched him nod slowly. He was as dear
to her as a child or a lover, for he had been both.
"You're upset."

"Benji called me this morning at the school. Danny's
getting worse."

"He won't come to Denver?"

"He says he wants to stay with Benji. He wants to die
at home. I can't blame him: they were happy together in
that apartment." He stared at the steam rising from his
coffee. "I couldn't do anything except hold him."

"That in itself is a great deal."

"Yeah, but I wanted to do more. I wanted to pull him
out of there, make him well, make him happy. But I
couldn't. I think that in some weird way he figures that
what's happening to him is just. He's wrong . . . he's just
wrong."

"But he knows he's loved now."

"Yeah." The snow that had caught in Kevin's hair was
melting now, dripping down his face, hiding his tears.
"Someday, though, I want to be able to help somebody.
I want to be like you, Chris."

She shook her head. "I couldn't have helped him either. Some things can be done, others can't."

"Then I want to know the difference."

"I think you do already."

He did not speak for some time. Finally: "Yeah. I
know."

*   *   *

Lisa checked her watch and crashed a cymbal with an angry flick of her wrist. "Forty-five minutes late. This is fucking ridiculous."

"Give her time," said Christa. She tried to occupy herself with her equipment, but she knew that the rest of the band was fuming.

"Look," the drummer persisted, "it's enough that we hear her mistakes, but if she starts flaking out on rehearsals, it'll get to the point where the audience hears it too."

"Give her time, Boo-boo."

"You've got to talk to her, Chris. I can't. I've tried. She just gets mad and tells me to shut the fuck up. I swear I'm gonna move out and find my own place. I can't take it."

Across the basement, Devi looked up. "Boo-boo's right, Chris." Her microphone caught a little of her voice and piped it through the monitors, spreading her sentiments, echoed and flanged, throughout the room. "We've had something pretty good going here, but Melinda's screwing it up. You need to talk to her. You're the leader."

"I thought we worked by consensus."

Monica burst out: "Oh, come on, Chris. You're the brains in this outfit. We wouldn't be playing if it wasn't for you."

Monica was right: the task rightly belonged to Christa. She had delayed this long because she had not wanted to admit that her unspoken and unrevealed plans were in jeopardy. Judith was possibly within reach, but Christa need a fully functioning band to win her. Melinda's problems hinted at the potential failure of the whole endeavor.

The bass player had become erratic and irresponsible, with violent mood shifts and bouts of unprovoked hostility. Perhaps more tellingly for Christa, she had terminated her harp lessons, a decision that had nothing to do with her teacher's tastes in music. Slowly, Melinda was closing herself off from her friends, rejecting the intimacy of the band and its music, dwelling more and more in a separate world of drugs, late-night rendezvous, and sex that bordered on sadism. If her insomnia had not returned, it was only because she was beating it down with pills.

"All right." Christa's voice was soft, almost drowned

in the hiss and whine of electronics that filled the basement. "I'll talk to her."

"Hey, anyone here?" came Melinda's voice from upstairs.

Devi leaned toward her microphone. "In the basement, Mel. Get your ass down here."

Melinda's playing was passable, but the rehearssal was tedious. Christa found it difficult to keep her mind on the music, and she sensed that the other women were only holding their anger in check because they were counting on their leader to handle the situation.

But the band was slipping away. No longer a cohesive unit, no longer sharing music as though it were the medium of a subtle lovemaking, Gossamer Axe was turning into an uneasy mix of hidden emotions, masks, and psychological games.

Monica's vocals were more raw than usual, and the tone of her voice made Christa wince. She was channeling her anger through her throat.

"Let's take that once again," said Christa when the song was finished. "I'd like a little more definition on your bass riff, Melinda."

"It sounds good enough for metal."

Christa took a deep breath. "Once more," she said. "Judas Priest is, if nothing else, precise. Please, Melinda. Try to stay with me."

"Okay. You say so."

With an effort, Christa pushed everyone through the practice, but the magic was not there. It was just a band rehearsal, no different from many she had had with Dark Power: something to be endured, like a hangover, or a drug overdose.

They were just finishing up, snapping off equipment and casing instruments, when Bill Sarah plunked down the stairs. "I let myself in, Christa," he apologized. "I hope it was all right."

Ceis would have warned her had a stranger intruded. Bill was a part of the band, and the harp knew that. "Fine, Bill."

Melinda eyed him suspiciously. "Something going on?"

"I'd like to talk with you all. Are you up for it?"

"Soon as my ears stop ringing," said Lisa. She slid her sticks into their case.

He waited until they had gathered in the living room. Christa handed him a cup of hot chocolate. "My, my," he said. "Chocolate. I can see there's a serious drug problem in this band." He did not notice that everyone's eyes flicked to Melinda. Neither did Melinda.

"Uh . . ." Lisa shifted on the sofa uneasily. "Yeah, sometimes we do a lot of . . . uh . . . coke, too. You know, the kind that comes in red cans."

It was a feeble attempt at humor, but it put Bill back onto his subject. "I want to talk about the band's future. It's fun to work with you, but I've got to mix a little business in here somewhere."

"So mix, Bill," said Devi.

"It's like this. You guys are doing real well here in Denver, but outside the metro area no one knows your name. Gossamer Axe? What's that? See what I'm saying?"

touring

Thank you, Ceis. I guessed. Christa blotted her forehead with the sleeve of her sweatshirt. "You want us to tour."

"You want to get anywhere, you're going to have to."

Silence. Bill cleared his throat.

"Listen," he said. "You're good. I've heard people comparing the Axe to Van Halen, and Christa to Eddie, Yngwie Malmsteen, and Gary Moore all rolled into one. You can definitely go places with this band. I'm asking you to untie my hands so that I can take you there. I'm talking exposure, I'm talking record contracts, I'm talking money."

Christa shook her head. Harper, guitarist: which did she want to be? She was not ready to make that decision.

"Yeah," said Lisa, "but we've been through this before. Last year I was on the road for more days than I really want to think about, and you know what I got out of it? My skin and my kit and five empty bottles of Rid. That's all."

"But—"

Melinda broke in: "This touring stuff is shit. If we're gonna make it, we can make it from Denver. We don't have to go on the road. We don't have to do anything."

Her tone was ugly, and Bill frowned. "What kind of fantasyland are you living in, lady?"

"I know what I'm doing."

Devi snorted under her breath.

"Hold," said Christa politely. "Please."

Melinda settled down, folded her arms, crossed her legs.

"I understand what you're saying, Bill," said Christa. "And I agree with you. But I've done some wandering myself, and I know that the comfort and the money are not good. This is our home, and we're not willing to give it up lightly."

"Tell you what, Bill," said Devi. Her head was up, and her eyes met Bill's. No more hiding for Devi. "Personally, I have no problems with, say, a weekend gig up in Casper or something like that. But if someone wants us to seriously tour, they're going to have to put some money up front. Enough to make it worth our while to give up everything for the road. They want us to trust them, they'll have to trust us."

Melinda sulked. "I still say it's shit."

Lisa gritted her teeth. "You want another manager, Mel?"

"Fuck off."

Lisa half rose from her chair, but Christa put her back with a glance. "Are you still willing to work with us, Bill? Given the restrictions?"

"Well . . ." He rubbed his forehead. "I'm a damned fool for doing business with people I actually like. Why can't you girls be the standard, unwashed metal band with delusions of grandeur? Then I could kick your cute little butts and bully you into doing what I want." He laughed, and there was no sting in his words. "But you're not." He threw up his hands. "Okay. Your ball." He rose, grabbed his coat, pulled out a notebook. "I'll just run through this to make sure. You're at Bonkers beginning Monday. Two weeks. Then I got you in at Journey North, and the Rock Exchange after that. Good money. They're all fighting for a chance to book the Axe. I'm trying for a concert at the Rainbow with Allencrain: remember me in your prayers." He stuffed the notebook back into his pocket. "I'm out of here."

The front door closed behind him. "Think he's pissed off?" said Lisa.

"Disappointed, more likely," said Christa.

Melinda was twitching in her seat. "Good riddance."

Christa's temper slipped. "Melinda, what in the name
of the Goddess is going on?"

"He's taking twenty-five fucking percent of our earn-
ings to do something that we can do ourselves."

"Come on," said Lisa. "We'd be playing Herman's
Hideaway without Bill."

"No we wouldn't. We got into InsideOut without him.
It's all connections, and I've got them. Record contracts
are connections, and I'm getting them. We can go anywhere we want, once we know the right people."

Devi had been listening, and the wall had risen behind
her black eyes. "Mel, this sounds just like Tom Delany's
spiel—"

Melinda was on her feet in an instant, screaming: *Don't
give me shit about Tom Delany.*"

In the silence left behind by her words, Christa could
hear the bare branches of the trees creaking and rustling.
A clump of snow fell to the ground with a soft thud.
"Let's call it for the day," she said softly. "We'll get
together again tomorrow. I think we can have the new
songs down by Monday." Almost as an afterthought, she
added: "Could I talk to you for a minute, Melinda?"

The others left, car doors slamming and engines crank-
ing in the cold for a few extra seconds before they caught.
Melinda glowered on the sofa.

"Can I ask you about the drugs, Melinda?" Christa
kept her voice gentle.

In spite of her agitation, Melinda's eyes were dull,
vacant. "Nothing much to say, is there?"

"That's up to you."

Melinda shrugged. "I'm just trying to do you guys a
favor, and you all come crawling down my throat."

She had said the same thing before: *I'm doing this for
you.* "How is getting stoned going to help us?" asked
Christa.

"I can't talk about it. Just leave it to me."

"Melinda, you're getting . . ." Christa struggled with
an unfamiliar idiom. ". . . totally . . . fucked up with this
stuff. It's not helping us. It's hurting the whole band, it
is."

Melinda lifted her head defiantly. "Back in September,
you said you didn't know a thing about the rock-and-roll
business, and I pushed you into starting this band. Now

you turn around and start telling me what to do. Just
because you can play a goddam guitar don't mean diddly.
You've got to get the breaks. Lemme handle things."

In her mind, Christa was confronting an arrogant Orfide
with the present Gossamer Axe. The bard would have
every reason to be scornful. *Judith!* "I'm going to leave
that up to Bill. Our job is to make music."

"Our job is to make money."

"Melinda!"

"Look, Crissy, you can play Polly Purebred all you
want as long as you're fooling around with harps, but
when you start playing with the big boys, you're going to
get eaten alive unless you're real clear about what you
want. I want bucks. I want to be up on stage someday
with a million fans reaching out to me. You got it?"

Christa felt cold. Her mouth was dry, and she could
barely form words. "I do indeed, Melinda."

"You can play with Bill if you want. Just let me handle
things my own way." She laughed, stood up, punched
Christa lightly on the shoulder. "Hey, one day you'll
thank me."

Christa bowed her head. "Surely . . ."

Melinda went out to her car, and Christa floundered in
a wash of horror. Her last chance for Judith was being
destroyed by Melinda's fantasies.

Almost staggering, she made her way to the kitchen.
The pale yellow walls seemed harsh and glaring as she
heated milk. "Ceis," she said, "it might well be the two
of us again this Midsummer."

The harp did not reply. Christa heard a footstep in the
hall. Monica. "Sorry," said the singer. "I hit the bathroom and you two were already going at it when I was
done. So I stayed where I was."

Christa leaned on the counter. "It didn't sound good,
did it?"

"Aw, Chris . . ." Monica came up, put her arms around
Christa. "This is rock and roll. It happens all the time.
People get crazy and go off the deep end. If it's not
drugs, it's boyfriends; if it's not boyfriends, it's motorcy-
cle accidents or something. There are other bass players
in Denver."

"There isn't time."

"What are we on? A schedule?"

Christa was crying. "Indeed, Monica. We're on a schedule. I've been waiting for two centuries, and I'm not letting this chance go by."

Monica looked incredulous. "Two—"

"Just believe me. There isn't time, and I've given up too much to go back." She recalled her words to Kevin: *Some things can be done, others can't.*

Snow thudded again outside, but this time it sounded different.

Ron

Monica gasped. "Who said that?"

Christa stared at Ceis through the open door to her studio. Monica? "A friend," she said, and she turned around just in time to see Ron's face, white and unshaven, pressed against the kitchen window.

Monica screamed. Christa threw open the back door and hit the snow running, but her foot found a patch of ice and she went down hard.

Ron was already gone. "You fucking dyke!" he shouted from the street. "Keep your lousy hands off my woman!"

If Christa had had any breath left, she would have shouted in reply, the Gaeidelg words rising up in a swift wave of angry eloquence. But she could only lie in the snow, fighting with an outraged diaphragm, as Ron drove away.

Monica helped her into the house, sat her down, and locked the doors. Christa's breath came back eventually, and she sipped at the warm milk that Monica put into her hands.

"Is this happening often?" she said when she could speak.

The room was warm, but Monica shivered. "Often enough. I think he fucks himself up with whatever his dealer has on sale, and then he comes looking for me." Turning away, she shoved her hands in her pockets. "You see in the paper about that woman who got shot by her husband?"

"I did."

"She left him, and he killed her. I'm wondering . . . I'm wondering if that's going to happen to me. Ron's crazy."

"Do you want to call the police?"

"I already called them. They took down my name, his

name, and that was it. Don't call us, we'll call you." Her dark skin was gray when she turned back. "So when do I get my bullet?"

Christa got to her feet, took Monica into her arms. "Never," she said. There was too much going on: pressure from Bill, idiocy from Melinda, anger from the rest of the band. And now Ron. "I swear it. It can't happen."

Monica clung to Christa like a frightened child. "I trust you, Chris. I hope to God you're right."

It was honest fear. Christa held her. "Do you want to stay the night?"

Monica's face was buried in Christa's shoulder. "Yeah. I need it." She looked up, her mouth working, her brown eyes vulnerable. "And . . . I think maybe you need it, too."

CHAPTER
TWENTY-TWO

The telephone dragged Christa up from a dead sleep that was the product of late nights and growing troubles. The clock told her that it was early afternoon. The continued ringing told her that she had forgotten to switch on her answering machine.

Day-old mascara stung her eyes as she pushed herself up and grabbed the receiver. *"Is Chairiste."*

"Christa?" Roger Best's voice.

She realized that her tongue had slipped. She had been dreaming of Eriu again. "Hello, Roger."

"Whew, you had me confused for a second. You ready to rock out with your new guitar?"

"It's ready?"

"I said I'd have it for the Equinox, and the wife says it's that. She's the astrology expert, so it must be ready."

The Equinox already. She had been so wrapped up in the band that the calendar was getting away from her.

"Come on down," he said. "I'll be here."

Thirty minutes later, showered and dressed, she was pulling into a parking space in front of Best's Guitar Laboratory. The cold air froze the damp ends of her hair when she left her car, and they clicked together like beads as she opened the door to the shop.

Roger was waiting for her, and he led her into the back room. On a table covered with a clean piece of dark blue carpeting lay her guitar, glistening as though with birth-waters.

"I thought about satin-finishing it," he said. "But I decided that it needed to shine."

Graceful and rugged both, the guitar was shaped as though by wind and water, and the grain of the woods gave a suggestion of Celtic knotwork that was all the more distinctive because it was present by nature and not by artifice. Roger had worked the willow wood of her harp into the body, neck, and headstock, and he had dyed it in shades of brown and green and amber, fitting the pieces together in such a way that the instrument would not have seemed out of place in a sacred grove, standing among its kindred, as venerable and as proud as any sunlit oak.

Every bit of her old harp had been used. Not a scrap remained. Even the bronze tuning pins had become a part of Roger's work.

Christa bent over the guitar. "Saille?"

"She's there, Christa," said Roger. "She's asleep, I think."

"It's right you are, Roger. I should have expected it." Still, she was a little disappointed that her old harp did not respond. Melinda was sliding into a pit, Monica lived in constant terror, the band was beginning to show signs of fragmentation, and her life as a harper was drawing to an end. If ever she needed the reassurance of old friends and of the familiar, it was now.

"There's an amp in the corner. Go ahead and crank it." Roger headed for the door. "I need to watch the counter."

She knew that he needed to do no such thing, but she appreciated the lie that allowed her to be alone with the guitar. "My thanks, Roger."

"Hey, anytime. I've heard you play. I'm glad you're going to use the best." He winked at his own pun.

Reverently, she put her hand to the guitar. Roger had left a strap on the table for her, and when she attached it and slung the instrument from her shoulder, she found that the neck was as she had wanted it, and the balance was perfect. Everything about it spoke eloquently of the fact that it had been made for her, not only in material and specification, but also in intent and in feeling.

The amplifier was warmed up for her, and she plugged in knowing that, up front, Roger was listening to see what the artist made of his handiwork. She heard the bell over the front door tinkle faintly, heard voices. She would have an audience.

Well, that was nothing unusual. These days, Christa Cruitaire always seemed to have an audience when she held a guitar in her hands. Much more audience than when she played harps.

The speaker had a chance to hiss only for a moment before she smacked out a power chord, held it, dropped its pitch with the tremolo bar, raised it until it shrieked. The back room shuddered with the wave of sound, but she was already shifting to the cascades of arpeggios and the double-stopped polyphony that had become her signature. The notes rippled out of the amplifier, washed through the room like molten metal, hung in the air like stars.

At first, she fumbled with the array of knobs that Roger had given her, but as the minutes passed, she learned their use and found that she had absolute control over the slightest tonal coloration. Alternately chopping out chordal riffs and weaving intricate and limpid melodies, she pressed power through the guitar, sent a grateful blessing throughout the shop and beyond.

Saille was not yet awake, perhaps, but it was certainly alive; and, finding no limits to its abilities, no niggling constraints to her technique, Christa allowed herself the pleasure of simply making music for a time, a blessing in itself. Too many rehearsals and performances had become trials of patience, too many band meetings had turned into shouting matches. Here was a rest, a haven from the strife; and into her music she put a memory of simpler times, when two women could sleep in one another's arms without fear and wake to a world washed clean by their love.

But, like a night of lovemaking, it had to end eventually. Her final arpeggio climbed up the neck, sweetening as it did so, until the last note rang out, shimmering: the gracious smile of a Goddess.

Her eyes were closed, but she heard applause. Roger was standing in the doorway, accompanied by a number of young men in ragged jeans and wild hair. She recognized one of them as Tony, the guitarist who had been in the shop when she had come to buy stain for a harp. Ages ago.

"It's beautiful, Roger," she said. "It's everything I imagined it could be."

And, driving home, the cased instrument leaning against the seat beside her, she went over what she had played, considered what might happen if the guitar awoke. She was not at present thinking of Judith or of Orfide. Instead, she was mulling over a more pressing and urgent problem, one that demanded a solution well before the Solstice.

Waiting at a stoplight, she rested her hand on the case. *Can you help me save Melinda?*

But the guitar was silent, sleeping in its dreams of potential and futurity.

Performance schedules were unaffected by the old Celtic holydays, and Gossamer Axe played that evening to a Saturday-night crowd eager to listen and to dance. But the absence of the customary rite for the Equinox nagged at Christa, and her discomfort was exacerbated by Melinda's poor playing and by the raging anger of the band. Even Monica, who was more concerned these days with Ron's possible unseen presence, was glaring at the bass player.

Melinda could not help but notice. Her gaze was fixed, sad, but at the same time angry and resentful: as torn and as miserable as Christa's.

There seemed to be little that Christa could do. The new guitar was responding well, but without an alert instrument, she did not wish to risk working magic on someone who—even though drug abuse had utterly changed her personality—was still dear to her.

But she was not sure that she would have been able to accomplish anything even had the guitar awakened in her hands that very moment. Melinda had made her choices, and nothing about her behavior indicated that she wanted to change. Ethically, even if Christa could indeed cure Melinda against her wishes, which was unlikely, she had no right to interfere with her free will.

Some things can be done, others can't.

Bitterly, she snapped her amplifier to standby at the end of the set as Melinda jumped down to the dance floor and pushed her way toward the back of the club. What was it this time? A couple shots of Jack Daniels? Or maybe a quick fix in the ladies' room, match and spoon keeping her company in the bare white stall.

Monica threw an arm about her. "Your ghost isn't around, Chris, so Boo-boo's going to keep me company. I'll be okay."

Christa gave her a quick hug. "Are you sure?"

"Yeah. She pumps iron, remember?"

Christa took her time doffing her guitar and setting it down. She felt tired, drained. The Equinox. She should have been at home, harping; but instead she was here, nursing a dying band.

Devi caught her eye, waved, pointed at the new guitar. *Nice axe,* she mouthed.

Christa smiled in return and descended to the dance floor with an air of tired resignation. Kevin was waiting for her at a dark table, hunched over a beer. He did not look up when she sat down.

Something had happened. He was crying. "Kevin?"

"I got a call from Benji just before I left the school. Danny . . ." His voice broke, but he had said everything.

"He . . . he went on ahead, didn't he?"

Kevin nodded. "I wanted to be up there with him, but Benji said he got real bad real fast."

The lights were low, and few patrons noticed as she held him while he wept.

"I wanted to help him."

"You did. As much as anyone could."

"It wasn't enough."

"He died loved, Kevin. He died in the arms of his lover. Can anyone ask for more?"

Kevin's sobs quieted after a time, but his eyes were red and sad, and the tears still glistened on his cheeks. "There's a bunch of stuff I'd like to make up to him. About twenty years' worth. You think I'll ever have the chance?"

"You'll see him in the Summerland, Kevin. And if you both think well of it, you can be born again together."

A trace of a smile found its way to his face. "I'd like that."

Lisa and Monica came by, tapped Christa on the shoulder. "We're on."

Kevin hid his tears so that they would not notice. Christa kissed him before she left. "Tonight, my big solo is for Danny."

Melinda's playing was worse during the second set. Even the patrons were noticing. Christa saw one or two dancers stop, look at the band, shake their heads. This was the wonderful Gossamer Axe?

Melinda stared straight ahead, pumping out notes that were but vaguely on time. Christa could only salvage the set by pulling together with Devi and Lisa, compensating for Melinda's inaccuracies by alternately overpowering her and following her lead. It was grueling, exhausting work, and though she was not overfond of large-scale, showy solos, Christa began hers that night with a sigh of relief. She would be the only one playing. She would have complete control. She could say what she wanted, however she wanted.

She swung into the opening licks, tossing off polyphony without thinking. Out of the corner of her eye she saw Lisa shake her fist at Melinda and throw her sticks on the floor. The drummer stalked away. Melinda vanished into the shadows.

Alone on stage, Christa forced herself to nod at the audience. Smiles were beyond her. She struck and bent a high note, held it, let it shriek as she went to a microphone. "A friend of mine lost a brother tonight," she said. "This is for Danny."

And she was off again, working her way through an intricate set of variations on the lament she had once played for Randy Rhoads. Her fingers blurred into rapid scales and ornaments, froze in place as she let the guitar cry out with grief. For Danny.

Kevin needed help too, however. And so did Melinda. And Monica. And, for that matter, Christa herself. As she wrenched her music out of the guitar, therefore, she began to add other themes, other scales and tonalities. The Equinox had arrived, bringing with it the promise of Spring, and she turned to it and its message, embraced it, celebrated its mystery with music from an electric guitar and a Laney stack driven to peak. Shouting out the mystery of the new season, she cast it throughout the club; and its benison enfolded her listeners like broad wings of solace.

Sensing a climax approaching, the other women returned to the stage. Melinda wobbled as she climbed the stairs, nearly toppled, but Christa's music held her, helped her up, put her bass on her shoulder.

Christa could not change Melinda, but she could probe; and gently, reverently, she used the last of her solo to search through the wreckage of her friend, looking for something that might show her that the Melinda she had known was not forever beyond her reach.

Acres of night, wastelands of despair and resignation. Christa pushed the music further, seeking Melinda, feeling with her own soul the sadness and the entrapment until she discovered, buried deep, a single spark of longing for another life. Mired in helplessness and fear, it was flickering, almost dying, but it was still there.

With a murmur of gratitude to the Patroness of harpers—whatever instrument they played—Christa went again to the microphone. "Okay, everyone. 'Break Down the Walls.' Stone Fury." She was changing the order of the songlist, but she started the opening riff and gestured for the others to follow. "Here we go."

Song or prayer: Which was it? Which did she want it to be?

Dawn hung in the air like an odor when Christa left the club. On the far side of the parking lot, Melinda was already pulling out, her Mustang spilling blue smoke to mingle with flecks of falling snow. Christa sprinted to her wagon and shoved her guitar cases into the back seat. Lisa had said that Melinda apparently spent her weekends with the man who was feeding her drugs. Christa intended to find out who he was.

There was little traffic on the gray streets save for the sanding trucks and the plows. Christa stayed far behind Melinda, hiding in the glare of her headlights, but Melinda seemed more intent on her destination than on what was behind her. Christa might have tailgated her without being detected.

Down University, out Orchard. Melinda led her into a neighborhood of expensive houses with yards that, even in the winter, were neatly groomed. As turn led to turn, Christa began to suspect Melinda's destination, and she was not at all surprised when the bassist stopped in front of the house in which Gossamer Axe had once signed a contract for a week at InsideOut. They had drunk champagne in celebration: their first gig as a new band.

The streets were cold and slick. Christa shifted to four-wheel drive as she drove home, wondering what she should tell the others.

Ceis was waiting for her when she opened the door, and it greeted her like the old friend it had become. *blessings*

"Blessings, Ceis."

Equinox

"Indeed." She laughed, but fatigue and strain made her voice brittle. "I'll shower and robe, and we can sit together for a while."

sleep There was compassion in the harp's tone. Christa had heard it before, but its presence always surprised her. The Sidh did not know compassion.

"I'll be all right," she said. "You made me eighteen. I should be able to go one night without sleep."

She thought for a moment of Melinda. How did she sleep tonight? What were her dreams like?

She put a hand to her face. Her eyes ached.

sadness

Christa nodded. "It's Melinda I'm thinking of, Ceis. She's in a bad way. I . . . I don't know how to help her."

music

Music and magic were the same thing for the harp. It knew no other way. Christa left her guitars in the living room and went into her studio. Ceis gleamed in jewel shades of amethyst and ruby, glinted with gold. "I don't have the power, old friend," she said. "The new guitar commands energy, but it's still asleep. You have the ability, but I'd need the volume of rock and roll to reach her."

The harp pondered. Christa went upstairs to strip off the glitter of heavy metal, to become, only again, the Gaeidil, the harper of Corca Duibne. She donned her robe facing the mirror, as though she needed the visual reassurance that Chairiste Ní Cummen had returned.

Dawn was growing rapidly when she sat down with Ceis, and the harp was a welcome presence on her lap. Seated in her studio with the scent of incense in the air, Christa could almost have believed that her life had returned to a time when harp students and ancient music had been her main concerns.

She sighed. Those days were far gone.

sleep

"I will, Ceis. I've already celebrated a little. I played some of the old hymns during my solo."

The harp was silent for a time. More and more, its place had been taken by patently new instruments, and now she was letting Roger Best's guitar usurp its duties in the Mysteries. She wondered if she had hurt its feelings.

"I'm sorry, Ceis," she said. "I needed the help. Danny died this afternoon. And Melinda's dying. Everything seems to be taking me further away from Judith. I don't know if I'll have a band come Midsummer. I don't know if I'll have anything. And it's my last chance."

She felt the harp struggling—an inner turmoil that almost thrummed the strings.

"Ceis?"

transfer The word came with an effort. Ceis seemed to be alive under her hands, rippling as though with ligneous muscles.

"Transfer? Transfer what?"

Again, a hesitation. *me*

"To . . . to what, old friend?"

The harp struggled even more. *guitar*

At first she did not comprehend the enormity of what Ceis was offering. But then she understood, and then she wept. Pressing her face to the wood, she thanked the immortal intelligence that was willing to give everything, even itself, to help her.

"Are you sure, Ceis?" She choked out the words. "That would indeed be the answer, but are you very sure?"

And for the first time in its existence, Ceis managed to verbalize itself in a full sentence that, although but a whisper in her mind, rang out as though the harp had been sounded from one end of its compass to the other.

I love you, Chairiste

CHAPTER
TWENTY-THREE

"That's the problem, Jessica," said Dennis. "The only well-respected source we've got in Denver is Carl Taylor, and he's not talking. I had a devil of a time just getting a copy of the demo out of him."

Jessica started on her third cup of coffee that morning. The brackish fluid smacked of an unscrubbed pot, but she hardly noticed. "What's in it for him?"

"He's screwing one of the girls in the band."

"So, out of gratitude, he keeps her in two-bit bars?"

Dennis pulled a chair up to her desk, sat, hooked one leg over its arm. "I've been skiing in Colorado for a few years, and Carl's always been there. He likes his women compliant, and he always has a hard time finding one who'll do what he wants. When he gets someone, he keeps her as long as he can."

"What does he do?"

Dennis shifted uncomfortably. "Well . . . he's a bit of a dealer."

"Is it even worthwhile to push this with Harry, then?" Jessica sipped at the coffee, became aware of its flavor, shoved it away. "If we finally get him to take the time and listen to the demo, and the band turns out to be a bunch of dopers, we've got nothing."

"Well . . . we'd have an expensive contract."

"And maybe a record, and maybe not."

"And maybe not." Dennis set fire to a cigarette. "But once you get the girl away from Carl, she'll probably do all right. A lot of metal bands are coming out against pharmaceuticals these days. Some counseling and a move to L.A. might do the trick."

Jessica picked up a cassette that lay on the corner of her desk. On the red label, neatly lettered in dot-matrix print, was the legend:

GOSSAMER AXE
Christa Cruitaire, Melinda Moore, Lisa Donnatelli, Devica Anderson, Monica Sanchez

For months now, the music she had heard at the Denver club had been haunting her, intruding into her dreams with unlooked-for images, into her voice with snatches of melody she eventually realized had come from a Gossamer Axe original, into her thoughts with a paradoxical sense of peace and fulfillment.

Ever since she had gotten possession of the demo tape, she had been shoving it under the nose of the head of Artists and Repertoire. And he had been patiently shoving it back at her. Harry Veltmann was not interested in titty bands—he had genuine hits to coax into existence—and nothing Jessica or Dennis had said had convinced him that the only factors that Gossamer Axe had in common with a titty band were instruments and reproductive plumbing.

"I want this band as much as you do, Jess," Dennis said. "But I can understand Harry, too. There's been a big crunch in the market. We've got to be real careful about where we put our money.

"You sound like one of those assholes down in accounting."

He thought, blew smoke at the ceiling. "Goddam. I do."

Still holding the cassette, Jessica stood up and went to the floor-to-ceiling window. Outside, Hollywood stretched off south and east, trickling gradually into the cluttered Los Angeles skyline. Below, the bestarred streets were dusty with age, shabby with the refuse of past wealth, trodden upon by the well-dressed and the derelict.

"The problem is," Dennis continued behind her, "we've cut back so much that we're depending too heavily on the respected-source rule. A&R isn't trusting A&R anymore. And Carl's got the Axe bottled up in Denver."

"What about Bill Sarah?"

"He's their manager. Of course he's going to say they're great."

"Kevin Larkin?"

"Dating the guitarist."

The music, angry and yet haunting, white-hot and yet flavored with something warmer than Jessica had ever heard from a metal band, drifted in the back of her mind. She had only heard it once, and it had become a part of her. Only once.

"Hang on," she said.

"Huh?"

"Let's pull a fast one." She turned around from the window, held up the cassette. "Let's run off a copy of this, stick on a label that just says *see Jessica and Dennis* or something stupid like that, and leave it on Harry's desk. He's bound to plug it into his deck eventually."

"Yeah, but what will that do?"

"Think back to when you first heard the Axe."

He thought, started to laugh. "Far fucking out."

Devi stood amid her equipment in Christa's basement, programming, discarding, altering the sounds she used during performances. Christa was pushing her guitar, pushing the band, attempting emotions and expressions that were usually ignored in heavy metal; and Devi felt compelled to match her, emotion for emotion, energy for energy. Struggling with sounds that began only as unheard ideas, she shifted waveforms, altered decay and attack rates, searched for and slowly found what she needed, what Christa needed.

She straightened up from her microcomputer and squinted with bleary eyes at her watch. Nearly eleven. It was a weeknight, and Christa's neighbors would be trying to get to sleep. She would have to finish up soon.

The upstairs door opened. "Devi? Do you want some coffee?"

"No thanks, Chris. I'm going to go home and crash in a few. Wait'll you hear this stuff tomorrow night at the club."

"It's good, then?"

"I think so."

She heard the warmth in Christa's voice. "Then it must be, indeed."

Since Christmas Day, when the harper had offered her a new life in the form of a cup of cider, Devi's respect for her, already great, had been growing. Christa had offered a hand and had pulled her out of the whirling montage of childhood abuse and bitter images, and it no longer mattered to Devi that what the guitarist had done was founded upon so ephemeral a rock as magic. The results were concrete enough: no nightmares disturbed her sleep now, and with a feeling of strength she went about her work, both at the music store and on stage.

Magic? Perhaps the magic was all in her head, a complex constellation of trust, belief, and desire. But then, that was perfectly all right with Devi, since her memories were all in her head, too, along with (she assumed) the temporary and unconfirmable thinnings of reality she had witnessed when Christa had played.

She changed disks in the computer and called up a set of parameters that she had, long ago, memorized. In the late '60s, the Doors had needed four musicians to perform "Light My Fire." Twenty years later, Devi could control the necessary instrumental forces from two keyboards.

Even after two decades, she still returned to the song, for to her it represented escape and freedom. She had sought solace in the organ solo when she was nine. Now she came back to it for relaxation, for the savoring of the transformation that allowed her to look back at the nine-year-old girl who was Devi and reassure her that everything would, in the end, be all right.

The computer sent exact duplicates of John Densmore's drums and Robby Krieger's guitar pouring out of the PA; and with a synthesizer patch that was a perfect clone of Ray Manzarek's dispassionate organ, Devi allowed herself the joy of escaping once again into the land she had discovered when she was nine. She might have been listening to the song in her parents' house, the big Zenith Radio sitting on the kitchen counter, its tubes—remnants of a dying technology for which Devi now had no use—glowing red and flickering blue. The sun-bleached curtains fluttered above the kitchen sink; and the plastic fruit in the bowl was frosted with the grease of too many hastily fried hamburgers.

But the memories were suddenly a little too real. Devi's hands moved of their own, recreating the music she had heard, but her thoughts took a disturbing turn. Her father stood before her again. "Devica . . ."

This time, however, Devi stood beside herself and took her own chubby hand. "Go away."

"Don't talk to me like that, Devica. I'm your father."

"You're a fucking pervert," she snapped. "Get away from me or I'll fix you good.

Instinctively, she was altering notes in the organ solo—prolonging dissonances, swelling volume, and heating up overtones more than the '60s had ever heard. The song was "Light My Fire," but the keyboardist was Devi Anderson of Gossamer Axe.

Her father stepped forward, tall—still taller than she, even though she was grown—reaching.

A fullness rose up within her, and she stomped on the volume pedal and smashed a wave of sound through the basement. Her father's outstretched hand turned abruptly into a charred ruin: shreds of flesh hanging in black tangles, bones splintered and seared.

Christa was calling. "Devi!"

With an effort, Devi pulled away from the keyboard and killed the programs. The speakers fell into silence. Christa's steps on the stairs sounded unnaturally distinct. "Are you—" Christa stopped at the bottom of the flight.

The air in the basement was strangely warm. Devi looked at the far wall, rubbed her eyes, looked again. In an area about the size of a man, the carpet that covered the sheetrock had been burnt black.

Christa reached out, touched the burn, drew her hand back quickly. "Your father?" she asked quietly.

"Yeah . . . I . . ." Devi tottered out from behind the synths, joined her at the burn. It radiated heat like a furnace. "How . . .?"

"I told you about magic once. You're a musician. You don't understand it logically, but your intuition knows how it works."

"*I* did this?" Thinking back, Devi recalled the rush of power that had enveloped her. Rage, wrath, righteous anger . . . all had blended together in the music, and she had lashed out at her father with the only weapon she had. "I . . ."

"Now you know why the Axe sounds like it does."

"Magic?"

"Indeed."

The convenient pigeonhole into which Devi had thrust the idea burst apart. "But that doesn't make any sense."

"It doesn't have to make sense," said Christa quietly. "Gossamer Axe doesn't make sense. For that matter, music doesn't make sense."

Years of habitual self-control stifled Devi's shakes, and
Christa took her upstairs and poured her a cup of strong
mead that moistened her lips and glowed at the back of
her throat like an old friendship. She coughed. "Okay,
Chris. Level with me. What's going on?"

Christa sat back in a kitchen chair, unconsciously biting at her lip. Her red hair, spiked and backcombed in
deference to rock and roll, seemed out of place now.
Devi had a sudden intuition that Christa was old. Very
old. Older than she really wanted to think about.

" 'Tis real, Devi. What I did last Christmas and what
you did just now are a part of the same thing. You can
use your mind to work magic, but you can amplify that
power with music."

Only the fact that she had learned to trust Christa kept
Devi from pushing back her hair and running for the
front door. "That's what you do, right?"

"It is."

"And . . ." Devi did not want to ask, but she was
proud: she wanted to be a part of Christa's work—not in
ignorance, but with full knowledge. "And the band . . .
something's going on there, too, right?"

Christa was looking past Devi. Into the future? Into
the past? "I'm going to need your help in a battle."

"Battle?"

"Of magic. Of music. First for Melinda—because I
need her, because I love her—and then . . . for someone
else I love."

Devi sat, unmoving. The mead burned in her stomach.
"Chris . . ." Christa had given her everything. Even, in-
directly, this new-found power. She set the mead aside.
"You let me know what you need, whenever," she said.
"You were here for me; I'm here for you."

"You're sure?"

Devi's certainly was as warm as the mead she had
drunk. "Yeah, I'm sure. Goddam, lady, you scare the
piss out of me, but I'm sure."

"Fire her, Chris."

Bill's voice was flat, definite, uncompromising. Christa
fought the impulse to curse him in Gaeidelg and hang up.
She was holding the band together in a net of spiderweb,
and he insisted on throwing his whole weight into the
meshes. "I will not."

"Chris, you've got to understand: things like this happen. You've got to replace Melinda. I saw the show last night, and she's killing you. And now you tell me that you don't even know where she lives anymore. . . ."

She passed a hand over her face. In fact, she knew quite well where Melinda had gone when she had moved out of the apartment she had been sharing with Lisa. But she would not tell Bill. "She comes to rehearsals," she said.

"Then what the hell are you doing with her?" He was angry. "You can't possibly be practicing."

"Give me time."

"She not worth it, Chris. Dump her. I know a number of female bass players, and any one of them would die for a chance to work with you."

But Melinda was family. Melinda was a friend. "Give me time."

"Dammit, Chris—"

"Give *her* time. By all the Gods, Bill, if you want to turn white-livered and run when the band's having some problems, go right ahead. But I'm seeing it through. The Axe played the way it did because we stuck together. Do you want to destroy that?"

Silence. When Bill spoke again, his tone was conciliatory. "I'm afraid that Melinda's already destroyed it."

"That's a possibility. Give me some time. Cut back on our bookings if you want, but just give me some time."

He was fighting his instincts, she knew. "How much time do you need?"

"Until Beltaine."

"Until what?"

"Give me until the first of May. That's . . ." She flipped the page of the wall calendar. "That's a Friday. Get us something for that weekened, starting that night. I promise you people won't forget the show."

He said nothing for a moment. Christa heard papers being shuffled.

"Bill?"

"I got a call from InsideOut," he said. "Carl Taylor wants you."

Christa smiled grimly at the irony and wondered what price Melinda had paid for the request. "That will do very well."

"You . . ." he sighed. "You won't let me down, will you?"

"On my word as a harper, Bill."

"You know, I believe you?"

She said good-bye and hung up feeling drained. For magic of the magnitude necessary to transfer Ceis into the body of the new guitar, she had to wait until Beltaine, the seam between the great seasons of winter and summer. But until then she had to hold the band together, and that was turning into a complicated proposition indeed. Devi seemed willing to support Christa's decisions; but Lisa, faced with a defecting roommate and a friendship gone sour, was at the point of leaving.

Christa spent the next several days talking to the drummer, both on the phone and over lunch, convincing her to postpone any final decisions about the band until after the first of May.

Lisa was depressed. "It just bums the shit out of me, Chris," she said. "This is the same kind of stuff I went through up in Montana. Now that Mel's gone and shacked up with whoever, I just feel like running away. You know she lost her job, too?"

Christa sighed, stared at her plate, shoved peas around aimlessly. "I did not."

"It's all going to hell, and I feel lousy because I can't do anything about it. My grandma said that magic would save my ass someday. Well, I'll tell you: I sure could use some magic right now."

"I could too," said Christa. She thought of Ceis and the task ahead of her. Ceis was saying nothing about the May ritual. Perhaps it was afraid. Christa could not fault the harp: she also was afraid. "Do you want to leave?" she said softly.

Lisa fidgeted with her bright orange work-vest. Aside from bursts of Italian temper, she was usually reticent, unwilling to verbalize conflicts or doubts. "That's just it. I want to stay. But I want to do something about Mel, too. She's a friend . . . and she's . . . just ripping me up . . ." She wiped her mouth with her napkin, swiped at her eyes while she did.

"Can you give me a few weeks?" said Christa. "I've a plan, but I'll need some time. We have a gig May first at InsideOut. My solo during the second set will become

rather intense. It might heal Melinda. Will you stay with
me and help?"

Lisa frowned. "What are you talking about?"

"Magic."

The drummer chewed over the word for a time. "Yeah
. . . I had a feeling that was it," she said slowly. "You've
been doing a lot of stuff that I haven't understood, but I
think you just explained it all." She considered, then
nodded. "Okay. Do your stuff, Chris. I'll be there. I sure
hope it works."

The knot in Christa's stomach loosened a little, and
she hugged Lisa as they parted at the restaurant door.
"Thanks, Boo-boo."

But that night, the phone rang. Monica. "He's back
again, Chris." She sounded genuinely frightened.

"What happened?"

"Nothing. It's just that . . . well, I've moved three
times now, and I thought I'd finally lost him. But he was
hanging around my door when I got home from work
today. The cops say they can't bust him unless he actually
does something that violates the restraining order. I don't
think they take me seriously."

The worry was draining Christa, but she had to hold
the band together. Three weeks to Beltaine, and then,
maybe . . .

"Do you think Boo-boo would let me move in with
her?" Monica said. "I'd feel safer that way. I mean . . .
Melinda's gone, and she could probably use some help
with the rent."

But that would make Melinda's defection too final,
and Christa wanted to leave the door open for her return. "How about . . ." She looked at Ceis, at the kitchen.
She had been living alone for two centuries, and the idea
that thrust itself upon her was an uncomfortable one.
How much did she have to give up?

Over the last nine months, she had asked herself the
same question about many parts of her life—her music,
her instrument, the persona with which she met the
world—and the same answer had struck her in the face:
Judith had given up her singing. Was there any alteration
at which Christa could justifiably balk?

"Why don't you come live with me?" she said to Monica. "My house is large, and you've slept here before."

Monica hesitated. "You're sure, Chris? I . . . I don't want to be any trouble. And you've got that ghost you told me about."

Christa was, in fact, not sure at all. "I'm quite sure. And Ceis is a friend. You can trust Ceis as you trust me."

Monica dithered for a moment more before she accepted. "Aw . . . shit, Chris. You're fantastic. Thanks. I haven't been sleeping, and—"

"Gather up your things, Monica. I'll come help you with the station wagon. You're moving tonight."

By midnight, most of Monica's possessions were in Christa's house. Much was still packed in cardboard boxes in the middle of the living room, but Monica had put enough necessities away in the spare bedroom that she could ready herself for work in the morning. Still a little embarrassed by her sudden intrusion, she joined Christa at the kitchen table for hot chocolate before bed.

"When I showed up on your doorstep last October," she said, "I didn't think it would come to this."

Christa shrugged inside her bathrobe. "I can't but say that I'm surprised. You didn't seem to like me when we first met."

"I was all hung up on—" Monica broke off, unwilling to say the name. "I was a kid. I didn't know what the hell I was doing. I still don't." She laughed, but tears still threatened to well up in her eyes. Abruptly, she looked around as though fearful of seeing Ron's face against the window. "Is Ceis on guard?"

"Fear not. Ceis is watching."

peace

The harp's voice was reassuring, like a kindly pat on the shoulder. "Rock and roll first, and now ghosts," said Monica. "My family's never gonna understand me."

"Is there a problem?"

"Nah . . . not really. They wish I'd be normal, and mama's sure this is just another phase I'm going through. But . . . shit, I've been going through phases all my life. And so has mama. I think that's what life is."

Child, adult; harper, guitarist; woman, priestess—Monica had said it all. "You are wise, Monica," said Christa.

Monica's dark skin took on shades of rose. "Dammit, Chris . . . there you go again."

"How so?"

"You . . ." Monica glanced at the window again, then turned back to Christa. "You make me feel as though I rate. Like I'm really someone."

Christa blinked. "But you are."

"Yeah, but, like I mean, more than the vocalist for the band, more than the front person . . ." Monica wrinkled her nose, struggled with words. "Like I'm someone just because I'm me. Monica Sanchez. A woman."

"But . . . you are."

Monica stared at her. "Where the fuck did you grow up, Chris?"

"Ah . . . in Ireland."

Monica looked at her patiently, like a precocious child who knew full well that an adult was being less than truthful. "C'mon, Chris. I went to East High and there were a couple girls there from Ireland. Fresh off the boat. Their parents didn't know what section of town to move into, so the kids wound up in school with a bunch of Chicanos and Blacks. The guys called them 'white meat' and were always hitting on them. They sure as hell didn't act like you. Scared little things, always going to church to say rosaries and stuff like that. Worse than my grandmother. No makeup. Straight hair. Wouldn't even look at a beer. Couldn't deal with their own bodies."

Christa sat, unmoving, unable to think of anything to say.

"You're just different, Chris," Monica went on. "You don't have to tell me anything you don't want to, but wherever you're from, it must be a pretty terrific place, cause you're sure as hell the best person I've ever met." She shrugged, still blushing. "I'm not gay, Chris, but I think I love you."

"I . . ." Generous as Monica was, Christa knew that the truth could shatter her. "I hope you'll remember that in a couple months."

Monica shook her head, puzzled. "What's going to happen then?"

Christa's eyes were as vulnerable as Monica's. "I'll need you."

CHAPTER
TWENTY-FOUR

On the last evening of April, Christa picked up the new guitar, snapped on her amplifiers and digital delays, checked her tuning. Across the basement, proud and upright in its stand, Ceis gleamed in the light of the fluorescents.

Christa had spent the last three weeks preparing for this working, meditating late at night with her arms wrapped around the harp and guitar, losing herself in the ambience of willow and bronze and plastic and steel until the material world—the sound of traffic, Monica sleeping in the guest room, the odor of the steaks she had cooked for dinner—had slipped away, and she had been conscious only of the instruments.

Ready, but still unwilling to start, she fiddled with the settings on the delays, assured herself that they were correct, then checked and rechecked to be sure that the amplifier was adjusted to give the bright, lyrical sound that she preferred. Everything had to be right tonight. Everything had to be perfect. Otherwise—

Chairiste

"Ceis?" Faced with the outcome of its decision, was the harp going to back out?

do

She set her guitar down, picked up the harp, cradled it in her arms. She rested her cheek against the old wood and felt the dampness of her tears.

do

Ceis could communicate only in single words, but Christa sensed that it was attempting to comfort her, to demonstrate its confidence in the working at hand and in her skills.

do

She looked over her shoulder at the still-sleeping gui-

260

tar. A harper? Where were her harps? One, much loved, had been sawed up into fragments and incorporated into an absurdly modern contrivance of steel strings and integrated circuits. Another, a dear friend, would tonight become a comparative stranger.

Symmetrically, perhaps fittingly, she had finished Kevin's harp and had returned it to him with a lesson that morning. She supposed that this night found him practicing in the dark, fumbling for notes with all the discipline and concentration that he had gained from his guitar, striving now for another kind of music, listening for magic.

Comfortable with the old Gods, trusting of himself, open and generous, Kevin seemed to her now more Gaeidil than Irish. Like the sun, he had waxed from winter to spring; and now at Beltaine, though he would not be with her to celebrate the changing of the seasons, he would himself greet the dawn in front of his mountain home with his own words and a cup of wine lifted at the gate of summer.

The world was full of change, and the same turning of the year that had brought Kevin his flowering had also, seemingly, dictated that Christa change her own form from the white-mantled innocence of a novice harper to the black leather and vengeance of a rocker. Monica had been right. Everything was just a phase. The seasons changed, and people did also. By what right had she held herself aloof so long from something so universal?

Chairiste

"Ceis . . ." She wept openly, rocking back and forth like a little girl in need of comfort, half hopeful and half afraid of what lay ahead of her that night.

do

"Indeed, Ceis," she whispered. "I'm delaying, am I not?"

She replaed the harp in its stand and tried to dry her eyes on her sleeve, but the leather would absorb nothing. She shrugged. There would be more tears that night: it mattered little that she began with a damp face.

She picked up her guitar, dropped the strap over her shoulder. "Ready, Ceis?"

do

"All right, old friend. Brigit bless."

If she heard the harp reply, she would lose her nerve,

and so she swung immediately into the opening licks of
the solo she had created for this working. Even, flowing,
strong, the music reached out to the harp and held it as
she had often held it in her lap.

The guitar sang, lilting out melodies that, at first, imi-
tated the sound of a harp with the clean ringing of plucked
strings. Gradually, though, Christa developed the music
into a roar of distortion that penetrated deeply into the
being of both instruments.

From the guitar she felt the soft seasons of the forests
of Eriu: cool rainy winters, warm summers that culmi-
nated in the blood of autumn. A willow tree grew near a
brook, sent down roots, lifted leaves, stretched branches
up into the clear, unpolluted air, waiting for someone to
come along with an idea, waiting for a young woman who
wanted to be a harper and who needed a tree to love . . . .

But there were other trees, too: growing in tropical
forests, making hard and unyielding woods out of the
violent life that teemed among rank moss and the sluggish rivers. They also waited—and dark, sullen men came
to cut them down and send them to other lands.

The deep, deciduous woods of New England that grew
within sight of still lakes mirroring unspeakably blue skies.
Trees. Waiting for a hand to shape them.

She saw Roger Best smoothing wood, soldering wires,
spraying and burnishing coat after coat of lacquer. . . .

The guitar was a complex involution of events and
processes brought together by fate, will, and need. And
Christa herself was as much a part of its existence as its
woods and metals and plastics. Were it not for her, for
Judith, for the Sidh, this guitar would not have been
made. But, in the same way, she stood in her basement
on this last evening of April, teetering on the threshold
of summer, because of this guitar. As much as it itself
had been summoned, it had called forth the Gaeidil.

Ceis, though, was something else, and Christa found
herself grappling with an entity that had no earthly history, that had sprung directly into existence just as the
first star had coalesced and kindled in the pitch of the
mortal Void. With a shriek of amplified guitar strings,
she stared utter nothingness in the face and saw, from
out of heavings and sudden brilliance, the inbreaking of
presence.

Teeth clenched, eyes shut tight against the vision that had taken her, throat contracted against a scream which her harper's pride dictated she would not utter, she faced the reality of Ceis and offered welcome and friendship to something she knew could rend her very atoms into a cloudy assortment of wave forms and probabilities.

She held a long, wailing note, stretched the string up, shook it, let it throb with an acceptance of whatever might come. That which was Ceis turned to her—could not but turn, was always turning—a consciousness unlimited by concerns of time or of life. It met her gaze with its own, returned her greeting, her acceptance, bowed to her need, gave itself.

For a moment, she was still Chairiste Ní Cummen. But, caught between the two extremes that she was attempting to meld, she slid into both, found herself making music under her own hands, discovered that she contained everything that was, that could be, in a blinding instant of union.

When she opened her eyes, Monica was bending over her, her dark face drawn and frightened. Christa blinked at her and tried to talk, but her mouth was not functioning. Monica swam out of view for a moment, faded back with a glass of water, and held it to her lips. The liquid flowed through Christa like electric current, its wetness and fluidity nearly overpowering.

Monica's lips had been moving, but Christa did not realize that she had been speaking until sound suddenly returned as though a switch had been thrown.

"—sus Christ! What the hell've you been doing? Chris, can you hear me? Wave your hands or something."

"I'm . . . fine . . ."

"Don't give me that jive, girl. I come home from *Psycho III* and find you in the middle of the floor. What the fuck's going on?"

The nouns in Monica's sentences slammed through Christa's thoughts like sledgehammers. She shook her head to clear it. Her hands were empty. Why were her hands empty?

She took the glass from Monica, held it as though her fingers encircled the weight of a planet, gulped the rest of the water. The world inched back toward normalcy. Monica helped her to sit up, and Christa rubbed her face with empty hands.

Empty . . . why empty?

The tang of ozone in the air slapped her in the face like a cold rain and she instinctively looked at her amplifier. It was on, its preamp indicators glowing red, but it was silent. Where was the usual hiss?

She stared at her hands. Empty . . .

With a lurch, she pulled herself to her feet and staggered to the Laney. Her boots crunched on pulverized glass as she stretched up on tiptoe to peer into the back of the amplifier head. Every vacuum tube in it had exploded. The inside of the head was littered with shards of glass and bits of tube elements.

"Serves me right . . ." she mumbled as she groped to turn it off. "I'll have to retube."

Monica had been hovering anxiously. She looked over Christa's shoulder. "What'd you do?"

"Poured the whole universe through my amp." Moment by moment, the room seemed to be growing more solid, no longer threatening to melt and flow into some other form.

"You been doing drugs, Chris?"

Christa sorted painfully through words, decided which she wanted to use. "Indeed not, Monica. Magic."

Monica looked more frightened. "This is out of my department."

"It's all right. You're safe. Ceis—"

Her hands ached. Empty. She grabbed Monica by her shoulders. "Where's Ceis?"

"The ghost? In the whole house, I thought."

"The guitar, Monica. Where's the new guitar?"

Monica's brown eyes were wide. "It was on top of you. I put it in its stand."

The basement blurred as Christa swung around, then settled into focus. The guitar gleamed in its stand, but to Christa's addled vision it seemed faintly transparent, as if it were an amber-colored window that looked into other places, other times. Stars floated in its depths, moons spun along their courses.

She ran to it, picked it up, cradled it against her breasts. "Ceis? Ceis?"

Inches from her heart, the guitar stirred.

"Ceis? Are you . . . are you there?"

Seconds crawled by as she strained her mind for a reply.

Chairiste

"Ceis . . ."

And as she hugged the guitar, she lifted her eyes to the place where the harp had stood. But instead of a shining instrument of wood and gems, she saw only a handful of gray dust that shuddered as though it found itself bereft of life and faded into the pale concrete floor.

Christa put Monica off with sketchy explanations about ghosts and magic. Monica was obviously not satisfied with the half-truths, but Christa could say no more. The band was already close to breaking up. To throw more difficulties into an already complicated situation made no sense.

Monica insisted that Christa go to bed immediately, and Christa insisted that she would do so only with the guitar in her arms. Monica shrugged: one more crazy thing she was not going to be told about.

It was a violation of trust, and Christa felt a pang of guilt. Monica had given her friendship and had brought a sense of youth and exuberance into her house. She deserved better than to be treated like a child. "I'm sorry, Monica," said Christa. "I really can't tell you. It'll have to be later."

Monica dropped her eyes. "You've been pretty straight with me before, Chris. Why the change?"

"I don't want to scare you."

"I'm not scared now? Girl, you haven't been looking."

A few hours of dead, dreamless sleep did much to restore the world to its customary appearance, and Christa awoke to find herself wrapped about Ceis like a vixen about her kit. In the kitchen, Monica had left her a pot of coffee and a note:

Chris—

I guess I should say I'm sorry. You've done a lot for me, and you got a private life too. I should know better than to push. Take it easy today. See you when I get home. Love.

She smiled as she read. *Take it easy.* She did not see that the next six weeks were going to be in any way easy.

Kevin called from the guitar school. "How did it go?"

"I blew out my tubes, but it worked."

"You two okay?"

"We are. Will you be able to run sound during my solo tonight? I'm afraid that the house engineer might become distraught and kill the PA or something."

"I know Fred. He won't mind me horning in for a few."

"Good. I have to get to work now, so I'll see you before the show." She caught herself before she hung up. She had birthed Kevin at the Solstice, and she was now watching him take his first steps. "How did your rite go this morning?"

"It was great. I wanted some music, but the harp's still a little more than I can handle. So I used Frankie's guitar and played the blues." He laughed. "Beltaine will never be the same. But, you know, I'm starting to understand what you and Frankie said to me. It's just like sex. It's just like everything. It all . . . it all flows together. It makes *sense.*"

She smiled. He was walking. "Happy Beltaine, Kevin."

"Brigit bless, Chairiste."

Her amplifier had suffered no damage save to its tubes, and after replacing them, she spent the day in the basement, practicing the licks and melodies that she would use that night. The guitar learned its new abilities quickly and worked with her to fine-tune the magic so that Melinda would be traumatized as little as possible.

"She'll need strength, Ceis," she said over lunch. "I think we'll all need it. Devi already knows about magic, but Boo-boo and Monica are going to see some disturbing things."

agreed

There was a different feeling to Ceis now, one that went beyond cosmetic matters. Over the years, the harp had learned passion, love, and friendship; and in melding with her, it had gone on to absorb something of the nature of the mortal woman who played it.

Christa sensed a hidden anger in it: anger at the Sidh, who held Judith against her will; anger at Carl Taylor, who was destroying a friend; anger at the smug complacency of Orfide; even a little anger at Melinda.

As she ate, she considered her own feelings. Yes, she

was angry, but anger at Melinda would be foolish. Melinda had been weak, and she had fallen. In much the same way, a young Gaeidil woman had once succumbed to a cocky disregard for caution and had lost everything, including her lover, as a result.

"Ceis," she said, "we have to be gentle with Melinda."

gentle

"Agreed? You know Melinda. She had harp lessons with me for months. And she's probably someone I knew at the harpers' school—she has dreams about it. You've seen her good side. She hurt herself years ago, and she never quite recovered. Be good to her."

compassion

"Indeed, Ceis. Compassion."

Monica came home from work, but said nothing about the previous night. She changed out of her office clothes and, together, she and Christa began dismantling equipment, preparing it for transportation to InsideOut for the evening's gig. Devi and Lisa showed up a little later and joined in.

"Where's Melinda?" Lisa grumbled.

"She'll be at the club."

"We have to move her stuff for her?"

Devi stood up behind a stack of cases, rolls of cables in her arms. "She's having a hard enough time getting herself around, Boo-boo."

"Yeah . . . yeah . . ."

"At least this way we know she'll be set up and ready to go."

"Will she be there, do you think?"

"Well . . ."

Christa picked up one side of her heavy speaker cabinet. Monica grabbed the other. "She will," said the harper.

"How do you know?"

"She'll be there."

Christa did not want to consider the alternative.

CHAPTER
TWENTY-FIVE

The club was empty when they set up, and, like a theater without an audience or motion-picture sets seen from the wrong side, the big room held a sense of hollow and unrelieved artifice. The backgrounds were, after all, just painted canvas, the props terrifyingly insubstantial.

Rock and roll was little different. Behind the glitter, the arrogant assurance of the young, the adolescent scorn for mortality, was an empty darkness in which prowled the unadmitted fears that propelled the music and the lights, that added a sense of urgency to the gyrations of the performers. *Run. Run while you still can. Age is coming, skeletal and grinning, and the world is a cesspool that is ever rising.*

But to that darkness, Christa had brought not only the courage and pride of an ancient culture that had put its trust in its people and its Gods, but also a compassion that was the product of ten-score years of lonely wandering; and when she struck her first chord that night—the ringing notes sustained by overdrive and digital delays long beyond anything ever achieved by a harp, feedback shrilling through upper harmonics until the sound coruscated at the edge of sight—she was lifting a voice to counter the age and the pollution: the defiant voice of a woman, a harper, a rocker who had come to heal.

Melinda was no better tonight. Her sense of rhythm was gone, and she played without feeling, mechanically pumping out notes as though her mind were elsewhere. Squinting into the lights, Christa made out the face of Carl Taylor at the edge of the dance floor.

death

"I forbid it, Ceis," she said between lines of the chorus. She kept a smile plastered brittlely on her face as she climbed on the drum risers and jumped down in time

268

with a massive chord that was a blue-white presence on the stage.

Lisa's eyes were wide. The magic was manifesting visibly. Christa dropped her high frequencies with a turn of a knob. Not until her solo.

During the break, Melinda disappeared with Carl. Christa waved the rest of the band into the dressing room.

"Do we have to keep up with this farce, Chris?" said Lisa. "Melinda's just the same."

"Wait for my solo in the next set. That's going to change." Ceis hung from her shoulder, glittering, beaded with drops of sweat.

"She means it, Boo-boo," said Monica. "Something's up."

Devi nodded. "I'm game, Chris. You won't hurt her, will you?"

Lisa stared at them. "What're you going to do?"

Christa regarded Ceis for a moment. "We're going to solve a problem," she said, lifting her head. "Melinda will try to disappear again when I start, so you all need to grab her. Hold her down, sit on her—do whatever you have to, but keep her on stage and out of sight. I'll tell the light man to keep the spot tight on me."

No one spoke. The canned music thudded through the door.

"Do you trust me?" Christa asked softly. "This is the only way I know."

Lisa said it: "We trust you, Chris. We're just damned glad you're on our side."

Melinda was late for the next set, and Christa's hands were tight on the neck of her guitar when she finally saw the bassist stumbling toward the stage. Lisa was tapping her foot—impatient or apprehensive, Christa could not tell—but Devi seemed calm. Monica hovered nearby as though for security.

Christa turned to the others, lifted an eyebrow. Lisa bobbed her head. Devi gave a thumbs-up. Sliding an arm about Monica's waist, Christa pulled the singer against her. "You all right?"

Monica's brown eyes were frightened. "This is part of what happened last night, isn't it?"

"That, and more," said Christa. "Sing as well as you

can, Monica. 'Tis all I can ever ask. But this time, sing for Melinda. Show her that we all care about her."

Monica nodded, put a hand to her throat, swallowed to loosen the muscles. With a small, strangled laugh, she whirled around to the club as the stage lights came up. "Here we go!" she screamed. "Boston! 'Hollyann'! Rock on!"

On the other side of the song, looming like a wall of water, was Christa's solo: ten minutes that would, by necessity, change everything. It might save Melinda. It might put an end to the band. Christa would not know until she played it.

Monica sang for Melinda. Christa heard the wellsprings of comfort in her voice. Devi's synths were rich, warm, and her brief keyboard solo shimmered like a beckoning hand of starlight. Lisa powered out the beat as though she saw the approaching flood.

Alternately crystalline and distorted, Ceis added its voice to the music. The song was about past times of innocence and belief, and through it, Christa called to Melinda, trying to rekindle something of those qualities in the bassist, to mirror them to her so that she might see what she could become once again.

"We were for life
And we would never
Concede it . . .
Hollyann."

Hollyann? Or was a different name on her lips tonight? Melinda? Maybe Judith?

"We held the line
Can you believe it?"

Her solo. The wave, breaking, thundered across the stage. Christa threw her volume knobs to full, stepped on the control pedal for her delays, swirled her sound into incandescence. Here was a harper from Corca Duibne, come now with music, with change.

As the spotlight narrowed in on her, she saw Melinda set down her bass and start for the edge of the stage. In a moment, Lisa had exploded out from her drums, piled into her, dragged her back behind a stack of speakers.

Melinda was struggling, but her cries were drowned out by the wall of sound from the PA and the stage monitors. Quickly, Christa shifted to a delicately structured countermelody that hovered between the dorian and the phrygian mode, twined like a growing vine, reached out and enveloped Melinda. Christa felt her friend jerk and lie still as her consciousness was smothered with blossoms.

Lisa looked up, her face white. "It's okay," Christa mouthed at her. The drummer shut her eyes and laid her head against Melinda's, and Christa plunged into the main theme of the solo.

Clearing the drugs from Melinda's system was comparatively easy: harpers in Eriu had been performing similar tasks for centuries, though they had been ignorant of the precise physical effects their music had wrought. But clearing a mind was phenomenally difficult. Melinda had never dealt with her previous mistakes, preferring instead to deny and run from them; and now she had become deeply addicted, with an addict's ingrained weakness. Any magic on Christa's part would, by necessity, have to reach deeply into her psyche and alter some basic assumptions.

Christa had ten minutes.

Those in the audience who saw her confident smile and watched her slender hands tossing off melody, lick, and ornament did not know with what deliberation she framed her music. Melinda's body twitched violently as Christa's spell felt through her flesh and blood and slowly converted the heroin and cocaine into a few simple sugars and trace elements. Double-stopping precise harmonies, Christa stabilized Melinda's breathing and heartbeat, held them constant until she was sure that her friend's body was echoing the rhythmic regularity of the music, then drove in again and blocked the withdrawal symptoms.

It took time. Five minutes left.

She shut her eyes and, carried by the music, entered Melinda, felt her identity, sifted through the wreckage. Left alone, the bassist would be dead in a few months. She had no reason to keep on living. She had realized that her dissoluteness was destroying the band, that Carl was going to cast her aside in another week or so, that all her efforts had gone for nothing. . . .

Sruitmor

Christa started and nearly lost track of her fingers. Sruitmor? The master harper of the Corca Duibne school?

What did he have to do with an abused young woman on a Denver rock stage?

Ceis?

The guitar replied by seizing the music and bending its timbres into a gush of energies that washed through Christa in a prismatic flood. She found herself facing the quiet lake to the north of the harpers' school. Melinda was there. Or rather, Melinda was all around her. Though fourteen centuries and thousands of miles separated Melinda from any trace of the school, Christa realized that this was the bassist's memory, not her own.

Holding to her dual consciousness—continuing her solo on the stage at InsideOut, she was at the same time standing on the ancient soil of Eriu—she saw approaching her a man clad in the azure mantle of a master of the *Cruitreacha*. His beard and hair were white, but his eyes mirrored the blue of the sea on a fine day. Sruitmor.

Four minutes.

He approached her, and she almost knelt; but he shook his head vigorously. "No time for that, Chairiste. Nor is it seemly for one master to kneel to another."

She blushed as she thought of the guitar she held. "I'm no master."

"Ach, you still talk like a farmer sometimes, Chairiste. Listen to the music you play. No novice could do that."

"I've not been initiated."

"You want another chalice pushed at you? Perhaps a wand with the proper Ogham cut into it?" Earthy and spiritual both, the master harper of Corca Duibne took her arm. "You don't need them. You know that. Walk with me. We have little time . . ."

Three minutes.

". . . and I must talk to you." Together they skirted the shore of the lake. As they passed, curlews flapped up from the reeds, their wingbeats stirring the water.

Christa examined her black spandex, compared it ruefully with Sruitmor's graceful robe. But she knew that she had no time for humility. She clasped her master's gnarled hand. "You're Melinda, aren't you?"

"I am," he said. "Come back for you."

"Why?"

His eyes lost some of their luster. "You've forgotten much, Chairiste. You remember your music, of course, but you don't remember how dear you were to me. Did you really think that an old man who had lost his only daughter to a fever could look at a young woman from the coast and not see some echo of his own blood? Did you think that I was so tolerant and encouraging merely because I recognized your talent?"

Christa wanted to embrace him, but she contented herself with his hand. "You were both father and mother to me."

"I tried. And I failed." His voice shook a little. "I should have foreseen that you and Siudb would go to find the Sidh."

"It was the action of a fool. And I am paying for it."

"I grieved when you vanished," he said. "We all grieved, but I . . . I wept because I had lost my daughter again."

Two minutes.

On the stage in Denver, Christa shifted into her most rarefied melodies: pointillistic licks that left in their wake only an aural impression of tension and of movement. *Change, Melinda. You can change.* Dimly, she saw the other women clustered around Melinda, and she gestured to Lisa with the headstock of her guitar. The drummer understood: the music was too intricate for solo work. It needed a beat.

Lisa climbed behind her drums, listened carefully for a moment, then, improvising, began rapping out a syncopated rhythm full of rim-shots and clanging ride cymbals, turning Christa's work from an abstraction into something concrete, something that could be danced to.

The sand of the lakeshore crunched under Christa's boots as she turned to her teacher. "What can I do?" she said. "You're dying. I have to cure you. How?"

Sruitmor regarded her calmly, though his tears dampened his beard. "I failed you, daughter. I failed to guide you away from your arrogance, which was a grievous mistake. I came back from the Summerland to try to help you, but I forgot the limitations of an incarnate personality, and I made further mistakes. Now I have almost done away with everything."

"What—"

"I need your forgiveness."

One minute.

Christa gripped his hand. "Master, you have it a thousand times over. If I'm anything today, if I have any chance at all of winning Siudb, it's because of what you gave me. I can't be perfect, nor can you. Surely the master harper of Corca Duibne knows that. If there is any regret between us, any sorrow or pain, I release you from it. I forgive you. You need to forgive yourself."

His face shone, and he bowed deeply. "The words of a master harper. You are indeed of the *Cruitreacha*, Chairiste."

"Now help Melinda."

He straightened. Though old, he held himself like a young man. "We will help Melinda together. Ceis? Once more?"

Sruitmor, the lake, the curlews vanished, and the stage came back. But Christa feld the presence of the master harper as surely as she held her guitar in her hand. With seconds left, she reached out to Melinda, flooding her with the knowledge that she was loved, sweeping away the mistakes and the failures.

We forgive you. Forgive yourself. If you need us, we'll be there. Come back. Come home. Come, now, quickly.

The bassist gasped, sat up, stared with clear eyes. Monica and Devi hugged her. Pale, shaking, Melinda turned to Christa, who had already begun the introduction to the next song. Christa grinned at the audience, held a chord, bounded across the stage to her friend. Just a part of the show.

"Melinda?" she shouted above the music.

"Chris . . ." Melinda was crying, mascara and liner streaking down her face. "Chris, what did you do to me?"

"I'm trying to help. Can you make it through this set?"

Melinda hesitated, looked at her bass.

Please, Melinda. For the sake of who you used to be. Play. Play music.

"Can you?" Christa shouted again.

With a grimace, Melinda grabbed her bass and spun up her volume knobs just in time to join in. Gritting her teeth to keep back the sorrow and the tears, she punched out the rhythm in perfect time.

The music sparkled. The magic was back. Gossamer Axe sucked in a deep breath . . .

. . . and lived.

Monica was only a little pale as she ran to the front of the stage, mircrophone to her lips:

*"Are you surprised to see me
Standing here at your door?"*

The song surged out into the club, a defiant shake of the fist at the powers that still remained to be battled. Monica's arm encircled Melinda's waist during the first chorus, and the bassist shared the singer's microphone, screaming out the lyrics:

*"I'm back
And I'm calling you out
So get your ass out here, boy,
'Cause it's time to get down
To the firing line!"*

Christa noticed Bill Sarah at a nearby table. As usual, he was wearing his business suit, looking very much like a lawyer, an incongruous presence amid the youthful bodies and tight jeans. She gave him a wink and a smile, and he straightened, returned a vigorous thumbs-up, and began applauding.

Beyond him, though, but for his familiarity almost lost in the darkness and the faceless young people come to listen and to dance, was Carl Taylor. He was staring at Melinda. He looked puzzled.

death

"Ceis!"

death

The guitar had absorbed something of her during their union, and although it was willing to treat Melinda with compassionate discipline, it had no compunctions about Carl. Christa realized that the lead break was upon her, knew that Ceis was fully capable of carrying out its wishes.

I forbid it, Ceis.

She might as well have bade the sea be still. As she started the lead, she tried to reduce it to common blues licks and minor scales; but the guitar was having none of it. She felt the music slipping away from her, felt Ceis taking control as it prepared to exact its own conception of justice.

Carl, unaware of the danger, was coming forward across the dance floor. He seemed puzzled by the change in Melinda.

Ceis whipped the lead into a fury of darkly minor riffs

laden with chromatic arpeggios. The lethal power built quickly, hovered in front of the PA speakers like an animate shroud, roiled with a terrible potency.

Melinda had seen Carl. Eyes wide and terrified, she backed away, withdrawing as far as her cord would allow. Carl smiled quizzically, took another step forward, waved at her.

Ceis struck. The guitar shrieked with wrath, and Christa had a momentary vision of a shaft of light, like a pale, spotted snake, darting at Carl, coiling about him, sinking its head into his chest.

The puzzled look did not leave his face, but one hand flew to his heart as he staggered back into the crowd. A dancer bumped into him, and he fell.

Someone turned and pointed. Carl was lost in the darkness, but people were suddenly gathering about something, something on the floor.

Lisa stirred and rolled over, listening as she had been listening ever since she had crawled into bed in the pre-dawn darkness, straining her ears even as she slept.

She sighed, rubbed at her eyes. She was not waiting for Melinda to get home. Melinda was home already, and in bed. Christa herself had tucked her in and kissed her good-night as though ministering to a frightened child; and, yes, Melinda had stared at her like a blond-haired moppet and had obediently closed her eyes.

The brash, cocky Melinda was gone. She seemed now to be a broken thing, a frail, young girl who had seen too much of the world and realized too much about herself. And although while onstage she had radiated confidence throughout the remaining sets, the mask had fallen away when she had put down her bass. She had stayed in the dressing room during breaks, staring silently at the wall, tears streaking singly down her face.

A truck rumbled by outside, and, in the silence left behind, Lisa heard what she had been listening for. She got up, pulled on a robe, and scuffed across the living room to Melinda's door.

The soft, gentle sobs of a young woman. Lisa paused with her hand on the knob. "Melinda?"

"Boo-boo?"

Lisa might have simply opened the door and entered,

but Melinda had arleady been intruded upon enough that night. She needed love, but she needed respect and privacy also. "Can I come in? Is it all right?"

Silence. Then: "Yeah."

Lisa found Melinda huddled in the big waterbed, her arms wrapped about a small harp that was dusty with long disuse. "You want to talk?"

Melinda's face was pale against the pastel sheets. "I can't seem to stay asleep," she said. "I keep dreaming that I'm in Carl's bed, and that he's coming in. . . ." She shuddered and made as though to pull the covers up about her shoulders.

Lisa tucked them in. "Carl? Carl Taylor?"

Melinda hung her head. The tears were still coming. "Yeah. He got me hooked. Used me like a washcloth."

Lisa's temper flared. "That son of a bitch. I'd like to—"

She broke off, staring. Carl Tayler had died that evening. A heart attack, the paramedics had said. But Lisa had seen something on stage that she had, at the time, dismissed as imagination: a pale streak of light darting from Christa's amplifier straight at the club owner.

Melinda did not notice her expression. "I really blew it. Bad."

Lisa dragged herself away from her thoughts. "It happens."

"I'm just a stupid bitch."

The drummer recalled all the anger that she had kept pent up for months. It was gone now, and she would have gladly given it up again and again if doing so would have made Melinda feel better. "It's over, Mel," she said softly. "It's done."

"What did Chris to to me? Do you know?" Melinda sounded almost afraid to hear.

"No," said Lisa. "I don't. She did something . . . with the music. She's talked to us about magic, and I guess for her it's the same thing. I don't understand it, but . . . well . . . she's a friend."

Melinda was a friend, too; and Melinda had been hurt, nearly killed, by Carl Taylor. What, Lisa wondered, would she herself have done? Nothing? When someone she loved had been so treated?

"You scared?" said Melinda.

"Yeah, kinda."

Melinda turned her face into the pillow. "I know she did the right thing, but, God, when that . . . that whatever-it-was hit me, it was like . . ." She shuddered as though she felt the soft blanket of unconsciousness crawling over her again. "I don't know what it was like."

"She cares about you, Mel." Lisa wondered how she could sound so reassuring when her assumptions about reality had been so thoroughly shattered.

"What . . ." Melinda's arm tightened on the harp. "What do you think she is? Or who? I . . . I don't know what to ask anymore."

Lisa shook her head slowly. "I don't know either. She just doesn't seem to be from around here."

"I asked her once what planet she was from. I thought I was joking."

Lisa tried to fit the pieces together and shrugged inwardly when she failed. "I guess she'll tell us about it when she's ready. But she's a friend. She's a good friend." There was pride in her voice. "I'd trust her with my life."

"Me too." Melinda lifted her head and blinked at Lisa with hollow eyes. "You guys . . . still want me in the band?"

"You bet."

No bravado here: only a stricken timidity. "Even after all the shit I pulled?"

Lisa reached out and touched Melinda's face. How would Christa say it? She did not know. She found her own words.

"Yeah," she said. "C'mon back."

CHAPTER
TWENTY-SIX

The light-blue Eagle lurched and bumped up the road in Gunnison National Forest. Sawtooth Mountain winked in and out of sight behind the aspens and the pines, but Christa did not have time to look. Winter had been hard on the road, and she was busy dodging potholes that threatened either to swallow the wagon or shake it apart.

"You say it gets worse ahead?" said Kevin. He studied the topographic map, then the scenery. His hand found the strap at the top of the doorframe, and he held on as the wagon swayed violently.

"Much worse," she said. "Here . . ." She swung the Eagle into the bushes, and Kevin flinched; but the bright green leaves fell away to reveal a pair of deep ruts separated by a swatch of high weeds and hemmed in by tall foliage. For a minute she followed the track, but then she braked to a stop, deliberating. The mid-May air was cool and fragrant with flowers; but the spring overgrowth had changed the land. She could not see her destination. "Ceis? It's confused I am."

The guitar lay on the back seat. *right*

She slewed the Eagle off the road, the four tires clawing for traction in the mud. The bushes parted. Straight ahead was the low cliff, and the lake—still, quiet, blue—lay at its feet.

Kevin whistled. "That's it?"

"Can you see the gate?"

"A little. The air over the water looks . . . different."

Two weeks of harping, and he was already seeing magic. He had the touch, and he had the talent, and if his parents had given him anything besides their fears, they had given him a little of the old blood. The former was gone, the latter was awakening.

She parked and stepped out onto the grass. Kevin

rounded the wagon carrying a small, battery-powered amplifier. "Will they hear this?" he asked.

"Who?"

"The twig-pigs. You're going to be making some noise." He hefted the amp. "Now that I think of it, you're going to be making a lot of noise come Midsummer. This is just a rumor, you understand, but I hear that the park rangers don't like having rock concerts in the forest."

"They'll not hear," said Christa. "They'll not notice us at all." Kevin's eyebrows lifted in surprise, and she explained. "Keeping folk from hearing what one doesn't want them to hear is one of the first things a harper learns, Kevin. Do you remember that air I taught you yesterday? The one that climbs up into the high strings and hovers there with the curious little suspensions? That's the beginning of the spell."

"You're teaching me magic?"

She lifted Ceis out of the back seat. "Surely. You're going to be a harper."

Blushing at the title, he followed her down to the shore of the lake, handed her one end of a guitar cord, and plugged the other end into the amplifier. "This has some on-board chorusing," he said, examining the controls. "And reverb. You want that?"

"I'll try the chorusing. And give me a little reverb." She dug a pick out of her pocket. "Crank it, Kevin."

Though small, the amplifier had a large voice, and the melody Christa played spattered off the rock wall that backed up the lake. She made no effort to downplay the visual effects of the magic: the energy built about her like a blue-lit fog, spread out on the ground, formed itself into a protective circle a thousand feet in diameter.

That done, she felt out toward the gate. As she had expected, it had shrunk noticeably in less than a year. The fact was distressing, but not fatal: with Ceis, and with the massed power of a rock band backing her, she would have little problem enlarging it to suitable proportions.

Ceis surged forward, urging, eager.

With a frightened jerk, she pulled her hands from the instrument. "Ceis. Old friend. You must work with me."
**

"You know better than that. A man lies dead because

of your vengeance." Her words were true, but there was
a sense of uncleanliness about them, for she could not
but say that she approved of the manner in which the
guitar had dealt with Carl Taylor. Gaeidil justice was
swift and decisive, but—in the eyes of mild little times—
brutal and vengeful. Caught as she was between the sixth
century and the twentieth, Christa could not but agonize
over the death.

Kevin came up beside her. "Ceis pushing?"

"It is." She unknotted the bandanna from her throat
and wiped her brow. Could she trust the guitar anymore?
Could she trust herself?

Kevin read her train of thought. "If you'd killed him
with your bare hands, Chris, would it have been better?"

"It would," she replied without hesitation.

"Why?"

"In the name of the Goddess, Kevin! The man didn't
have a chance!"

"Did he give Melinda a chance?"

A sticky question. "I don't know," she said. "Maybe
in Corca Duibne I'd have an answer. Hard it is to be a
Gaeidil among another people. The world's changed."
Almost pensively, she hefted the guitar. "I've changed,
too."

She looked about her. The sky was as blue as any that
Eriu could have boasted, the trees as straight, the water
as cold and clear. And yet a difference was blazoned
upon the land as brightly and unmistakably as the white
contrail of a jet streaked the azure vault above her head.
Not for the first time, she wondered how she would
explain it all to Judith. She could not even explain it to
herself.

"I hope she'll be happy here," she said softly. Kevin
picked up the amp, put his arm about her, led her back
to the car.

Kevin took the wheel for the long drive home, but he
seemed thoughtful. He had grown up, but he had also
grown backwards. He was seeing the world in light of old
memories and was, perhaps, as much in conflict as she.

His eyes were on the road, but he seemed to be looking beyond the asphalt. "What happened to us, Chris?"
he said at last. "To Ire—to Eriu? It's . . . I mean, it just
. . . went away."

Went away. Went far away. For all that Eriu had influenced modern ways, it might never have existed. "I wasn't there to see it, Kevin. I was with the Sidh. I missed the changes."

"Any ideas?"

Christa shifted, reached back between the bucket seats, and laid a hand on Ceis. "I've thought about it. I've a few ideas."

"Tell me. It sounds crazy, but I miss it."

It did not sound crazy to her at all. "I've told you about the cycles," she said. "The big ones that make up the seasons. That's what we're celebrating on the holydays: the way winter gives way to summer, which in turn yields back to winter. It's a circle. Well . . . a spiral, really, but think of it for now as a circle."

If Gossamer Axe was a circle, it was turning once more. Bill Sarah was happy, and had even apologized to Melinda for some of his words—Melinda, on her part, bursting into tears and returning the apology—and the gigs were building up again.

"A people is a circle, too," Christa went on, still thinking of the band. "Everyone is a part of it, and everything flows around it. Commerce, religion, art . . . all depend upon one another."

Not surprisingly, the women of the band had become her family, her circle; and by necessity, their beliefs, their loves, their joys and sorrows mingled inseparably. Melinda's tragedy was the band's tragedy. Monica's fear was shared by all. Christa's need . . .

Mid-May. Only a little over four weeks left. Time for confessions, revelations: the final test of the band. Would it hold together?

"Chris?"

She pulled herself back to the present. "I'm sorry, Kevin. My mind's wandering."

"If this is painful for you . . ."

"Not at all. I saw something once that gave me a clue about what happened. When I lived in London in the 1860s, I traveled about, trying to learn something of the people I'd found myself among. In a museum I came upon a reliquary from Monymusk, and there was piece of circular knotwork design on one of the bosses that I found disquieting. I looked at it for a long time. I wanted to know why it bothered me.

"It finally struck me that the entire design was perfectly symmetrical save at the top. Instead of replicating the rest of the loops, the line bent down and took a different turn. The symmetry, the circle, was destroyed."

She wondered whether, in telling Gossamer Axe who and what she was, she would complete the pattern of the band . . . or destroy it.

"And what did that tell you?" said Kevin.

"This: that so long as Eriu was a circle of people, she could not fall. But with time came other beliefs, other ways. Patrick and the Christians were only the last, but in many ways the most telling, for some of their beliefs were similar to those of our own religion. The poets and the *filid* drew one parallel after another, and eventually most everyone forgot just where the differences were. A single loop in the pattern that was Eriu was forever altered, and the circle was destroyed."

Kevin stared ahead through the windshield. "Forever?"

"Until we learn to trust the Gods again."

"You think they'll forgive us?"

Would Melinda forgive her? Would the rest of the band?

"Chris?"

"The Gods will forgive anything," she faltered, "given true repentance, and true love."

A scream, taut, wailing. It resounds across the darkling hills of the Realm, echoes hollowly off the pools and the gardens, settles menacingly into the courtyard of the palace. The Sidh look up, startled. Orfide's hands freeze upon the golden strings of his second-best harp.

No, not a scream. No throat, mortal or immortal, could produce such a sound. It knows no flesh, no touch of blood or bone. Metallic, gleaming, it holds within its sustained trembling an edge of steel.

Suddenly, it is gone. The courtyard is silent. Orfide finds his hands motionless. He pulls them away from Clesac's strings. Lamcrann rises, taking refuge in the endlessly repeated gestures of formality. "We are honored, master bard, by your song."

Cumad has not risen. Orfide doubts that she sees anything, so enmeshed in dreams of change is she. Her eyes might as well be windows into the starless—

He glances quickly up to the dark heavens.

—into the starless sky, for all the emotion they show.

Orfide looks at Siudb. She is not even aware of him. She also has heard, but what significance the sound has for her, Orfide cannot guess. But neither can he fathom the expression of hope that plays on her face as, hand in hand with Glasluit, she strolls off into the gardens that surround the palace.

Christa dropped Kevin off at his home in Indian Hills and returned to her house late in the day to find a familiar, battered Mustang parked in front. As she lifted Ceis from the back seat, Melinda got out of her car and approached, a blue harp case slung from her shoulder.

"I was out looking for work," Melinda explained timidly. "I got tired of filling out applications, so I thought I'd drop by."

She seemed younger now, with the unsurity of one who was new to the world. Only when she had a bass in her hands did she seem at all familiar. Offstage, without her music, she was another person: innocent, perhaps, but sad also, and perhaps a little damaged.

Christa put an arm about her shoulders and guided her toward the front door. Melinda, in some ways, was a child again: her child. "Have you been waiting long, Melinda?"

"An hour or so . . ." Melinda blinked her blue eyes, looked appreciatively at the blooming rosebushes to either side of the door. "I hope . . . I hope it's all right."

"Surely. Come in and be welcome. You brought your harp?"

"I . . ." Melinda did not speak until Christa had shut the door behind them. Standing in the dim hall, she hung her head. "I wanted to ask you if you'd take me back as a harp student. I learned a lot from you. I guess . . ." Her lip trembled. "I guess I didn't learn enough."

"We all make mistakes, Melinda. There is no shame in that."

"I can't believe that you've ever blown it as bad as me."

"Indeed I have, Melinda. Much worse, in fact. Someday . . ." And that day, Christa knew, would have to come soon. Within a week. "Someday I'll tell you about it. And you may indeed be my student again. I'm honored."

But as Christa led the way to her studio, she noticed that the light on her answering machine was blinking. She let go of Melinda's hand and punched the play button.

"Chris," came Bill Sarah's voice, "I've got news for you. Adria Records just called. They want the Axe. We're talking big, big money . . . in advance, just like you wanted. I know these guys. They're serious. We're all going out to Los Angeles tomorrow morning: the tickets are waiting for us at Stapleton. Now, pick yourself up off the floor and call me back, pronto. Got it?" A brief pause on the tape. In shock, Christa looked at Melinda, who had pressed a hand to her mouth. Bill's voice came back. "I guess I knew this would happen eventually." He laughed. "Love you all. Now *call me!*"

The shock faded too quickly. Torn, panicked, Christa stared at the machine. The tape beeped, then spooled on in silence. Melinda lowered her harp to the floor, covered her face with her hands, sobbed.

"Did you hear?" Siudb has led Glasluit well out of earshot of the palace, and the open expanse of lawn about them ensures that they will not be surprised.

"I did," he says. "It was . . . terrifying."

"I think Chairiste had a hand in it."

"But . . . how?"

Siudb shakes her head. She has practiced for what seems an eternity, and her fingers are sore, her long nails eroded and frayed at their striking edges. She feels that she is prepared, and she is willing to take the sound as a sign—from the Gods or from Chairiste—that the time for escape has come.

She looks at the gown she wears: shimmering gossamer and iridescent lace. "I will not do as I am. Have my clothes been kept? The ones I wore when Orfide took me?"

"They have. I know where they are."

"Then, beloved Glasluit, I pray you fetch them for me the next chance you have, along with my harp." He folds her hands in his, and she kisses him lightly. "It is time. Let us prepare for the mortal lands."

Lisa was cautious: rather than quit her job, she used her sick time. Devi, equally careful, wheedled a leave of absence from the music store. Still, as they waited at the airport gate for the flight to California, Christa saw eagerness in the set of their shoulders, heard it in their quiet conversation. For years, her bandmates had scrimped to make the rent, had played for little money and less recognition, had hoped that, someday, their chance might come. And it had.

The morning mist left the runways, and the sun slanted shallowly through the tall windows. Beside Christa, Monica zipped up her leather jacket. "Jeez, they believe in air conditioning, don't they?"

"Did you convince your boss to let you come?"

"Nah. He wouldn't go for it. So I quit." Christa looked surprised, and she went on. "I fill a hiring quota, and I know how to be pretty meat. If this doesn't work out, I can find another receptionist job easy."

But Christa could not find another band. And she was frightened—terrified—that the contract *would* work out, that Gossamer Axe would suddenly have records to make, tours, commitments, and no time . . .

Melinda was sitting off by herself, staring at the runways as though they were roads that would take her anywhere but home. Christa gestured to Bill and he rose, joined her, spoke to her casually.

. . . and no time to rescue Judith. The gate was in Colorado, not in California, New York, or Japan. Gossamer Axe could take her far away. But if she left the band, she would have nothing, and Judith would be gone forever.

She shivered and zipped up her own jacket. Her hair flamed against the black leather, and the *failge* glowed softly at her wrist. At her feet, Ceis rested within its flight case.

"But, you know," said Monica, "I think this is gonna work out."

Monica was right. Much as Christa wanted to deny it, she knew presciently that the contract offer would be good, that she would have no plausible reason for objecting to it. Gossamer Axe would be signed within days, and the advance check would be in their hands within a week.

During the flight, she reclined her seat and pretended to sleep, but her thoughts were racing wildly. If the offer was good, she would have to sign. There was no doubt about that. But neither was she willing to doubt that, come Midsummer Night, Gossamer Axe would assemble by a lake in Gunnison National Forest to battle with immortals.

The limousine at the doors of Burbank Airport told Christa that Adria Records was wooing them. Guitar case in hand, she regarded the long white car, wavered a little, nearly fell.

Bill caught her arm. "Have you eaten, Chris?"

She could not remember.

Lisa and Devi leaned toward her. "Chris? What's wrong?"

"It's . . . it's too much . . ."

"She needs to be fed," said Bill. "We all should have something more than airline food. This could get pretty intense." He gave instructions to the driver to take them to a restaurant, and he threatened to spoon-feed Christa himself if she did not eat.

Christa ate mechanically, without tasting the bland food; and then she found herself in Hollywood, in the spacious lobby of a tall building. A woman came toward them, introduced herself as Jessica Conway, and escorted them up to the main offices.

The oak door led into a world of thick, plush carpeting, chrome furniture, floor-to-ceiling windows. It was all designed to intimidate, but Christa was beyond such emotions. *Judith. Judith.* The name hammered at her, and when she faced Harry Veltmann, the head of the Artists and Repertoire department, she was close to tears.

The figures Harry quoted were large, the benefits excellent, the offer—on the whole—kingly. What Adria Records asked in return was not unexpected.

"We're talking five albums to start off with," said Harry. "We usually make it two, with the band on probation, so to speak, since first albums usually don't do too good. Van Halen did better with Warner, of course, but Van Halen was an exception."

Lisa looked up. "So is Gossamer Axe."

Harry nodded, thoughtful. "I believe you. That's why we're making it five."

"Five is okay. We can give you five."

"Christa?" said Harry. "How is your original material? Can you handle five LPs?"

Christa looked at the guitar case at her feet. Once, she had been a harper. But her harps were gone. In their place . . . "I . . ." Save for Melinda, who kept her face averted, the women were looking at her with pleading expressions: *Don't mess it up, Chris.*

She gasped as though she had swum up from the bottom of the sea. "I can," she said.

Harry's next words crushed her. "You can go out and look at some studios today. We want you comfortable, but we want to start in two weeks."

The room blurred. Christa fought with the vertigo. "Two . . . weeks?"

"Fifty grand apiece? Up front?"

"Two weeks?" she cried. "But . . . but I . . . we can't . . ."

Harry, on the surface, was unruffled. He stared at her for a moment, evaluating. "Okay, Chris. Give me a date."

"Ah . . ." Christa looked at her bandmates. Melinda was plainly frightened. Lisa was frankly puzzled. Monica, as usual, was leaving the details to others.

Devi regarded her calmly. "This has something to do with what we were talking about, right?"

"It does." Christa's voice was hardly audible.

"Chris?" said Bill. "Harry's open. Make an offer."

"The . . ." She had to name a time for her world to change forever. But, with Judith by her side, she could face anything; without her, nothing would matter. "The . . . the first of July."

"Good enough," said Harry. "You got a lawyer out here, Bill?"

"Damn straight. The best. Geoff Swanson."

"I'll have hard copy on this by noon," said Harry, "and Geoff will have it by closing time. Can you rush him a little?"

Bill laughed. "If I pay him enough."

There were rooms waiting for them at the nearby

Hilton, all expenses paid, and Harry suggested that they take an hour or two to rest. Jessica escorted them back to the limousine and saw them off, but, waiting at the curb, she touched Christa on the shoulder. "I need to thank you," she said.

"Thank me?" The others had already entered the car. Christa and Jessica stood alone, the passing traffic masking their words. "For what?"

"For your music," said Jessica. "With all this business talk, some things don't get said. I heard you play in Denver. You made me feel different. You made me feel proud." She smiled. "Thanks."

Jessica had just paid her the highest compliment a harper could receive, and it pulled Christa out of her whirl of thoughts like a friendly hand. "Brigit bless, Jessica," she said softly, and, as she turned and entered the limousine, she found that she could face her bandmates' questioning stares with comparative equanimity.

CHAPTER
TWENTY-SEVEN

Just after dinner, Melinda rapped softly on the door of Christa's hotel suite and stuck her head in. "Chris," she said softly, "we're having a band meeting in me and Lisa's room. Could you . . . uh . . . come?"

Christa nodded, picked up Ceis, and followed Melinda down the hall. Since she had boarded the United flight that had brought them to California, she had been expecting this. She had hoped that she would be the one to decide when and where to tell the band of her origins, but the record contract had taken the matter entirely out of her hands.

Melinda paused at the door. "This wasn't my idea."

"We're still friends?"

"Yeah, Chris." Melinda bent her head. "I know it's gonna be weird. But we're still friends."

They entered the room hand in hand. The others were already there. Lisa's expression was that of a woman about to check the contents of her fuel tank with a lit match. Devi had apparently advised her to use a flashlight. Monica plainly did not want to know, but in light of the trip ahead, felt that it was necessary.

Christa sat down on the edge of Lisa's bed. "I'm here."

Lisa fidgeted. "Chris . . ." She looked at Devi. Devi looked back. "It's like this. We . . . uh . . . always knew that you had some personal things in your life. Like plans or something. You know, stuff you didn't want to talk about. But with this contract and all, it seems to be getting in the way, and we're thinking that . . . uh . . ." She turned to Monica as though for encouragement. Monica shrugged. Lisa plunged on. "We're thinking that maybe it's time for you to tell us what's going on."

Ceis lay in Christa's lap. She stroked the smooth wood, idly snapped a switch back and forth. "It is, surely."

Melinda had huddled in a big chair by the window, her face buried in her knees. She did not look up.

"You all know that I didn't grow up in America," said Christa. "I told you that I was from Ireland. I must apologize. It was not quite a lie, but it was close enough." Her tongue fought her, but she mastered it. "I was born in the sixth century. Ireland wasn't even Ireland then. We called it Eriu, and I was trained as a harper. Trained in magic."

She went on. She told them about Judith, about the harpers' school, about the Sidh. She described the two hundred years of survival, the battles with Orfide. The tale could have gone on for many hours, but she kept it short.

"I'd given up hope," she said finally. "But Melinda introduced me to rock and roll, and I knew then that at last I'd found something that could defeat Orfide. The rest . . ."

No one spoke. Lisa looked stunned; Devi, thoughtful. Melinda was clutching her legs so hard that the tendons of her hands stood out taut as bass strings. Monica seemed sad, almost sympathetic.

"The rest you know. I have to fight Orfide this Mid-summer. That's June 21. I . . ." Christa's voice broke. "I hope you'll come fight beside me."

Silence. At last, Devi spoke. "You've always been honest with us, Chris."

"I have. I am being so now."

"I know."

A police helicopter slowly traversed the night scene outside the window, strobe light flashing whitely. Down below came the sound of a car horn, its pitch rising and falling as it Doppler-shifted past the hotel. Melinda stood up, shaking, and ran for the bathroom. The door slammed behind her.

Christa sighed. She had forced Melinda enough. She would not intrude. "What say you, then?" she said to the others. She felt weak, dizzy: the strain of the last two centuries was catching up with her.

"I was a fucking mess when I first met you," said Devi bluntly. "You saved my ass." She got up, went to Christa, held out her hands. Christa took them. "I believe you, Chris. I'm with you."

"But that's impossible," said Lisa. "Stuff like that just doesn't happen."

"You're saying that Chris is lying?"

"No, but . . . I mean . . . What the fuck happened to common sense?"

"This is rock and roll, Boo-boo," said Devi. "Common sense went out the window a long time ago."

In the bathroom, the toilet flushed, but Melinda did not reappear. Lisa looked at the door. "You don't think she'll . . . hurt herself, do you?"

Christa shook her head slowly. "She can't. Not after what I did to her on Beltaine."

Monica finally spoke. Her eyes were moist, and her words came out with a nervous giggle. "It all fits together, doesn't it? The way you act, and the stuff you couldn't tell me. And the ghost, too, right? Is Ceis in on this?"

"Ceis was the ornate harp in my studio, Monica. But the night before Beltaine, Ceis entered my new guitar, and the harp was no more." Christa held up the gleaming instrument. "This is Ceis."

peace

They all heard it. Monica laughed again, a little hysterically, and Devi put an arm about her. Lisa blanched.

"That was the guitar? It talks?"

Christa nodded.

The drummer stared for a moment, then fainted.

Christa dropped Ceis onto the bed and saved her from toppling out of her chair. Lisa recovered quickly enough, but her brown eyes were bewildered. "Jesus Christ! You came up with some weird shit, Chris. Couldn't you just be gay or something like that?"

"I *am* gay, Boo-boo. It's for to save my lover that I need you."

"Yeah . . . well . . ."

Devi stood before her, hands on hips. "You running out on us, Boo-boo? Or are you going to help us kick some Sidh butt?"

The drummer put her face in her hands. "Oh . . . God . . . my grandmother was a witch, and that was bad enough. Now my bandleader turns out to be a . . . a . . ."

Monica spoke suddenly: "A friend? Is that it, Boo-boo?" She tottered to her feet. "Chris is my friend. When I needed help, she took me in. Shit, she went after Ron like a buzz saw the first time I showed up. She didn't have to do that. And if I can handle ghosts, I guess I can handle anything." She turned to Christa. "You gonna mind if I ask lots of dumb questions?" Christa shook her head. Monica hugged her. "You must have been hurting like mad all this time," she said, and Christa clung to her, her face against the stiffness of bleached-blond hair.

Melinda came out of the bathroom, face washed, strands of hair dripping around her face. She leaned heavily against the doorframe. "I'm okay, Chris. Just real scared."

Christa did not let go of Monica. Kevin was a thousand miles away, and the warmth of human flesh was a comforting reminder of friendship and love. "Are you frightened of me?"

Melinda brushed drops from her cheek. "I've been scared since I first met you. You always knew what you were doing, and I didn't. Sure, you fucked up, but you've been trying to fix it ever since, and that's a damned sight more than I ever did."

Christa waited.

"Count me in," Melinda said abruptly. For an instant, Christa saw a flicker of robes the color of a summer sky and piercing blue eyes that flashed, stern and kind both. Melinda turned toward her bedroom. "I'm gonna sleep," she said. "See you in the morning, huh?" She stopped at the door. "I haven't had any trouble sleeping lately, Chris. Did you fix that, too?"

Christa shook her head slowly. "You did."

Devi waited until Melinda had closed the door, then turned to Lisa. "We're waiting, Boo-boo."

The drummer stared helplessly. "What the fuck am I supposed to say? This is unreal."

"So is MTV."

"I don't live in MTV!"

"You do now."

Lisa's curls had turned damp. She lifted a strong hand and wiped at her brow. "Oh . . . God . . . grandma . . ."

"I won't push you, Boo-boo," said Christa. " 'Twill be rough at Midsummer. Orfide is a skilled bard, and he will throw everything he can at all of us."

Lisa deliberated. "My grandma said that magic would save my ass someday, Chris. Are you up for it?"

"On my honor before the Gods," said Christa, "I

pledge my protection to you all, to the best of my powers, in this world, in all the Worlds, for as long as I have strength to call my own." The oath did not sound as imposing in English as in Gaeidelg, but her tone conveyed her sincerity.

For some time, Lisa said nothing. Then, finally, she took Christa's hand. "Okay. You got me, Chris." She looked at the guitar where it lay on the bed. "Ceis?"

Lisa

With a glance at Christa, she forced a nervous smile. "My . . . my friends call me Boo-boo."

They signed the contract two days later. The terms were generous, much more so than Bill or the band could have expected. Adria Records intended to keep the Axe happy.

"What puzzles me," said Harry Veltmann as he offered a fountain pen to Christa, "is that no one even mentioned the idea of . . . uh . . . recreational substances in the contract." He did not see Melinda flinch. "That's a first for me. We've had other bands—"

"We don't do drugs," said Devi abruptly. "It's out."

"You . . ."

"Well," said Lisa, "maybe aspirin." She took Melinda's hand protectively, grinned at Christa. "Usually we just stay high on life. It's like, uh . . . magic."

Christa smiled thinly as she inspected the nib and signed her name. Unknown to Bill and Jessica and Harry, Gossamer Axe had pulled together to face a task much harder than cutting a record or touring. The business of rock and roll stardom was as nothing compared to the battle that would be waged beside a still lake in Colorado. Still, she felt almost lighthearted. The band was solid. Only the Sidh remained, and she was confident.

"I look at it this way," said Lisa that afternoon. They were back in the limousine, traveling from studio to studio, looking for one in which they would record their first album. "If we can beat the Sidh, we can sure as hell beat Budokan. Or Red Rocks."

Devi sipped at a can of pop and glanced at the glass that separated the passenger section from the driver. He could hear nothing unless they flipped the intercom switch.

Her jeans squeaked on the leather seat. "What can we expect from Orfide, Chris?"

"Physical death is the least worry," Christa replied. "He might try to kill me, but most likely the worst you will face is madness . . . and the knowledge of failure."

"So we could all be crazy," said Lisa. "So what's the big deal? Rockers are nuts anyway."

Christa heard the apprehension beneath her words. "We have a few weeks ahead of us," she said. "In that time, think about yourselves, try to confront your fears. Try to heal any old wounds you've suffered. Orfide will strike there first."

Devi looked darkly at the passing buildings. "If he has time."

"Don't dismiss his abilities, Devi. He is powerful."

Devi finished her soda and crunched the aluminum can one-handed. "So is a fifteen-thousand-watt PA."

Kevin had buried his brother in the spring, and, standing at graveside, placing his boutonniere on the polished lid of the casket, he had known that he was also burying his own past. Surrounded by Danny's friends—singles and couples who leaned upon one another for reassurance, their eyes damp and red—he felt no connection save with the body that was lowered into the earth; and even that link evaporated as the weeks lengthened and he took up his guitar and his school once more.

Now, he had Christa's past, and her people, and her Gods; and after she put his harp into his hands, he found his memories dissolving, his childhood swept away. He dreamed of Corca Duibne, and if he had a beginning, it was in Eriu, at the edge of the sea. His parents, his schooling, his guilts—all were fading like old pictures left too long in the sun.

Frankie alone remained vivid. In the swirling images of dream, the old black man seemed as much a part of the Gaeidil as white-haired Sruitmor, and the contradiction of race and locale disturbed Kevin not at all. The old slide guitar responded gladly to him now, and its power was as strong as stone, as fragrant as fertile earth—a living invocation of the bluesman's art.

Dave Thomas, Kevin's fellow teacher, heard the difference in his playing. Frequently, he poked his head into

Kevin's office and listened to him milk his unamplified Stratocaster for all the emotion it could give, exploiting the smallest nuance of tone and timbre.

"You sound hot, man."

"I have a good teacher."

Dave blinked. "You planning on playing out one of these centuries?"

The Gaeidil pursed his lips. "Thinking about it. Haven't found the right people, haven't found the right gig."

"Do it, man. Look what happened to Christa. She's in L.A., having a ball, and they're showering money on her."

"I know." Kevin smiled, propped his feet up, flashed through a series of licks.

"You were her teacher, Kevin."

Kevin's smile grew broader, and he laughed. "Nope. Never." He swiveled his chair around to face Dave. "Take a look at this," he said. "You take the phrygian mode—which is a woman's sound, because it generates life—and you mix it up with the plagal form of the locrian. You just hold it there." He reeled off a scale and turned it into arpeggios while he talked. "Doesn't that make you feel dizzy?"

Dave was clutching at the doorframe. "What the hell are you doing?"

"It's life and death balanced together. It's magic."

"You're outta your ever-loving mind." And Dave retreated to his office at the other end of the school.

Kevin sighed. He was beginning to understand the magic, but he had no direction for it. In Christa's hands, the same scale would have a purpose; in his, it was merely a parlor trick that made Dave dizzy. Once again, he was courting stagnation. What could he do with himself?

A band? Maybe. But he thought that perhaps it was Christa's job to lead a band, to be a star, to take her healing and her love and spread it throughout the world. His own life beckoned him down another path, though he could not yet make out what might lie at its end.

"I'm gonna do something," he said to himself, turning back to the window from which, months before, he had watched a red-haired girl walk down the street with a harp. "I just don't know what it is yet. Maybe at Midsummer . . ."

*   *   *

True to her words, Monica asked questions, but Christa found them anything but foolish. The dark vocalist wanted to know about Christa's childhood, about her life in Eriu, and, strangely enough, about her religion, the worship of the old Gods.

Christa was puzzled by Monica's interest, but she explained as best she could. Eyes shining, Monica listened, her chin cupped in her hands and a faint smile playing about her mouth. To Christa's eyes she looked at times impossibly and unnervingly like Aoine, the Priestess.

"Why are you asking, Monica?" she said during the flight back to Denver. The contract had been signed, the studio chosen, the checks distributed. Much as the 737 hung midway between heaven and earth, Gossamer Axe was suspended between two phases of its career: no longer a local Denver band, it was about to step into another, much larger world.

" 'Cause I like it," Monica replied. "People have been giving me gas all my life. You're telling me about this place where everyone fit in, and someone like me was treated decent. If I'd lived in Eriu, if I hadn't been told all my life that I had to have a man, I wouldn't have gotten mixed up with someone like Ron. And even if I did, I would've been strong enough to tell him where to get off all by myself. And I wouldn't still be so scared of him." She sighed, reclined her seat, settled back with her eyes on the ceiling as though she saw there a vision of a green land. "Sounds nice. Especially the part about the Goddess." She smiled. "I always liked the Virgin Mary. Jesus and God were okay, but Mary was it for me. Except that she always seemed a little wimpy. Now, the Goddess makes sense. Kinda like the Virgin Mary with balls."

Back in Denver once more, Bill arranged for a rehearsal studio. The facilities would be better than Christa's basement could offer, he explained to the band, and there would be recording equipment available. They could polish their music and prepare for the studio in Los Angeles.

It was a fine idea, but cutting a record occupied only a small part of their thoughts. If they rehearsed night after night, working well into the small hours of the morning, refining technique and—now that Christa admitted it openly—magic, they did so for the benefit of an immortal audience.

And, as they rehearsed, they could not but talk about their goal. Christa described her lover and her ways, and Judith slowly became an absent member of the band, one who was missed even by those who had never known her, one for whom Gossamer Axe would passionately battle.

"Will she be able to handle 1987?" said Monica one night as she rode home with Christa. "I mean, there's a big difference between Eriu and America."

"I've thought about it greatly," said Christa. "Judith is strong. Stronger than I, I sometimes think, since she gave up a part of herself to stay with me at the school—something I don't think I could have done. It will not be easy, but I believe that, with the help of all of you, it won't be impossible."

Monica regarded her in silence for a while. "You . . ." Her voice was full of wonder. "You must really love her, Chris. I don't know anyone else who'd do what you're doing."

"She's everything to me."

"Yeah . . ." Streetlights passed, signals changed from red to green, stop signs glowed out of the darkness. When the Eagle bumped up into the driveway, Monica had not spoken for a long time.

Christa turned to her, puzzled: Monica looked sad, and the soft smile on her face only intensified the sadness.

"Monica?"

"I guess I'm jealous, Chris."

"Of me?"

"Of Judith. You love her. I . . ." Monica looked away, her lower lip quivering. "I wish you felt the same about me." With a nervous laugh, she passed her hands over her face. "Listen to me, will you? I thought I was straight."

Christa reached out, touched her gently on the arm. "I . . ." Living together as they did, they had grown close. Closer than family. Closer than sisters. "I thought you were, too."

Monica bit at her lip, took Christa's hand in her own, and, trembling, placed it upon her breast.

CHAPTER
TWENTY-EIGHT

The skies over Denver were dropping rain and hail as Gossamer Axe prepared for a Memorial Day weekend gig at Lavish, a club in the northern part of the metro area. The record contract was already bringing sizable changes to the band, for a crew of three roadies now set up most of the equipment, and Bill Sarah had hired permanent technicians to handle a larger PA and a computerized light system that complimented the new backdrop and lightweight drum risers.

Other changes, though, were also manifesting, and as the wind rattled the windows of the dressing room that Friday night, Christa donned her stage clothes and makeup with a feeling that something was wrong. As she finished her hair and bent over to pull on her boots, she caught Devi looking at her.

"You feel it too?" said the keyboardist.

"I do. What's happening? Do you know?"

Devi shrugged and began lacing up her skin-tight blouse. "I was out in front having a beer when the people started coming in. Did you know we're deserters?"

Lisa caught the word. "Deserters?"

"Yeah. We signed on with Adria, got lots of money, and now we're running out on Denver. At least that's what they're saying. Don't expect the crowd to be real luvvy-duvvy."

"Oh, great . . ." Lisa clipped suspenders to her spandex pants. "Just what we need."

"It happens. Small-town mentality."

Methodically, Christa finished donning her boots and looped several lengths of chain about them. Her brow was furrowed.

Monica put her arms around her. "Hey, Chris. Take it easy. We're still doing real good. I saw Ron get hit with a two-liter bottle of Coke in a bar out in Commerce City. Knocked him flat. At least we don't have to worry about anything like that."

Her perfume and her presence made Christa smile. Theirs was no headlong, passionate affair that left them trembling at one another's touch. Rather it was the fitting culmination of a slow growth of esteem and affection, the embrace of friends who found in the sharing of their bodies the fulfillment of a simple love that desired merely to touch, to be held, to give.

With a wicked grin, Monica kissed her on the cheek. "No," she said as Christa, laughing, moved to wipe off the lipstick. "No. Leave it. Let 'em wonder."

The club manager knocked on the door. "Five minutes, girls."

"Okay," Lisa shouted. But she muttered to herself after he went away. "Girls. Shit."

Monica was fixing her lipstick. "They didn't call us that in Eriu, did they, Chris?"

"You were a girl only until you were brought into the circle of women and presented to the Goddess," said Christa. "From then on, you were a woman."

Lisa was nodding. "I can dig it."

Monica's face said that she wanted to know more. Christa had grown to recognize the quiet smile, the bright eyes. The singer might have been hearing about a beloved home and family that she had left when very young. "When did that happen?"

"When you had your first period."

"Is it . . . was it hard?"

Christa picked up Ceis and strummed a chord to check the tuning—a needless gesture, since Ceis took care of its own adjustments. "There are men's mysteries, and there are women's mysteries," she said. "I can't say which is harder."

"That wasn't what I meant." Monica had turned suddenly shy. "I want to know if . . . well . . . like you could still do that."

"Monica?"

"For me. I mean . . . can you adopt me or something?" Monica's brown eyes were earnest.

"You . . . wish to become a woman of the Gaeidil?"

"Yeah. That's it."

Her family. Her kindred. It was assembling itself out
of various races and backgrounds, called by bonds of
friendship and love. " 'Tis not unheard of," said Christa,
swallowing the sudden lump in her throat. "In the old
days, the whole clan would have to accept you, and the
Sabaid, the council, would have to approve." She shrugged.
"But I'm all that's left of the old days. And so I'll have to
take on the role of *Sab*, and . . ."

She smiled, folded Monica in her arms.

". . . and approve you with all my heart. Come Midsummer, with Judith among us, we'll call you Gaeidil and
woman. And then, counting Kevin, there will be four of
us in the world."

Monica hugged her. "Thanks, Chris. Y'know, I feel
like I'm finally getting to where I should've been all
along." She grinned, indicated the other women with a
flick of her eyes. "Give 'em time," she whispered. "There'll
be more."

Devi's appraisal of the crowd was quite accurate. At
previous gigs, the audience and the dancers had ema-
nated a sense of playful acceptance, a willingness to
participate in the creation of a good time. Tonight, the
listeners separated themselves from the stage with a wall
of aloof disdain.

Melinda felt it, and she began to grow a little afraid.
While she relished the sense of well-being that was hers
while she made music, the first set would end in a few
minutes, and she would have to put down her instrument. She had no idea how she would deal with a hostile
audience when all her defenses had so effectively been
smashed to bits.

No, she admitted, the bits had been there already.
Christa had merely cleaned them out. It was as though,
after a long vacation, she had returned to her apartment
to find the carpets shampooed, the walls painted, the
broken-down furniture repaired and reupholstered. Christa
had moved her into a clear mind, but Melinda had not
lived in it long enough to call it home.

The set ended. No applause, no cheers. Melinda put
her bass aside and plunked down the stairs from the
stage, the hot passion of the music running out of her as

though through a bullet hole. She saw Christa open her mouth to call to her, but she turned away.

She was no longer certain exactly who she was, could not remember her own mannerisms, was not overly sure whether a given memory should yield a sense of joy or of pain. She had lost all sense of the little comforts with which she had once provided herself—favorite foods, cold beer, a good-natured, flirty dance with a young buck—and, in fact, had only a tenuous grasp on pleasure.

She bummed a cigarette off the girl at the front desk, vaguely remembering that she had once, years before, smoked. But the first drag told her that here was another habit that was gone, that the instinctive revulsion she now felt for drugs of any sort included nicotine. She tossed it into an ashtray.

"Hey, Melinda."

She had to sort through memories that seemed not quite her own until she matched the man's face with a name. Tom Delany. "Hey," she said dully.

"I heard about your contract. Jeez, that's pretty hot."

She nodded. "Thanks."

Tom still talked too fast. "You must be running around with a pretty fast crowd out in California. Bet they've got bucks."

She shrugged. "I guess some of them do. I wouldn't know."

He glanced over his shoulder, edged around until he stood between Melinda and the rest of the lobby. "Listen, Mel. I've got this band, and we're really hot. The demo sounds terrific, and I know for sure that one listen is going to send the labels sky-high. I just need you to push it for me."

"I don't understand."

"Don't play stupid, Mel. You're in. You're signed. You need to play my demo for Adria. Hey . . ." He grinned. ". . . they'll probably cut you in on our contract. You know, finder's fee or something."

Melinda shook her head tiredly. "I'm sorry, Tom," she said softly. "I just want to be left alone."

"What the hell are you talking about?"

"Get yourself a good manager, play music, and enjoy it. If you're supposed to make it big, you will." She started to walk away, but he grabbed her jacket.

"Listen, girl, you owe me. You stole my Strat, and your band bumped mine out of a gig at InsideOut after the holidays. You owe me big. If it wasn't for the fact that you were fucking Carl Taylor, it'd be me that was signed, not you."

His words battered at her. She shook her head. "Please, Tom. Let me go."

But her sad voice did not move him. "You damned bitch! You're just like all the rest, screwing your way to the top." He shook her in cadence to his words. "What kind of drugs they give you out in L.A.? Good stuff, I bet."

"Please . . ." The tears were coming. She was alone. She had only herself to blame. For everything.

"Look here, slut—" But his words were suddenly choked off as a small white hand seized his hair and jerked him away from her. He fell back onto the carpet.

Devi stood over him, her black eyes hot and bright. "Leave her alone."

He was not listening. He got to his feet and reached for Devi with both hands. The keyboardist's eyes flickered for a moment as he took hold of her arms, but then she lifted a leg and, with deliberate precision, kneed him in the groin.

Tom doubled over and went down. The bouncer arrived a few seconds later and threw him out.

Devi held Melinda as she sobbed. "It's okay, love. You're safe."

"Is that what I am, Devi? A slut? Did I just sleep around so we could—"

"You're Melinda," said Devi. Her voice was warm and reassuring, almost like Christa's. "You're our friend. You made some mistakes." Gently she guided Melinda back toward the stage. "Time to put them behind you. Come on. We're up again."

"The audience . . ."

"Fuck 'em. They don't know good metal? Too bad."

The fire of the music was slow to build this time. Still trembling, Melinda played competently, firmly, with all the power that Christa could have wanted; but though she knew that Devi was right, she felt empty, sad, shaken.

The passion still had not returned when, midway through the second set, she looked down at the dance floor and

saw Ron, Monica's old boyfriend. Haggard and unshaven, he stood directly before the stage.

He had a gun.

Fighting as she was with the hostile crowd, Christa did
not notice Ron until he had raised the revolver. She
almost froze, but Ceis kicked her into action, and she
ran to protect Monica.

But Ron was already pulling the trigger.

Monica had half turned to flee, but the first slug caught
her in the chest and spun her around to face Ron just as
the second ripped her cheek open. She crumpled, her
legs folding up beneath her. Her head bounced hollowly
on the stage.

Ron pivoted and took aim at Christa. She felt an
impact as she dropped to her knees beside Monica, but
the bullet had embedded itself partway in Ceis, stopped
as much by the hard woods as by the intelligence resident
within them. A few feet away, Melinda threw off her
bass and, with a running leap, piled into Ron, dropping
him to the floor only a moment after Ceis, enraged, had
smashed him back with a blow as from a fist.

Christa bent over the singer. Monica's face was a mass
of blood and torn flesh, but her eyes were open.

"Chris . . ."

Someone was calling for the police, someone else for
the paramedics, but Christa left the technicalities to others. With a healer's instinct, she knew that Monica was
dying. No power of medicine or magic could heal quickly
enough the damage that had been inflicted upon her.

Christa set Ceis aside and gathered Monica into her
arms. Monica's wounds were bleeding freely, but shock
had dulled the pain. "He got me, Chris . . . like I
thought . . ."

"Monica . . ."

"I'm gone, huh?"

Honesty alone was appropriate. Christa nodded slowly.
"I'm here."

"I . . . I know you are." Monica's eyes glazed, but she
seemed to pull herself back. "Where do we go, Chris?
When we die? What did you call it? I can't think."

"The Summerland. The Land of Youth. *Tir na nOg.*"

"Can I . . . go there? I don't want to wind up in heaven or something. I want . . . to see you again."

"You can," said Christa. "You're one of us now. And you'll see me again." Faintly, as though from a distance, she heard sirens growing louder, more urgent.

Monica gripped her hand. ". . . dark . . . can't see . . ."

"Monica, I love you. Follow the light."

". . . sorry I didn't get a chance to meet Judith . . . I'll wait for you . . ." Monica's eyes widened then, and she almost smiled. ". . . allí está . . ."

And she was gone. Gently, Christa lifted a hand and traced the Ogham of rebirth on Monica's forehead, then bent and kissed the still, warm lips.

"I am the resurrection and the life; he who believes in me, even if he die, shall live; and whoever lives and believes in me shall never die."

Monica was buried in a Catholic cemetery at the edge of the city and within clear sight of the Rocky Mountains. The weather was mild, as though to spite the gray clouds that dappled the blue sky, and the grass was fresh and green with the spring rains.

It was a Christian ceremony, but Christa felt no rancor towards the priest who read the antiphons and the verses over the casket, for he spoke for the living: Monica's parents, bent like storm-broken trees; her brother standing stiffly in his full dress uniform, heedless of the tears on his cheeks; the rest of her relatives and friends. Monica—the real Monica, the Monica Christa knew—had long since fled to the Gods she had chosen freely for herself.

The band stood among the mourners as witnesses to their love and the music they had made. Devi's face was hard, Lisa and Melinda wept freely with their arms about one another; and though Christa had already grieved, had already said her farewells in Gaeidelg the night before, still she leaned on Kevin's arm, her vision blurry and shifting, for she was burying a kinswoman that morning.

I'll wait for you, Monica had said.

When the service was over, Christa went to the grave and stood there for a moment, head bowed, voice as soft as the whisper of aspen leaves.

*"Inmain lem do ruidiud rán,
Inmain do chrut caem comlán.
Dursan do dál dedenac,
Tussu d'éc, missi d'anad."*

She placed a bough of evergreen among the flowers and departed, the hem of her Kinsale rustling across the grass.

Afterwards, Kevin left to meet with his students, and the women gathered at Christa's house with Bill Sarah. In his dark suit, Bill looked even more like a lawyer than usual, and his polished shoes creaked as he sat down in one of the big chairs in the living room. His eyes were red. "I've never done well with funerals," he said.

Christa, who was pouring coffee in a kitchen that seemed too silent without Monica's voice and laughter, heard him. She nodded to herself. In two hundred years, she had seen a great deal of death, but it was never easy. And this death . . .

They spoke of simple things, touching now and again on Monica and what she had given to each of them. Christa dropped her modern persona enough to speak of the Summerland, and of Monica's promise to wait. Lisa, Melinda, and Devi understood, and though Bill did not, he nodded in approval.

Toward afternoon, though, he finished his coffee and stood uncomfortably. "I hate to do this," he said, "and I feel like an asshole, but I need to talk business."

"It's okay, Bill," said Lisa. "We've got obligations. It's not just us anymore."

Bill looked relieved, but not much. "I talked with Harry and Jessica the other day. They both would have been out here for the funeral, but they couldn't get a flight."

"What do they want to do?"

"They're willing to wait," he said. "They said to go ahead and take six months, get yourselves sorted out, find . . ." Bill bent his head, plainly unwilling to say the words.

"Find another vocalist, right?" said Devi tonelessly.

"Yeah."

Christa passed a hand over her still-tearing eyes. "I don't want to think about that now."

"Tell me one thing, though," said Bill. "Do you think you'll all want to stick together . . . as a band?"

Melinda spoke quietly. "You have to understand, Bill. This isn't just a band. This is a family. We've . . ." A deeper sadness crossed her face. "We've stood by each other when things got rough. That's not going to change."

"The way I see it," Lisa said slowly, "Ron was aiming to kill the band, too. If we knuckle under and give up, he'll get just what he wanted."

"What's going on with that son of a bitch, anyway?" said Devi.

"He's been arraigned and formally charged," said Bill. "Bail's high. He can't get out."

"Is the DA going for the death penalty?"

"He doesn't think he can get it."

Christa's eyes flashed. One of her clan had been murdered. There were certain penalties, certain traditions of the Gaeidil . . . whether the district attorney considered them possible or not.

The phone rang, but she made no move to answer. "The machine will catch it. It's probably another reporter. I'm done with them."

"I'm surprised they're not at your door."

Christa snorted softly. "They can't find my door."

Bill stared for a moment, then shrugged. "Shall I tell Harry we're still a band?"

"Yeah," said Lisa. "We'll get through this. We'll do it for Monica."

Devi clenched her fist. "Right on."

Bill bade them farewell and went down the brick walk to his car. Only Christa could see the cirlce of blue light about her house flare for a moment as he passed through it.

When she turned away from the window, she realized that the others were watching her. "I said that we'll get through this, Chris," said Lisa. "I meant that we'll get through all of it, including the Sidh gig."

"Question is," said Melinda, "can we do it without Monica?"

"The magic is in the music," said Christa. "The voice makes it more real to the conscious mind, but I'm not overly concerned about Orfide's conscious mind."

Devi seemed to be running over songs in her mind. "What about cues? Vocals are good for that."

Lisa nodded. "But could we find somebody who could do it without freaking?"

Christa shook her head. "I don't believe we can. Not with the time we have. I don't sing very well, but my voice has strengthened since we began playing out, and I think I can do well enough to fill the need." She laughed sadly. "Fitting it is, I suppose: Judith gave up her singing so as to follow me to the harpers' school, and now I must sing with all my heart in order to free her from the Sidh."

Lisa plucked at her dress. "Looks like we've got some heavy-shit rehearsals coming up. Let's go change clothes and get on it."

"For Monica," said Christa.

Lisa stood, took Christa by the shoulders, looked her in the eye. "For Monica," she said. "And for you."

Monica's absence at the rehearsal was an empty ache in the music, like a missing limb. Together, fighting back emotions that ranged from anger to tears, the four women began to hammer out the final decisions regarding the music they would play for the Sidh.

"We'll do the songs first," explained Christa. "I set them up that way. 'Firing Line' is designed to breach the gate and issue a formal challenge to Orfide. I've a slow synth and guitar prelude to it, Devi, that I'll use to muster strength. Some of the covers we've been playing will also be useful."

"I want to see this dude's face when we hit him with 'Metal Health,' " said Lisa.

Christa's smile was thin. "And I also. But, more than likely, Orfide will come to understand the structure of the songs and will counterattack in ways that we can't answer without sizable improvisation."

"We can handle that," said Melinda.

"Indeed, I have no doubt of it. But as I've said before, don't underestimate Orfide."

"What about 'Light My Fire'?" said Devi suddenly. "The solos. I've seen what they can do."

"I did not plan to use that piece, but it's one well worth having in reserve. Can you play that under stress?"

"Shit, Chris, I played that when I was nine years old, and you know what was going on then. I can play it in the middle of a napalm attack."

Christa met her eyes. "Devi, I beg you, be careful of your anger."

"I know what you're saying, Chris, but you can't deny that you're mad, too."

"I am indeed. Just be careful."

"Gotcha." But Devi's eyes were hot.

Christa had no one to drive home, no one to drive home to, and she stayed in the rehearsal studio after the others left. Monica's microphone was still clipped in its stand to the side of the room, and although Christa had stood by her grave that morning, she could not but think that, out of the corner of her eye, she could see a familiar flash of peroxide-blond hair.

Over the months, painstakingly, she had been slowly peeling back the layers of enculturation that she had suffered to grow for the last two hundred years. The Gaeidil, once swaddled in wrappings not at all her own, had gotten her hands loose, had found her voice again. At Christmas, she had freed Kevin, but she had also freed herself. Monica had turned to her, a child seeking a people and a religion that would take her in and love her; and Christa, in welcoming her, had found her own beliefs and loyalties strengthened.

One of her clan lay dead by the hand of another.

Without speaking, Christa picked up Ceis and threw the volume knobs of her amplifier full on. She had rebuked the guitar for its vengeance, but she wished now that she could take back her words. To some actions there could be only one reply.

With a clean, precise anger that she thought she had reserved only for the Sidh bard, she began to play.

CHAPTER
TWENTY-NINE

Pale faces, silvery voices. The Sidh are engrossed in a
revel, torchlight white as frost spilling over tables heaped
with pallid food, reflecting in deep cups of colorless wine,
shimmering in platinum hair. The air is saturated with
the bell-like laughter of innumerable, bloodless throats.

From the dais at the end of the banquet room, Lamcrann
watches and listens, but he does not himself participate.
Orfide is playing well, but even the king detects a note of
desperation in his music. It is as though the bard is
pursued by something, and madness lurks in the depths
of his eyes.

Orfide will not speak of it, denies, in fact, that there is
anything wrong. But Lamcrann knows that the bard, like
Cumad, is foundering in thoughts that, by right, should
never enter the mind of a Sidh.

Perhaps he is right, then, he considers slowly. *Perhaps
the mortal is not good for this place. Perhaps she should
be altered.* He imagines Siudb as a tractable, willing par-
ticipant in the Realm, contemplates her presence in his
bed, wonders for a moment what her rough, mortal skin
would feel like when coated with rank sweat and pressed
against his own opalescent flesh. If she could be made
willing . . .

Lost in his own thoughts of change, he is hardly aware
that Siudb has quietly left the room, led by Glasluit to a
small chamber near the door to the courtyard. There she
finds her harp and the simple clothing she wore when
Orfide first bespelled her. Silently, she strips off the
hated gown of gossamer and light, dons the loose shirt
and tunic, the trews and shoes, slips over all the white
mantle of a novice harper. She is tall and proud as she
takes up her harp.

310

"Now," says Glasluit, "to the grove and beyond. And then . . ."

Siudb hugs him, gripping him about the waist as though he is indeed a man of her own people. This is not Sidh flesh she feels through his shimmering raiment. No, this is sinew and blood and solid bone and, she fancies, the good, reassuring odor of a male body. "Let us go, then."

She holds out her hand, and he takes it. Together they ease out into the darkness surrounding the palace and, under cover of the ornamental hedges, run for the myrtle grove. Behind them, the sounds of the revel continue, but Orfide has stopped playing.

. . . and it's a beautiful morning here in the Mile High City, taking us into an almost-perfect weekend with just a touch of some late afternoon thundershowers to liven things up. Temperature is sixty-two degrees, going up to a high today of eighty-five. Saturday and Sunday going to be much the same, with some scattered afternoon clouds, continuing hot into Monday, so keep those six packs cold, and I'll see you all out by the pool. Coming up, here's one from Bon Jovi . . . 'Dead or Alive' . . . on KAZY, Denver. . . ."

Christa awoke at the first words and lay, eyes closed, listening to the song and to several others that followed. The room was warm with the soft air of a midsummer morning, was filled with the scent of the roses that twined up the trellis on the front of the house.

When the commercials started, she turned the alarm off, dropped a light gown over her head, and went downstairs to make coffee and breakfast. A full day was before her: a long drive, hard work, final arrangements. Tomorrow night, beside a mountain lake, Kevin would power up the sound system, and the Sidh would hear a challenge from mortality that would shatter their complacent existence forever.

As she stirred the oatmeal, she swallowed and felt her throat experimentally. The last days of rehearsal had been hard on her voice, and she had gone to bed hoarse. Guitars could be tuned, strings could be replaced, volume and tone knobs could be adjusted, but a singer's instrument was flesh and blood, and, in spite of healing spells, was prone to pain and wear.

The soreness was gone this morning. That was good. She would have to sing tomorrow night, a necessary but poor replacement for a member of the band who could not be present.

She looked up from the stove. "Blessings, Monica," she said to the empty kitchen. "Be well."

Even after a month, the vocalist was still a presence in the house, a memory that warmed the rooms. Christa wondered that she had never noticed how lonely she had been before Monica had come to stay with her. The Gaeidil were a clannish race—people taking care of one another, contributing to the well-being of a larger whole that, in turn, helped its members. A Gaeidil in isolation was unthinkable, and yet Christa had been so for two centuries.

No more, though. She had the band. And Kevin was with her. And Monica, though dead, was nonetheless family: honored appropriately . . . revenged appropriately.

blessings

Ceis distracted her from her thoughts. She was grateful. "Brigit bless, Ceis."

Through the door to her studio she could see the guitar leaning in its stand, as radiant as it had ever been in harp-shape. Even Ron's bullet had not detracted from its beauty. She had taken the instrument back to Roger Best for repairs, and he had, at her request, merely smoothed the wound and polished the slug flush with the surface. It winked at her in the light, a metallic spot of brilliance against the rich wood tones, a reminder of much-loved kindred and the vengeance of the Gael.

"I'd like to see her again," she said to the guitar. "Just to be sure she's all right. I hope she found the Summerland."

The latch of the front door clicked.

Kevin

He entered with a backpack, his harp, and Frankie's guitar, setting all three down in her living room before he joined her for breakfast. "For luck," he said when Christa asked about the guitar. "It's been with me everywhere, and if I'm going off to fight the Sidh, it's coming with me."

"You're sure you still want to do this?"

He buttered his bread slowly and deliberately. He reminded her of her father. "Hey look, Chris, can you imagine what those techs of yours would do down in Gunnison? They're okay guys, both of them, but . . . well . . . they're not our people." He chuckled. "At least not yet."

" 'Twill not be easy for you, even though you've seen magic."

"Easier with me running sound than with anyone else." Kevin had been mumbling through the bread, but he now swallowed it and continued in a clearer voice. "I'm just glad I can do something. I've been sitting around, twitching, feeling like there's something that I've got to do. Maybe this is it." He looked at his watch. "When are the ladies showing up?"

"In a few minutes. We loaded the truck last night, and Boo-boo's stopping by the studio to get it. Devi will take our clothes and personals in her van."

"What about a generator?"

"We rented a big Allison diesel powerplant."

Her words trailed off as she looked down the hall to the front door. When she reentered her house on Monday, would Judith be on her arm? Or would Christa Cruitaire be, again, alone?

She held a staggering weapon in her hand, but Orfide was himself unbelievably powerful. She believed in rock and roll, and she believed in herself, but she could not but think that heavy metal had but evened the odds between her and the bard.

Kevin took her hand. "Courage, Chris. If rock and roll can't get Judith out of there, nothing can."

She was still looking at the door. "It's greatly I'm afraid of that."

The caravan proceeded southward along U.S. 285. In her rearview mirror, Christa could see Devi's white van and, farther back, the big truck they used for transporting their equipment. Immediately behind her Eagle, swaying heavily on its four-wheeled trailer, was the Allison generator, a lumpy bulk beneath its canvas cover.

Their schedule gave them plenty of time, and they stopped at the diner in Fairplay where Christa had once harped. Bobbie was still there; but Christa had altered her hair and her clothing, and so to the waitress she was only another rocker, the band was no more than a band, the journey but a trip that was taking them through the center of the state to . . . somewhere else. Another gig, another few dollars in a smoky bar in Taos, or in Albuquerque. It was all the same to Bobbie.

She served them hamburgers and asked them about the band with a smile that indicated that she did not believe a word of what they said. But rock and roll was playing on the radio, and the music of Gossamer Axe would one day be sandwiched into the playlists along with the Bon Jovi and the Van Halen and the Loverboy. Maybe, Christa thought as she finished her coffee, maybe Bobbie would someday hear the love and remember that not all tears were shed in sorrow. And maybe that would make a difference. Her harps were gone, replaced for the most part by guitars, but maybe that was for the best.

Kevin went up to pay the bill, and Melinda and Devi vanished into the bathroom. Lisa touched Christa on the shoulder. "Hey, come on, Chris. We're going to do it. We're going to get your girlfriend out."

"Thanks, Boo-boo."

"I mean it. I feel good about this." Lisa smiled out at the highway and the trees. "All the shit I put up with in all those other bands, the hassles, the crummy beds—it was all getting me ready to go and do something real. I think I understand what grandma meant now." But a shadow crossed her face for a moment, the same shadow that, now and again, touched them all. "I just wish Monica was here."

"And I also."

Lisa regarded her somberly. "Ron . . . died in his cell the night after we buried her," she said softly. "The paper said he killed himself."

"Monica was family," Christa said without looking at her. "Murder brings its inevitable penalty."

Lisa dropped her eyes. "That's the way you feel about us, huh?"

"It is."

Lisa was silent. Finally: "That's all I wanted to know."

"Boo-boo?"

Lisa stood up and pulled on her windbreaker with firm, definite movements. "I feel the same way about you."

Toward late afternoon, they reached Gunnison National Forest, and Christa turned the Eagle over to Kevin. With Ceis plugged into the little battery amplifier, she sat on the back seat, weaving a spell of unseeing about the three vehicles. A large truck with *GOSSAMER AXE* painted on the side in two-foot, uncial capitals would normally attract a good deal of attention in a national forest, but a ranger looked right at it without noticing.

At the edge of the meadows that surrounded the small lake, they pulled up and cut their engines. The big truck swayed once, then settled in. A meadowlark called, likewise a jay. Swifts streaked through the clear air, fighting for insects.

Lisa swung down from the cab and joined Christa by the shore. "That's it?"

Christa was examining the gate. In the light of the westering sun it roiled and swirled above the water. Just on the other side, almost within reach, was Judith. "It is," she said.

"Right. Let's get started." Devi and Melinda had already opened the back of the truck, and Kevin was helping them to unload the portable stage. Lisa started off to join them, but turned for a moment back to Christa. "I meant what I said at lunch. You put it all together for me, too."

"My thanks, Boo-boo."

Lisa went to help the others. Christa faced the gate, hands on hips. In spite of her worries, she felt unaccountably good. If love and loyalty had anything to say about it, Orfide would have his hands full tomorrow night.

She heard Monica's words again, whispering as though on the breeze that rippled the surface of the lake. *Give 'em time. There'll be more.*

The thought was a warm glow. With or without Judith, Christa would welcome them.

Music had given her much: the touch of harpstrings, the blazing fury of electric guitar, a band, and, maybe, Judith. As she had at the Malmsteen concert, she lifted a fist into the air. *"Rock and roll."* An edge, as of bright metal, glinted within the words.

The stage was in place by twilight, ringing fully a third of the circumference of the lake, a raised aluminum platform covered with nonslip vinyl sheeting. Access stairways led down toward the equipment truck, and Lisa and Kevin had already muscled some of the larger PA speakers into place.

Afterward, Melinda took Christa's wagon up to Gunnison and returned with what Christa said was enough Kentucky Fried Chicken to feed a band of *Fianna*. But the day had been long, the work hard, and for all the chicken they left they might well have been Gaeidil warriors.

Sprawled on the grass, they watched the last traces of light fade from the sky, marveled at the brilliance of the stars, listened to the sounds of crickets and night birds. Lisa was sitting with her arms wrapped about her drawn-up knees, and she peered off through the darkness. "Should I be seeing something out by the lake?"

"Like what?" said Christa.

"Like the gate or something? What am I supposed to be looking for?"

The gate hung above the water, as faintly luminous in the night as it was shadowy during the day. "Don't look *for* something," said Christa. "If you look *for* something magical, you'll never see it. Just look. Unfocus if you want. It's not your eyes you want to use, really."

Silence. "Yeah," said Lisa at last. "I think I know what you mean." She caught her breath. "Oh, shit. Now *I'm* seeing this stuff."

"Well," said Kevin, "why not? It's real."

Another silence. Then: "Yeah. I guess so."

Melinda shrugged. "We'll be seeing a lot more tomorrow night, I guess," she said softly. Devi put an arm about her shoulders.

After dinner, the women prepared to drive back to a hotel in Gunnison, since Kevin was of the firm opinion that sleeping on cold ground did not improve the quality of rock and roll. He himself would camp at the sight.

"I'm used to it," he said as Christa attempted a final protest before she joined the others in Devi's van. "I do it all the time. Real Colorado boy. Don't I look like John Denver?"

She laughed. "It's ashamed I am to sleep in a bed while you have to—"

He shook his head violently. "Someone's got to stay here and keep an eye on things, and you've got to be up to par tomorrow. No screwing around with Gaeidil pride. This is important. You sleep. I'll be fine."

"It's well," Christa said at last. "A word though: don't leave the meadow. I've ringed it with a spell of confusion so that we won't be interrupted. If you leave, you won't be able to find it again."

"No problem. It's too dark to find anything even without the spell."

The van bounced up the faint road, and Kevin waved at the taillights until they winked out amid the bushes and trees. The engine noise faded and left him in the meadow with the sounds of insects and the lap of water.

As when, shortly after he had first met Christa, he had stood outside his mountain home, listening, he heard again the intricate symphony that was the working of the world. He smiled: by the grace of the Gods, and by Brigit's hand, he had come to consciously participate in this music, adding his own small melodies and ornaments, fitting himself into the score . . . and occasionally taking a solo of his own.

He had a solo coming up tomorrow night, he was sure. The music that went on around him and the feelings of the world—of the many Worlds—were pointing ahead to it with all the certainty of a twelve-bar blues progression that turned about on the dominant fifth and swept back to the tonic for another round as the Band Leader smiled and nodded to him with all the warmth of a Midsummer sunrise. *Yours, Kev.*

He did not know at present what he would play. But he was a musician—a rocker and a harper both—and when the time came, he was sure that the music would be there.

For an hour or two, he watched the stars, watched the flickering of the gate above the water, listened to the music. And then he crawled into his tent and went to sleep.

A league out, and a foot above a tall man's head.

Chairiste Ní Cummen stares out at the ocean, wondering if what the storyteller said was true. She hopes that it is, that the Druids' tales of the Summerland, the Land of Youth, *Tir na nOg*, are also; for she has a friend there that she wants to see again.

She turns around to her father's house. Wicker-woven and new-thatched, it lies surrounded by the steading and ringed by an earthen bank. Beyond lies the land of Eriu, green and golden in the sunlight, and in the distance a smudge of smoke testifies to the presence of another house, where Siudb dwells with her family.

And on and on. Eriu lies like a velvet comforter spread by the hand of a Goddess, surrounded by seas of water both white and blue. Her land. Her home.

Now the Sidh mound rises up in the Midsummer evening, lit by moonlight and starlight. Chairiste and Siudb can hear the sound of a revel. Music and silvery laughter loft up into the air from the Realm, leading their thoughts into other places, other Worlds, until . . .

Too late, Chairiste notices the archway of darkness that has opened in the hill. Ron strides toward them, revolver in hand, eyes full of madness, and he aims the gun at Siudb. His finger tightens on the trigger.

But when Chairiste turns, Siudb is not there. Her place has been taken by Monica, who, ignoring the apparition from out of the barrow, takes Christa's hand and leads her off into a brighter land, sunlit and warm. The singer is clad in her favorite T-shirt and jeans. Her peroxide-blond hair gleams.

They walk together through a copse of silver fir. The path they follow crests a hill and opens out into a broad lawn that sweeps down into a valley. This country is endless, woven of river and mountain, of clear air and sunlight.

This is not Eriu. It is another place, of earthly happiness, dear to the heart of every Gaeidil born . . . or adopted.

Monica sidles close to Chairiste and wraps an arm about her waist. "I wanted to see you again," she says. She laughs, embarrassed. "Selfish, huh?"

Chairiste touches Monica's face. She shakes her head. "Never."

"I managed to swing this dream. Everyone kinda laughed, but it was nice laughter. You know, like we'd do in the band with each other."

"Is it well with you?"

Monica nods. "The people here are real good to me.

They talk straight, just like you. They don't seem to mind that my skin's dark. A Celt's a Celt, they say."

"Oh, Monica . . ,"

Monica's eyes are brimming. "I wanted to see you. I wanted to let you know that I'm okay. We can't do this real often, but hey, it's something, isn't it?"

Chairiste nods, takes Monica's hands. They are as she knew them in life: small and brown, the nails painted a color that Monica always called *fuck-me red*. Christa kisses them and folds them together between her own. "We're playing for the Sidh tomorrow."

"Yeah, I know. That's another reason. I left you kinda quick, and I wanted you to know that everything's all right between us. You gave me some of the best nights I've ever had, and you really made me feel good about it all. We're cool. Don't let Orfide give you any shit. I love you. And I know that"—Monica smiles through her tears—"that when you get here with Siudb, I'll love her, too. We'll probably terrorize the place. They'll be glad to see us go."

For another minute, Monica stands before Chairiste, and then she is gone, slipping out of the dream as quickly as she slipped out of life. For an instant, Chairiste is alone in the Summerland. She almost wishes that she could stay, but even in the land of the dead she is as far from Judith as she is in life.

Christa woke to the morning sunlight that glared through the blinds of her hotel room. A knock came to her door. "Hey, Chris," said Melinda. "We're going for breakfast. Do you want to come?"

Midsummer Day.

CHAPTER
THIRTY

The lights and revelry of the palace are distant and faint.
Siudb and Glasluit have penetrated far into the rolling
hills and grasslands, farther—again shattering the patterns, the sameness that holds the Realm in thrall—than
they have ever traveled before. Here, the groves and
streams shift in form even as the eye looks upon them,
and the sky, though dark, feels uncertain. Flickers, as of
ice or gems or nothingness, blink from the blackness
suddenly, and as suddenly vanish.

"Undisturbed we will be here," says Glasluit.

"Are you afraid?"

He glances about nervously. "This is no longer my
land. I do not belong here. I am . . . disturbed."

Siudb cannot blame him. Her own heart is beating in
fear. There is much that she must do, and opening the
gate is the least of the task ahead of her.

Gently, she touches his face. "What you will, my
friend," she says. "I will not be the prideful Gaeidil in
this, demanding unquestioning loyalty and valor from my
friends. I can speak only for myself. I must go. My love
awaits me."

"My love . . . stands before me," he says softly. "If my
nature betrays me, I will remember you always . . . with
whatever memory is left me in whatever form I might
take."

"You have a great heart. A great heart creates a soul."

He takes her hand. "I pray you are right."

Ahead, a stone outcropping proves fairly substantial. It
overlooks a gentle slope that, though it leads down to
absolute darkness, is spotted with wildflowers. Siudb sits,
leans her harp against her left shoulder.

"Ah, little friend," she whispers to the willow wood.
"Who would have thought it?" She presses her lips to the

soundbox. Her harp: humble, inexpertly made, much beloved. Once it was an emblem of her sacrifice to Chairiste. Now it is a symbol of achievement.

Her first chord rings out like a summons to battle. The very rocks appear suddenly to be listening. The darkness ahead of her flickers with violet light.

Swiftly, the music infiltrates the substance of the Realm, pries at it, works it into a loose suspension of realities. Then, straining her shod feet into the ground to anchor herself, Siudb reaches through the appearance of the Realm and feels through the many possibilities that lie beyond it. She finds one that is filled with homely memories and thoughts. Her world.

She cannot see it, for the gate is not yet realized, but she knows it is there. Smiling at the thought of home in whatever guise it might array itself, she strikes up the melody that will blend the two sides of the gate and open it to vision and to feet.

But something is going subtly wrong with the spell. Under her hands, the strings of her harp seem to be moving of themselves, sustaining too long at one time, damping too quickly at another. The gate begins to dissolve even as she strives to make it more real.

She glances up. Glasluit is not in sight.

Stubbornly, she bends her will to the harp once more, battling the recalcitrant strings. But the magic is inexplicably failing.

She smashes out a chord to clear the air, tries again. Now, though, her hands are losing their feeling. Moving her fingers becomes an effort, as though she is fighting infinite fatigue.

Brigit!

And now she hears the sound of another harp, for her own has fallen silent. The veils of magic drift over her, deadening her body, and in another few heartbeats she is frozen in place, her hands still lifted to play, as though she is a statue of a harper.

Footsteps swish through the grass. She cannot even move her eyes to see. Orfide comes into view with a half-dozen guards. His face is much paler than she remembers, and there is a look in his eyes that reminds her of corpse-light and the slitherings of unnamed things.

He does not speak. He gestures to the guards, and as

though she is verily a piece of stone, they lift her bodily
and bear her back to the palace.

Night fell slowly over the mountains with a long, lingering twilight that turned the surrounding ridges into
ragged strips of airbrushed cardboard. The sky was clear,
and as dark set in, the stars came out—singly, in clusters—
constellations switching on as though toggled from some
master lighting board.

In full stage clothing and makeup, her hair backcombed
and spiked out until it was a crimson mane that glittered
in the multicolored stage lights, Christa dropped Ceis's
strap over her shoulder and plugged in. The chains looped
from her belt and around her boots rattled crisply in the
night air, and the *failge* at her wrist clinked with a muted
music of their own.

On the other side of the stage, Melinda's Fender Precision gleamed like a sword of jet, and the lights shimmered
across its strings. The bassist lifted her hand to give her
lead guitarist an okay sign, and her studded leather gaunt-
lets flashed in fiery coruscations.

Devi was loading her programs. Bent over the micro-
computer rack-mounted above her keyboards, she stared
intently at the screen, now and then tapping in instructions. The red LED on the disk drive finally winked out.
She nodded to Christa.

Lisa crashed a cymbal. "Come on," she yelled. "Let's
get this party cookin'!"

At the mixing console behind the stage, Kevin brought
up the volume faders. The PA speakers hissed when he
switched in his headset mike. "Ready when you are,
Chris."

The stars were bright. The lake and the cliff were
fading into the evening. A trout plashed in the water.
The waning moon had not yet risen. In the distance,
flickering on the edge of vision, the barrier that Christa
had erected the day before burned blue-white. No one
outside the circle would disturb them, no one would
hear them.

Christa felt warm and comfortable, confident, almost
cocky: after so many gigs, her stage persona manifested
itself automatically. She had but to don her stage clothes,
pick up her guitar, hear the hiss of an active PA, and she

was Chris Cruitaire, lead guitar for Gossamer Axe. With a familiar grin, she grabbed her microphone. *"You guys ready to rock?"*

"Right on!"

Lisa pulled her microphone boom into place and pitched her voice into a nasal whine: "Gee, Yogi, Mr. Ranger's going to be mad at us."

They all laughed. At Kevin's touch, the stage lights brightened and shifted from red to blue to yellow as Lisa laid down a fill and left the sound of her cymbals shivering in the air. Christa pointed to Devi. The synth player put her hands to the keys and began a slow introduction full of eerie whispers and fragments of melody.

At the proper moment, Christa entered the music with the guitar, lofting out a long, wailing lead line. From the stars above, from the earth beneath, from the water and stone about her, she drew such energies as would smash an entry into another universe and funneled it into her music.

The spell built, taking the form of a huge arc of light. It spanned the lake from one side to the other, filling in slowly with ghostly flashes of pale fire. Christa risked a glance at her bandmates and found them staring at the materializing gate.

"God*dam* . . ." Lisa's voice, awe-struck.

Christa stretched a note, held it. The lake was suddenly no more, its place taken by a luminous floor of mist and cloud. "Are you still with me?" she shouted into her microphone.

"To the end, Chris. Brigit bless."

Devi's eyes were dark as she stepped on a volume pedal, and Christa found that the available energy had suddenly doubled. The synths and guitar built. Thunder rumbled from Devi's sampling keyboard. The gate and the floor solidified. Melinda brought up her volume and stood with her hands poised over the strings.

Ceis was roaring now, shrieking out a song that chiseled at the barriers between Christa and the Realm, etching the gateway with lines of yellow fire that burned and sparked and snapped with all the brilliance of a wounded star. In another minute, the veil between the Worlds was thin, weak, ready for breaking.

Christa nodded. Lisa lifted her sticks and smacked out a four-count.

Siudb has been deposited like a block of marble on a stone bench to the side of the great hall. She can see nothing other than what is directly before her eyes: columns, dark windows that have never known anything of daylight, bas-reliefs that tell stories of cherished and unending monotony. Now and again, a bright robe flicks into vision, or a guard stands in her line of sight, his pale Sidh face watching her carefully for signs of escape. But there can be no escape: Orfide's spell holds her frozen.

The bard himself stands behind her, his harp in his hand, watching the reactions of his king to the proposal he has set forth.

"It does seem," says Lamcrann, "that yours is the only way."

"Otherwise," replies Orfide, "this will happen again and again. Cumad is affected by this subtle madness. Who knows how many others have been touched? Glasluit . . . well . . ."

"What has become of him?"

"He ran off into the shadows."

Inwardly, Siudb is raging against the spell that holds her, but she is helpless. She cannot move. She cannot harp. She cannot even sing.

O Mother of All, help me!

Lamcrann circles the wayward Celt, stroking his chin. Orfide, he knows, is right. Cumad is nearly mad with thoughts of stars and suns and the passage of time, Orfide is drawn and frayed from his battles, and he himself—yes, even the king of the Sidh!—is growing weary of this sunless place, of flowers that neither bloom nor fade.

And Siudb could be his. Her nature need not be changed greatly. Only a little change, the smallest of transformations. The Realm would be safe then, and she would be happy. Oh, she might rail and complain still, but her words would be ineffectual: merely the whining of an overindulged child.

"Do it then," he says.

Faint, but plainly audible over the sounds of the revel, comes a rumble as of thunder. A wisp of melody floats through the hall, circles in the air, hangs like bright fire.

Lamcrann looks toward the door. Orfide's hand tightens on his harp. Siudb sits, frozen, motionless.

"What is that?" asks the king.

"Nothing."

More thunder. The melody returns, stronger now: wailing, screaming into upper octaves. Impossibly high overtones claw at Sidh ears with razor talons.

Siudb is suddenly hopeful. The instrument is alien, the strangely haunting music totally foreign, and yet she thinks that she knows whose hand is on the strings.

"Why do you say *nothing*, bard?" asks the king. "My ears do not lie."

Orfide ignores him and starts for the door to the courtyard; but he perhaps can be forgiven his discourtesy, for the music is growing louder, resounding through the palace, shaking the foundations of the building.

Another crash of thunder. Orfide is running now, a presentiment growing on him in spite of his denials.

The music is a rain of heat on his face as he steps into the courtyard. Other Sidh are there, dragged by curiosity or fear from their amusements; but Orfide hardly notices them, for the wall that separates the courtyard from the gardens has vanished. In its place is a towering archway of fire, a latticework of blazing strands that burn as though the very air has been ignited. As Orfide and Lamcrann watch, a fragment falls away, chiseled from its place by the hammer-blows of sound. Another falls. And another. Through the gaps, they see another sky, one filled with stars.

The music builds to a crescendo—roaring, deafening—and is suddenly augmented by the thudding of bass notes and the crash of percussion. The gateway explodes as though struck with an axe, and showers of sparks fly as the curtain that separates one universe from another crumbles, revealing a world of blazing, parti-colored light; of threatening figures clad in leather and steel, chains and studs; of music that cascades into the Realm like molten iron tipped, fresh and hot and white, from out of a furnace.

The fat, searing chords pummel the Sidh, thrust them back; and now a voice lifts up, thin and reedy, but full of menace. Lamcrann thinks he recognizes the singer—a woman with a mane of hair the color of an angry sunset, her face painted and vivid with sensuality and power, her body glad of life, swaggering and arrogant with mortality.

Orfide himself has no doubts. He knows now. Chairiste has returned.

"Are you surprised to see me
Standing here at your door?
Thought that it was all over between us, huh?
Thought you could forget about it all?"

He does not understand the language, but the music speaks in terms he cannot fail to comprehend. This is a challenge: battle to the death.

"I'm here
And I'm calling you out
So get your ass out here, boy,
'Cause it's time to get down
To the firing line!"

The red-haired woman leaps into the air, her agile hands already blurring into a solo of moving harmonies and changing chromatics that Orfide cannot track. But the music is battering him, ripping at his ears, at his brain; and the vocals return, venomous, full of contempt.

"Did you really think I'd just
Give up and walk away?
Did you really think I could?"

By the time the song ends, his mind is fuzzy, likewise his vision. But he shakes himself roughly in body and in spirit. He is a bard. He has been challenged. He will defend his Realm.

For a moment, the women on the stage are silent, and then Chairiste steps forward, chains rattling ominously, *failge* glinting as she points at Orfide. Her words roll out across the courtyard, echoing and swirling as though shouted by an angry Goddess.

"All right, you son of a bitch: *let her go!"*

Leaping, bounding, juggling her instrument with all the casual flash of a seasoned guitar hero, Christa had nonetheless been as piercingly aware of the pale Sidh faces turned toward her from the gaping hole she had smashed into the Realm as she was of the startled expressions of her bandmates. But though the music had faltered at the instant that the gate shattered, it had come back strongly. Lisa had whooped behind her and added a fill that Christa recognized as a show of support. Devi had permitted herself one of her rare smiles. Melinda had pumped grimly on her bass, her hands fluid, moving.

The song finished, her challenge uttered, Christa watched Orfide shake himself free of his stunned disbelief and step forward out of the shadows. He recovered quickly, but the ironic smile he assumed seemed a trifle brittle.

"Why, if our dear Chairiste has not returned to us," he said. "She seems to have taken up with mountebanks. Such coarse entertainments find little favor here at court."

"What's he saying?" asked Lisa.

"He's insulting us, Boo-boo."

"Uh . . . yeah. Tell him to go blow himself."

Christa smiled thinly. "Oh, be assured, I will." She switched back to Gaeidelg. "I have come for my lover. Bring her out."

"Your lover?"

Christa did not reply. She put her hands to Ceis, popped off a harmonic that stung the ears even of the veteran rockers, and jerked up on the tremolo bar. A high pinnacle of the palace exploded into powder with a dull flash of light and rained dust on the heads of the Sidh. "Siudb," she said when the echoes had died away. "I am sure you remember her."

A guard brought a stool for Orfide. He seated himself and put his harp on his lap. "I believe, *crossain*, that this calls for individual combat." He looked meaningfully at the other members of the band.

His name-calling meant nothing to her. "I believe, bard, that I am interested in results only. Individual combat be damned." Christa fingered Ceis again and was satisfied when she saw a number of the Sidh shrink back. Part of the battle was already won. "You might consider giving her up peacefully . . ."

Orfide struck a chord, but before his spell had time to manifest, Christa was at her microphone. " 'Metal Health'! Let's go!"

Lisa was already pounding out the opening fill, and the first chord hit Orfide like a spear in the chest. The bard reeled.

I'm an axe-grinder, a pile-driver,
Mamma says that I never, never mind her.
Got no brains, I'm insane

Teacher says that I'm one big pain . . ."

A pick scrape chain-sawed its way out of the PA; and as Christa kicked in the full overdrive of her amplifiers, the bard winced and shut his eyes in pain.

But he was still playing. Christa felt his spell reaching out, trying to deaden her thoughts, and even though she continued with the Quiet Riot song, she was altering chords and changing rhythmic values to create a counterspell that twisted Orfide's own magic against him.

The bard was taking no chances: he was fighting at strength. Had Christa been equipped only with a harp, she would have been hard pressed. But the massed sound of Gossamer Axe roared like a breaker into the Realm, shredded Orfide's music, rebounded off the palace walls with such force that a number of the assembled Sidh looked up to see if perhaps the whole structure were coming down upon their heads.

"Bang your head!
Metal health will drive you mad!"

And so, seemingly, it would, for Orfide nearly fell from his stool as the energy buried him. Lamcrann held him upright until he recovered; and with a determined crease to his brow, the bard set his hands to the strings again.

Christa threw speed and pyrotechnics into her solo, letting him know what he was going to face if he continued the fight. Orfide was subtle, she knew. Best to make him capitulate before he could think of a suitable defense.

"Bang your head!
Wake the dead!"

The song hammered at the Sidh. Some fled, others cowered in the shadows of the palace; but Orfide fought back, reweaving the fabric of Christa's magic, battering it aside with block chords that, even though they could not be heard above the PA, had power and strength behind them.

But Christa was winning. Each subsequent song only increased her command of the battle, and when she saw Orfide playing and did not feel any effects, she assumed that she had at last mastered the bard.

She smashed out a last chord. "Had enough?"

Orfide stood up. "You have fought well, Chairiste Ní Cummen." His voice was, as always, dulcet, a steel blade

balanced between each word. "But your continued bel-
ligerence puzzles me. You have no lover here."

Christa blinked, felt a sudden sickness in her belly.
"What do you mean?"

"Siudb Ní Corb decided long ago that her lot will be
better with immortals," he replied. "She has become one
of us."

"I do not believe you."

The bard shrugged. "Then ask her yourself."

He gestured at the door of the palace, and a figure—
longed for, familiar, loved—emerged. She was clad in the
gossamer garments of the Sidh, her brown hair lustrous,
her dark eyes bright and flashing.

"Siudb!" It was all Christa could do to keep from
throwing off her guitar and rushing to her.

But the girl smiled softly and shook her head.

CHAPTER
THIRTY-ONE

Siudb remains on the stone bench in the great hall, frozen, immobile. But though she cannot move, she can feel, and when she hears Chairiste's words rolling into the palace through the open doors, her heart leaps.

Outside, Orfide is fighting for his life; inside, Siudb begins to wage another kind of war as she strives to work herself free of her magical bindings. Chairiste's attack helps, for though terrifyingly loud, the music is nonetheless haunting and human and rooted in the same magic of release that Siudb so desperately needs.

Seizing upon fragments of melody, Siudb throws them against the spell, concentrating on the forefinger of her left hand. It rests against a string, long nail hooked over the bronze wire, immobilized in the act of striking. Her throat is unresponsive, but she is singing a silent counterpoint to the foreign words that batter the Realm:

Rowan finger, Oak finger,
Ecstatic finger twined with Ivy . . .

And, just as one of her guards shifts his position to stand next to her, the finger twitches itself free, flexes, sounds a note that is lost in Chairiste's pounding music. The spell collapses, but Siudb stifles a cry of relief. Though they are disorganized by the painful volume, her six guards are nonetheless quite capable of restraining an unarmed woman, Gaeidil though she might be.

Cautiously, she examines the nearest Sidh. His eyes are glassy, his jaw clenched. Accustomed only to the soft whisper of Sidh voices and chime of harpstrings, he is unprepared for this onslaught.

But he is still armed, and I have no weapon. Glasluit, where are you?

An almost sacrilegious thought strikes her, and for several minutes she regards the small, stout harp on her

lap. Its bronze wires glisten in the light of the torches, and
the twenty-nine tuning pins stand like a row of spikes
along the length of the harmonic curve.

One of her guards covers his ears and runs from the
room. Five left.

She herself made this harp. She has wept over it,
longed for it. By dint of untiring work, she has succeeded
in becoming a harper. And now . . .

O my friend.

The harp seems to hear her thoughts. From the wood
radiates a gentle reassurance. *Do it.*

A crescendo of sound tumbles through the room, and
Siudb moves, rising suddenly, swinging the harp like a
club into the face of the nearest guard. The blow is such
that the harp shivers and splits, but the Sidh's sword is
already falling from his strengthless fingers.

Siudb is no master swordswoman like Scathach or Aifé,
the teachers of Cu Chulainn, but she knows how to fight,
and the Sidh are soft and unused to the rigors of combat.
Snatching the sword, she falls upon the guards; and soon
all but one are lying motionless upon the ivory floor.

The last, though, is determined. "Come now, young-
ling," he says. " 'Tis best to stop this foolishness."

The sounds of magical battle have died down outside,
Siudb shakes her head in the freezing silence. "By all the
Gods, you will see me dead first."

"Come now—" But as he passes before a pillar, his
words choke off. He stiffens. His eyes grow wide for an
instant, and then he topples to the floor.

Glasluit stands behind him, his sword bloody. He regards Siudb for a moment, hangs his head. "I ran away."

"You came back, and at the best time."

"I ran away."

Chairiste's stricken voice carries into the hall: "Siudb,
are you sure? After all this time, are you . . ." As grievous as her tone is to Siudb, the gentle reply from just
outside the doors of the palace is even more unsettling,
for it is her own voice, with a touch of Sidh inflection.

"Mother Goddess!"

Glasluit steps forward. "Orfide's magic . . ."

They start toward the doorway, running, but a chord
from an unknown instrument rises up like a wall of green
water and smashes into the palace. It plows into them,

dropping them to the floor. Glasluit is holding his head, crying out, his words buried in the music. Siudb struggles onward, crawling across the ivory, her nails breaking on the slick floor as she fights for handholds. "Chairiste!"

Judith stepped away from the door, her garments whispering in the hush that had fallen over stage and palace. Christa stretched out her hands. "Beloved . . ."

"I have come to say good-bye, Chairiste. I think it is better this way. You have lived in the mortal lands so long, and I have been in the Realm. I could not wait any longer. I had to take friends where I found them."

Devi watched and listened. Both Christa and Judith were speaking Gaeidelg, but she understood: Christa's work had gone for nothing.

It happened. It always happened. Devi herself, abused by her father, had been unable to trust enough for intimacy, and so had made a practice of non-involvement. But friends and acquaintances had supplied her with enough vicarious experience that she was hardly surprised when Christa's lover had appeared only to deny her.

"Siudb, are you sure? After all this time, are you . . ."

Devi could see the grief cutting deeply into Christa's face. It had cut her before, when she had cradled the dying Monica in her arms, but its strokes tonight were infinitely more telling, more cruel.

"I am sure," said Judith. "You'll find others you love, Chairiste. Be well. I must go now."

Maybe, Devi reflected, this was better. Christa had always been someone who was unmistakably real, and her words and actions, in marked contrast to the prattling of the average rocker, invariably carried weight and substance. Judith was not like that at all. She had none of Christa's presence and solidity. In fact, she seemed as unreal as the unreal Sidh, and if her sympathies had changed so easily, then—

Devi lifted her head suddenly. She was shouting before she could think. "Chris! This is a bunch of bullshit! That's not Judith! That's a fake!"

Christa turned, her face streaked with tears.

"You said nothing changes in the Realm!" Devi continued. "So how can she change enough to dump you? Orfide's just trying to pull a fast one!"

The guitarist shook her head, stunned, uncomprehending.

Devi was already changing computer programs, calling up the full voice from every synthesizer she had and assigning them all to her main keyboard. She threw the volume faders all the way up and her hands descended on the keys. The chords she summoned were thick, ferrous, gritty with the crunch of overdriven guitar, fluid with pulsing waveforms.

Two licks, three licks, and the likeness of Judith became hazy. Another few seconds, and it faded entirely.

Devi stopped playing. "You son of a bitch!" she screamed at Orfide. "You keep dicking around with my friends and I'm gonna fry your ass!"

The bard seemed disconcerted for an instant, but he sat down again. His fingers went to his harp.

Devi felt the world shift around her, felt the touch of magic on her skin. She fought, but the stage and the palace both vanished, and their place was taken by something both familiar and frightening.

Her old bedroom. Her father's house.

She was nine years old again, her fingers pudgy with baby fat. Standing in her nightgown, she stared at the slowly opening door.

"Hi, princess," said her father. "Mama's out shopping."

"Get away from me."

"Now, is that nice?"

"I blew off your hand," she said, looking around for her keyboards, not finding them. "I'll do worse this time."

But her voice faltered. Though she knew that she stood on a stage in Gunnison National Forest, she was unaware of anything save her old bedroom. Orfide had trapped her in the past.

Her father moved quickly, grabbing her hands and shoving her back onto her bed, pinning her with the full weight of his body. "You're going to be nice, or I'll have to punish you."

Was Christa helping? Was anyone?

My keys. Where are my keys?

Clothesline was being knotted about her wrists, her nightdress lifted. Large hands prodded at her body.

Her mind almost blank with pain, Devi fought the illusion in which she had been wrapped. Blindly, she reached out to the keyboard that lay, unseen, before her. She could not hear, but her fingers knew their way, and, haltingly, she started out with the rhythm of the song that had sustained her throughout her hellish childhood, added the solo . . .

The bedroom flickered. She had a glimpse of the stage. Christa was calling out to Melinda and to Lisa: " 'Light My Fire.' Jump in with Devi."

Orfide redoubled his efforts, but though the bedroom came back, it was transparent now, an overlay through which Devi could see her friends fighting to help her. Her childish wrists were pinned, but her adult hands were loose, and the Doors' song flowed ever more freely.

Devi's father lifted his head, met her eyes. Behind his face was that of Orfide.

"All right, you bastard," she said. "You're on my turf now."

And with flourishes and fills, she tore the image of her father apart, bundled the bloody shreds together, and threw them at the bard. Stomping on her volume pedal, she sent the arid, precise butchery of her solo into the Realm and watched the Sidh run for cover.

Orfide, eyes closed, brow knotted, played on, a trickle of blood winding down his cheek.

The massed chords are gone, but what has taken their place is worse, and the music from the unknown instrument is a knife in Siudb's ears as she staggers to the door of the palace. Orfide and Lamcrann stand in the courtyard, but her eyes are drawn to a place of light and brilliance beyond the Realm.

For a moment, she hardly recognizes her lover. Her red hair a shaggy mane of curls and spikes, her body clad in black leather and flashing studs, Chairiste might well be twisting her strange instrument in her bare hands, wringing sounds from the wood and steel as though from her own heart. A few minutes ago there was despair in her voice, but now her face is set, her eyes hard and unyielding. She chops out chords, shrills harmonics, and, with seeming indifference, blasts away large chunks of the palace, knocking off towers, splintering doors and windows, fragmenting walls and buttresses.

Christa's voice rolls across the debris. "Give her up!"

Orfide shakes his head, continues. There is desperation in his playing now, and he claws at the harpstrings, his nails cracked and broken, his fingers bleeding.

One of the women with Chairiste—black-haired and slight, but standing as tall as the High King's champion—sees Siudb, smiles, lifts a fist in salute. Her costume is bizarre, but her smile tells the Gaeidil everything.

"We must run," Glasluit shouts above the hurricane of sound.

"We cannot," replies Siudb. "The years await us on the far side of the gate. I am not sure what they will do to you, but I know they will kill me."

"Then let us put an end to this foolishness." Lifting his bloody sword, Glasluit steps toward the bard.

Orfide, though, has seen them. A few feet from the bard, the lad halts, paralyzed. His flesh begins to melt from his bones, running down to the pavement in streams of phosphorescence. He cannot move, he cannot speak, but his eyes are full of screams.

Siudb tries to go to him, but she is knocked away as though by a fist. Stunned, she falls against a pile of rubble, and as she struggles to her feet, she has a last look at Glasluit's face before the flesh sheets off it and leaves him to stare pleadingly out of a bare skull. He falls, smoking, and his remains smolder slowly.

Two of the guards seize Siudb and disarm her. Orfide is on his feet. "I will do the same to your lover unless you withdraw, Chairiste Ní Cummen."

"Try it." Chairiste stands now at the border of the Worlds, commanding, implacable. "Try it, ghost among ghosts."

" 'Twill be your woman who is a ghost."

"Try it." Chairiste's hands are already moving, laying down a barrage of sound. The very foundations of the palace tremble, and an entire wing collapses as Orfide rushes to counter.

Melinda tried to keep her mind on her playing, reminding herself that Christa knew more about her opponents than anyone else. This was a gig, she told herself.

Christa had been talking to the bard in Gaeidelg, but now she went off again into fast-changing improvisations. Melinda knew the guitarist's style and how she put chords and scales together, and she followed with her bass, supporting the music, lending strength to the woman who had taught her the ways of the harp . . . and saved her life.

The stage was alive with energy that crackled in Melinda's hair, sparked from her bass strings, tingled up her hands. But as the music went on, as Orfide clawed at his harp, as Christa plunged into mazes of rarefied diminished chords, Melinda wondered where she was going to be tomorrow. Dead? Maybe. She had seen what had happened to Judith's friend. But it seemed to her more likely that, her usefulness at an end, she would find herself alone, without a band, without friends, without guidance.

It made sense. Christa could not possibly have replaced her in the few weeks between Beltaine and Midsummer, and so, quite logically, had allowed her to stay on as a tame puppy who could be depended upon to come when called, to respond gratefully to a dog biscuit, to play bass when needed.

'Tis true, a voice seemed to whisper in her ear. *She will be done with you tomorrow, and then you can go back to your little apartment, and your insomnia, and your Led Zeppelin records, and no one will hear from you ever again.*

Tears were starting from Melinda's eyes, and the scar on her heart threatened to split wide open.

No one at all, until the police find you with your wrists cut open, of course.

Melinda faltered. The bass line went wide and dropped out. Christa glanced back at her, startled, and Orfide's energy surged toward the stage.

But then Melinda saw the bard looking straight at her, and she suddenly knew the origin of the voice and the despair. Madness, Christa had said. Physical death was the least worry.

Melinda's spirit, broken since Beltaine, rallied abruptly. The bass line came back. "No way, guy," she muttered to the voice. "I can hack this shit. Chris is my friend. She

stuck with me. And I'll be damned if I'll let her down
now!"

Christa looked back again, and Melinda, eyes blurry
with tears, gave her a nod.

"Love you, Chris," she mouthed.

Christa's smile was like a warm embrace, and Melinda
felt herself coming back. Maybe she was a fuck-up, but it
seemed that, in Christa's world, fuck-ups got another
chance.

Pumping out a cannonade of bass notes, she fired
Christa's harmonies straight at the Sidh bard.

Christa had been able to breach the Realm, and she
had leveled some sections of the palace, but though she
strove mightily, supported by the full output of the band,
she was still unable to touch the bard himself. Devi had
succeeded, for the cut in Orfide's forehead still bled, but
there was no time and no opportunity to ask her what she
had done. Quite probably she would not be able to
explain.

Throwing out the beginning of spells and turning them
suddenly into something else, Christa sought to catch
Orfide off guard, but he followed her effortlessly, match-
ing her chromatics with abrupt modal shifts, expanding
his tactics to include the full voice of his harp: all the
modes, rather than the few customarily used for defense
and combat. It was a testament to his immense skill that
he could turn even the phrygian and lydian scales, both
normally associated with life and healing, into weapons.

He shifted from one mode to another, working plagal
and authentic forms equally. Christa recognized the oscil-
lation of his bottom notes: a fourth up, a third down, a
fourth up, a third down. Something about his playing
made her uneasy, though.

Judith stood in the grip of Sidh guards, but Christa had
no time even to exchange glances with her. "Kevin: up
the treble at five kilohertz," she said into the microphone, and the sound from the PA changed instantly,
transforming the music into a lance of white fire that
darted out at the bard from the many speaker cabinets.

Orfide remained bent to his task, progressing methodically through the modes: plagal form, authentic form;
plagal form, authentic form. Countering, Christa matched

his playing and found herself forced to attack and defend using the same scales.

Chairiste

"Huh?"

spiral

Ceis's warning came almost too late. Orfide was using the spiral of modes with the intent of killing her with her own music when he finally teased her into the locrian mode's string of diminished intervals. Already, Christa realized, her hands were growing cold, her thoughts turning of themselves to winter and the inevitable passage into death.

She shifted keys immediately, but she was already too far into the spiral, and her thoughts dragged her back toward oblivion. Against her will, she was considering the attractiveness of the proposition, for—after two centuries of living, after fourteen hundred years of history— death beckoned seductively.

She looked ahead to the locrian mode that waited for her. To the Sidh, it represented eternal negation; but Christa was mortal, and she saw beyond it. There were always beginnings, she thought, even in the spiral of the modes. Monica had died, but she would be reborn someday; and the locrian was itself merely a prelude to rebirth in the ionian, to living in the dorian, to giving life in the phrygian, to experiencing the mystery of the lydian . . .

And she saw then that she could break through the cycle—by living it. At Midwinter, she had rebirthed Kevin. Now, at Midsummer, she would do the same for herself. She had been a harper; she was going to be a rocker. It was inevitable. Her life lay not behind her, but before her.

She brought her cold lips to the microphone. "Everyone: we're going to do the blues, metal style. Van Halen: 'Ice Cream Man.' Where Eddie jumps in with the solo. On my signal."

Orfide's locrian mode started up. Christa's vision was blurring. She felt her heart falter as the bard's spell tightened around her.

Brigit . . .

But Orfide's final note would be the fifth of the blues progression, the root of the chord that turned everything around and brought it back to the beginning; and 'Ice

Cream Man' was a raucous tribute to adolescent sexuality: irreverent, leering, full of nothing but life and the promise of a good time.

And just as Christa felt the glimmering of light that promised Summerland and rest, she dragged her spirit up by its throat and forced her lungs to squeeze out a scream: *"Now!"*

The cold and the grave vanished with the first power chord, and Christa tossed off licks and tremolo-bar dives, fragmenting Orfide's spell as she swept through keys with an arrogant disregard for harmonic convention. With her hands now on the core of the bard's magic, Christa threw it back at him and saw desperation etched in his posture as he frantically worked to dismantle what he had assembled with such care.

The rest of the Sidh shared his fright. They fled into the gardens and took cover within the shattered palace. Judith's guards, too, were affected. They had crowded back, releasing her. The Gaeidil stood alone a few yards from Orfide. A fallen sword was at her feet.

Slowly, deliberately, Judith bent and retrieved the weapon, then advanced. Lamcrann made as if to stop her, but she backhanded him and knocked him to the ground.

The bard suddenly seemed to become aware of Judith's presence, and Christa felt his magic veer suddenly to the side. The same spell that had killed Glasluit launched itself at Judith.

It was blown away like so much smoke. At Christa's shouted command, Kevin threw the master volume controls to full, and she jammed Ceis's headstock against the stack of PA speakers, letting the feedback build and join with the magic. Orfide, breaking at last under the terrible electronic assault, let go of his harp and put his hands to his head, his mouth opened in an unheard scream as Judith's sword clove his skull.

The bard jerked with the impact, and then the feedback split him open, rending flesh and bone. His harp fell, clattered and bounced on the tile, and was followed closely by his body.

Christa pulled her guitar away from the speakers and spun down her volume knobs. The stage grew silent save

for the hiss of active speakers and the sobs and wails of
the Sidh.

Kevin looked over the edge of the stage, shook his
head, sighed. "Poor devils."

Christa looked at him, startled, almost angry. "What
are you saying, Kevin?"

He shrugged. "Look at them. They're terrified. You've
got your lover, Chris, but they've just lost everything.
I've got to say it: I pity them. They probably feel about
the same as I did when my folks got through with me."
He fell silent, as though his words had made him
thoughtful.

Not a single Sidh moved. Casting the sword aside,
Judith picked her way across the debris-littered ground,
her hands and arms bruised and scratched, her white
harper's mantle stained with blood. At the edge of the
Realm, just at the foot of the stairs that led up to the
stage, she stopped.

"Beloved," she said hoarsely, "will you help me cross
this threshold? I . . ." Her eyes turned tragic. "I have no
harp."

Christa looked down at her. So close now. The battle was
over. Just one more spell. "I will, Siudb, with all my heart."

Devi came in with synthesizer swells, and Christa began the song that, long ago, she had composed for this
one hoped-for purpose. Her voice was nothing like Monica's, but her emotion made up for the lack, and though
she had put the words into Gaeidelg so her lover would
understand them, she knew that, even in English, their
meaning would have carried effortlessly.

"I do not know how to praise you, O my love,
For I am no master poet who can claim the twelve
branches.
Your hair in my hands was sweet as new milk,
Your lips against mine like the rich mead of kings.

"Baile and Aillinn could not meet in life—
Only the apple and the yew spoke of them
In speech that brought them together beyond death.
But I am Chairiste Ní Cummen and I can better that.

"Unlooked for, maybe forgotten, I have come
To win you, who, once won, graced my arms

With your presence.
Unthought of, perhaps despaired, I return
From lands which, though mortal, are alive
And waiting for you."

At the foot of the stairs, Judith raised her arms as though to embrace the magic that washed over her in a purifying flood, cleansing her of the effects of the Realm, wiping away the years that would have taken her life; and to Christa it seemed that, though dawn was still some hours away, the Midsummer sun might well have been shining already, bringing with it the joy and gladness of the longest day.

The last chords faded. Judith, free, slowly mounted the steps. Trembling, Christa handed Ceis to Melinda and went toward her lover amid the whine of electronics and the rattle of chains.

For a moment, Judith stared. "Oh, Chairiste," she whispered. "How you have changed."

"Have I?" Ceis had taken extra years from Christa's age, but much had happened in the last two centuries, even in the last year: wandering, and sacrifice, and disappointment . . . and death. "Have I?" Her eyes were streaming.

Judith reached out a hand, but then, with tears and a shake of her head, she fell into Christa's arms, filling the long, lonely ache with the solid, undeniable presence of her beloved.

CHAPTER
THIRTY-TWO

The palace of the Sidh was in ruins: towers knocked off jaggedly as though with a club, walls blasted with holes, entire wings leveled. The courtyard was filled with glass and shattered stone, benches were tumbled and broken, and imperishable tile had been cracked and scorched. Glasluit's body still smoked like phosphorus where it had fallen. Orfide's corpse was inert and shattered, unrecognizable.

Her arms still full of Judith even after many minutes, Christa opened her eyes to the destruction. Kevin had put it well when he had compared the Sidh's desolation with his own. The immortals stood in scattered clumps, staring with empty eyes, hands seeking hands in something that was, for the first time, no mere dalliance, no superficial gesture, but rather an honest expression of fear and hopelessness.

Lamcrann stepped forward. Christa faced him with Judith at her side. Unwilling to let go even for an instant, she kept her arm about her lover's waist.

"Well, Gaeidil, you have won," said the king. "And if there was a debt between us, you have collected it."

Even in defeat, he was proud. Christa felt a grudging admiration for him. "You could have released her," she said. "You could have made it simple for yourselves."

"Ah," said Lamcrann, "but you mistake us for mortals. We are as we are. We cannot change."

"Glasluit changed," said Judith.

"Orfide changed, too, Lamcrann," said Christa. "At the very last, he was not fighting as a Sidh. He saw his death coming as clearly as any mortal thing."

The king regarded Orfide, Glasluit, the shattered palace. "And so, it appears, do we all."

Poor devils. Christa realized that she was echoing Kevin.

She had, in killing Orfide, laid waste an entire world. Without the bard's magic, the Realm would gradually disintegrate, and the Sidh would face terror after terror as dissolution advanced upon them.

Kevin ascended the steps to the stage. Devi nodded to him. "Good job, Kev."

He smiled thinly in reply. Christa stretched out a hand to him, and he joined her and Judith at the front of the stage, wrapping a long arm about them both.

"I'm glad you made it," he said to Judith. "Welcome to Colorado." She blinked at his English, thanked him in Gaeidelg. Kevin indicated Lamcrann. "What's he saying?"

"He says that I've killed them all."

"Yeah . . . I thought so." He mused for a minute. "What are you going to do?"

Lamcrann held himself regally. "Will you give us leave to depart, Chairiste Ní Cummen?"

"Wait," she said to the king. "Please . . ." Compassion had arisen, and, with it, courtesy. "Please wait for a moment." Lamcrann's eyebrows lifted at her tone of voice.

"You going to just dump them now?" said Kevin.

She spread her free hand. "I don't know what else I can do."

"I can think of something."

Christa sensed his meaning. "Kevin, you can't. You'd be lost forever."

He shook his head. "Not forever, I think. Not with that place changing as much as it is now." He stared at the Realm, at the Sidh. "Can't you feel it, Chris? Six months ago I needed to change, and you changed me. The Sidh need to change, too. I can do it. I know I can."

"How?"

"Music. I couldn't help Danny, I helped Melinda a little, and I ran sound for this gig; but it's time to move on. I'm going to take the blues into the Realm, Chris, and I'm going to help some people who need it, just like you brought your music to rock and roll and turned things around for everyone who heard you."

Lisa suddenly called out from her drums. "Kev, are you sure about this? That place is a wreck. Look at it."

He was standing straight, like a Gaeidil man. His decision, Christa knew, had been made from the heart, and he would not be swayed. Stubborn Celts.

"Yeah," he said. "I'm sure, Boo-boo."

Judith had been listening. "Chairiste, who is this? What is happening?"

"This," said Christa, "is Kevin Larkin. He is my teacher and my friend, and he is kindred. He . . ." Her voice broke. Kevin was leaving. But he was right: it was something he could do. Magic was flowing through his playing already. In the Realm, it would come to him all the more effortlessly. "He is going to help the Sidh."

"Willingly?"

"It is so."

Kevin embraced them both. "I'll lose my nerve if I stick around too long, so I'm going to grab my stuff and head on out. Judith . . . Siudb . . . I'm glad I got a chance to meet you. Take care of Christa. And . . . Chris . . ."

She looked up at him.

He smiled. "I can tell that she's worth everything we put into this. Brigit bless." Letting go, he went down the backstage steps quickly and vanished in the direction of Christa's Eagle.

Lamcrann was still waiting, arms folded. His head was bowed—in thought or in defeat, Christa could not say for sure—but he lifted it when she spoke.

"What do you want, O king of the Sidh?"

"Leave to depart."

"There is one among us who would give you more. Much more. You have but to ask for what you desire."

Lamcrann looked suspiciously at her, then shrugged. "I believe I want what any king wants for his people: happiness, prosperity, peace."

"You have them, then."

Kevin was coming back up the steps with his backpack, his harp, and Frankie's guitar. He paused to thump Lisa on the back, kissed Devi and Melinda, then approached Christa.

"Last chance to back out, Kevin," she said.

He shook his head. "I'm not backing out. This is the best thing I've done since I let you take me to bed Christmas morning." He smiled. "Can't you feel it?"

Unwillingly, she nodded. "I can."

Lamcrann eyed Kevin. "I cannot order you, mortal. But I will not beg."

"Chris?" said Kevin, and she translated. "I'm not asking you to beg, Lamcrann," he said. "I'll come of my own will. But things are going to change. Big time."

Lamcrann seemed to understand. Kevin descended the front stairs and crossed the courtyard to his side. He bowed to the king and to the Sidh, then turned to the stage. "Rock and roll," he called. "I'll see you all in the Summerland, if not before."

The scene was blurring to Christa's eyes, and she clung to Judith. "A good friend?" asked Judith.

"And a lover," Christa whispered. "I could not have rescued you had it not been for Kevin Larkin."

But Kevin had seated himself with his harp. "I think I can do this myself, Chris. Closing up is easier than opening, isn't it?" He struck two chords and set off bravely into an air.

"Farewell," Christa called when she found her voice, but the lake and the cliff had returned, and the word echoed off the rock wall and played in the ripples of the dark water.

Devi shut off the PA. The silence left behind was profound.

peace

Christa smiled through her tears, took the guitar from Melinda. "Thank you, Ceis."

"Ceis?" said Judith. "But Ceis was . . ."

"It is a strange world you have come into, Siudb."

Judith looked around at the stage, the women, the equipment glowing with LEDs, the lights. High above, a jet crossed the black sky from north to south, blinking red and blue and white, moving among the stars. She tracked it for a time, then dropped her eyes. "How long has it been?"

Christa hesitated. "Fourteen hundred years."

"O Brigit."

Melinda set her bass down and approached slowly. "Chris . . . tell her it's going to be all right. We'll help. She's not alone."

Judith looked confused. "These are . . ."

Christa called them forward. Her band. They had stood with her through fear and death. "These are my friends," she said with pride. "This is our family."

As though peering beneath the makeup and the leather,

Judith regarded each of the women searchingly as Christa introduced them. This was nothing like the clan she had known in Eriu; but she must have felt the acceptance, the sense of family that was a product not of blood, but of will and loyalty, for, one by one, she took their hands in a firm clasp. "I am honored."

Lisa held her grip the last and the longest. "Hey, Chris," she said, "haven't you been telling us that your girlfriend could sing?"

"Chairiste? What is she saying?"

Chris felt a pang. "She is asking if you can sing."

If grief flickered over Judith's face, it was only for an instant. "Tell Boo-boo that, indeed, I can sing." She turned to Christa, and there was acceptance and forgiveness in her eyes. "Tell her that I am a singer."

Bill Sarah was on his way to bed when the phone in his office rang. It was not late, but he hurried back downstairs so that Kelly would not be disturbed.

"Hey, Bill." The woman's voice was familiar and strange at the same time. "What's shakin'?"

"Who is this?" Who would be calling his office number on a Sunday night?

"Melinda Moore. Gossamer Axe."

Which explained the strangeness. Melinda sounded bright and alert, cheerful and upbeat. "Where the hell have you guys been?" Bill demanded. "I've been trying to call you for two days. No one's been home."

"Uh . . . we were . . ." She muffled the phone, and he heard indistinct voices. Melinda came back. "We took a vacation."

"With all the equipment?"

"Uh . . . yeah . . . that . . ." More muffled voices. "Bill, can you do me a real big favor? Like, for the whole band?"

He was instantly suspicious. "I'm not guaranteeing anything. What is it?"

"Can you just . . . uh . . . not ask?"

His managerial instincts rebelled. Dammit, he was representing the Axe, and if the girls were going to go running off and taking outside gigs without telling him, they had better be prepared to 'fess up.

But intuition told him to put the instincts aside. There

was obviously something going on, but after working with the girls for six months, he was learning to let them have their way. Christa had helped Melinda, and that was good. Now the whole band had vanished for a week-end, and that . . . well . . . that probably was not *bad*. . . .

"All right, Melinda," he said reluctantly. "I won't ask." More voices in the background. "Where are you, anyway? It sounds like a party."

"Kinda. We're at Christa's house. We just got in."

"Is Chris there?"

"Well . . ."

"Let me talk to her."

"She's . . . in bed."

"But it's only ten o'clock! Is she sick?"

"She's fine. Real fine. She's just in bed."

Stranger and stranger. Bill pursed his lips and examined the ceiling. Melinda was silent. Good. Let her sweat. He suddenly remembered that she had been the one to call. "So what did you want?"

"We've got a vocalist."

"Yeah? Who?"

"Her name's Judith. Judith . . . uh . . ." Someone—it sounded like Lisa—called out a name, and Melinda relayed it. "Judith Clairaide."

"Weird last name."

"It's Irish." Melinda laughed, and it was a free, clear sound, even over the telephone. "She's pretty neat. Fits right in . . . like family. And *damn* but she can sing."

"So what do you want me to tell Harry and Jessica? How long does she need to get your songs worked up?"

"Chris said to give her a good four months. Until Samain."

"Four months? Why so long?"

"Well, she's kinda fresh off the boat, and she doesn't know English yet."

"Melinda . . ."

"Hey . . . trust me, huh?"

She was talking quickly, but without the nervous self-deception that had once characterized her. *C'mon*, she was saying. *Play with me. Give it a shot.*

Bill did not like games, but Christa had a good head, and if she said that this Judith what's-her-name was all right, then that was enough for Bill Sarah.

"Okay," he said. "I'll go for it. But tell Chris to call me first thing tomorrow morning, will you?"

"You got it."

He paused for a moment before he hung up. "By the way, Melinda . . ."

"Yeah?"

The Axe was back in business. All of it. "You sound real good. Keep it up."

A moment of silence. He could feel her smile. "Thanks, Bill. I'm getting there."

Christa opened her eyes while it was still dark. The room was warm in spite of the open window, and the air was scented with roses. The waxing moon splashed into the room, and the streetlight made leaf-patterns on the wall.

For a few minutes, she drifted up from the depths of sleep. Denver. Her house. The Fourth of July had just passed with the band and Bill Sarah laughing around a barbecue in the backyard. July . . .

Judith . . .

Gasping, she sat up, searching. But her bed was empty no longer, and her lover, peaceful in repose, lay curled up at her side: dark hair falling over dark lashes, spilling over the pillow and sheets. Judith stirred, murmured, reached out in her sleep, and pulled Christa back down.

Christa touched her with a trembling hand. They had been together now for three weeks, settling into blissful routines; but she still had difficulty believing and accepting that Judith was really, after two centuries, in her arms. She had fought for so long that fighting had become instinctive, a habit to be unlearned only with determination and work.

Judith was doing quite well, accepting everything from microwave ovens to Mexican food with a kind of amused puzzlement, her fears tempered and even eclipsed by her relief at being, once more, in mortal lands and in the company of her lover. She now donned 501s and T-shirts with the same ease as she had trews and tunics, and with the help of a little magic, her command of English was growing daily. She even enjoyed rock and roll: if Bill Sarah had had any reservations about the new vocalist, her screaming performance of 'Firing Line' on the Fourth had done away with them.

"That's one fantastic lady you've got," he had said to Christa at the barbecue.

"My thanks, Bill. I know." And Judith's dark eyes had sparkled at Christa over a hamburger and a glass of iced tea. The shadows of the apple and the yew had been dark, but Judith had been sitting in the bright Colorado sun, the highlights in her hair shining golden.

In the moon-washed bedroom, Judith stirred again, cried out softly. Christa shook her gently awake. "A dream, beloved?"

"Oh, Chairiste . . ." Judith sat up, stared at the clock radio and the window, felt the sheets of the bed. Christa saw the relief flood into her. Denver. 1987. She was safe. "I dreamed I was still in the Realm," said Judith, the Gaeidelg words tumbling out into the night. "That Orfide was about to . . ." She shuddered. "If you had been any later, that illusion he sent to speak to you would have been no illusion."

"But it did not happen so."

"It did not." Judith rubbed at her eyes, tried for a smile. "And, anyway, that it was but a dream helps much. I did not dream when I was in the Realm. I did not . . . I did not even sleep, now that I think of it."

Christa pulled her down, folded her in a soft embrace. "Welcome home, Siudb."

Judith kissed her. "You must call me Judith now, beloved. Else I will not get used to it."

"Does the name displease you?"

"It is comely enough. And everyone here can pronounce it. English is strange, but the ladies are helping me greatly. Boo-boo is teaching me to swear." Judith smiled in the moonlight. "She says that it is required of a rock singer."

"Well . . . I suppose you might say that." Christa's thoughts went to Monica, who, for all her Latino origins, had possessed an incredible command of English invective.

Judith lay silently for a while. "I myself often think of Glasluit. And about Kevin. I hope he is well. He is a noble man."

"Truly. I . . ." Monica was gone, and so was Kevin. Christa had not finished grieving for either, and the tears still came. Monica, though, was safe and happy. Kevin . . .

"The Sidh are honorable in their own way," said Judith as though in reply to her thought. "That much I know. They will treat Kevin with the respect he deserves." She laughed softly. "I did not think that I would ever be able to say that of the Sidh. I was captive, and angry."

"And rightly angry."

Judith rolled over, her lips to Christa's cheek. "I am angry no more."

"Are you happy? Even though this place is so strange?"

The old language, craggy and liquid both, came freely to their tongues. It was an intimacy and a luxury they permitted themselves only at night. But Judith put her mouth to Christa's ear and, in perfect English, whispered: "I love you, Chris. And I'm very, very happy."

Christa wept still. But she wept for joy.

Kevin wears a robe of lace and embroidered knotwork. The old slide guitar is in his hand, and about him, the courtyard is clear, the debris long ago shoveled together and carted away. Beneath the partially repaired walls of the palace, the Sidh have gathered to hear him play.

They listen in the twilight to mortal music, to songs and melodies thick with the grease of life and death, pungent with sweat and deep passion. They listen to the blues scraped out of a guitar with a pick and an old Coricidin bottle.

Kevin's voice is rough, but the Sidh are not displeased. At first, their interest was in his novelty—a strange mortal come to take the place of their bard, bringing with him even stranger music—but they now hear the blues as the blues, and tonight they gather around him willingly.

The sky is full of stars. They appeared sometime after Kevin arrived, but even the mortal cannot remember when they flashed out of the darkness in unfamiliar constellations. Like the Sidh, he simply accepts them, for they are fitting and lovely, and they seem to make this twilight world a part of a much larger universe . . . one that most surely contains Colorado, and Christa, and the others that he loves.

He plays on.

He has been busy since he arrived, using powers both magical and mundane to help the Sidh repair their home and deal with the signs of change that, heartbeat by heartbeat, encroach on the Realm. Flowers have blossomed . . . and have died. Trees have shown signs of growth. The palace itself looks subtly different, as though the walls that Kevin has raised partake more of solidity than did their predecessors.

The blues.

Lamcrann and Cumad, hand in hand, listen. The queen's eyes are clear, and her head is cradled on the king's shoulder. They have grown together, these two, and their love has been an inspiration to the others.

The wind freshens, rustling the leaves, stirring the pennants and the oriflammes; and there is a sense of cleanliness and life about it. A tang, as if of the sea, is in the air.

Kevin, still playing, looks up. The stars have grown fainter. The sky has lightened, and, at the distant horizon, it has paled to a soft blue that is streaked with crimson and pink, with gold and white-violet. As the wind stirs again, he breathes deeply and feels the changing of the world.

Lamcrann and Cumad have risen, and so—garments whispering, voices murmuring—have their people.

The horizon grows brighter. The Sidh look to their bard for reassurance. He nods, smiling. This is the reason he has come here. This is why he forsook the mortal lands. This is his healing, his giving, his love.

The blues carries bittersweet through the air. An arc of brilliance lifts above the edge of the world and sends the shadows fleeing before it. The sky is a deep azure, the wind cool, betokening morning, and the mortals of the Realm turn to witness and greet the glory of the First Dawn as the sun—resplendent, golden, shining—

—*rose*.

ABOUT THE AUTHOR

Gael Baudino grew up in Los Angeles and managed to escape with her life. She now lives in Denver . . . and likes it a lot.

She is a minister of Dianic Wicca; and in her alter ego of harper, she performs, teaches, and records in the Denver area. She occasionally drops from exhaustion, but otherwise can be found (grinning happily) dancing with the Maroon Bells Morris.

She lives with her lover, Mirya.